Terry Williams is an ex-teacher living in the Staffordshire Moorlands, close to the Peak District National Park.

He is married and has three children.

A Lay reader within the Parish Church, he enjoys solving cryptic crosswords (or any other puzzle for that matter), reading, hill walking and repairing the unmendable.

He has always had an interest in the mysterious and unexplained.

Terry W. Ki—— (signature)

THE
FINAL INSANITY

T. G. Williams

The Final Insanity

Vanguard Press

A CIP catalogue record for this title is
available from the British Library
ISBN 1 843860 90 2

*Vanguard Press is an imprint of
Pegasus Elliot MacKenzie Publishers Ltd.*
www.pegasuspublishers.com

First Published in 2004

**Vanguard Press
Sheraton House Castle Park
Cambridge England**

Printed & Bound in Great Britain

Dedication

To Hilary, Ruth, Peter and Rachel
Who have always believed in me

Chapter 1

"Train up a child in the way he should go…"

Proverbs 22:6

Ken Howard stood by the school gate and watched as the children scuffled and pushed their way back into the outside world, disappearing along the litter-strewn streets into the gloom of a wet Thursday afternoon. He pulled his raincoat collar together against the penetrating drizzle and heaved a sigh of relief as the last of them passed from view, punching and kicking at each other. Turning away from the gate, he saw the mass of the school building bulking against a huge bank of black, rain-filled clouds. There were already lights illuminating the steamy windows as the cleaners went to work, fighting a losing battle against the accumulated debris of the school day, brushing and calling to each other along echoing, deserted corridors. At one time the school had been a showpiece of glass, concrete and plastic, the politicians' pride and joy. As those politicians had moved on, leaping like mountain goats to the next pinnacle of photo opportunity, the money, once so lavishly poured in, had dried to a mere trickle, and the school had been left to fend for itself as best it could. The years had not been kind, and it now looked run down and seedy.

Walking back across towards the main buildings, he lifted his hand in silent farewell as two of his colleagues passed by in their cars on their way home to start their Christmas holiday. The end of the Autumn term was always a difficult time, with the children, so full of their own importance, noisy and all too eager to be away from the authority and order which the school tried so desperately to maintain. The dark evenings at the end of the longest school term didn't help. Both teachers and children

11

were glad to see the back of each other.

"It's been getting worse recently, too," he thought, as he pushed through the glass front doors and climbed the stairs to his office overlooking the staff car park. The children's behaviour seemed to be deteriorating rapidly, they were more violent and aggressive, and no one else seemed to matter to them. Their attitude was one of complete indifference to any other person's feelings or whether they inflicted pain or not. "Putting the boot in" was an everyday occurrence – a natural event. You did it to others before they could do it to you! It was an attitude which sickened him and made him wonder where it would all end and whether there was an answer to it. There were those amongst his colleagues who recognised that it was happening, but shrugged it off as a natural circumstance of life. To Ken, that attitude represented the thin end of the wedge. Tolerated bad behaviour could only lead to worse behaviour, but he knew that, for some, their only method of survival was to turn a blind eye and maintain a low profile.

Settling down in the worn but comfortable chair behind his desk, he looked at the pile of paperwork he had to get through before he too could start his holiday. It wasn't large, as he had worked lunchtimes and late into every evening over the last week to try to clear his desk before term ended. He hadn't quite managed it. There was always more coming in. Being deputy head at a large city school was not an easy job. The discipline side of it was probably the hardest, as the children of today seemed to be used to getting their own way and did not take to being disciplined at all easily.

He had not always wanted to become a teacher. Upon gaining his degree, he had decided to travel, and had obtained a position with an engineering firm as a sales representative, which entailed visiting potential customers overseas. The cut-throat world of business, however, soon lost its appeal, and he had looked around for a more rewarding career. He had chosen teaching, and at first it seemed to be exactly what he had always wanted, finding the contact with young minds to be both stimulating and satisfying, and their interest and enthusiasm brought a breath of fresh air into his life. Over the years, however, things had changed. The children themselves became unwilling to co-operate and their attitudes seemed to harden. No one wanted to make the effort required to explore new areas of knowledge, and open hostility could be seen in their eyes. The attitudes he had once seen in the hostile world of business were now all too apparent in the young people he taught. As his career advanced he was brought into contact with this side of the pupils more and more often. Eventually he saw that their hostility was turning to aggression. He was becoming ever more involved in a world he could not understand.

It had gradually dawned upon him that the behaviour he saw in the young was not solely confined to them. Adult behaviour was also changing. He recalled recent news items which highlighted this disturbing tendency in human behaviour. Reports of inhuman aggressive behaviour were all too common. Tourists being shot dead on city streets. Snipers firing indiscriminately at passing cars. Heavy objects being dropped from motorway bridges or placed in the path of mainline trains. The terrorist attack upon the World Trade Center. Motiveless random killings, often involving young children, and not always as the victims. Bombings in such places as Bali, rape and mindless violence were now seemingly accepted as part of everyday existence. He was also aware that mankind was not the only recipient of its own destructive tendencies. The animal kingdom had not escaped unscathed. There were numerous reports of various animals being mutilated, set on fire, or slaughtered for no apparent reason. The more he thought about it, the more instances of this type of incident sprang to mind, and the less he understood the mentality of the people who perpetrated such vile acts.

"Man," he mused, "just doesn't fit the pattern of life. No other animal kills or maims just for the pleasure of it. In all of creation he is the odd one out."

A knock at his door jerked him out of his reverie.

"Come in."

A slim mousey girl in her early twenties, wearing the obligatory tracksuit which marked her down as one of the games staff, poked her head around the door.

"Oh, Mr Howard," she began, edging into the room, "thank goodness you're still here. I think you ought to come and have a look at the boys' toilets down by the sports hall. Mr Rollins sent me…" Her voice trailed off into silence.

Pushing himself wearily out of his chair, he followed her down the echoing corridors to where Jim Rollins, the head of P.E., was waiting, along with the brown-coated school caretaker, Ron White.

"They've gone an' done it again!" began Ron as soon as Ken came in sight, pushing open the door to the toilets. "Made a right job of it this time!" He was obviously fuming.

Ken led the way in, closely followed by Ron.

He turned back towards the door.

"Did you catch anyone?"

Jim shook his head.

"No, I just noticed the water coming under the door as I passed," he rubbed his left ear pensively, "But you can tell who it was."

Ken nodded in his direction.

"It's OK, Jim, I'll take it from here. No point in you two hanging on. Go home and have a good holiday."

And to the girl, "Thank you, Miss Jones."

He turned back to survey the scene. Toilet doors had been ripped off their hinges, and great holes kicked through the partitions. Rolls of toilet paper stuffed down one of the toilets had caused it to overflow as it had been repeatedly flushed. Two other toilets, totally shattered, littered the floor with white shards, and the automatic flush pipes over the urinal had been ripped from the wall so that the water flooded onto the floor. The paper towels in the dispenser had been set alight, the smoke from the still smouldering fire painting a black petal on the white wall behind. The wash hand basin below had been ripped from its mountings and smashed into the urinal, completely shattering one of the glazed earthenware panels. Anything which could possibly be damaged had been. Aerosol cans had been used to sign the destruction with the usual graffiti. 'Gozzo Rules', 'Death to the Greasers' and the simple word 'Kill', were a few of the milder examples of the artistic offerings of those who had

14

caused this destruction. Others were much more graphic, calling into question the parentage of certain members of staff, or stating what their fate should be. The language was crude and violent.

It was obvious from the graffiti who had committed this act of vandalism, but, Ken knew that upon being questioned, they would vehemently deny it. "After all," they would say, "who would be daft enough to leave their own names behind?"

He felt that he was fighting a losing battle. All authority had been wrested from the hands of people like himself, and the children knew it!

"More waste of taxpayers' money. They want a good thrashing, the kids of today. Never did me any harm." grumbled the caretaker, as Ken made a mental note of the damage, and the names daubed on the walls.

"Mindless," Ken agreed. "Right, I've finished here. No point in getting the police in. The young louts just laugh in their faces these days. Get someone in to repair it and I'll leave a note on the Head's desk so that he can sort out the necessary paperwork" When he gets back from Tenerife!, he added under his breath. "It will be next term now before we can do anything about talking to the culprits."

As he left to return to his office Ken could hear Ron, cursing and swearing softly to himself as he made a start on cleaning up the mess.

The sound of a radio tuned to one of the pop programmes echoed emptily down the corridors towards him, the voice of the disc jockey interrupting the crude lyrics of one of the latest 'hits' with suggestive comments, in a vain attempt to be trendy and humorous.

"What chance do we have?" he asked himself as he re-entered the sanctuary which was his office. He could feel the beginnings of a headache building behind his eyes, and sat for a moment with his elbows on his papers, hands pressed against his eyes, savouring the darkness it brought.

Half an hour later, his paperwork finished, Ken Howard, Deputy Headmaster of Crossburn Community High School, Coventry locked up his office and headed out into the wet

December night.

His car was quite close to the main door, and before getting into it he checked to make sure his luggage was still under the floor of the hatchback. One never knew these days; even the deputy head's car on the school car park was fair game for a bit of extra pocket money. He also checked the wheels to ensure that the wheelnuts had not been tampered with – a not unknown occurrence at the end of a term.

"Perhaps the term has gone on too long and I'm painting too black a picture." he thought, but deep down inside he knew that this was not so. Things really were getting worse, and the pace was accelerating.

The journey which lay ahead was now the only obstacle standing between him and the seclusion of the cottage where he would spend the Christmas holiday, well away from the hustle and bustle of busy school life with all of its attendant irritations and stresses. Two and a half weeks of blissful isolation before he need face a class of children again. Thus it was that he heaved a sigh of relief as he accelerated away and watched the lights of the school disappear from his rear view mirror.

As he edged into the main stream of traffic and drove through the city the rain, which had been intermittent all day, began to fall more steadily, and the already heavy evening traffic slowed to a snail's pace. The streetlights and car headlights reflected back from every wet surface, making firm outlines difficult to see. Brakelights flared from time to time and horns were sounded irritably at ever increasing intervals as groups of youngsters simply walked into the road, causing vehicles to brake suddenly to avoid hitting them. Having achieved their aim they would saunter arrogantly across, causing the same disruption to the flow of vehicles from the opposite direction. But for the slowness of the traffic there would have been more than a few accidents.

"Youngsters!" Ken thought, "I don't know what's got into them these days!"

But the more it happened, the more he noticed that not all of the jaywalkers were youngsters. More and more often adults could be seen risking life and limb with the same disruptive tactics.

It took him an hour to reach the northern suburbs and, although traffic was still heavy, most was now going in his direction and speed picked up slightly. Again he was able to put the problems of children to the back of his mind and anticipate Christmas spent at his holiday cottage high in the lonely hills above Kelden in the Pennines, north of Skipton. He had been looking forward to it since the beginning of September, and had made arrangements with Mrs. Grindle, who lived in Kelden with her husband, and who looked after his cottage, to open it up for him the moment term ended. He could see, in his mind's eye, the huge fire that would soon be blazing in the hearth, and the small table lamp left on for him casting a warm welcoming glow through the curtains, tightly closed against the rain which now lashed the windscreen of his car.

Approaching the outskirts of Lichfield he again saw the brakelights of the cars in front and the occasional flash of hazard warning lights. Slowing to a halt, he peered through the rain-streaked windscreen to see if the cause of the hold-up was apparent. About a hundred yards ahead the blue flashing lights of an emergency service's vehicle pierced the gloom, contrasting sharply with the oranges and reds of car and street lamps. Whether it was a police car or an ambulance he had no way of knowing. He sat and waited, wondering how long it was going take to clear, turning on the radio to see if he could pick up some traffic news. Soft classical music surrounded him, helping to ease away some of the tension. There was no traffic from the opposite direction, so whatever had happened up ahead had obviously blocked the whole road. A short while later an ambulance came howling past on the opposite carriageway, heading for the scene of the accident.

By now, a few of the cars in the line ahead were turning around and heading back to make their journey home by another route. As he didn't know the area well enough to join them, Ken could do nothing but listen to the radio and wait for the obstruction to be cleared.

The occupants of the terraced houses which lined the road at that point, attracted by the disturbance, had been out to see what was going on, and some were now filtering back to their homes. He turned off the radio, unbuckled his safety belt and leaned over the passenger seat to wind down the window to ask what had occurred.

"Some idiot shot out of a side road, straight in front of a tanker," an elderly lady informed him. "Tanker swerved right into a bus coming the opposite way. Couple on the bus killed outright, seven or eight injured, and the tanker driver in a pretty bad way. Car what caused it all disappeared without a scratch. Didn't even stop!" she said disgustedly, "Wants 'angin' 'e does – if they ever catch 'im."

She turned away and headed back to her home. Ken rolled up the window again and hoped that he would soon be able to get through. He had been travelling now for two and a half hours and his journey had only just begun.

"Perhaps I should have taken the M6 north," he considered, immediately dismissing the idea – hating motorway driving and knowing what the M6 could be like at this time in the evening. He was probably better off where he was. It was another fifteen minutes before the line of traffic began to move again.

When he reached the site of the crash Ken saw that the rear of the tanker, which had been travelling in the same direction as he was, had been moved over to allow the queue to squeeze through. One policeman was waving them on, while a number of others were holding back the fair sized crowd of onlookers who had gathered.

"People seem to revel in a disaster," he thought as he drove carefully past, "The more gory it is the more they seem to enjoy it."

He had hoped that by now he would be nearing the end of his journey but he was nowhere near his destination and it was almost eight o'clock.

The best thing to do, he decided, would be to take a break and perhaps get a bite to eat. After all, there really was no hurry and there was no one waiting for him. Ken Howard was still single. It was not that the opposite sex found him unattractive, or he them, it was just that whenever a relationship seemed to be developing he found something about the girl which he did not like or some attitude which repelled him. In short he had never found the perfect woman for him. He still held out hopes that some day he would meet her, as he often found a bachelor existence somewhat lonely.

He had intended eating when he reached the cottage but that was obviously going to be much later than originally planned. There was an attractive little inn on the road between Bakewell and Hathersage standing by the River Derwent, which he had often noticed and had long promised himself that he would visit at some time. This seemed like a perfect opportunity.

After clearing Lichfield the traffic had thinned leaving the roads quieter and so he made excellent time, pulling onto the car park of the Shipley Arms at about eight thirty. There were a number of cars already standing outside, but not so many that the pub would be too crowded.

On entering the bar he saw that the interior of the inn was as cosy as the exterior had promised. Light from the enormous open-hearth fire glowed warmly from the lustrous dark wood panelling which lined the room. Tasteful watercolours, carefully lit, were strategically positioned on the panelling and the whole room was indirectly illuminated to exactly the right level to highlight these features. The bar, in one corner of the room, was unobtrusive, but neat and well kept.

"Evening, sir!" called the landlord as he approached the bar, "And what can I get you?"

The landlord was a clean looking, elderly man, with a thin grey moustache, well trimmed. Wearing a blazer with a regimental badge on it and a smart diagonally striped tie, his thinning grey hair well groomed, he blended in perfectly with the surroundings.

Ken ordered half of bitter and a beef sandwich, and while he waited for the food to arrive (freshly made, no pre-packaged food here, he noted), he leaned on the bar observing that there were seven other people in the room. There were three couples, middle-aged and obviously enjoying each other's company over a quiet drink in familiar surroundings, and one older man sitting in the corner by the fire. He too looked comfortable in his place, almost as if he was part of the decor. These people belonged here. There were sounds of other customers in another room off to his left, probably a mirror image of this one, but this was where the regulars drank in comfort. Here they could be at ease and find peace.

When his sandwich arrived he ordered a second half-pint to go with it and took it over to the fireplace, sitting in the corner opposite to the older man, who looked up as Ken sat down.

Ken nodded. "Nasty evening."

"Aye, it is," the man responded, "an' goin' to get nastier if I'm not very much mistaken."

He was wearing a heavy tweed jacket and corduroy trousers. His raincoat and hat, folded neatly on the back of one of the chairs, were steaming slightly as they dried in the warmth of the fire. His left hand rested on the top of a gnarled, well used walking stick, and Ken was surprised to note that the back of the hand was much smoother than one would have expected in a man of his apparent age. He was obviously an outdoor man, well-wise in country ways. He took a draught from his pint pot, wiping his mouth on the back of his hand, an action which did not seem to fit Ken's assessment of him, before speaking again.

"Come far?"

"Coventry." Ken warmed to his friendly companion.

"Not a good night for travellin',' this. 'Specially traffic bein' what it is. Lot of mad heads about."

The man didn't waste words.

Ken snorted. "I know, I was held up by an accident caused by one. That's why I stopped here for a break," he offered.

"Goin' far?" again the question was concise.

"Just north of Skipton. I've got a holiday cottage up there."

He was enjoying the conversation across the fireplace, and felt entirely at ease with this man.

"Arr! Long way that at this time a' night," the man rejoined, "You ought to stay here for the night. Andy'll put you up."

Ken was sorely tempted. He really felt very comfortable here, but his own little cottage also had its charms.

"Oh, I don't know that I could do that, I really wanted to get there tonight."

"Nobody waitin' is there?" It was more of a statement than a question. There was more to this elderly man than there seemed.

Ken looked at him closely but the man held his gaze with his steady blue eyes.

"No, there's no-one waiting, but I really think I ought to get there if I can."

The man nodded, seeming to regard that as the end of the conversation and settled down again to his own thoughts, but from time to time he would look up from under lowered eyelids and scrutinise Ken with a strangely penetrating gaze.

As he ate Ken could not help but compare the warmth and security of his present surroundings with the hostility and violence of the world he had just left beyond the door of this establishment.

He was just finishing the last of his drink and thinking about getting back on the road when the door burst open and a group of four people dressed in black motor cycle leathers shattered the calm with their entrance. In their early twenties, the two young men were obviously out to make an impression on the girls with them. Their language was loud and crude, and their impatience was obvious as they waited for the landlord to come and serve them.

"Shop!" one of the men shouted, banging the bar with one of the empty glasses that stood there.

"Come on, mate, we haven't got all night. We've got better things to be getting on with!" He leered at one of the girls, making obvious gestures towards her, and they all burst into fits of raucous laughter.

The barman bustled through from the other bar, wiping his hands on a small striped towel.

"Now then, what will it be?" he asked.

"Four pints of whatever passes for ale around here," said the larger of the two men, "And make sure you fill 'em right up. Like to get our money's worth, we do."

"Straight glasses for the ladies?" asked the landlord.

"Ladies?" guffawed the man, "These ain't no ladies."

Again the group dissolved into bawdy laughter.

"No," he continued, "Give 'em ones with handles on. It'll be something for them to get hold of!"

Once more the laughter was loud and raucous. The drinks

were dispensed, and the payment was thrown down arrogantly upon the bar. The landlord took up the coins and made a point of counting them carefully as he rang the amount into an old fashioned till before returning to the other room.

The pleasant atmosphere of the room was now a thing of the past. This group had brought the world which Ken had left behind flooding back. Having gulped down their pints they immediately began to bang their glasses on the bar top.

"Oi! Same again, mate!" yelled the second man, leaning far over the bar and waving his glass at the landlord, who was obviously busy in the other bar.

"It's all right, Dad, I'll see to it."

Through a door to the rear of the bar walked a most attractive girl. She was in her mid twenties and was dressed in a crisp white blouse and black skirt. Her blond hair, cut in a fringe, fell, bell-shaped, almost to her shoulders.

"Oi Dad!" bellowed the man, "Where have you been keeping this one, then?"

And to the girl, "Never mind about the beer, love. You come round here and join us."

"No thanks." she replied. "There are other customers to see to." Her dislike of him was obvious.

"Ooh, no thanks there are other customers to see to!" mimicked one of the girls, parading primly round the group. "You're not good enough for the likes of her, Stevie."

"Not good enough, eh? I'll show you how good I am."

Reaching over the bar he grabbed the landlord's daughter by the wrist and started to pull her towards him.

"Hey!" shouted the landlord, coming round into the room, "Cut that out!"

"And what if I don't?" asked Steve belligerently.

"Then I shall have to ask the darts team in the other room to help me throw you out." replied the landlord coolly, lifting the bar flap and coming round to confront the group.

"And I'm sure we would all be only too pleased to assist them," said Ken quietly, getting to his feet and starting to move towards the group.

Deep down inside he hated violence, but he knew that this

type would usually back down when the odds got too long. He was a well-built man, and had kept himself fit by training and indulging in field sports. Rugby had never been to his liking, requiring an aggressive approach which he had always failed to find within himself. His activities on the track and field had given him the type of physique which usually deterred any would be antagonists. His whole teaching career had been built on bluffing out situations such as this. This one proved to be no exception, and Steve decided that a strategic withdrawal was called for.

"Let's go!" he shouted.

In one movement he released his hold upon the girl, picked up his empty beer glass from the bar, and flung it at the optics display on the rear wall. It crashed into an ice bucket on the shelf below the optics, scattering ice in a thousand different directions. The glass shattered into tiny pieces.

By now the other men in the room were on their feet and moving towards the bar, but the group were obviously used to situations like this, and, pushing the landlord roughly out of the way, they overturned a table into the path of Ken and the others, and ran swiftly out into the night, screaming abuse as they went. At that moment, having heard the commotion, the darts team appeared from the other room. The landlord had not lied when he said that they were next door – he had simply neglected to mention that not one of them was under retirement age! Even so they were willing to join in the chase as the men in the room also made for the door.

"No!" shouted the landlord, picking himself up off the floor and brushing down the knees of his trousers with his hands.

"They're not worth the trouble. Let them go. If you catch them there's not much the authorities can do to them, and then they'll only be back for revenge. Besides, one of you may get hurt, and I don't want that on my conscience."

It went against the grain to let such people go unpunished, but Ken knew what the landlord said was right. They would probably get off with a fine, and when they came back they would bring their friends. He picked up the table they had overturned and went back to his place by the fire to collect his things. The tranquillity of this refuge was totally shattered so he thought it best to be on his way. He turned to nod goodnight to the old man opposite and saw that he was looking at him with those extraordinarily piercing eyes.

"Not right in the head, that lot," said the man, as they heard the sound of high-powered motor cycles scream off into the night. The words seemed to fit the situation perfectly, but it was not until much later that Ken realised that the other had been speaking the literal truth.

Chapter 2

"I will lift up mine eyes to the hills…"

Psalm 121:1

The car park outside the inn was quiet, with no sign of the troublemakers. The wind was rising and the cloud cover, now very low, made the night even darker than before. The way to his car was lighted by the warm glow falling from the windows of the inn. He climbed in, started the engine, and began to back out of the parking space. It was immediately apparent that something was wrong. The car, usually very smooth and responsive, displayed an uncharacteristic resistance to motion. Putting on the handbrake he got out again to look for the fault and found to his dismay that the rear offside tyre was absolutely flat. This just wasn't his night. He set about changing the wheel and had just jacked up his car and was removing the second wheel nut when it slipped smoothly off the stud and rolled away into the darkness. Feeling carefully around to try to locate it, his hand brushed against the tyre on the car next to him. That too was flat. His curiosity aroused, he examined the cars nearby. Some of them also had flat tyres. The fleeing group had observed that they had not been pursued and taken time to vent their anger against the landlord on his customers' cars.

After he discovered where the missing wheel nut had rolled to, and before finishing off his wheel change, he returned to the bar to let them know what had happened. In all seven cars had had their tyres slashed. Something large and very sharp had been driven through the walls of them. Just as he was replacing the hubcap the rain began again, this time being driven before an ever-increasing wind. He ran back in to wash his hands, and as he came out of the washroom, the landlord's daughter approached him to offer a drink 'on the house' to thank him for helping and to make up for his experiences. He was again tempted to stay, and he now secretly wished that he had not been so quick to reject the old man's suggestion, for although she could not be called beautiful, there was something very appealing about the gentleness which shone in her eyes, but as it was now getting late, the weather turning bad, and still having a long way to travel, Ken reluctantly declined. He waved goodbye to those who were lucky enough to be still inside and returned to his car to resume his journey. One or two men were still struggling to complete their repairs in the rain as he drove off into the darkness.

The traffic was now very much lighter and the lateness of the hour meant that there were fewer heavy goods vehicles on the road to impede his progress. Passing through Matlock, he soon skirted Sheffield, took the A616 to Huddersfield and progressed rapidly on towards Skipton.

The weather had deteriorated steadily as he travelled north, and the thought of being safe and warm behind the stout walls of the cottage became ever more attractive. To reach this haven by mainly major roads meant a lengthy detour and so it was that he decided to take a short cut he had noticed on the map, but had never tried before. It meant some steep climbs on very minor roads, but he was certain he could find his way, and it meant lopping at least half an hour off what had now become an extremely long and wearisome journey.

Soon after passing through Skipton, he turned off the main road and began his ascent into the hills. Ten minutes later, disaster struck! Rounding a sharp right hand bend, the headlights of his car picked out the tangled branches of a small tree, brought down by the gale. It was lying across the width of the road, completely blocking the way ahead. On such tracks as these, his speed was not great and, by breaking heavily, he was able to stop before actually hitting the obstruction. He was now faced with a number of choices. The road was too narrow to turn the car around, and so he could reverse back until he found a wider spot to turn around in, retrace his route back to the main roads and take the long way round, or he could sit here until morning and hope that some help would arrive, or he could try to squeeze past the barrier (there was some space to the right between it and a drystone wall) and thus continue his journey with only minor damage to his paintwork.

Putting the car into reverse he backed away from the branches to get a better look at the situation. Peering into the darkness through the rear windscreen he found that the reversing lights hardly made any impression upon the gloom. His first option was an obvious non-starter, and besides, his cottage could only be a few more miles ahead of him. He therefore decided to try to go around the obstruction.

Engaging first gear, he swung the wheel to the right and edged the car warily forward. The branches scraped against the bodywork as he carefully pulled onto the grass at the roadside. There was not as much room as he had thought and his side of the car was dangerously close to the drystone wall that bordered the road. He went ahead very slowly indeed. The front of the car was now clear of the main branches and he edged gingerly back towards the paved surface. It was then that the engine surged to a crescendo as the rear tyres lost their traction and the wheels began to spin wildly on the rain soaked verge. He quickly eased up on the accelerator and the car lost its forward motion. He pressed the accelerator again, but the rear of the car began to sink as the wheels became ever more firmly embedded. Slamming the clutch to the floor he took his foot off the accelerator and tried to size up the situation. He saw that, because of the close proximity of the drystone wall to the tailgate, he did not dare to rock the vehicle backwards and forwards in an attempt to extricate it. As he sat watching the driving rain slice through the headlight beams like shining metal rods, he realised that the options open to him had narrowed themselves to one. He could do nothing about the situation but sit there until morning and hope that a Good Samaritan would come this way. Cursing his bad luck, he turned off the ignition and tilted the driving seat back, preparing to spend a long, lonely, and somewhat cramped night within the confines of his vehicle.

As the sound of the engine died, the noise of the storm

became tremendous, and the westerly wind, which had gathered strength as it rushed inland across Morecambe Bay and over the hills of the Forest of Bowland, buffeted and rocked the car with ever increasing gusts. He doubted whether he could sleep in such conditions and was therefore surprised when he suddenly awoke to an eerie silence. He was cold and cramped and so he turned on the engine to warm up the heater before getting out of the car to stretch his legs.

The wind had died, leaving a thin drizzle in the air which made an already cold night even colder. Many miles to the south the glow of a large town, probably Manchester, could be seen reflecting from the heavy, low clouds. There was no other visible light. Glancing at his watch he noted that the time was 2.25 am. – he had slept for about two and a quarter hours in the storm.

The cold, damp atmosphere soon drove him back into the car, where the efficient heater was now producing a pleasant warmth. Having nothing else to dwell upon, he stared out into the blackness and his mind returned to the train of thought that had occupied him for much of the evening. What was it within Man that caused him, more often than not, to go wrong? This was a beautiful world, with the potential for being a real paradise, but the greed and selfishness of man was driving him to destroy that potential. Beautiful countries such as Yugoslavia had been ripped apart by war, neighbour against neighbour fighting for a land that would not be worth having when the fighting was over. It had happened before. Two world wars had been fought for the 'freedom' of the nations. A freedom to go on producing more and more arms in order to fight another war for 'freedom'. There were those who actually encouraged such wars in order that their fortunes might be made by the sale of arms. There was much that was evil in Man!

Ken had been brought up by religious parents and he remembered a quotation made by Paul in his letter to the Romans: "the good that I would do, I do not: but the evil which I would not do, that I do." At least it went something like that. The problem had always been there, right from the beginning. Man did not seem to be able to help himself, and now it seemed to be coming to a head. There were of course the obvious exceptions, Mahatma Ghandi, Mother Teresa, St Paul himself, but these seemed to have been few and far between. He would never have put himself on a par with these, but Ken also hated violence and tried to prevent it amongst those with whom he came into contact. He had always managed to bluff his way out of situations where violence was called for, as he had back at the inn earlier that night. Most people enjoyed their violence in one form or another. Boxing, blood sports or just ever more violent television programmes, were just some ways in which man sublimated his own violent tendencies. In his mind Ken could hear the words which the old man in the inn had spoken earlier in the evening. They seemed to echo, going round and round inside his skull...

"Not right in the head...in the head...in the head...in the head."

He was brought out of his reverie by a curious sensation that there had been some subtle change in his surroundings and for a short while he could not work out what that change was. Drops of rain still pattered against the roof of the car – no change in the weather. What could it be? Something was different. It took a little while to realise that the darkness was no longer absolute. His surroundings were getting lighter.

"Can it be morning already?" he asked himself.

A glance at his watch showed him that the time was only 3.10 a.m., much too early for dawn. He climbed out of the car again and there before his unbelieving eyes was a sight he had occasionally read about – but always with scepticism. His jaw dropped and he stood with the cold December rain falling unheeded around him, struggling to accept what he was seeing.

Approaching, at an unbelievable speed and from a great height was the source of the light, growing ever more intense as it drew closer. It stopped and hovered in the air before him with the base of the light source roughly level with his eyes. There was no heat, and though the object appeared to be spinning, it did not seem to disturb the air. He had no way of gauging its size, as he could not tell how far away from him it was. The light was brilliant white, but there appeared to be other colours within it, spinning and twisting indistinctly, and forming no regular pattern. He realised that he was face to face with an object the existence of which he had always doubted. Here in front of him was a UFO, an Unidentified Flying Object. He was awe-struck, and he could feel his mind struggling to accept what his eyes told him lay before him, and recoiling from it. Man has always feared the unknown, and this brilliant light seemed to pierce his very being, entering into him and bringing all his hidden and deep-rooted fears to the surface. Panic lay just below that surface – and he could sense it edging closer…!

***

When he came to his senses, Ken was sitting staring through the windscreen of his car at the rain that was once again lashing against it. He had a thumping headache and his eyes felt sore. Had he fallen asleep and dreamed about the penetrating light? Checking the time he saw that forty minutes had passed since it had appeared. Perhaps it had all been a dream and he had never got out of the car at all. It was then that he made a further discovery. He was soaked to the skin! He must have been outside the car, and the mysterious light had been there. What then had happened during the past forty minutes?

For the second time that night he became aware that there was something about his surroundings which was not as it had been, without being able to discern what that difference was. It took some minutes for him to realise just what it was that was troubling him. The car was no longer tilting backwards, and the branches of the fallen tree were not scraping and screeching against the rear windows and bodywork, even though the wind had again risen to gale force. He warily opened the driver's door and started to climb out once again, being careful not to slip on the wet grass – only to receive yet another shock. There was no wet grass for him to tread on – only solid tarmac. His car was firmly back on the road!! Ken's head began to swim as he struggled to come to terms with what had just taken place, and he slumped back into the driver's seat, the knuckles of both hands, which gripped the door frame ferociously, standing out whitely. His head was reeling; panic once more rising within him, his breath coming in short gasps as he felt sanity slipping away.

Realising that he had to take hold of himself, he fought to regain control. He forced his hands to relinquish their hold on the bodywork and return to the steering wheel, then, lifting his legs back into the car and closing the door, he turned on the headlights and saw that the road ahead was clear! He glanced at the driving mirror. In the glow from the taillights he could see the waving branches of the fallen tree whipping wildly in the wind a metre and a half behind the rear of the car. Immediately, his one overriding thought was to be clear of this place and reach more normal surroundings in which to try to regain his sanity. Carefully slipping the car into first gear and, in a state of complete shock Ken set off on what he hoped would be the final short leg of his journey.

Afterwards he found that he could never remember driving that final six miles or so. His mind was in such a state of turmoil that he drove on autopilot until he reached the sanctuary of his cottage in the hills. Parking the car on the small gravelled patch to one side of the building, he stumbled round to the front door, fumbled the key into the lock while the rain cascaded down his face, dripping off his nose and chin. Throwing open the sturdy oak front door he almost fell into the welcoming familiarity of the cottage he had begun to think he would never reach.

The lamp left on for him by Mrs. Grindle was still burning, but the fire was well and truly out – nothing but light grey feathery ashes in the grate. The thick walls of the cottage had, however, retained most of the warmth they had absorbed during the previous evening, and it was quite warm enough for him to be comfortable as he stripped off his wet clothing, dried himself upon the warm, fluffy towel from the airing cupboard and climbed into a fresh change of clothing. His luggage was still in the car, and he was glad that he always kept a few things here at the cottage. Here at last was normality, and there was no way that he was venturing out again tonight into the hostile world beyond the front door.

He rekindled the fire, and having poured himself the large

malt whiskey he had promised himself what seemed an eternity ago, and savouring its smoky flavour, he sat down in his favourite armchair in front of the fireplace to try to make some sense out of the events of the last twelve hours.

It was not easy to relax his mind and body after all that had occurred, but gradually the warmth from the fire and the drink began to take effect. He began to see the events of the day like a kaleidoscope in his mind's eye. The wreckage in the toilets, individuals stepping into the traffic and causing it to brake wildly, groups of people seemingly enjoying the spectacle of a gory accident, his thoughts on the aggressive nature of mankind in general, the incident in the bar, the slashed tyres, and finally the blinding light deep in the hills of northern England.

Through it all he could hear the words of the man in the inn – "Not right in the head...not right in the head," and oddly, just before he nodded off to sleep, it all seemed to make a peculiar kind of sense.

He awoke to find the grey morning light filtering through the still-drawn floral curtains, competing with the light from the lamp on the table by his chair. He eased himself into a standing position and walked over, stretching and yawning, to open the curtains and let in the daylight. Looking out of the window, he saw that the rain was still falling and low grey clouds scudding along in the wind blanketed the tops of the hills. A thoroughly unpleasant morning, but standing here safe in the womb of his cottage he could relax and enjoy the wildness of the day. A look at the clock, as he strolled back across the room to turn off the table lamp, told him that it had gone ten o'clock. Noticing that there were still some thinly glowing embers in the grate, he bent down to put a few small sticks onto them and topped the sticks with a couple of smallish logs. The action of bending down caused a flash of pain behind his eyes. The headache of the previous evening had not entirely disappeared, and its renewed presence brought the memory of the strange events only a few miles south of here flooding back to him.

His thoughts on the matter were a little clearer this morning. He had obviously seen something, and that something had physically moved his car back onto the road. It must therefore have been capable of developing quite a lot of power.

"What if it was radioactive?"

The thought leapt unbidden into his head.

"How high a dosage might I have been exposed to? Perhaps I ought to visit one of the local hospitals and have a check up."

Even as these thoughts chased each other through his mind, he knew with absolute certainty, that there had been no radioactivity. He didn't know how he knew this, but he was totally sure that it was so. There would be no need for any hospital visit.

He braved the weather and fetched his luggage from the car, inspecting the damage to the paintwork caused by the fallen tree as he did so. One or two of the scratches were fairly bad and he made a mental note to get a coat of primer onto them, as soon as the weather allowed, to prevent rust gaining too firm a foothold. He would have the damage repaired properly by a local garage after Christmas. Returning indoors he unpacked his shaver and freshened himself up before thinking about food. In the kitchen he found the sandwiches which had been prepared for him last night. Although they had been covered by a tray cloth they were now rather dry and unappetising. He took them and put them onto the bird table adjacent to the kitchen window before dashing back into the shelter of the kitchen. They might just attract a few unusual visitors when the weather cleared. Mrs. Grindle knew his tastes and had stocked up the refrigerator accordingly. He always left the cottage with the store cupboards well provided with non-perishable food. All in all he was well provided for and he had seen that the local bird life would also dine well – if they dared brave the weather for it.

He soon had the aroma of grilled bacon and percolating coffee wafting throughout the house, and it wasn't long before he was satisfying his appetite with a hearty breakfast of bacon and eggs, followed by highland oatcakes, washed down with a large cup of good hot coffee. He now felt at peace with himself. He still hadn't made complete sense of his experiences, but he had the feeling that his mind was coming to terms with the events he had witnessed, and he would eventually realise what it all meant.

After breakfast he made a conscious decision to spend the

first day of his holiday in complete isolation from the outside world. He did not have television or radio in the cottage, preferring to cut himself off from the depressing events which made the news headlines these days. He found his holidays were much more refreshing that way. It was thus that Ken Howard missed the catastrophic events which were to take place in the world beyond the protective hills.

Chapter 3

"...for the arrow that flieth by day..."
Psalm 91:5

He spent the greater part of the day peacefully enjoying pottering about the cottage, carrying out the odd repair left over from his last stay. A compact but powerful generator which was housed in an outhouse to the rear, for use when the local power lines were down, had been acting up a little during his last visit and as this was no spot to be in without some form of lighting, he spent a few very happy hours tinkering with it, cleaning filters, replacing plugs and generally lubricating anything that moved. At the end of the time he had it running as smooth as silk, and was feeling very satisfied with himself. There had, however, been a couple of odd little incidents during the repair.

The first of these concerned the spark plug. When he came to remove it he found that at some time during his absence water had dripped onto the area around it and it was well and truly rusted into its seating, and, try as he might, he was unable to free it. He gave up his attempt with the plug spanner and went out to the car for the socket set in order to apply more leverage. When he came to fit the socket onto it he noticed that the plug in fact felt quite loose, and was greatly surprised when he found that he could now turn it with his fingers! He supposed that he must have loosened it with his final attempt with the plug spanner and that he hadn't noticed at the time. Shrugging it off as one of those things that happen from time to time he went happily on with his work.

The second incident was not so easy to explain. This concerned a small screw which had to be inserted into a rather awkwardly placed hole on the underside of the generator, pushed along to the end of the casing and then the thread located. Time and time again he balanced the screw on the end of a Philips screwdriver and attempted to insert it into the hole, and time and time again it would either catch the edge of the hole and drop to the floor, or the threads would fail to engage and the screw would drop out again as he removed the screwdriver. In the end frustration got the better of him and he set both the screw and the screwdriver down on the floor together in order to consult the generator manual. It was no help at all, showing where the screw had to go, but not explaining how to get it there. Discarding the manual he turned back to resume his task. The screwdriver was exactly were he had left it but the screw was nowhere to be seen. He searched desperately around the area where he knew that he had left it, but all in vain. The screw had completely disappeared. He returned to the house and fetched a torch in order to shine the light beneath the generator to see if it had rolled under there, but the screw was nowhere in sight. In desperation he shone his torch up into the hole where the screw should fit, and to his absolute amazement, there it was sitting neatly in place! On trying it with the screwdriver he found it to be properly situated and perfectly tight. The skin on his scalp crawled and just for a moment the headache behind his eyes returned and then died back to the vague presence which had been there all morning. The rest of the work proceeded without incident and the smoothly running generator helped him to put these incidents temporarily from his mind

His next job was to be the clearance of a slight air lock in the central heating system. The open fire in the living room was a superfluous luxury – but one which he was unwilling to forego, and it certainly came in handy last evening, warming up the house, and providing the hot water which he needed. He had asked Mrs. Grindle to leave the heating off so that he could clear the lock before he started the system up again. Before commencing this task however, he decided that a cup of coffee and a bite to eat would not go amiss.

The bread bin yielded up a delightfully crusty loaf and he resolved to say a special "thank you" to Emma Grindle when he next went down to the village. She never missed a thing. The perfect companions to such bread were Wensleydale cheese and pickles, both of which were in plentiful supply in the cupboards.

After lunch he took his second cup of coffee and stood by the open back door to watch the thin drizzle which was riding on the now dying wind. He breathed deeply, filling his lungs with the sweet clean air of these hills, flushing out the tainted fumes which passed for air in the city. The sound of shotgun fire was borne to him across the hills and valleys that separated him from the nearest village, some two miles away. Somebody was having a pre-Christmas hunt and by the sound of it, a large one. It struck him as a funny sort of day to be out on the hills hunting, but he knew from experience that people did do odd things at odd times. "There's nowt so queer as folk," as the old north country expression says.

He placed his dirty dishes in the sink and set about clearing the air from the central heating. This was a straightforward job and left his mind free to wander. The incidents with the generator had unsettled him. Perhaps there were some ill effects from last night's 'light' after all. Perhaps he was now subject to blackouts and was not aware of them. Could people continue with their work during a blackout – even doing things which proved difficult whilst they were fully aware? He just didn't know, but he rather doubted it. Again even as these thoughts were passing through his head, his mind told him that there was a logical explanation for what had occurred and that there was nothing wrong with him. Of this he was absolutely certain and again he felt comforted and his anxiety dispersed.

The rest of the afternoon was spent on the many small jobs that had accumulated over the summer. Nailing down a loose tread on the stairs, filling the log box by the hearth, oiling the squeaky hinges on the kitchen door, and countless other such trivial tasks. Occasionally the sound of gunfire would drift across the hills to him, sometimes sounding fairly close and at other times quite distant. On two occasions, when it sounded closest, he went to the upstairs windows to get a better view of the area, but could not see any activity. By the number of shots he had heard he reckoned that someone was either making a determined effort to rid his farmland of vermin, or else they were planning to hold a fair sized dinner party – with game as the main course.

As the light faded and evening approached the gunshots became few and far between but did not die out completely until quite late. Whoever it was certainly had the bit between his teeth and showed a high degree of persistence.

He cooked himself a steak from the freezer for his evening meal, and with that inside him began to wonder if he should drive down to the village for a pint at the local. On looking outside and seeing the rain still coming down he was persuaded to stay with his original plan and spend the whole day in isolation. He was not ready to face the world again yet, particularly on such a miserable evening as this. Stoking up the fire he fetched a cold beer from the fridge and carefully poured it into a tall glass before settling back into the comfortable depths of his favourite armchair. He had been intending to read Tolstoy's 'War and Peace' for months and now he found both the time and the inclination to make a start on it.

Every so often his concentration was disturbed by a distant bang and once he thought he even heard an explosion – very remote and muffled. He persuaded himself that someone was having a firework party and he vaguely wondered what they were celebrating. He found it difficult to become engrossed in his book as he could not completely forget about his experiences of the previous evening and he kept getting up and crossing to the window to peer into the darkness to see if any lights were visible in the sky, but there was nothing to be seen other than unrelieved blackness beyond the glass.

Around eleven o'clock he took himself upstairs to bed. His headache had all but faded, and, after undressing, he sat for a while in the window of his darkened bedroom, again looking for any signs of lights in the sky. He recalled that there had been many other accounts of UFO sightings, all involving some sort of 'light in the sky', in the lonely Pennine hills.

Now that his mind was on the subject, memories of what he had read or heard came back to him. It was as if someone had dipped a stick into a still, deep pool stirring up the mud at the bottom. The result for him was that long hidden memories were now being brought to the surface. He recalled reading about the encounter which a police officer had experienced in Todmorden back in the 1980s. He too had come face to face with an inexplicable 'light' whilst driving alone in his panda car in the early hours of a winter morning, looking for a 'missing' herd of cows. He too had found that, when the light had suddenly disappeared, he was sitting in his car a hundred yards or so further down the road from where he had stopped to observe the light with no recollection of how he had got there. For a while Ken pondered the mystery. The similarities between the two encounters were striking, but there was no rational explanation that he could think of to fit the facts.

He continued to look out into darkness, mulling over what he had remembered, but saw nothing beyond the rivulets of raindrops that merged together and ran down the windowpane. Eventually his eyes became heavy and so he climbed into bed and fell into a deep sleep almost as soon as his head touched the pillow. He had passed the first day of his holiday as he had intended to, totally alone, and in complete ignorance of the terrible events which had occurred in the world beyond his lonely hills.

He awoke the following morning with the sun streaming in through the bedroom window and was surprised to see from the clock by his bedside that he had slept for a good ten hours. This was at least three hours longer than normal and a sure sign that the stresses of teaching were disappearing more quickly than he could ever have expected. It usually took him at least a week to begin sleeping properly again after the end of term.

He enjoyed the luxury of not having to get out of bed for a quarter of an hour or so before he began to feel guilty about wasting such a beautiful morning. All traces of the previous day's headache had gone, and he felt exceptionally refreshed, alert and ready for anything. Rolling out of bed he went over to the window, unlatching it and throwing it wide open. The view was magnificent. The air was so crisp and clear that every breath felt like a draught of water from a cold mountain spring.

The sun had just cleared the top of hills to his left, and was casting enormously long shadows from every rock, tree and bush in its path. The hills to his right met the sunlight head-on and every feature of them could be seen with crystal clarity. He would never tire of these magnificent hills with their ever-changing moods. This was the enchantment which had drawn him to this secluded spot in the first place. In front of him, two miles away and slightly to his right he could just see the tops of the trees of the wooded hillside which ran down to the village of Kelden, his nearest settlement. Beyond the trees, rising in the still morning air was a plume of smoke. "I was right," he thought. "Someone was having a bonfire party last night." He hoped that they had enjoyed themselves.

A trip down to the village today to replenish his provisions was going to be a necessity. He was especially short of fresh milk. The timing of the day, however, mattered not at all. This was a day to be savoured – not hurried.

He enjoyed a leisurely start, a relaxing shower followed by a hearty English breakfast. As he was cooking he made a mental note to pick up some more of that excellent, home-cured, smoked bacon from the shop while he was down in the village. Afterwards he stood in the open kitchen doorway, leaning easily against the doorpost, surveying the glorious vista spread out before him and enjoying the last of his breakfast coffee. He really did feel amazingly good this morning; the weight of the world seemed to have been lifted from his shoulders.

Heaving a deep sigh of contentment, he turned to go back inside and prepare for his trip to the village. As he did so his attention was caught by the sound of a jet aircraft, flying at high speed. He knew that the Air Force often used hilly areas to train their pilots in low level flying, but on this particular morning he was irritated that the tranquillity of the hills should be shattered by this high speed pinnacle of man's technology in the field of mass destruction. Irritated though he was, he could not help turning to watch as it swooped and dived in the cloudless blue of the sky, the sun striking bright sparks off its polished surfaces as it flashed along, weaving and dodging. There was something abnormal about the behaviour of this particular aircraft. Usually these planes would flash by and be gone in a moment leaving a trail of rolling thunder and scattered sheep behind them, but this one was flying much more slowly as if searching for something.

Pilot Officer John Ramsey was in a blind rage. There had been a minor disagreement with a fellow officer just before he took off, and, instead of evaporating away as he flew his Tornado, as such things usually did, it had simmered and boiled inside him until he was totally consumed by it. Behind him his navigator was blissfully unaware of the situation which was building until the aircraft banked and turned for a second pass over the hilly landscape below them. By the time he had reached these northern reaches of the Pennines, the pilot's mind had snapped. All he was now aware of was his total hatred of mankind. All the way north he had been setting up the aircraft's armament systems, and when he had seen the Land Rover moving up the hillside as he swept majestically over, he had arrived at his decision. Banking sharply and climbing, he brought his aircraft round for a second run in, flipping the safeties off the rocket launchers as he did so. Ignoring the urgent questioning of his navigator, he lined up his sights on the now stationary vehicle, and pressed the firing button. As the missile leapt forward, Ramsey noticed that one of the occupants of the vehicle had, with some sixth sense, leapt from the cab and was even now diving for cover behind a rocky outcrop some twenty or thirty metres beyond the Land Rover. There was no time for a second missile and the pilot reacted in the only way his deranged mind could think of. He pointed the nose of the plane directly at the outcrop and the cowering figure behind it. The last thing he heard before the Tornado hit was the terrified screaming of his navigator as he tried in vain to eject.

***

Back at his cottage, Ken Howard reached inside and took down the binoculars that he always kept handy, hanging on a hook just inside the doorway ready for a close look at any unusual bird. Focussing them upon the plane, he was just in time to see a flash from the underside of one of the wings, and a trail of smoke shot off in front of the plane. The pilot had fired one of his missiles! Unbelievingly he followed the trail of the missile and was astounded to see it plunge into the side of a Land Rover which had been crossing open ground near the top of one of the hills. The vehicle disappeared in an enormous ball of flame and black smoke, pieces of burning wreckage flying high into the air leaving their own individual trails of smoke arcing behind them. The sound of the explosion reached him seconds later, but he hardly noticed it. The plane had followed the missile down, and whether it had been hit by a piece of flying wreckage, or whether the pilot was just inexperienced he didn't know, but the plane flew straight through the pall of smoke and directly into the hillside beyond. The explosion this time was gigantic with a tremendous fireball of orange flame mixed with black smoke which rolled heavenward. The noise, when it reached him, was ear shattering but by now he had dropped the binoculars and was standing with his hands over his ears in automatic reaction to the events.

He was in total shock at what he had witnessed. A British Air Force jet had fired a missile at a farm vehicle in the Northern Pennines and then crashed!

"These things just didn't happen," he told himself. "Not here – not in England!"

His eyes, however, told a different story. These things had happened, and he had been a witness to them!

For a while he was frozen to the spot, his mind numb with horror. The crash had occurred on a hillside beyond the village, some three or four miles away as the crow flies, but a good distance further than that along the winding Pennine roads. By now some of the village people would be speeding as fast as they dared towards the scene of the crash to see if they could help. From what he had witnessed he doubted whether anyone within a quarter mile radius of the crash stood any chance at all of survival, so intense had been the fireball.

He came to with a jolt, realising that he ought to go down there and at least offer his services to the locals. Pausing only to pick up his car keys, he ran back through the house, leaped into his car and, gunning the engine into furious life, sped off toward Kelden.

Chapter 4

"...nor the pestilence by night."

Psalm 91:6

Reaching the main road in record time he turned right towards the village, and was surprised to note that there were no other vehicles in sight. This was Saturday and there was usually quite a bit of local traffic. Lumbering farm lorries fetching and carrying goods and livestock to neighbouring market towns, but today – nothing. The roads were deserted.

Kelden itself was compact and well hidden, nestling deep into its valley, well protected from the storms which often lashed across this region. One came upon it suddenly, without warning. One minute you were driving on a country road, the next you were amongst the houses. Ken was therefore totally unprepared for the sight that met him as he rounded the last bend and entered the village.

What he saw can only be described as a scene of utter devastation. Much of the village was in ruins, with some of the houses blackened and smouldering. The plume of smoke, which he had seen earlier and assumed to be from the remains of a bonfire, was in fact from these smouldering remains. He immediately braked to avoid running into the rubble and abandoned cars which lay across his path, and sat bolt upright, staring straight ahead, hands gripping the steering wheel fiercely, to take in the scene before him.

"What on earth has been happening here?" he thought. "Where is everyone?"

The crash on the hillside was forgotten. The mystery of what had happened to this village and its inhabitants now occupied the whole of his mind.

He turned off the ignition and immediately an intense silence descended, broken only by the occasional crackle of burning timbers, or the rattle of slipping masonry as the supporting wood beneath burned through and allowed it to settle. Both sounds echoed strangely in the otherwise silent street.

"But where have the people gone?" he whispered to himself, desperate to hear a sound but at the same time afraid to disturb the cathedral-like silence. He stared wildly around frantically trying to think where they might be hiding. He had friends in this village, being a part time inhabitant here ever since he had bought the cottage some ten years ago, and he had become accepted as a member of it – as far as anyone who wasn't born in those close-knit northern communities ever is.

"The village hall, or the church, that's where they'll be," he thought to himself.

He decided to try the hall first as that was on the main street. A visit to the church would mean a detour into the back streets of the village and, until he had learned more of what had happened here, that did not appear to be a very good idea. Taking a deep breath, he opened the car door and stepped out onto the road surface. He did not slam his door, but closed it as quietly as he could. Even so the click it made on closing sounded deafening to his ears and seemed to rebound from building to building as it fled into the distance.

A delivery van, skewed across the road a few yards ahead of him, blocked much of his view of the street surface itself and as he approached it to get a better view, his feet crunched on broken shards of glass. Glancing to his right he noticed that most of the windows were shattered. The irrational thought that the plane crash on the hillside above the village might have caused all of this flashed through his head, but the burnt-out shell of what had been the hardware shop to his left refuted that. This damage must have occurred quite a few hours before the plane had crashed.

Skirting the front of the van he stared down the street. Bodies lay everywhere. Most of them were on the pavement, huddled against the shop-fronts or in doorways, some singly but many in groups. One or two were lying in the road. All appeared to have died violently. Many had gunshot wounds. This is what he had heard yesterday! There had been a wild hunt going on, but the quarry had not been game or vermin, it had been the people of this once peaceful village. He was revolted. Men, women and children, some of them personal friends of his, slaughtered indiscriminately as they went about their daily life.

He continued cautiously down the street keeping well to the centre. He had to know if there were any survivors amongst so much death, and to see if he could spot any clue as to who or what had caused such a massacre. Shop fronts had been smashed in and there were signs of looting. Some of the bodies had the spoils lying close by them and others actually lay within the wreckage of the window displays. One small body was that of a young girl not more than about twelve years old. She had been shot in the back as she fled and had fallen on top of the video recorder she had been carrying.

The village hall was on the left-hand side, about three-quarters of the way down the main street, set slightly back from the road with a small lawn containing the war memorial in front of it. It lay just beyond 'The Feathers,' the local he had contemplated visiting last evening. As he passed the pub he saw that it had not escaped unscathed. Windows were smashed and there were a great many shattered glasses lying about in the road outside. By now he was feeling distinctly in need of a stiff brandy to counteract the shock, and so he cautiously approached the doorway and peered inside. The familiar bar, where he had spent many a long winter evening in the company of friends, was devastated. The furniture lay in splinters all over the room, and hardly a piece of glassware remained intact. Blood from some of the bodies lying there had soaked into the carpet. George, the landlord lay sprawled across the bar, eyes glazed and staring. His neck had been broken. Scattered around among the bodies was an odd assortment of farm guns and spent cartridges lay everywhere.

Searching amongst the wreckage behind the bar he failed to locate a single unbroken bottle. However, he did find a case of whiskey and a couple of bottles of brandy on a shelf in a storeroom behind the bar area, along with a box containing some new half pint glasses. Opening a fresh bottle of brandy he poured himself a generous measure into one of the glasses and gratefully gulped it down. Taking the rest of the bottle with him, along with a bottle of Scotch (he would certainly need them later when the full horror of all this had sunk in), he went back out of the storeroom. Reaching for his wallet he realised that he had not picked it up when he rushed out of the cottage. Conscience would not let him leave without paying for the goods, and so he left an IOU written on a beer mat on the till and made his way back, blinking, into the sunlit street. When someone came along to clean up this mess they could contact him for payment.

The village hall was deserted although there were signs that someone had been there. Overturned tables and chairs were strewn around the room, and plates of sandwiches and small cakes had been scattered around and trodden underfoot. Bloodstains on the walls and floor told him that whoever had taken refuge here had not escaped the carnage. He found their bodies in the small yard just outside the back door of the hall. Amongst them were Emma and Bob Grindle. Both appeared to have been stabbed. Some of the victims seemed to have been killed by having their heads banged against the wall of the hall or the rough tarmac of the yard. All were elderly and in the hands of some of them were makeshift weapons, one of which was the knife that had been used to butter the sandwiches. There were traces of both blood and butter still on it.

"Of course," he remembered, "Friday night had been Old Time Dance night for the senior citizens club. Emma and Bob Grindle had often enthused about it."

Someone had burst in and massacred these old folks while they were enjoying themselves at their weekly Old Time Dance.

There was nothing he could do here and so he went back through the hall and out into the street again. There were only a few more houses and the filling station before the village came to an abrupt end. Beyond the filling station were just two de-restriction signs and the lonely road heading south east into the hills.

The sight of the filling station reminded him that his car was, by now, probably very low on petrol. He would need to fill up again before he went back to the cottage. This would mean either negotiating the length of the debris strewn street or going back the way he had come, taking the road through the hills, and coming in from the other direction. He doubted whether he had enough fuel for the latter course of action, so the street it would have to be. On the way back to his car, he called in at the village stores and picked up enough provisions to see him through the next few days, packing everything into a couple of strong carrier bags he found hanging behind the counter. He doubted whether the mess would be cleared up before then. When they arrived the police would probably cordon off the village for at least a week. He was about to leave his IOU by the till when a sudden thought struck him.

"What would the police think when they arrived to find the whole population of Kelden brutally murdered, and my IOUs lying around all over the place? They would probably arrest me immediately and then I'll spend this holiday locked in the depths of some police station being questioned at regular intervals on a matter about which I really know nothing. No! Far better that I come back when all this is over and settle my debts then."

Carefully propping his carrier bags in the shop doorway he went back down to 'The Feathers' and retrieved his IOU.

On his return to the shop he noticed that two of the bodies lying in the roadway were very close together and lying in such a way that it would be impossible to get the car past without running over them. This he could never do, and so he had no option but to drag them out of the way.

His stomach turned as he approached them as there had been a great deal of blood, but the brandy had done sterling work and he held on to his breakfast. He recognised one of the men immediately as one of the local shopkeepers. He was covered in deep gashes – the obvious cause of his death. The other man was lying face down and when Ken went over to move him he saw that he was holding a heavily bloodstained axe firmly in his right hand. He had no doubt that here lay the killer of the shopkeeper. He started to drag him out of the way and as he did so he accidentally rolled him over. Ken was thunderstruck! Here lay another man he recognised! In life the two men had been firm friends, and his body was also covered in deep gashes. Underneath the body lay a second blood-encrusted hand axe.

In blind horror Ken ran back to the car, dived in behind the wheel and slammed his hand against the door locking button. He double checked that all the doors were securely locked before letting out a great gasp of breath. His panic had been so complete that he had been holding his breath since he started running. Slowly he regained control of himself, forcing his breathing to become more even and waiting for his heart to stop pounding against his rib cage. His mind refused to accept what his eyes had seen. Such things just didn't happen! There must be another answer, but, try as he might, he could see no other conclusion to be drawn from the facts as he had observed them. The two men had indeed been firm friends, but it went deeper that that. These two had worked together for years in the family hardware shop in the village. They had, in fact, been father and son, and it looked very much as if they had stood face to face and hacked each other to death!

A quotation from somewhere forced itself into his mind.

"Now the brother shall betray the brother to death, and the father the son, and the children shall rise up against their parents and cause them to be put to death..."

"...They're not right in the head...!"

The more he saw the more he realised that this village had not been invaded from the outside. These people had done this to themselves. He dug his fingernails into the palms of his hands, using the pain to try to provoke rational thought. His instincts screamed for him to turn round and get as far away from here as fast as possible, and he actually had the engine running and had reversed a few yards before he remembered the petrol situation and jammed his foot on the brake bringing the car, screeching wildly, to a halt once more. He really had to get himself back under control.

A glance at the fuel gauge showed him that he would not get far if he did run. The needle was well down into the red section. There was nothing else for it, but to proceed with his original plan and drive down the main street to the filling station at the far end.

Breathing deeply to control his fear he edged the car forward, mounting the pavement where necessary to avoid obstructions. When he got to the point where the two bodies needed to be moved fear welled up in him again. His skin crawled and the hair on the back of his neck prickled. The bodies were no longer blocking his way, but lay to one side of the road – still in the same positions relative to each other as far as he could tell, but now well out of the way. He forced himself to remain calm and as he urged the car forward he saw, out of the corner of his eye, the two carrier bags he had put down in the shop doorway. Much as he needed the contents of those two bags, there was no way that he was going to leave the fragile security that his car offered to retrieve them, and so he drove on.

As he pulled onto the forecourt of the filling station, he saw that he had had a stroke of good fortune. If it had been closed when disaster struck, then all would have been locked up and he would have been unable to work the pumps, but the station had been open. All he had to do was switch on the correct pump and fill up.

An inspection through the windows of the forecourt shop suggested that it was unoccupied. There were, however, areas that were hidden. Indeed there were a couple of doors on the rear wall which presumably led to storage rooms and toilets. Ken was therefore extremely cautious as he pushed open the door and went inside. So far he had not seen any survivors, but someone must have been last.

Searching around as quietly as he could he soon located the pump switches and, just to make sure, depressed them all. Returning to his car he jammed the nozzle into the filler pipe, and, using a roll of paper left on the forecourt for customer use, he wedged the trigger on the nozzle fully open and quickly climbed back into the relative safety of his car to wait for the tank to fill. In doing so he noticed that the two carrier bags which he had left in the shop doorway were now sitting comfortably on the back seat!

He put his hands up and clutched his head, feeling as if he were going out of his mind, a headache once again pounding away behind his eyes. For what seemed an eternity he sat there in frozen terror and there is no telling how long he would have remained in that state had not a shadow fallen across the steering wheel of his car.

Looking up with a start he saw a wild-eyed, dishevelled looking man staring in at him through the passenger side window. Seconds later the newcomer was tearing frantically at the door handle and hurling abuse at Ken, huddled inside the vehicle. The man's face, hair and clothing were spattered with a great amount of congealed blood. When he found that he could not open the door, he reached down and raised a double barrelled shotgun which he aimed at Ken through the closed window. Ken thought that his last moment had come but, as a wave of pain surged up behind his eyes, he saw the gun jerk upward and the shot just cleared the roof of his car. In his terrified state, Ken had not dared switch off the engine of the car while it was filling up and now he was able to take full advantage of this by flooring the accelerator and letting out the clutch in an instant, causing the car to leap forward and screech wildly away before the gun could be brought to bear and the second barrel discharged. During this sudden acceleration the petrol pump nozzle jammed firmly into the car's petrol cap opening and, though it distorted the bodywork considerably, it held tight, ripping the pipe from the pump body and trailing it behind the swerving car like a thin green snake, leaving a trail of petrol in its wake. The wild eyed gunman seemed to be having trouble bringing the gun to bear on the rear of the fast disappearing car, while petrol gushed in torrents from the damaged pump, spreading quickly over the forecourt and onto the road. Eventually the gun came up and the man got off his second shot.

Ken glanced into the driving mirror just in time to see the flash as the gun discharged. The rear windscreen of the car crazed over as the shot hit it, turning a milky white and almost immediately it glowed orange. Finally it caved inwards altogether, accompanied by the sound of a gigantic explosion, as the flash from the gun set off the petrol which lapped around the feet of the gunman. To Ken the events of the next few seconds appeared to take place in slow motion. First of all the car slewed madly sideways caught in the ferocity of the blast, coming to a halt sideways on across the road. In a single action Ken slammed open the door and dived from the vehicle.

Looking back towards the scene of the explosion through the side window of the car he had seen a thin finger of flame snaking along the path of petrol left on the road by the trailing filler pipe, towards his own petrol tank. Rolling as he hit the road he was immediately on his feet and after a couple of gigantic bounds he dived for the safety of the ditch, just as his own vehicle exploded. In his mind he could still see the glimpse he had caught of his would-be assassin, writhing and rolling, engulfed in the flames from the burning petrol station. This, however, was no time for resting. Ken realised that he had to put more distance between himself and the conflagration. Immediately he was back onto the road and sprinting for the bend about seventy metres distant. He only just made it. Collapsing onto the verge beside the road just around the corner, he felt the ground shake and simultaneously heard the mighty explosion as the filling station's underground storage tanks went up.

For a while he lay on his face and hugged the ground, sobbing helplessly in reaction to his experiences of the last few minutes, but gradually he was able to regain his hold upon himself, and, as the sobbing died away, he considered his situation. He was certainly very vulnerable in his present position should another would-be murderer appear, and that circumstance seemed to be one that was distinctly possible, for the man who had tried to shoot him had been no stranger to the village, but a local farmer with whom he had shared a drink on many a winter's night in the village pub. This man had no reason for wanting him dead, yet Ken had seen a blind murderous rage in his wild eyes when he had pointed the shotgun in his direction. From the evidence he had seen it appeared that the whole village had been struck down by the same madness setting neighbour against neighbour and father against child. What had caused it all he had, as yet, no way of knowing, but he knew that if anyone remained alive they would come looking for the cause of the explosion and, finding his burning car with no body inside it they would, in all probability, come looking for him. They might, of course, take the gunman to be the owner of the vehicle but he could not rely on that. In any case, he could no longer assume that anyone who came to investigate would be friendly, and it was therefore imperative that he found a less exposed position than this roadside verge.

Taking stock of his position he saw that he was in a fairly narrow gorge where the road passed between two walls of rock. By the side of the road ran the stream that had originally cut the gorge, a stream which, Ken knew, ran behind the houses on the south westerly side of the village. Scrambling off the paved surface he dropped down to the side of the stream and, screened from the roadway by a large holly bush, sat down on a rock to formulate some sort of a plan for extricating himself safely from his present somewhat precarious situation.

Downstream from here the hills stretched on for a good number of miles before any other settlement, and taking that way out, bruised and shaken as he was, did not present a very appealing prospect. Upstream lay the village and all the unknown danger which it held. By now he was feeling the cold. The brandy he had drunk had completed its work and had dispersed throughout his body. He was also beginning to feel the effects of shock and the punishment which recent events had inflicted upon his nervous system as well as upon his physical body. Finally he made the only choice open to him. He had to return to the village, by way of the stream, and there he could obtain whatever he needed to keep body and soul together. It was also obvious that he now needed another car if he wished to get out of the area.

Returning to the village by way of the stream was not as easy as it at first sounded. The recent rains had swelled the waters to a point where the small muddy path was, in places under a good six inches of water, and the rushing sound of the torrent made distant noises very difficult to hear. When he reached the place where the filling station had stood on the opposite side of the road he proceeded with such caution that he dropped to his hands and knees where there was little undergrowth, risking the mud and cold water rather than detection by anyone who had come to investigate the fire. Thus it was that when he came to the first of the houses, Ken was in a very sorry state. He had lost his footing on the muddy path a number of times and so, covered in mud, dripping wet from the knees down, and in a very jumpy frame of mind from the many noises, heard or imagined which had caused him to dive for cover, he re-entered Kelden.

Most of the side roads on this side of the village terminated at the stream. A tarmac path had been constructed between it and the back gardens of the houses that bordered it to provide access for the residents. This path made the walking easier but Ken felt very exposed on it, imagining that the rear windows of each house masked hidden eyes and he was alert to any sign of occupation. Twice sudden movements caught his attention and he ducked into whatever cover was available, but on both occasions these proved to be from curtains flapping in the breeze through broken windows. The damage to the village was not quite so apparent from the rear, but Ken was distinctly aware of the smell of smoke that hung in the air.

He came at last to a place where his progress was blocked by a high stone wall; the stream gushing out of a low archway skilfully constructed by some long dead craftsman. This, Ken knew, was the churchyard wall, and it marked the point where he must return to the main street if he wanted to pick up the items which he now needed more than ever. He was cold, tired, cut, bruised and very frightened as he turned right and walked up the path which led alongside the wall back towards the central thoroughfare of the village.

To his left, beyond the wall lay the churchyard, and on coming to an open gate, he went through it and found himself quite close to the rear corner of the church building. The structure was not large as church buildings go, but it was solidly built of grey gritstone, weathered almost to black by the wind and rain. Its form was standard Church of England, dating back to the eighteenth century. This was a traditional place of refuge, and Ken thought that if any of the villagers had escaped from the slaughter, this was where he might find them, and the welcome might prove to be friendlier amongst any surviving church folk.

He pushed open a side door which led into the choir vestry and stepped warily inside.

Passing through the small vestry, which smelled of musty hymn books and choir robes, he approached the door which led into the main body of the church. Despite the bright sunlight outside, the interior was dim and it took a moment or two for his eyes to grow accustomed to the low level of light. The church had proved to be no sanctuary to those who had taken refuge there. Bodies littered the pews, and again there was evidence of a battle from within rather than an invasion from without. The stout main door of the church had been barricaded on the inside and this was still in place. The killing must have started amongst those who had taken refuge here. Having fortified the front door they had also locked all the other entrances to the church. When the madness struck the last one left alive had unlocked and left by the door by which Ken had entered, although Ken had no way of knowing this at the time.

There was nothing he could do here, and the inside of the thick walled building was even colder than the air outside. Ken's mud-caked, sodden clothing was freezing cold against his skin and he knew that he must get warm soon or else risk hypothermia. A movement at the back of the church caught his eye, and he swiftly ducked down behind one of the pews. After a while he risked peering over the pew back. The movement was still there. Something was swinging gently too and fro in one dim corner. Cautiously he moved towards it, and as he did so he heard the words "Oh no, oh no, oh no..." repeated very very quietly over and over again, and a feeling of absolute terror reached into his mind. The terror however was not his! Someone else was in great fear and he, Ken, was sensing that fear!

As he drew closer to the movement, he saw that it was the figure of a man, swinging with his feet some distance above the floor. The man was wearing clerical robes. The vicar had ended his days strung up on a bell rope, probably by members of his own congregation. As he approached the slowly swinging figure the feeling of terror increased and the words degenerated into an unintelligible gabble. Then Ken saw the foot. It was quite small and was clad in a trainer. It obviously belonged to a child and was sticking out from behind a bookcase that contained the service books. This also seemed to be the source of the sounds.

He approached the bookcase slowly and as he did so the owner of the foot tried to draw it further in, but there just wasn't any more room. Gently pulling back the heavy bookcase, Ken peered behind it. Immediately there was a piercing scream, followed by the words "I'm going to die. Oh please don't!" and then absolute silence as the child lapsed into unconsciousness through sheer fright. The external terror which Ken had felt also disappeared, only to be replaced by a terror of his own. While the child had been screaming and uttering those last words, Ken had had a clear view of its face. The terror was caused by the fact that, though the sounds had been audible and obviously came from the child, the child's mouth had been clamped firmly shut the whole time!

Ken was now shivering uncontrollably, as much from fright as from the cold. He had met, and dealt with, so much that he couldn't understand today that he just had to get away to somewhere safe and think. Sweeping up the unconscious child into his arms, he stumbled back through the church and out into the bright sunlight. Throwing caution to the wind he hurried directly towards the main street again. The sunlight revealed that the child was blue with cold, having spent at least the last twelve hours hiding in the church, and obviously needed attention fairly rapidly. Setting his light load in the doorway of the shop where he left the shopping bags earlier, Ken re-entered the premises, hurrying through the door at the rear and dashed up the stairs leading to the flat above the premises. As he expected, the flat was unoccupied. Locating the bedroom, he stripped the duvet from the bed to wrap the child in. In the wardrobe he found a heavy winter coat to wrap around himself. Returning downstairs he rolled the child in the duvet and then went back into the shop to fill up a couple more carrier bags with provisions, including some spirits from the small off licence section he had missed earlier.

The main need now was for transport. On inspection, the cars in the street were either damaged or had no keys in the ignition. Ken racked his brains for a solution. It was then that he remembered the garage where he had sometimes had his car repaired. It lay in one of the streets behind the shops almost opposite where he now stood. If at any time he had been unable to collect his car before the garage had closed for the night he had an arrangement with the proprietor to have the car left locked outside the workshop, and the keys hidden for him to collect later. With any luck...! He dashed across the street and down the side road opposite, then turned right into the street behind the shops. Outside the workshop doors stood a fairly new Range Rover, and tucked inside the exhaust pipe was a key! He took the key and opened a small locked flap set high in the double doors of the workshop. Inside the flap was a small compartment containing the keys to the Range Rover. Ken just couldn't believe his good luck. After all that had happened this day, fortune at last seemed to be smiling on him. He could not have picked a better vehicle if he had had a whole showroom to choose from.

Driving back to the High Street, he laid the child along the front seat, placed the shopping bags on the floor, climbed back into the driver's seat and headed slowly back along the route he had taken into the village some six hours ago. Once clear of any obstructions he pressed the accelerator hard down and headed for the comparative safety of the hills with as much speed as he could muster.

Chapter 5

"For then shall be great tribulation…"

St. Matthew 24:21

The cottage, when he reached it, seemed like a haven of peace in a hostile world, and Ken felt like he had been away for days rather than a matter of hours. Realising that it might now prove dangerous to advertise his presence, he parked the Range Rover carefully out of sight around the back, carried the still unconscious youngster into the house and laid him on the couch in front of the fireplace. The light was fading fast, but before he turned on the lamp, Ken fetched an old blanket from the airing cupboard and draped it over the window. A lighted window could be seen for miles in these hills and he did not want to attract any unwelcome visitors, should anyone be roaming around with murder in his heart.

His next job was to light a fire, for although the central heating was now on, it was only set to provide background warmth, not the real warmth of an open fire, and the child needed such warmth even more than Ken did. Having seen to that task, he checked that the boy was comfortable and then took himself up to the bathroom for a hot shower.

Passing the full length mirror on the landing, Ken stopped in amazement. No wonder the child had been so frightened of him when he had entered the church. His clothes and hair were caked in thick brown mud, which had dried in streaks on his face where it was mixed with blood from the many small abrasions and cuts which he had not noticed until that moment. The only difference between himself and the man who had tried to kill him earlier was that there was no wild, murderous rage to be seen in Ken's eyes, but the child would not have been aware of that in the dimness of the church.

The shower hurt. Ken's body was a mass of abrasions and bruises, and already he could feel his muscles beginning to stiffen up from the prolonged punishment they had received during the day. No activity he had ever undertaken had left him feeling as he now felt. He had just finished and was dabbing at his sore body with a soft towel, when there was a piercing scream from below, followed by a wild incoherent gabbling sound. Wrapping the towel around him, Ken leapt down the stairs two at a time, his body protesting at the sudden return to strenuous activity. Throwing open the sitting room door, he bounded in, to find the child still lying on the couch, eyes tightly closed, and rolling his head from side to side. The gabble subsided, to be replaced by a description of what had taken place in the church. Ken looked at the child in amazement and he felt the hair on his neck prickle again, for though the words were clear as a bell in his ears, the boy uttered not a single sound.

"What I'm hearing are the child's thoughts." The thought struck him like a thunderclap and for a moment his own mind reeled, then he pulled himself together and made a determined effort to listen.

"They're coming… Come on Mum, into the church before they catch us. We'll be safe there. I wonder where Dad is…? They'll be here soon… let's help barricade the door… No, no this isn't happening… Why are you all fighting each other? Don't try to stop them… No, oh no, leave him alone… What are they doing…? They've killed him… They've killed him… They've all gone mad… Oh help me, God… They've hung him on the bell rope… He's just swinging… swinging… swinging… They're all killing each other… must hide… Swinging… swinging…"

As the thoughts died away into silence, the small boy's eyes opened momentarily before he once again drifted off into unconsciousness.

Ken's own mind was in turmoil, with a thousand and one unanswered questions jostling for position in his brain, tumbling over each other as they sought their own answers. One thing was clear, and that was the fact that so much which had happened seemed incredible and outside normal experience that all must be examined with a completely open mind to try to make some sense out of it.

"First things first, though," he said to himself. "I suppose I ought to phone the police and let them know what's been going on here."

Picking up the telephone, he dialled 999 and waited. The phone on the other end rang and continued to ring, but there was no answer. Cold fingers ran up and down Ken's spine. This was almost unheard of. Eventually he replaced the receiver, and having looked up the number, he dialled the police station in Skipton. After a short delay he got the engaged tone, and though he held on for several minutes the line failed to clear.

"Something big must have happened to tie up 999 operators and police phones in the area," he thought.

He went back to the couch and looked down at the child. The boy appeared to be about twelve or thirteen years old, with a thin face and straight brown hair, cut in an unfashionable fringe. His eyes, Ken had seen when they fluttered open, were brown. He was dressed in an army-style khaki pullover with patches on elbows and shoulders, blue jeans and trainers, although all of these were now hidden by the duvet. Ken was relieved to see that there was now much more colour coming back into the thin features.

After climbing into his pyjamas and dressing gown he tried the numbers again with precisely the same result. He had just replaced the receiver for the second time when once more his mind was filled with the sound of the boy's thoughts. This time however the boy was more in control although still very frightened. Ken felt him drifting back to consciousness as he approached the couch. The boy's eyes opened and stayed open and Ken felt the swift surge of panic that ran though the young mind. He stood a good two metres away from the couch, held up his hands to show that he was not holding anything dangerous and then spoke very quietly.

"Don't worry, you're safe now."

At the sound of a quiet voice the panic in the boy's mind subsided, but apprehension remained.

Still in a quiet voice,

"I'm Ken, what's your name?"

"Jamie" flashed the thought, although the boy remained silent.

"Well, Jamie…" said Ken,

The panic was immediate and total.

"How does he know my name?" was all that Ken could make out among the garbled thoughts.

Again Ken set about calming the child, not making any move that could be considered threatening. Once more the panic subsided as the boy realised that his life was not in danger.

In the child's mind was hunger, and this reminded Ken that he himself had not eaten since breakfast time and it was now almost seven in the evening.

"How about some soup?" he asked.

The mind response was an immediate acceptance – but the boy still did not speak.

Learning quickly from his mistake, Ken ignored the boy's thoughts and continued,

"I'm going to make some for myself, I'm starving. Would you like some?"

This time the response was a nod.

"Right," Ken grinned, pleased that he had at last handled the situation correctly, "I won't be a minute."

In the kitchen, as he heated the soup, he caught more of Jamie's thoughts as he wondered where he was, how he had got here, and what was going to happen to him, and this allowed Ken to work out just what to talk about when he went back in. Returning to the front room, he set the two steaming mugs of soup side by side on the small table that was set between the couch and his chair and sat down.

"Now be careful and drink it slowly. It's hot." he said, keeping his voice soft and friendly.

Jamie struggled into a sitting position and cupped the mug in his hands, taking regular sips of the hot, meaty soup, and gazing into the fire, all the time wondering where he was. The apprehension however was gradually disappearing, and was being replaced by a tenuous strand of hope.

A second mug of soup was offered, accepted and brought

in, and it was while this was being despatched that Ken tried again.

"What's your name?"

This time the boy was more forthcoming.

"Thomas James Croxten," his voice was gruff, and he spoke in an almost inaudible whisper. He appeared to have forgotten Ken's faux pas in using his pet name a few moments ago, and Ken tried to reassure him.

"Well, Thomas James Croxten," he said, "I'm Ken Howard, and this is my home. There's no need to worry, you're perfectly safe now, and you're welcome to stay as long as you want to," and then, after a pause to allow time for this to sink in, "Do you live in Kelden?"

Ken felt it coming and moved over to sit by the boy just before the dam burst. Huge sobs welled up from deep inside the child and Ken held him close and tried to comfort him as the release of tension surged out in a flood of natural childish tears.

The tears continued for quiet some time, washing the fear out of his system, but when they eventually subsided, they had done their healing work and the child seemed ready to talk.

"M... M... My friends all call me Jamie," he stuttered, eager to add Ken to that select band.

He was obviously very disturbed by recent events, being unable to understand why the things he had witnessed had happened. On many of the points Ken was as much in the dark as the boy himself, but he did get a much clearer idea of what had taken place in the village from his account.

It seemed to have started at around lunchtime on Friday, when one of the locals went into 'The Feathers' and started an argument with another man in the bar. Jamie did not know any of the details, but it seemed to have been over one of the local girls. A fight had broken out, and one of the protagonists had been stabbed. People took sides, forming up to defend the party whose version of the truth they believed. When the police had arrived to make an arrest, they themselves became the targets of the hostilities. Their car was burned and the two officers taken hostage. From there it all seemed to snowball. The whole village seethed with unreasoning hatred. Some groups, like the elderly,

61

appeared to have been less affected than the rest and had tried to continue with their normal activities, others, like the ones in the church had tried to cut themselves off from it, but the madness was able to penetrate locked doors and before long the murder in the heart of man boiled up into action, and the wild indiscriminate killing began – even amongst those in the church.

Jamie had seen it start there, with one of the churchwardens bludgeoning an elderly choir member to death with the heavy metal cross from the communion table. Instinct had then taken over and he had crawled into his hiding place and kept well out of the way. He had seen them hang the vicar, and then turn upon each other. The young had not been immune, although Jamie himself did not seem to have been affected. Children of all ages had attacked anyone in sight until they themselves died at the hands of someone else. He did not know how long it had lasted, but eventually he had heard lone footsteps dying away towards the door by which Ken had entered, bolts being drawn back, and then a long silence, punctuated only occasionally by distant shots and screams from outside. He had not dared move all the long night, despite the cold and hunger, and when Ken had come in Jamie had thought someone had returned to ensure that no one remained alive. Seeing Ken in such a state in the dim light of the church had only confirmed this impression and he had uttered that soundless scream just before unconsciousness claimed him.

When he had finished his account, Jamie turned to Ken, with his mind asking the question,

"Why did it happen?"

It was then that Ken realised that the thought projection was selective. Throughout Jamie's account only odd thoughts had escaped to amplify his story, and all of these were at points where the emotional stress was greatest. The mundane thoughts did not break through. It was as if the boy's mind was functioning on two different levels, with the high level thoughts being broadcast, and the low level ones remaining hidden. When he reached the part of the narrative where Ken had appeared in the church Jamie's thoughts had indicated what he had thought of Ken, and it was then that he realised that the boy had no idea that some of the contents of his mind could be heard.

A sudden alarming thought struck Ken. How far did these thought waves travel? Supposing others could also hear them and were, even now, being guided towards the cottage? As he thought this, a second realisation came to him. There had been no reaction from the boy to Ken's alarming thought. The logical conclusion therefore was that Jamie was not able to receive thoughts – only broadcast them!

All of Jamie's thoughts had now subsided to the lower, unheard level. It was imperative that Ken should be able to discover the range of the thought projection, and so he suddenly stood up and made for the kitchen door. The sudden activity alarmed the child, and Ken could pick up his thoughts again as he went through the kitchen and into the night beyond. A few metres from the house Ken was relieved to find that the thoughts rapidly died away and became inaudible after a few paces. Just to make sure he started back. The thoughts rose in 'volume'. The range was only a few metres and would probably not be picked up on the road which ran past the smallish front garden of the cottage. This brought considerable relief to Ken and he relaxed and went back in to the boy, carefully locking and bolting the back door after him. There may not have been a beacon of thought guiding unwelcome visitors in, but one never knew who was at large in the night and the experiences of the day had taught him the need for caution.

On his return, he was soon able to reassure the boy that there was no cause for alarm, and the frightened thoughts died away again. Suddenly Ken was aware of how tired he was. The punishment his body had absorbed was now giving rise to a thousand and one small aches and pains, and that body was also crying out for sleep. Before he could indulge himself, however, there were still a few things left to attend to. He ran a warm bath for the boy, and while Jamie relaxed in it, Ken prepared a hot water bottle and made up the bed in the second bedroom. He looked out a pair of his own, far too large, but soft and clean pyjamas for Jamie to sleep in, and, when the child was snug and dry, gently tucked him up in the soft, warm bed. The boy was totally drained by his recent experiences, and was asleep almost before his head hit the pillow.

Before getting into his own bed, Ken tried to contact the police once more, but the results were identical to those of the earlier attempts. The phone in the Skipton police station was still engaged and the 999 service did not answer. This disturbed Ken, and when he at last climbed into bed, despite his tiredness, his troubled thoughts kept sleep at bay.

"What on earth," he wondered, "is going on?"

The plane crash, which had sent him hurrying down to the village in the first place, was almost unbelievable, but the fact that there did not seem to have been any indication of a search for the missing Tornado was totally inexplicable. In fact, on reflection, Ken realised that he had not seen any other aircraft at all that day, including airliners. Normally the sky would have been crossed by any number of high level vapour trails, and he did not recall seeing a single one scarring the cloudless blue of the sky. Granted he had been rather preoccupied but he was normally pretty observant, and surely a helicopter or some other search aircraft would have been sent out once the fighter had disappeared. The RAF usually knew where its aircraft were at any given moment.

There was also the inexplicable lack of through traffic. Kelden was not on any major trunk road, and the nearby A1 took a great deal of the traffic, but the village usually had its fair share passing through, Today, however, Ken had not seen a single moving vehicle other than his own. The happenings in the village itself, were also beyond his capacity to explain. True, his perception was that violence had been getting worse lately, you only had to read the newspaper accounts of rioting after football matches to be aware of that, but a whole community going mad – it was unheard of! Or was it? Somewhere at the back of his mind Ken had the disturbing thought that this, or something like it, may have happened before, but he was unable to pin down where or when.

As his thoughts jumbled through his head, Ken remembered 'The Light'. Surely that could not have been a coincidence. It must have had something to do with recent events, but what? If the light was what drove people insane why hadn't he been affected, and where did Jamie fit into the picture? How too could he account for the loose spark plug and the small screw? And why had his would be assassin missed at such close range?

With such thoughts Ken drifted into a fitful sleep which was haunted by strange troubled dreams of Emma Grindle chasing him with a carving knife, shrieking like a banshee for his blood, and he himself running headlong down the village street, with cars, bodies and piles of rubble all conspiring to get in his way and slow him down. When he ran into them it was like struggling through treacle, and Emma, who seemed to have no trouble at all with the obstructions, was gaining on him. Suddenly he was on a battlefield with exploding petrol pumps all around him and ragged white sheets dangling from the branches of dead, riven trees. The sheets slowly rotated and were seen to be robed clergy hanging by the neck, their faces blue and bloated as they swung gently to and fro. An aircraft shrieked in towards him and Ken could see the crazed face of the pilot as he aimed the needle sharp nose directly at his chest. Diving for cover he found himself falling infinitely slowly towards a spinning white light, flashed through with streaks of orange and blue.

He awoke with a start, bathed in sweat. From the spare room came the sound of coughing.

"The boy's caught a chill, sitting for so long inside that icy church," he thought.

His eyes felt sore and his body protested as he struggled to turn over, pulling the bedclothes tightly around him. Sleep however evaded him and his mind returned once more to his earlier theme.

"Silmoor. That had been the name of the Devonshire village where the neighbours had fought a pitched battle against each other for no apparent reason, resulting in many deaths a couple of years ago," he remembered. News of it had been suppressed at the time, but accounts had leaked out through gossip and hearsay, "...and wasn't there something about a massacre in a place called Hungerfield...?" With these and other similar thoughts running through his brain, Ken slowly drifted back into sleep, accompanied by the sound of fitful coughing from the other room.

Awakening the following morning was not a comfortable

experience. His head throbbed and there did not seem to be an undamaged spot on his whole body. Where joints and muscles did not ache, bruises, cuts and abrasions made their presence felt with varying degrees of painfulness. Forcing himself upright, he swung his legs over to sit on the side of the bed, listening intently to the sounds of the morning. The wind had arisen again during the night and was gusting around the cottage, seeking out every unsealed opening by which to gain entry. His body protested vigorously as he stood up and crossed to the window, drawing aside the curtain to peer out. The blue skies of yesterday were no more, having been replaced, during the night, by low grey clouds which scudded across the hilltops. The rain, however, was holding off so far. Nothing seemed to be amiss outside, so Ken let the curtain fall back into place, picked up his dressing gown from the bedside chair, and, pulling it on, followed the sound of coughing into the next room.

As soon as he saw the boy he knew that all was not well. The child's face was flushed, and his eyes, when he opened them to look at Ken, had a feverish brightness about them. Ken sat on the edge of the bed and felt Jamie's forehead. It was hot and dry, although the boy's pyjamas and bedclothes were soaked with perspiration. The few thoughts which escaped from his mind were extremely muddled and of very low intensity.

Ken went downstairs and brought the boy a glass of water, which Jamie accepted gratefully, but when asked he indicated that he wanted nothing to eat. Digging out his last pair of clean pyjamas from the airing cupboard, along with fresh bedding, Ken took them back to the boy's room, and soon had him tucked up warm and dry again. The coughing intensified each time the child was moved, and it was obvious to Ken that the boy was in need of some sort of medication.

By now he was ravenous, the soup of the previous evening, sustaining at the time, being no substitute for solid food. A substantial breakfast was called for, and he was glad that he had taken the time to go back for that second lot of provisions. As the bacon cooked he nipped back up to Jamie's room to see if he had changed his mind about food, but the boy, still looking hot and flushed, was dozing again.

Over breakfast Ken came to a decision. There was no chemist in Kelden (he was not sure that he wanted to return there if there had been), and something had to be done for Jamie, therefore a trip to a larger town was necessary. Whilst not being particularly large, Skipton seemed the obvious choice, and by going there he could kill two birds with one stone. When he had again tried to phone the police in Skipton, during the cooking of breakfast, he had found the line to be engaged once more. A personal visit would solve that little problem without the need for any further attempts at phone calls.

After he had cleared away the breakfast dishes he returned to Jamie's bedside, but the lad was still dozing and, by his breathing, was in some distress. Ken washed, shaved and dressed as quickly as he could, choosing serviceable mountain walking gear. He was determined that, after the events of yesterday, he was going to be prepared for any eventuality. He chose a thick warm winter coat to wrap Jamie in, putting heavy woollen socks on his feet and finally re-wrapping him in last night's duvet before carrying him out and laying him on the rear seat of the Range Rover.

After packing his rucksack with all he could think of which might prove useful on the trip, Ken made the house secure and returned to the vehicle. Sitting in the driver's seat, with all the doors securely locked, he spread out a local Ordnance Survey map on the seat beside him, and considered his route. There were a number of different options, but the shortest by far was the route he had taken through the hills on the way up. His one worry there was the fallen tree, but he thought that one of the local farmers was sure to have removed it over the last two days. These hill roads were lonely – but not that lonely! He therefore decided to take a chance and return to Skipton that way.

It was much easier to navigate by daylight and so Ken, breaking his own unwritten rule of isolation, turned on the Range Rover's radio to see if news of the events which had occurred in this area had reached the outside world. The radio, however, appeared to be broken, for though he tried frequency after frequency all that came over the speakers was the hiss of white noise. Turning the radio off again he concentrated upon his driving. From the back seat came the sound of Jamie's coughing, now deep and hacking, and his breathing was sounding fast and shallow. This, along with the fact that there were now only a few stray thoughts escaping, and those being muddled and jumbled, seemed to indicate that the boy's condition was not good, and it worried Ken.

Eventually they reached the place where the fallen tree had temporarily blocked Ken's progress on his northbound journey, and his heart sank as it came into sight. The tree was still fully across the road, blocking any further progress. Braking to a halt, he got out to examine the situation. The obstruction was not as large as it had appeared in the dark, but it was still too big to move single-handed. The roots to Ken's right were still partly embedded in the earth. He went over to examine the other end. There to the left of the tree were the deep ruts marking where he had spun the back wheels of his car, and in the daylight he could see just how deep they were. Peculiarly, however, there were no tyre tracks leading from those ruts back onto the road surface. Except for the two lighter tracks left by the front wheels, the grass was unmarked. This was yet another mystery to add to the inexplicable events of the last few days.

The sound of coughing from the interior of the Range Rover reminded Ken that he had no time to indulge in idle speculation. He had to devise a method of removing that tree! Perhaps if he could find a long enough lever he could move it enough to get past. Looking around, he noted that nothing in the vicinity presented itself as being suitable. He therefore went around to see what was contained in the rear of the Range Rover, and his eyes lighted upon a possible solution. There lay a neat coil of stout rope. It was but the work of a few minutes to attach one end to the tree trunk near to the top and the other to the chassis of the vehicle. Engaging four wheel drive, he slowly backed away. The rope tightened and began to stretch as it took the strain, but gradually the tree began to move, pivoting on the embedded roots, and pulling clear of the other side of the road. When he judged that there was enough room to get past Ken stopped, then eased forward slightly to slacken the rope off. The knots had pulled tight with the load, and it took a little while to free them, but one never knew when a rope might be useful, so he was not abandoning it. Getting it free at last he threw it into the back of the car, jumped back behind the wheel and eased forward past the tree, glancing again at the dead-end wheel ruts as he did so. Once past the obstruction, he roared off towards Skipton and, he fervently hoped, normality and help for Jamie.

Chapter 6

"In a dream, in a vision of the night..."

Job 33:15

Turning left onto the main road, he headed quickly for the town. They had not gone far, however, before a small group of stationary vehicles appeared up ahead. Ken groaned inwardly as he drew nearer to them, for here, repeated on the approaches to Skipton were the same sights which had met him as he entered Kelden. A minor accident had occurred at a road junction, but it had not stayed minor for long. Those involved in the bump had got out of their vehicles, and the usual argument over blame had ensued. Tempers had boiled, sparking the madness, the results of which were there to be seen in the form of the bodies of at least some of those involved. It had not ended there though as passing motorists, stopping out of curiosity had become embroiled, and the death toll had mounted.

Ken did not know these details, but the results were clear to see. It was obvious that some of the drivers had used their cars as weapons, crushing groups of fighting people into the bodywork of their own vehicles. Whether anyone had escaped or not it was impossible to tell. Trails of dried blood led to bodies lying away from the vehicles, but they appeared to have been made by those people whose body lay at the end of the trail, either trying to escape or pursuing someone else, even though they themselves had sustained fatal injuries. The sight was sickening and, for Ken, depressing in the extreme. No longer could he think of this madness as a localised phenomenon, contained within the village. It obviously had a much wider field of influence.

"How far does this thing extend?" he asked himself.

He had no idea, but however far it went he had to get

beyond it and seek medical help for the child. First, however, he knew that he had to enter the town, despite the risks involved, and seek out a pharmacy to see if he could find a medicine which would be of help, at least in a temporary capacity, to Jamie. The road was still passable and he was able to ease the Range Rover around the carnage.

As he drew nearer to the town, such sights became more common and, entering the built-up area, he saw that here was a repeat of Kelden, but on a more horrifying scale. Events seemed to have followed the precise pattern of those in the village. Keeping a wary watch out for any signs of movement, he drove slowly into the town, heading for the chemist's shop which he had used on earlier and happier visits to the town. By the time he reached it, Ken knew that this was not going to be the short shopping expedition he had planned. He had no idea how far he was going to have to travel before he found help, and he realised that he might not even reach the security of his cottage again before nightfall. With this realisation came another, the provisions he had made for the trip were hopelessly inadequate. He had to be much better prepared for any contingency in future!

By now Jamie was drifting in and out of sleep and during the more wakeful periods his coughing intensified, and only the occasional stray thought escaped. Ken parked the vehicle in the centre of the wide street immediately in front of the church. On his last visit this had been a bustling market place with plastic sheeted stalls of all descriptions stretching down both sides of the wide street. Leaving Jamie locked in the Range Rover; Ken took a last searching look around, and hurried over to the shop.

The sight which met his eyes was, by now, a familiar one, with glass from smashed bottles littering the floor and horizontal surfaces. He could not, however see any bodies. Moving deeper into the interior, glass crunching underfoot, he quickly located the paediatric section of the medicines, which had escaped relatively unscathed, and searched until he found one which purported to deal with high temperatures. Putting a few bottles into the carrier bag he had brought with him for the purpose, he looked around again for any medication which might be of use, avoiding those which were kept in the pharmacy as he had no idea which of them might turn out to be dangerous, and choosing the more well known brands of antiseptics and analgesics. By the time he was ready to leave, Ken had a well-stocked and very comprehensive first aid kit.

Moving to the shop doorway, he risked a quick look up and down the road. On seeing no signs of life he made a dash for the car and quickly scrambled in, closing the door quietly, and locking it behind him. He then lay across the front seats, his eyes level with the top of the dashboard and only the top of his head visible through the windscreen, watching the road in front of him, and with the aid of the wing mirrors, behind him for any movement. If there were any marauding killers still at loose in the town, they were not going to take him unawares. When he was sure that his vehicle was not being approached, he raised himself up into a sitting position, and then clambered over the back of the seat to join Jamie in the rear. Sitting the semi-conscious child up, he poured out a measure of the thick, pink fluid and pressed it to his lips.

The boy took it, and the words "Thirsty. So thirsty…" sprang into Ken's mind. He gave the boy a second measure of the medication, and as he replaced the cap on the bottle he looked around for somewhere to obtain a drink for him. There was the usual cluster of shops surrounding the chemist's. Next to it was a shop, which specialised in high-class pastries and beyond that a milliner's, followed by a small cafe. All of them, like the chemist's, showed signs of damage.

The cafe appeared to offer the best bet, and Ken cautiously drew the Range Rover down to it, checking the street again before moving out into the shop. This one was far worse than the chemist's had been, with enough bodies piled inside to indicate that a pitched battle had taken place here. Smashed glass lay everywhere, hardly a bottle seeming to have escaped. The smell of rancid milk was almost overpowering, indicating that some time had elapsed since it all took place. Ken judged, from the state of the dried blood and the sticky residue from the spilt liquids which lay around, that the madness had struck here at about the same time as it had started in Kelden.

The scene was quite horrific, and Ken could imagine the

frenzy of destruction which must have been going on here before at least one crazed mind turned to thoughts of death...!

Although most of the glass bottles had not survived, there were quite a number of soft drinks which came in plastic containers, and a good number of these were lying about in the debris near the counter. Some were far too gory to take, having been lying in former pools of blood, but there were one or two which had been protected by the counter, and it was these to which Ken helped himself.

He was just about to leave the shop when the unmistakable sound of a gunshot, from somewhere close by, stopped him dead in his tracks. It was followed, almost immediately, by a second, which sounded as if it came from a different gun. For a second Ken stood rooted to the spot. The realisation that neither of the two shots had done any damage anywhere in the vicinity helped him to re-activate his frozen muscles and risk a quick glance down the road in the direction from which the shots seemed to have come. Movement some distance away caused him to jerk his head rapidly back into cover and hold his breath, listening intently. No bullet came his way and so, presuming that he had not been seen, he risked a second look.

A little further down from his hiding place a smaller thoroughfare branched off the broad market place. A huddled, grey-haired figure was crouching behind some ornamental wrought iron railings on the steps of a building on the left of this smaller side road about fifty metres away. The building lay on the opposite side of this road. The crouching figure was looking down this smaller thoroughfare away from the shop where Ken was hiding. As he watched, the figure raised a rifle, took very careful aim, and fired a shot into the shops opposite. A thin scream rang out and Ken edged his eye further round the doorframe to get a better look. He was just in time to see a second figure hobble out of a doorway on his side of the street and start to advance on the first one. One arm hung down limply at the left side, but the other was bringing up a shotgun to bear on the still crouching figure. There was a loud click as grey-hair tried to get off a second shot. The figure appeared to have forgotten to reload and the mistake was a fatal one. Struggling to stand upright, perhaps to reach more ammunition from a pocket, the old lady, as Ken now saw her to be, caught the full force of the shotgun blast in the chest and her body was hurled backwards onto the steps behind her. The figure with the shotgun, who, Ken now observed, was also a woman, turned and hobbled down the street in the other direction, screeching with rage and pain, her left arm hanging limply dripping blood, right arm dragging the shotgun along the ground behind her. She disappeared into one of the many alleyways which led off that side of the road. The madness was not over yet it appeared. There were still those who had survived and were apparently intent upon ensuring that no one else did!

Ken waited for a few minutes until the sounds of her screeching and ranting had faded into the distance before he went back to the Range Rover and gave Jamie some lemonade to drink. The medicine already seemed to be having an effect, for the boy did not seem as hot as he was, and appeared to be a little more alert.

"I can't see you very well," he whispered, "Things are all blurry."

The words were superfluous for Ken had suddenly caught a flash of the inside of the vehicle as seen through the boy's eyes, and he could actually feel the child's headache, and, despite the drink, his still raging thirst. Then it was gone again, but that short contact made it clear that pictures and feelings were now being transmitted as well as words, but it was still all one-sided. No matter how hard he tried; Ken did not seem able to transmit any thoughts to Jamie.

Suddenly rousing himself Ken realised that he was in a very perilous position and wondered if he should go and collect the rifle which the elderly woman had dropped when she had been shot. He dismissed the idea as quickly as it had formed. He had never liked guns or any other weapons for that matter, and seriously doubted whether he would be able to kill another human being, even to defend himself. It was not that he was a coward, he could be as courageous as the next man should the occasion call for it. It was just that he had never equated bravery with killing. Quite the opposite in fact; the most courageous act in Ken's eyes was that of a man or woman who walked into a dangerous situation knowing that they would never resort to killing another human being, even if the failure to do so meant their own certain death. A gun would be useless. It was certainly no deterrent to the killers at large, and he himself could never use it. It would simply be excess baggage and nothing else.

A course of action now had to be decided upon, and there were a number of options which presented themselves. Ken tried to make a mental list of his priorities, but it was not easy to concentrate, knowing that hostile eyes could be watching and that an unexpected and unprovoked attack could come from any direction. He knew that his first priority was to find medical help for Jamie, although he now had no idea where to look for this help. The madness had spread much further than he had expected and he knew that the situation in Skipton was probably worse than it had been in Kelden.

He decided to press ahead through the town, heading south to see if Keighley had fared any better. Knowing that the woman with the shotgun had disappeared in that direction made him jumpy as he drove slowly on, although he knew that she had already discharged both barrels and that her injured arm would make it difficult to reload. Still, she might have managed it, or there could be others around. It would pay to be extra cautious from now on. Jamie was showing signs of great distress on the rear seat and again Ken halted the vehicle. It was obvious to him that the child needed to relieve himself and so Ken helped him out into a shop doorway and kept a watchful eye on the street whilst the boy did what he had to. On helping him back into the car, Ken noticed that everything the child had been wrapped in was wringing wet. Leaving the boy locked in the vehicle Ken made a quick foray into a nearby store, emerging with as much dry clothing as he could carry. A second expedition into an electrical store also provided a number of items which Ken hoped might prove useful in the near future.

Jamie had drunk a good deal of lemonade while Ken had been inside, and was obviously still very thirsty. Ken put him into some of the clothing he had just obtained before driving on.

As they continued through the town, their progress was

occasionally obstructed by crashed vehicles or groups of bodies and a detour into the side back streets had to be negotiated. On one such detour Ken drew up as the kerbside and dashed into a shop he had spotted, to re-emerge a few seconds later with two warm-looking sleeping bags, which he threw into the back before continuing on his way.

Once clear of the town Ken decided to stop to reassess their position. He had pulled off the road, a little way up a track where they were well screened from any passers by, and as he sat and thought he broke out two of the pork pies he had brought with him from the cottage. Jamie did not feel well enough to eat, and so Ken put one of them back into the pack and tucked into the other one. It had taken much longer than expected to clear Skipton as there had been a major pile-up on the road he wanted to take, which had meant back-tracking and finding a way around it. This had not proved easy, as there seemed to have been a major battle in that area and Ken could not bring himself either to get out and move the many bodies which lay scattered around the streets, or to run over them. It was therefore well past midday by the time they had stopped and Ken was hungry. Jamie continued to drink and pass water with monotonous regularity.

The distance between Skipton and Keighley was not great, but Ken had to stop the car three more times for Jamie to climb wearily out and relieve himself. His coughing had continued, but this was not what was now causing Ken concern. He had come across these symptoms once before in his teaching career, and if what he had begun to suspect was actually the case then Jamie was in urgent need of help, and the sweet drinks he had been taking would only be making things worse.

Even before they reached it, Ken knew that Keighley was a disaster. From some miles away he had been able to see the great plumes of smoke rising to meet the low grey clouds which had been threatening rain all day. As he came in sight of the town the clouds decided to deposit their cargo in the form of a fine drizzle and this did nothing to raise Ken's spirits as he saw the devastation which had once been Keighley. Fire had ravaged a major portion of the town and some areas were still alight, burning buildings throwing up great fountains of smoke and sparks as their roofs collapsed.

There seemed little point in entering the town, as there could be no help from this quarter. He did stop, however, at one of the houses which stood alongside the road on the outskirts. The yawning front door and the corpses of two elderly people lying just outside it indicated that the house was probably unoccupied. Taking the empty plastic bottles from the Range Rover, he found his way to the kitchen and filled them with fresh cold water. He was now nearly one hundred per cent certain that Jamie had developed diabetes and he had to stop pouring sugar into the boy's system.

No one knew for certain why some children developed this condition, but it was thought that a cold might prove to be the trigger in those who were predisposed towards it, and Jamie had certainly fulfilled that condition! Ken also knew that diabetes could be controlled, but that the diabetic's life hung in the delicate balance between carbohydrate intake and the injection of insulin. Without treatment, Jamie's life expectancy was less than a fortnight! With this thought Ken made up his mind. He had to get the boy well clear of all this and into the hands of a competent doctor as soon as possible. There was little point in wandering from town to town only to find the same in each one. He needed to put some distance between them and this spreading madness. He therefore decided to head south again, to his home in Coventry to seek aid there.

His plan was to avoid towns as far as possible, and join the M62 to the south of Bradford, then use the motorway network to reach Coventry by way of the M1 and the M69. Once on his home territory, he knew where the hospitals were, and the two of them would have a refuge from the cold grey December drizzle in his Coventry home.

His plan was destined to fall at the very first hurdle!

The drive to the motorway took a little longer than anticipated, with crashed and abandoned cars being the main obstacle and regular stops for Jamie adding to the delays. One major road junction near to Queensbury was completely impassable; being totally jammed with wrecked and burnt out cars. Finding a way around that took a little more time, but eventually Ken found himself at junction 26 where the M606 and the M62 converge.

It was immediately obvious that the motorways were going to be unusable, at least until the two of them had travelled far enough south to be clear of the effects of whatever had caused the madness. It must have been during the rush hour that it had struck, for the scene which lay before him now was worse than anything he had experienced so far. The motorway was a mass of wrecked vehicles stretching as far as the eye could see. This had been motorway madness taken to the limit and beyond! It was obvious that much of the carnage below him had been caused by vehicles travelling at extremely high speeds ploughing into those which had already crashed. Many of the vehicles were so compressed between heavy goods lorries that it was impossible to believe that a car could fit into so confined a space. Others were so inextricably bonded together by the vast impacts that had taken place around them that it was impossible to determine which part belonged to which car or even what make or model they had been in the first place. Before him lay a mass graveyard where many thousands of motorists had died in the biggest pile-up Ken had ever seen.

Climbing out of the Range Rover he put up his anorak hood to protect against the persistent drizzle and stood and gazed in disbelief at the scene before him while Jamie again answered the call of nature. The most frightening aspect of it all was the total silence. Ken had often appreciated silence while walking alone in the hills, but he knew that there were now very few places left where there was a total absence of man-made sound. One could usually hear the rumble of distant traffic born on the wind to even the remotest outposts. But here even that was absent. They could well have been in some remote desert, rather than on the edge of an enormous conurbation. Intermittently there came to their ears the barking of a lone dog, echoing strangely down deserted streets, and then dying back into silence. He was just about to turn away when a thin keening reached his ears, and Ken realised that not everyone involved in this terrifying 'accident' had died outright. Someone down there was still alive.

Warning Jamie to keep the doors locked, he set off to investigate.

Many of the victims were still in the mangled remains of their vehicles. The lucky ones had died instantly. As he clambered over the wreckage Ken saw many stomach-churning sights. Men, women and children trapped in the wreckage of family cars, having died in agony as their lifeblood drained away from mangled lower bodies. One man, face crushed up against the windscreen of his van, had been impaled on the steering column by the lorry which had totally crushed the rear three quarters of his vehicle. The blood streaks left by his fingers as they had scrabbled against the windscreen testified that he had not died instantly. People who had escaped from their vehicles had not got far before something else managed to hit them! He closed his mind to such horrors as he sought the source of the sound.

After what he guessed to be about a quarter of a mile of slipping and scrambling over the rain-slicked wreckage, he judged that he was getting close to the sound. It seemed to be coming from beyond a large white van that lay just ahead of him. Rounding the front of the van, Ken was confronted by an absolute jumble of wreckage and for a moment he simply stood there, wondering where to look. The keening had stopped as he negotiated the van but as he stood looking about him it started again with renewed intensity. It seemed to be coming from the back of a silver saloon car which had come to rest under the rear of a large lorry which had been carrying heavy engineering components. The front of the silver car was not visible, having been totally crushed under the lorry's rear end. It had been forced there by the BT service van that had rammed into the boot. All that remained of it was the rear passenger section, and it was from here that the sound originated.

Ken approached cautiously and looked in through the shattered offside rear window. There sat a well-dressed, middle-aged man, who had obviously been on a chauffeur-driven trip when all this had occurred. He sat, half turned away from the window, hunched up, hugging himself. His keening showed that he was in pain. Beyond him, on the rear seat, lay a well used, leather brief case and the empty remains of the limousine's cocktail cabinet. The driver's seat, complete with driver, had been driven back by the force of the impact, trapping the man in the rear by his legs and preventing his escape from the car. He had been trapped there now for almost two days with no food and the cold of December days gradually seeping into his body. The pain from his crushed legs must have been terrible. It was probably only the alcoholic drinks from the cocktail cabinet which had kept him alive for so long. The stench from within the confined space caused Ken to recoil from the opening. The man inside turned, his attention caught by the sudden movement, and Ken leaned forward once more to see if he could help. The man's response was instantaeous. With surprising speed he thrust his arms through the remains of the window to grip Ken by the throat, ignoring the pain as his arms scraped against the glass shards which projected from the window surround. There was a look of absolute hatred in his eyes as he tried to pull Ken's face onto the jagged glass, and strangle the only person who could possibly help him. In his weakened state, however, he was unable to resist as Ken pulled away, gently prying the hands loose from his throat and scrambling back out of reach. A look of cold fury appeared in the man's eyes as he continued to reach out in Ken's direction, cursing and swearing horribly as he did so. There was no way that Ken could help him. All the man could think of was murder, and he did not care that his intended victim was also his would-be rescuer.

It went completely against Ken's nature to leave the man, but there was no way he could release him, and to stay would only endanger Jamie and himself. It was with regret that he made his way back to the Range Rover over the slippery surfaces of the intervening vehicles closing his ears to the screams of frustrated fury emanating from the wreckage behind him.

By the time he regained the firm, solid surface of the roadway his many falls had given him a fine collection of bruises to add to those from his previous expeditions. The fine rain had penetrated his clothing and he felt cold, wet and thoroughly miserable. In his depressed state he considered returning to the cottage, letting the boy die and taking his own chances at lying low until outside help arrived. He began to suspect, however, that such help was not going to be readily available, as this madness was more widespread than he had first thought. He also knew that there was no logical reason why he should continue to move southwards. If the south had fared any better than the north, he would surely have seen some indication of it in the form of air reconnaissance, and he had seen absolutely no movement either in the air or on the ground since the ill-fated Tornado. It was at that point that despair almost overcame him, and he was just reversing the Range Rover prior to turning back and retracing his route north when he felt an almost overwhelming desire not to give up, but to return to Coventry using the route he had taken on his journey north.

"Was that only three days ago?" he wondered aloud, "It seems like a lifetime!"

He was glad that he had had the forethought to obtain fresh clothing as they had passed through Skipton, and he took the opportunity to dry himself off and change his clothes before he resumed his trek south.

The journey progressed slowly, with frequent stops for Jamie and endless diversions to avoid blocked roads, so that by the time darkness began to fall they were only just west of Sheffield on the edge of the Peak District National Park.

The urge to keep heading south was still there, but Ken knew that he had to stop and rest for a little while at least. His body was still very sore from his experiences in Kelden, and his newly acquired bruises and scrapes only added to his discomfort. Besides that, his nervous system had taken such a pounding over the past two days that he was absolutely exhausted, and he did not relish the thought of navigating his way around the obstructions, which he would surely meet ahead, in the dark! In addition to this his headlights would act as a beacon for any hostile eyes. He also disliked the idea of spending the night in the confines of the vehicle exposed out on the roadway. The rain, which might have been a slight deterrent to any marauding individuals had died away as they had progressed southwards.

It was with these considerations in mind that he turned off

deeper into the hills just as the light was waning. After a few minutes driving he saw what he wanted. There, sitting high on the flank of a hill was an isolated farm. He stopped the Range Rover and dug out the binoculars from the rucksack beside him. Examining the farm through the gathering dusk, and detecting no signs of life, he decided that he had to take a chance and move before the darkness closed in completely, forcing him to advertise his presence to the whole area by the use of his headlights.

Five minutes driving time brought him to the farm track, and, revving the engine, he turned into the gateway and sped up the track as fast as he could. He hoped that a fairly noisy approach would bring anyone who might be inside the buildings running out to see who was coming. All the people he had so far disturbed had been only too eager to make their presence felt, and he would far rather meet any assailants here in the open than to have them lying in wait to ambush him when he entered the buildings.

As he roared up to the front of the house he could dimly make out a number of shapes lying in the open yard before it which he recognised as bodies. Their positions seemed to indicate that they had been fleeing the farmhouse when death overtook them. No lights were visible inside as Ken climbed out into the fast fading twilight.

Keeping the vehicle between himself and the open door of the house, he reached back into the car to take out the torch he had placed ready on the seat, and switching it on, he laid it on the bonnet of the Range Rover, pointing it directly into the doorway. No shots came his way, and there was no movement that he could see. Breathing quietly he waited for a few minutes, and, when there was still no movement, he picked up a second torch and made his way round the rear of the vehicle towards the farmhouse – using only the dim, scattered light from the first torch reflected back from the building.

Flattening himself against the gritstone wall of the house, Ken waited for his breathing to become easier and less noisy again before edging towards the doorway. Still there was no sound or movement from within. The most dangerous part of the approach now lay before him. On entering the house he would be framed in the doorway with the lighted torch behind him. Anyone waiting inside with a gun pointed at the doorway could not fail to miss him. Taking a deep breath, he risked a quick glance around the doorframe, jerking his head back to safety as fast as he could. No response. He therefore eased through the door sideways, keeping his back pressed to the doorframe in order to present as small a target as possible, and flattened himself against the side wall of the hallway. As he did so his foot caught against something which went skittering away into the darkness. Looking down in the dim light he saw a number of spent cartridges from a twelve-bore shotgun scattered around the floor. This is where the gunman had stood, firing on those who had tried to escape from him. There was still no sound from within. The torch outside cast long shadows into the corners of the hall, but it gave enough light for him to see a flight of stairs stretching away from him occupying the left hand half, and two doorways in the right hand wall, presumably leading to the rooms on that side of the house. A third door at the far end of the hallway must lead to the rear, while a fourth, between himself and the stairs, gave access to the room which lay on the other side of the wall against which his back was pressed.

It was pot luck which one he tried first. He guessed that the one on the opposite side of the hall at the front of the house would be the sitting room or lounge, while the one which lay behind it could be the kitchen or dining room. The door to that room was slightly ajar and it was this which helped him decide to examine that one first.

Changing sides in the hallway threw a gigantic ogre-like shadow down onto the wall at the far end. Keeping his back firmly pressed against the wall he edged slowly sideways towards the slightly open door. When he was within arm's length of it he stretched out his right hand and pushed it fully open, keeping his body well back against the wall. The creak as it swung open sounded deafening in the silence of the house, and caused Ken's heart to thump in his ears, but there was no reaction from within. When his heart had settled down again, he switched on the second torch and threw it through the doorway, quickly following it in and dodging to the other side of the room from that where the torch had rolled. The beating of his heart thundered in his ears once more as he took in the scene. The torch had rolled across the floor to finish up resting against the side of a man's body lying face down in a pool of dried blood. The sight was not pretty, as most of the back of his head was missing. Ken stood transfixed hoping that he was not to be next in line, but the house remained as silent as the grave. He shuddered at the thought.

When he was certain that he was alone in the room, he retrieved the torch from its grisly resting place and swept it around. There was a window set in the rear wall, and he quickly crossed to it and drew the heavy curtains. No light should escape through these once he switched on the room lights, and there was probably only the deserted hillside behind the house anyway. He surmised that there would be few out on the hills to see it on a bleak December night such as this, but saw no point in taking unnecessary chances. Closing the door to the room, he located the light switch and clicked it on. The room remained in darkness. The torchlight, which continued to illuminate his surroundings, would have to suffice as he carried out further investigation. The man on the floor was dressed in a light brown boiler suit and smelled strongly of manure. Ken decided that here lay the owner of the farm. Sticking out from under the body was what was unmistakably the stock of a shotgun. Steeling himself to look at the man's head, he was forced to the conclusion that the wound was self-inflicted. The farmer, after standing in the doorway of his farmhouse, and shooting his fleeing family, had sat down on an upright chair in his own kitchen, placed the barrel of a shotgun in his mouth and pulled the trigger. The spattered stains on the ceiling and wall behind where the chair had been served to confirm this.

In an odd sort of way this eased Ken's worries. Up until this point he had been concerned about where the last ones left alive could be. Now it looked as if some of them at least, when they had killed all they could, turned their weapons upon themselves. The thought brought him a certain measure of comfort, and allowed him to become much more relaxed as he moved around the house. Returning to the hall he discovered that the door at the end led into the farm buildings to the rear of the house, and not wanting Jamie to discover the grisly remains should he choose to go into the kitchen for a drink during the night, it was into these that he dragged the body, after wrapping it in the large rug from the kitchen floor.

Examining the remainder of the downstairs rooms, he found the one immediately in front of the kitchen to be the farmer's office, well kept and orderly, while that on the other side of the hall was a spacious, comfortable sitting room which extended the full depth of the building from front to rear. The wall opposite the door held two windows, one on each side of a large chimney breast. In the fireplace stood an artificial fire. He noted with some relief that this was gas-fuelled, as his inspection had revealed that there was no electricity in any of the rooms he had tried. He lit the fire, using the matches from behind the clock on the mantelpiece, before making a quick but careful inspection of the upstairs rooms assuring himself that there was no one else in the house.

Returning to the car he retrieved the first torch and carried Jamie inside, laying him on the couch in front of the gas fire. He then went back out again and took the provisions he had gathered throughout the day, including the two sleeping bags, from the car, which he carefully locked before returning to the farmhouse, securely bolting the heavy front door behind him.

The gas fire was very efficient, and Jamie, after visiting the bathroom and drinking more and more water, but refusing food, soon fell into a fitful sleep, wrapped in his warm sleeping bag. Ken, despite his bone-aching tiredness, found sleep harder to come by. He had eaten a good, but cold meal from the contents of the farm's well-stocked larder, but he could not shake off the urgent and inexplicable urge to continue southwards with all haste.

The farmhouse stood high on the hillside and the views in front of it must be magnificent by day, he thought. Perhaps the night time view would show him where the nearest civilisation lay. He went upstairs to one of the front room windows and seating himself upon the window seat with his back resting against the side frame, gazed out. Here and there in the blackness he could see what appeared to be bonfires burning, while away to his left was an enormous conflagration, half hidden behind intervening hills. The size of it could be judged by the glow which was reflected on the low rain-filled clouds. It seemed that a whole town or maybe a city was ablaze! He guessed that it was probably Sheffield. Awesome though the extent of the conflagration was, the thing which struck dread into Ken's mind, however, was that in all the vast blackness before him, there was not a single artificial light to be seen!

This, in effect, served to confirm his ever growing suspicion that whatever this madness was, it had been total and catastrophic. With no one left to supervise the equipment, when a failure occurred it caused a major breakdown, which perhaps overloaded other parts of the system causing further breakdowns. The result was that failures occurred at an ever increasing pace, spreading like ripples in a pool. Civilisation, built up over thousands of years had been stripped away in a single night and the savagery, which had always lain just below the surface, had come to the fore. Now that the process had started, it would continue. The electricity had already gone. How much longer would the gas and water continue to flow? He had no idea, but he thought that he ought to make provision for when supplies were no longer available. Life was going to be a great deal more difficult from now on. There was also the problem which the thousands upon thousands, perhaps even millions of dead bodies were going to pose eventually. Pretty soon now they would start to decompose, and then any survivors would face an ever-increasing threat of disease.

"This must surely be the end for the British as a nation," he thought, but he refused to carry that on to its logical conclusion and consider what it meant if this peculiar affliction were not confined solely to mainland Britain.

"But why haven't Jamie and I been affected?" he pondered, "and are there any others…? Has my experience with the 'light' anything to do with all this…? What was the cause of the odd incidents on that first day at the cottage and in Kelden, and were these linked in any way…? How was it that I can hear some of

Jamie's thoughts, and why am I feeling such an urgency about returning to Coventry?"

Questions such as these whirled and chased each other endlessly through his head, but, as yet, he could find no answers to them.

***

He awoke with a start, cold and cramped, with the noise of a crash still ringing in his ears. He was just beginning to wonder whether it was real or part of a forgotten dream when a second crash sounded from below. The sounds were coming from the room where he had left Jamie. Ken strained to try to pick up a thought from the boy, but there was nothing. He did not know whether to see this as a good or a bad sign. Turning on his torch, he dashed from the room, descended the stairs two at a time and, noting that the front door was still firmly bolted, threw open the door on his right. The room was dimly illuminated by the flames from the gas fire, and as Ken swept the torch around it was quite plain that there was still only the child inside – and he was still sleeping, although he was rolling his head from side to side in an agitated manner as if troubled by bad dreams.

As the torch continued to swing around its beam fell upon the remains of a smashed vase lying to one side of the fire, and there, on the opposite side, a second, also in fragments. Ken remembered seeing them sitting on the mantelpiece when he had been searching for the matches earlier. He shone the light to where they had been and was just in time to observe a large brass candlestick, one of a pair which stood at opposite ends of the shelf, start to quiver, shake violently and then upend itself to land with a resounding crash among a set of fire irons which resided on the hearth below. This crash awoke Jamie, and Ken, feeling the terror in the boy's mind matching that of his own moved over to the couch and took him in his arms. The child's arms went around Ken, and there they sat, hugging each other for mutual comfort until the terror subsided.

There were no further mysterious movements, and gradually the capacity for rational thought returned. There was too much happening too rapidly for it all to be coincidence. There had to be a link, but for the life of him Ken could not see what that link could be!

"Perhaps it was the light."

The thought was there in his mind, but Ken knew that the thought had not been his. It had come from Jamie!

Incredulously Ken held the boy at arm's length and stared at him.

"What did you say?" the thought had formed in his mind, but he held the words back, knowing what had happened the last time he had replied to one of Jamie's unspoken messages.

"Perhaps it was the light." The thought came in loud and clear.

Ken's head spun as the realisation struck him. The boy was now receiving as well as transmitting thoughts!

"What light, Jamie?" He tried to hide the panic in his mind as he silently asked the question.

"The one outside last night. Didn't you see it?" was the equally soundless response.

"No, I must have missed it. When did you see it?"

"Well, you were going upstairs. I could hear you, and I was feeling thirsty again so I got up for a drink. Then the room started to get very bright, and I looked round at the window and there was this light…"

Jamie's jumbled thoughts described what he had observed, but the words were unnecessary, for there, in Ken's mind, was a clear picture of what the boy had seen, and it was almost exactly what he himself had seen on that lonely hill road only three nights and a lifetime ago.

Ken hugged the boy to him again, and, with both deriving mutual comfort from shared thought processes and the certain knowledge of mutual friendship, trust, and a tiny embryo of love, a wave of exhaustion swept over them and sleep claimed their minds.

Chapter 7

"For how long shall thy journey be?"
Nehemiah 2:6

As he emerged slowly out of a deep and apparently dreamless sleep, Ken became aware that there were sounds of movement outside the house. Carefully and quietly, so as not to disturb him, he slipped his arm out from under the sleeping boy's form and eased himself gently off the couch. The room was very warm, but he felt a chill run down his spine as the sound came again. Someone or something was definitely moving around out there. Rubbing the arm on which Jamie had been lying to bring some life back into it, he crossed to the window at the front of the house and carefully fingered back the heavy curtain to leave a tiny slit through which to peer out without being seen. During the night a thick fog had descended, and at first all he could see was a uniform greyness with only an indistinct patch of darker grey to indicate where the Range Rover stood. Gradually, as the mists swirled to and fro he was able to make out a number of low moving shapes on the gravelled area to the front of the house, a little way beyond the parked vehicle. A snarling, snuffling sound reached his ears.

"Dogs! Was someone tracking them with dogs?"

The thought sent a pang of fear though Ken, and this, communicating itself to the boy, disturbed him, causing him to half awaken. Ken turned away from the window and looked back at the child, trying to think soothing, pleasant thoughts. Jamie, comforted, drifted back into light sleep, thus allowing Ken to concentrate solely upon the situation outside. It struck him that this thought contact had very definite advantages, and should he ever be able to return to teaching, it would certainly prove useful, although that possibility now seemed to be getting ever more remote.

Peering out through the slit between the curtains, he waited for the fog to give him a better view of the situation. From time to time visibility cleared slightly as the mists, driven before a slight wind, rolled lighter areas across the hillside. During these times he was able to make out the vague shapes of the dogs. There seemed to be eight or nine of them as far as he could tell, and they appeared to be totally disinterested in the farmhouse. If anyone had them under control then it was a very loose control for they seemed to be in a pack scuffling around and snarling and snapping at each other with the occasional yelp from an animal low down in the pecking order. It occurred to him that these were the first animals he had come close to since the disaster and he wondered if they had been affected by the madness. From the pack outside it would appear that they had not, for they did not seem intent on killing each other. Only man seemed to have had a predisposition towards that particular activity.

Fascinated, he concentrated upon their movements to try to ascertain what was going on. Eventually the wind blew a much clearer patch across the front of the house, and Ken was able to see what was happening. The dogs, having lost their owners now had to fend for themselves, and had gone back to their ancestral roots, forming into packs once more. Foraging for food together, they had returned to the habitation of their former masters, where they had found the bodies in front of the house and were, even now, engaged, literally, in biting the hand that once fed them. Hardened as he had become, over the last few days, to the many aspects of violent death, what he saw happening outside sickened, but fascinated him, and he was only able to tear himself away when the fog returned and hid the sight from his gaze.

For a moment he considered rushing out into the open and chasing them off, but what good would that do? He could not help the person who was receiving their attentions, and even if they went and did not turn on him, they would only return or find someone else as soon as he was out of sight. He therefore turned away from the window and busied himself with preparing for the day, trying to ignore the sounds which drifted in from outside.

Checking the clock on the mantelpiece, he saw that the time was still only eight thirty.

"Good," he thought. "We can still travel a fair distance today, providing the fog soon clears, and we can get to the car."

Strangely, though, the urgency over travelling south that had been driving him on recently no longer seemed to be present. He felt curiously empty without it, and it was almost with a sense of relief that he felt it return, as strong as ever, part way through the morning.

The sounds of the dog pack gradually died away, and Ken risked another look outside. All he saw was the fog, as thick as ever, completely undisturbed by any signs of movement. With the conditions on the roads as bad as they were it would be tantamount to suicide to attempt to travel in this weather. If they were lucky enough not to run into the obstacles they came across, finding a way around them would prove vastly difficult and time consuming under such conditions. They had already saved quite a lot of time on their journey by being able to spot road blockages before they actually reached them and so make the necessary, and often tortuous, detours. In fog, that would not be possible. Far better to stay put and wait for visibility to improve. It would be safer in the long run.

During the morning Ken busied himself with preparations for their continued survival. Beyond the room into which he had moved the wrapped-up body, he discovered a small but clean and neat dairy, containing four or five milk churns. These, on examination, also proved to be spotlessly clean. Using a length of already connected hose which was hanging in a coil on a white painted wall next to the tap, and thanking his lucky stars that the water supply had not failed yet, he filled up a couple of the churns with water to the point where he could just lift them. These he manhandled back up the hall to stand just within the front door.

In the sheds beyond the dairy he found the animals. Half a dozen hungry-looking cows and three horses. These he turned loose, after opening all the gates to the fields and hillside. He also opened the doors to the hay barn. Far better for them to have the chance to fend for themselves in the countryside than to starve to death in their sheltered accommodation. For a moment or two he considered whether the horses might not prove a better mode of transport than a car, enabling them to go across country, but the raw dampness of the day and the fact that he had not ridden a horse in years made him decide otherwise. Besides, Jamie was not at all well and the horses would severely limit how much they could take with them. It might come to that in the future, but for the moment the warm interior of the Range Rover was a far more inviting prospect.

In the yard behind the house he discovered a large propane gas tank. The mains gas supply could well have failed and might even now be fuelling the enormous fire beyond the hills, but this hill farm was immune to that particular disaster. He filed this away as a piece of information which may well prove useful in the future.

By mid-morning he had achieved what he could by way of providing for their departure. The hallway of the farmhouse was piled with as much equipment and supplies as he thought the Range Rover could carry. At one point in his scavenging he had come across a number of five-gallon fuel cans, two of which were full. On checking, however their contents turned out to be diesel fuel for the tractors, and he needed petrol for the Range Rover. He did, however, take two of the empty cans to fill up should the opportunity present itself. Throughout the morning's activities he had continued to feel the urge to be on the move, but had been able to push it to the back of his mind. Now that all was prepared, it returned like a nagging toothache that would not let him rest. He therefore decided to load up the vehicle so that they could be ready to move out the moment the fog lifted.

After first checking to make sure the front of the house was clear, (as far as the limited visibility enabled him to), he unbolted the heavy front door and gently eased it open. Slipping into the clammy wetness of the day, he was halfway to the car when, with a low growl, a grey figure off to his left raised itself from the prone position it had been in, and slowly advanced towards him. Answering growls came from various points of the compass in front of him, but as yet only the one dog was visible. He knew that if he made a dash for the car, the animal could be on him long before he reached it. He therefore stood his ground and turned to face the approaching dog. He had heard it said that dogs can sense fear. He therefore tried to think confident, dominant, even aggressive thoughts in order to display to the animal that he was not frightened of it. He simply stood there, stock still, staring fixedly at it and tried not to display any sign of relief when, with a whimper, the dog turned and slunk back into the fog, tail between its legs. Further yelps and whimpers from all around indicated that the others had followed suit! With all of the events of the past days, Ken had lost much of his capacity for surprise. The threat from the dog pack had receded for the present, and he simply accepted that, adding it to the list of oddities that had occurred, to be examined at a later date.

Now that the dogs no longer posed a threat, he carried on with his proposed task of backing the Range Rover up to the door of the farmhouse and proceeding with the loading of the stockpile from the hallway.

Eventually all was crammed in or strapped to the roof rack, and with the cessation of physical activity, the call south reasserted itself with a vengeance. Jamie, who had spent the morning lying on the couch and complaining of an enormous headache, also felt it, and even though his head ached abominably and he was constantly in and out of the toilet and drinking copious amounts of water, he was eager to be on the move.

So it was that, after an early lunch, and against his better judgement, Ken found himself behind the wheel once more, and trundling slowly down the track, away from the farm and back into the unknown. The fog was patchy, and once they had regained the road, Ken imagined all sorts of movement within it as they headed back to their intended route, but nothing actually materialised to impede their painfully slow progress. Even at such a low speed it was difficult to follow the line of the road, and required total concentration as they descended out of the hills, and Ken's eyes soon began to ache, having very little upon which to focus. He was just about to give up and return to the farm to wait for the mists to clear when he observed that he could dimly make out the shapes around him. The lower they got the thinner it became until eventually they emerged into clear air. Ken could have kicked himself. The farmhouse had been high enough for the cloud base to have been below it. The valleys had probably been clear all along and he had failed to realise it.

"The whole morning wasted," he thought. On reflection, however, he realised that, far from being wasted, the morning's activities had probably been far more useful than rushing off totally unprepared would have been. At least they now had supplies and water to last for quite some time, as well as a comprehensive array of emergency equipment. The enforced delay had provided badly needed time for constructive planning and preparation.

Their progress was much the same mixture of delays and detours as the previous day's had been. A blockage in Hathersage caused them to detour west of the intended route with further blockages pushing them ever further west. The route south was proving harder, and longer than ever Ken had imagined it would be. His encounter with the dogs had made him much more aware of the plight of animals now that man was largely absent from the scene, and he wondered how they would fare in the wild. Many, he knew would just go under, having become too dependent upon their owners, and the ones which had been tied up or shut indoors would even now be facing slow and certain death from starvation, if indeed death had not already claimed them at the hands of their owners, or as their homes had burned down around them. The lucky ones were those who, like the dogs at the farm, had been free to roam. They would adapt. Only the weak would die, the rest would return to the wild. This was the law of the jungle. The fit would survive. He was not so optimistic about mankind's chances. It was at that moment that he came to the realisation that life from now on was possibly going to become a whole lot lonelier than ever it had been in the past. Jamie's chances of survival looked far from good at this point, and Ken was not at all sure that he would want to go on living once he was alone.

He was probably not concentrating on his driving as closely as he should have been, for, on rounding a sharp bend in the road, his problems in that direction were almost solved for him, as immediately around the bend, and slewed completely across the road, an enormous tanker lay directly in his path. Braking wildly, as he swung the wheel hard to the left, the car hit the tanker broadside and lurched to a halt to the accompanying sound of tortured bodywork. Ken was thrown against the driver's door by the impact, his head hitting the window, and a deep velvety blackness descended to envelop his senses.

**

A persistent regular clicking sound echoed in his head, accompanied by a painful throbbing as he swam up out of the blackness. When he opened his eyes the light stabbed painfully into his skull, causing him to close them again immediately. There was a sticky, warm wetness down the right hand side of his face. All he wanted at that moment was to slip back into unconsciousness, but that did not happen. There was pain in his head which wasn't his, mixed with jumbled frightened thoughts of death.

"Jamie! Jamie, are you all right?"

A confused feeling of relief swept over him, coming from the bundle in the back seat. Jamie had thought that he, Ken, had been killed!! The boy himself had sustained no more than a badly bruised shoulder in the crash. The persistent regular clicking again forced itself to Ken's attention, and he looked around for the cause. The engine had stalled on impact, and the clicking, he determined, came from the direction indicator which must have been knocked on when he was thrown sideways. He turned it off and switched off the ignition. The silence was broken only by the faint sounds of hot metal cooling.

After sitting for a while to make sure that no bones were broken, Ken leaned over and examined his head in the rear view mirror. A scalp wound was bleeding profusely, as was their wont, but otherwise there seemed to be no serious damage. He wondered if the same could be said of the car. There was no way that either of the two offside doors could be opened, being jammed up tight against the tanker, and so, holding a clean handkerchief to his head wound, Ken eased himself across the front seat and climbed out through the passenger door.

Examining the front of the vehicle, which was close to the rear of the tanker, he saw that the impact had been mostly absorbed by the body panels, and that there appeared to be little or no mechanical damage, with the front wheel passing underneath the tanker bodywork. The front offside wing, however, was badly crumpled into the tanker bodywork, as was the bonnet above it. The headlight and indicator light had both been crushed out of existence.

Walking round to the rear, he saw that the crash had not been quite sideways on, and that there was about three hundred millimetres (Ken thought of it as a foot) of space between the rear offside body panel of the Rover and the tanker. With a little careful manoeuvring he might well be able to separate the two vehicles. He climbed up and looked into the cab of the tanker. The driver was still there, but unmistakably dead, and, Ken saw, on the other side of the tanker lay the mangled wreck of a dark blue saloon car, half thrown over the drystone wall at the roadside by the impact. Its driver was lying on the road, having been catapulted bodily through the windscreen. By the angle of his head, and the size of bloodstain around him, he too was dead. The saloon car had serious damage to the passenger side, and Ken knew without looking that he would find blue paint on the front wing of the tanker. Both vehicles had been on the wrong side of the road, and it looked very likely that the tanker driver had been using his lorry as a weapon, with fatal consequences for all concerned.

There was a smell of petrol in the air, and Ken hoped that he had not damaged the tank on the Range Rover. A quick examination showed that it was still intact. The smell was coming from the tanker, and with a leap of his heart he realised that it was a petrol tanker. Looking underneath it he could see a spreading pool of liquid being fed by a small but steady stream from the main tank. He offered up a silent prayer of thanks that there had been no sparks!

Climbing back into the car, he turned the key. The starter engaged, but the engine wouldn't turn. Ken almost panicked, at the thought of being stuck here and then with a sigh of relief he noticed that the gears were still engaged from the crash. Pushing the gear lever back into neutral, he tried again. This time the engine roared into life with no trouble at all.

"Think," he told himself. "Calm down and think, or you'll never get out of this."

Before attempting to pull free, Ken took Jamie and laid him in the shelter of a wall around the bend in the road, where he hoped that the boy would be safe should there be a spark and the leaking fuel ignite. If that were to happen he hoped that there would be a chance for him to get clear, but he would certainly not have enough time to stop for anyone else.

Engaging four wheel drive, and putting the car into reverse gear, he revved the engine and slowly let out the clutch. The engine protested wildly as it tried to drag the tanker back with the car. The two were very firmly enmeshed. He depressed the clutch again to prevent the engine from stalling. That tactic not having worked he tried a different one. This time he revved the engine even higher, and then let out the clutch fiercely. For a second nothing happened except that the engine note dropped, and then, with a tearing of metal he was free, the Range Rover shooting backwards, engine screaming, and almost ramming the wall behind it on the far side of the road. Looking back at the tanker, Ken saw that he had sacrificed only minor components from the bodywork, tearing them out of the Range Rover body, rather than the tanker. Even as he watched they tinkled onto the road surface and rolled aimlessly around. Thankfully he noted that there was no fire.

His door was well and truly jammed shut, and so he had to use the passenger side doors again to retrieve Jamie and wrap him up warmly on the rear seat once more. Examining the damaged side of the car he saw that the metal was so distorted that the front wheel was now totally exposed, and he would probably not be able to use either of the doors on that side again. To some extent that alarmed him as he did not want to have any avenues of escape blocked should he be attacked. He resolved to look out for a replacement vehicle as soon as possible.

He was just about to drive away when he realised that he had not extracted all that he could out of the situation. Here he was with a half empty fuel tank, and capacity for another ten gallons in the empty cans he had brought, sitting right beside a tanker full of petrol. Though the silent urge to move on was very strong, he fought it for long enough to siphon off enough petrol to fill up all he could. Once this was accomplished, he set off again driving much more carefully, to find yet another way around.

They eventually rejoined the main road just north of Matlock, and Ken realised that he had no wish to take the main road through the town as there was a fairly long stretch just beyond it which was bounded on one side by the river, and on the other by the Heights of Abraham which offered no chance of a detour should it be blocked. The wisest choice would be to detour before going into Matlock and, hopefully, save some time as it was once again getting well on into the afternoon.

This detour also proved to be a lot longer than expected with many blockages, and he was well south of Matlock before he was able to rejoin the main road. Almost immediately another crash site caused him to return to the minor roads, emerging again just to the north of Belper. As he had been driving along the sideroads around Matlock, it had started to rain once more, and the spray from the offside front wheel, no longer contained within a wheel arch was being flung out and blown back to deposit its load of mud upon the windscreen. The wipers were putting up a valiant fight, but it was a losing battle. The loss of one headlamp was also going to add to the difficulties when darkness descended.

Ken was therefore starting to search for a place to spend the night, when he realised that the urge to travel south was no longer there and did not seem to have been with him for some time. The urgency now seemed to be to return north! Tired and confused he drew up by the roadside. He had driven all this way under the most difficult conditions possible only to discover that he had made a mistake. But surely not! He could not have imagined the compulsion, for he still felt it, but now it was pulling in exactly the opposite direction. Suddenly he recalled the gentle eyes of the girl in the inn he had stopped at on the evening before the world collapsed around him. That was reasonably close to here; it was on the way back northwards and at least he now knew which of the roads to avoid. If at all possible he would make that inn his base for the night and perhaps see if the girl had by some miracle also escaped the 'mad death' as he now christened it.

Reversing his direction with a sweeping u-turn, he accelerated away, northwards this time, as the light slowly began to deteriorate.

***

The Shipley Arms was more difficult to locate without its welcoming lights, and Ken might have driven right past had it not been for the fact that a voice in his mind called him to stop. Thinking that the call had come from Jamie, he applied his foot onto the brake pedal and the car slowed to a halt as he asked over his shoulder,

"Do you want to get out again, Jamie?"

There was no reply, and turning on the interior light, he looked around at the child. Jamie was sound asleep, curled up in the rugs on the back seat.

Just as it dawned upon Ken that he no longer felt any urge to travel, the voice came again.

"Bring the boy inside."

It was then that Ken recognised that he had stopped directly opposite the Shipley Arms, and swung the wheel over to drive onto the deserted car park. He also realised that inside the building was someone who was also able to communicate through thought, but it was with great disappointment that he realised that the person speaking to his mind was male!

99

Chapter 8

"...and there the weary be at rest."

Job 3:17

The voice came again. "Bring the boy in, he needs help."

Still Ken hung back, having had too many near scrapes to rush into anything.

"How do I know I can trust you?"

This thought communication was a useful way of avoiding danger. You could talk without being too close.

"What other choice do you have?"

"I could drive out of here."

"Then the child would die." It was a simple statement of fact.

"Besides," the silent voice continued, "I thought you wanted to see Susan again."

There was a trace of amusement behind the thought.

"Is she there?"

The mental gloom suddenly lightened a little and the thought was involuntary, but at least he now knew her name.

"Why don't you come in and see?"

In his mind, Ken knew that this was no trap. Or was the man inside clever enough to be able to project that feeling too? He was too new to this type of communication to know what the possibilities were, but by now he was too tired and shell shocked to worry any more. He manoeuvred Jamie out of the car and carried him towards the patch of blackness which was the building. He had picked up a torch from the car, but was reluctant to use it for fear of giving away his position to a would-be attacker.

The door was closed but not locked, and he had some

difficulty locating the handle in the absolute blackness that now surrounded him. Even when he did locate it he found it impossible to manage with the boy in his arms. As he was attempting to shift Jamie's position to allow more freedom of movement, there was the sound of the latch being raised. Startled, Ken leaped back, poised to make a dash for the car, but nothing further happened. Stepping forward again he put his foot to the door and pushed. The heavy oak door swung back on well-oiled hinges to reveal a rectangle of blackness which was slightly darker than the surrounding building. There appeared to be no movement within it. Whoever had opened the door for him seemed to be keeping well out of sight. Ken wondered why, but taking a firm grip on his courage, he stepped inside out of the drizzle.

The interior of the inn was dark, cold and totally silent. It appeared deserted although Ken knew that this could not be so. The room he had been in before had been through the door to his right and this was the direction he now took. Once in, he stood for a moment to let his eyes try to adjust to the dark.

"Where now?" he thought.

"Come over to the bar," came the reply, "but be careful, it's a bit of a mess up there."

Ken risked a quick sweep of the torch and immediately turned it off again. The voice was right. The room was not as it had been when he had last been here. The tables were strewn about, and there was some smashed glass. It was not, however, as bad as some of the places he had been in, and there did not seem to be any bodies. His quick glimpse with the torch had given him a rough idea of where the main obstacles lay, and he only barked his shins once on his approach to the bar.

"Now look behind the bar. You'll need your torch again!" advised the voice.

He seemed to know just where Ken was, what he was doing, and what equipment he carried!

The flap between the bar area and the room proper was up, and as Ken stood there he shone the torch around once more. There was not much damage here, although most of the liquor had disappeared, and Ken wondered if he should go through the

101

door the girl had entered by when he was last here.

"No. The trapdoor down to the cellar!" the thought voice went on, "Come on, you're almost here."

Sweeping the torch beam over the floorboards, he located the outline of the rectangular trapdoor. To one end of it was a pull-ring set in a circular recess and the keyhole for a Yale lock. The area around the lock showed signs of being hacked at with a sharp instrument. Laying Jamie carefully on the floor to one side of the trapdoor, Ken gripped the ring and pulled. Nothing happened. The trapdoor was locked.

"Sorry!" The word sprang into his mind.

At the same time there was a click and the trap moved upwards a little way. Again he gripped the ring and pulled. This time it swung upwards easily, revealing a flight of steep wooden steps leading down into the cellar which was illuminated by a flickering orange glow. There was still however, no one to be seen below.

Questions burned in Ken's mind.

"Why does he want me down there? Why doesn't he show himself? Why didn't he come to meet me outside? Who on earth is he and how does he know all about me – and Jamie too?"

"You'll soon have all the answers you want. Don't worry, come down the steps." The mind-voice was very close now, friendly and reassuring, and Ken felt sure that he knew the person behind it, although he could not yet identify who it was.

Coming to a sudden decision, he laid the trapdoor right back against the floorboards, and gathering Jamie into his arms again, carefully descended the steps into the cellar, leaning back against them as far as he could to counterbalance the boy's slight weight. Just as he reached the bottom he was startled by the sound of the Yale lock re-engaging as the trapdoor swung quietly shut above his head. Looking wildly around to see who had closed it, Ken's eyes lighted upon a solitary figure sitting propped up on a mattress at the far end of the cellar.

The man made no move to get up, but spoke softly as Ken stood there cradling the sick boy.

"Its OK you're safe now. You can relax."

The spoken words brought a blessed release and Ken

realised that he had been holding his body rigid. He almost collapsed as the tension drained away, for here before him was the old man he had been talking to in front of the roaring fire in this very inn just before the world fell apart.

He stood his ground and took in his surroundings. The cellar was lit by two hurricane lamps hanging from the old wooden beams. One of them was over at the end to his left, hanging between himself and the old man, and the other was just in front of him near the foot of the steps. Wine racks threw the corners of the room and the spaces between the racks into deep shadow. The cellar was pleasantly warm in comparison with the rooms above and Ken saw a paraffin stove flickering away near the man's makeshift bed. Behind the steps and slightly to the right, was the stillage with the barrels of beer resting in neat rows stretching away into the darkened recesses of the rest of the cellar. Polythene pipes led from some of them up to the bars above. Stacked around the walls were piles of boxes containing, if the labels were anything to go by, many different kinds of tinned and non-perishable food. Looking up at the trapdoor above and slightly behind him, Ken saw that it had recently been fitted with two stout bolts on the underside. Although no one had been anywhere near them, the bolts were now firmly in position! Someone had prepared this place well in advance.

The man on the mattress gave him time to become familiar with these new surroundings before he spoke again.

"Why not put Jamie down over here? He must be getting heavy."

He patted the mattress beside him.

Ken realised that he was still holding the boy in his arms, which were beginning to ache, and he felt irrationally grateful for the reminder. He sensed that there was no danger here and so he did as the man suggested, laying the boy on the mattress by his side.

"Is the girl still upstairs?" he asked. "Was it she who opened the door and closed the trap after us?"

"Oh no, there's no-one up there."

"Then who...?" Ken was cut off in mid-question.

"All in good time. Now at this moment you look awful

enough to give anyone a fright!" commented the man, pleasantly, and passed Ken a mirror from the small table standing beside the mattress. Ken reached down and took it from him.

Looking into it he could not believe it was his own face which was reflected there. He was hollow eyed and drawn, and there was congealed blood down the right-hand side of his face and in his matted hair. A great multi-coloured bruise lay around his right eye and across his forehead. The last few days had certainly left their mark.

"There's soap and water over in the corner."

The man indicated their location with a nod of his head.

"Boil yourself some hot water if you like. Oh, and there are toilet facilities in a little alcove down past the stillage. There's a sheet hung up across the end of it but you'd better whistle in there if you don't want to be accidentally disturbed."

Ken saw that there was indeed a wash stand where the man had indicated and next to it stood a good camping stove and a plentiful supply of gas.

"Sorry I can't help, but I'm having a little trouble getting around at the moment."

Ken saw that his legs were bound tightly together with thick bandages.

"Came a cropper on the stairs over there," he said, "I'm pretty certain one of them is broken."

Ken also noticed that there was now little trace of the local accent he had spoken with during their first conversation, and that the man did not appear to be as old as he had first seemed.

"There will be time to find out more about that later on," he thought to himself, "I'd better get cleaned up first."

He filled a kettle from a tap on the wall next to the wash stand, and put it on to boil. While he was waiting for it, he decided to fetch some of the fresh clothing he had in the Range Rover to change into.

"Be careful, and use the torch as little as possible," the man called after him as Ken climbed the stairs once more, "there are still some of them who haven't gone under yet left out there."

Ken wondered how he knew what was going on outside

when he was stuck away down here.

"There's a lot you don't know yet!" the thought came as he made his way back to the Range Rover.

The trip to the car passed off without incident, and Ken recovered as much as he could carry from the vehicle, after moving it to a position directly in front of the inn door to make access easier. Once back in the security of the cellar, he put the hot water to good use in making himself look and feel more human. During this operation he noticed that the man was lying back on his pillows, eyes closed, and his hands were both on Jamie's head.

As he was towelling himself dry, he went back to the side of the mattress and, as the man seemed to be asleep, opened up a camping chair he found propped up against the wall, and sat down, grateful for the chance to relax his aching body.

He was still sitting there when he awoke. His head had lolled back and he had a crick in his neck. His throat felt dry and he was sure that it was his own snoring which had awoken him. Changing position caused every joint in his body to protest, but he gradually eased himself into a more upright position. As his eyes focused he saw that there were now three people sitting on the mattress, regarding him with some amusement. There was the old man, Jamie, looking more alert that Ken had ever seen him, and the girl with the gentle eyes, Susan.

Ken sat bolt upright when he saw them, wincing when his back complained at the sudden movement. The three before him burst into peals of laughter. This was the first laughter he had heard since all of this nightmare had started, and it was music to his ears. Here there was at least a semblance of normality, and normality, being in very short supply, was what he needed most.

He had no idea of the time or how long he had slept. He still felt tired and groggy and the side of his head was throbbing, but now he needed some answers. As the many questions he had chased each other though his head, all three before him held up their hands as if to shield themselves from the barrage.

"Hold on, hold on," cried the man, "We'll never get anywhere like this. Let's just settle down comfortably with a hot drink and I'll tell you what I know of what's happened. Then, if you've still got any questions, I'll try to answer them for you."

Susan went over to where a kettle was simmering on the camp stove.

"Coffee OK for you?" Her voice was light and pleasant, as she looked Ken directly in the eyes.

Ken was almost tongue-tied, feeling like a schoolboy. He nodded.

"Yes please," he managed, feeling a complete mess.

"And hot chocolate for Jamie?" she asked the boy.

Ken interposed, "Better not. I think he's diabetic."

"Not any more he isn't," said the man with a knowing smile towards the boy.

"What do you mean? Are you a doctor?" asked Ken, puzzled that the boy seemed to have recovered so speedily.

"No, I'm not a doctor exactly. Just hang on a minute, till we've all got our drinks and then I'll explain," the man offered, "and just for the record my name's Donald. I keep seeing myself pictured as 'the old man' in your mind, and I can't say that I like it very much."

Susan handed round the drinks and unfolded another of the camp chairs for herself, setting it down next to Ken's, half facing him, as they all settled down to listen to what Donald had to say.

"I know that there are many things which don't make sense to you at the moment," he began, "and yet other things which have taken place, for which you have rationalised an explanation. Whatever you may think lies behind the events of the past few days, I have to say that I doubt if any of you have come anywhere near the real truth!"

He settled himself more comfortably against the pillows behind him before continuing.

"I must apologise to Susan first of all for keeping her in the dark up until now, for this explanation will also be new to her. Each of us here has had very similar experiences. If we had not, then we wouldn't be here, but probably lying dead out there with most of the other inhabitants of the world we once knew."

And in reply to Ken's look of surprise, "Yes, this 'mad death', as you have so aptly named it is a global phenomenon. Nowhere has escaped it. I say 'nowhere' and not 'no-one',

106

because we ourselves, and a few others like us have obviously not been affected. To explain why, I must tell you a story.

"I am sure that each of the grown-ups here has had the feeling that man has never fitted into the pattern of this world. His greed and killing instincts belonged to him and him only in all the animal kingdom. Oh yes, animals do kill each other, but only man kills his own species for financial gain or just for the thrill of it. Throughout the whole of this world man has always been the odd one out.

"At the dawn of history, mankind had many more inherent powers than modern man has. He was able to communicate by thought, and to a limited extent, control his environment and inanimate objects through the power of his mind, but above all he was totally non-aggressive and gentle. The linking of minds made for shared experiences, and pain in others was as real as pain in themselves, thus rendering them incapable of inflicting it. Their children were not born with this ability. They were very much like we have always known children to be, acting out their aggression, but in their case it was always under the complete control and guidance of adults, who had been specially trained to deal with them. The part of the children's brains which contained the extra powers and the gentleness of the race did not open until the child entered adolescence. This 'opening' or triggering of the dormant portions of the brain was as natural to them as growing body hair or becoming aware of the opposite sex. From that time on they were completely whole.

"Then came a change, a mutation if you like. After a thousand years of perfect coexistence with each other, a few children were born to the race who never fully developed, whose brains never opened up completely, and who retained their aggression as their bodies matured. The mutation seems to have affected only a very tiny number of individuals and then disappeared again as mysteriously as it came, but the damage had been done and, of course, it was not until the affected individuals reached adolescence, and their dormant areas failed to open up, that the difficulty became apparent. These individuals were segregated from society as much as possible and the scientists tried every method they could think of to try to

107

trigger the change. Sadly, nothing worked! There was absolutely no artificial means of opening up the dormant areas of the brain.

"While the numbers remained few, they were kept together on an island set aside for them, but as the years passed the group reproduced and the abnormality was passed on. The mutation bred true, and much too quickly for comfort. Within the original race, conception was automatically controlled by the minds of the couple concerned. No fertilisation took place unless that was what both partners wanted. In the mutants, or 'unenlightened' as they came to be called, no such control was possible, and so conception, and the resultant childbirth, was far more frequent.

"This posed quite a problem for the race in general. Here, growing amongst them, were the seeds of their own destruction and if the problem was not tackled early then they would be unable to deal with it at all. They were faced with a number of choices. They could sterilise all the unenlightened so that no more births would occur; they could maintain the status quo and so accept the end of the race as they knew it, or they could find somewhere else for the mutants to live, where they could do no harm to the race from which they had sprung. They rejected the first option on the grounds that they would be denying a full life to those who were, after all their own offspring, and they could not tolerate the thought of killing – even the, as yet unconceived, children of the unenlightened. The thought of destroying the unenlightened themselves was anathema to them. The final choice was to find an alternative place for their mentally crippled brethren to live.

"The complete interaction between minds had allowed man to develop scientifically at a very fast pace indeed, and the race had long ago ventured into space. They therefore began to search for a new planet upon which the mutants could develop and live out their lives in their own way. Eventually one was found on the far side of the galaxy and the unenlightened were transported to it, under sedation. The planet they were placed upon was young, pleasant and contained no human species upon its surface. That planet was Earth!"

Donald paused to sip from his coffee and to allow the full weight of what he had just said sink in. The faces around him were grim, but no one felt inclined to break the narrative.

"I can see from your faces that you understand the implications of that," he continued, "We are the descendants of that mutant race! We were not left to fend completely for ourselves to start with. A few of the more hardened individuals stayed amongst us to help where they could, but none of them could tolerate a long-term stay. They simply could not cope with the aggression and brutality of their charges."

"And you are one of those who came to help." It was more of a statement than a question from Susan.

"No, not exactly," Donald went on. "You see, it was found that, from time to time, one of the offspring of the mutants would revert back to type. There was no rhyme or reason behind it. Their brains would trigger and open up to their full potential, and aggression, which never figured very largely in the makeup of these individuals, would totally disappear from their characters, leaving them terribly vulnerable in this violent world. It did not quite follow the same pattern as in the original race, but could occur at any time from the onset of adolescence. That, my friends is what has happened to us. It is most unusual for there to be three of you to trigger so close together, both in time and location, but I can only suppose that whatever factors sparked off the 'mad death' also triggered the changes in your brains which allowed you to survive it."

The room was very quiet in the flickering glow of the lamps as each of the trio considered the facts which had just been presented to them.

Eventually Ken broke the silence.

"How did you know? About us, I mean." He waved his hand to indicate the three of them.

"Oh, there was nothing very difficult about that," replied Donald. "You told me yourselves."

"Us? How?" This time it was Susan's turn. Donald turned to look at her.

"The change always follows a fairly predictable pattern," he explained. "The first signs are that the subject starts to 'broadcast' telepathically a few days before it actually happens. Both you and Ken were coming in loud and clear on that first evening."

And turning to Ken,

"That's why I tried to persuade you to stay, if you remember. I could see you were both attracted, and I knew by then what was coming for both of you, but that's all water under the bridge now. You know what happened to you next. Both your's and Susan's brains were triggered very close together in time. The opening up of the dormant areas of the brain is always accompanied by a stimulation of the visual cortex. It is not understood why, but the subject experiences something similar to seeing a very bright light. After you have 'seen the light', a phrase with which I am sure you are familiar, you lose awareness for some minutes, during which all of the previously unused parts of your brain are activated, and, in some small way, tested. Peculiar events seem to occur around you which appear to be inexplicable when awareness returns."

Ken remembered his moved car and the tumbling candlestick at the farmhouse, and he was unable to prevent the word forming in his mind.

"Poltergeists!"

"That's right," Donald confirmed. "Poltergeist activity has long been associated with children, although there are many more reports of poltergeist activity than there are children who achieve the change. I can only presume that some of them actually come very close to change, the activity ensues, and then their brains are unable to sustain the process and they revert to what is seen as being normal in this world. For a tiny minority, which includes yourselves, the process continues and you regain the powers of our original race.

From that point on you are able to receive telepathically as well as broadcast, and you have limited telekinetic powers, although to start with it is all a somewhat painful experience as you exercise the previously unused areas of your brain. Severe headaches are the usual penalty."

Again Ken remembered the spark plug and screw incidents, and in a flash of insight he burst out, "So that's why the madman at the garage missed!"

They all knew what he was talking about, the picture which

flashed through his mind being graphically clear.

"Of course," Donald went on. "In moments of crisis we tend to use our powers instinctively as you did when you mentally jerked his gun upwards, but, without the proper training, they are very limited and weak compared to what they could be. Now that we are all together we should be able to improve things."

Both Ken and Susan were looking puzzled.

"OK! Time for some questions," offered Donald, noticing their expressions. "Fire away! Susan? Ladies first."

"Well," she began, hesitantly, "we now know that we can share thoughts."

Donald nodded.

"Why is it then that you had to explain all this to us. I mean, why couldn't we just see the explanation in your mind right from the start?"

"Easy ones first, eh!" said Donald, laughing, "Well, I think telepathy would be intolerable if all of us could receive every single thought from all those around us, and so we seem to be able to think on two different levels. The thoughts we want to share are kept in one compartment, and the ones we want to keep to ourselves are in another. At first it is difficult to control, with some thoughts slipping out by accident and others remaining masked, but you soon get the hang of it. We are therefore able to choose which thoughts we share and which we keep to ourselves. We cannot, however, mask our feelings; you would know immediately for instance if I tried to lie to you. I chose to communicate by speech at this particular time for the simple reason that man has always been afraid of silence, a state which would exist in here without our conversation. I therefore used the method of speech to convey all of this in order to keep silence at bay and so bring you a much needed degree of comfort."

Ken nodded.

"But what about all of this?" He asked, indicating the well-stocked cellar. "How did you know?"

"The eventual outcome was inevitable. The aggression within earth-man was so great that he was bound to destroy

111

himself eventually. He has tried often enough in the past with his wars and weapons of mass destruction but he always managed to draw back from the brink. This time there was no way out, for the destruction came from within each individual, and not from without. The mutation peaked at some critical point and that particular branch of mankind was finished. What we have lived through over the last days was, to the unenlightened, the end of the world. A few of the most aggressive individuals may well have survived out there, but they will not last long with the disease which will result from so much death, and whenever two of them meet, they will fight to the death, and even the victor may die of his wounds. If not, sooner or later he will die at his own hands. That is the way the madness takes them.

"I have been aware of its approach for some considerable time, a matter of years. The signs were there for all who knew what to look for to see. I therefore laid very careful plans. I first bought this inn, and installed Susan and her father to keep it for me, as I needed all my time to make my preparations. I had no idea then about Susan's 'potential', that was sheer coincidence. Over the years I have gathered together all you see around you for this particular purpose. Susan and her father thought I was a crank preparing for a nuclear attack, but, as I owned the establishment, they humoured me."

Susan's cheeks flushed at the recollection, and Ken thought how it became her – which caused her to blush even more. Donald smiled at them both and continued.

"When I knew about you and Susan I had to make some last minute additions but I managed that easily enough. It wasn't until the madness struck that things went slightly off course. By then Susan had developed and we could communicate by thought over a limited distance. Even so I had a very difficult job persuading her that she must abandon her father," (here a great sadness emanated from the girl) "and she was not finally convinced until he tried to kill her. Luckily I was there and was able to bundle her down into the cellar before he could get to her. As I tried to follow he grabbed at me and in pushing him away I slipped on the steps and broke my leg. Susan had the presence of mind to close the trapdoor before he could recover himself and follow us down; otherwise neither of us would have been here to tell the story. We heard him hacking at it with something or other for a while, and then there was the sound of more footsteps up there and he stopped. We have only been able to guess at what happened next."

He paused for a while and Ken could feel him projecting comfort and security in Susan's direction.

"Anyway," he went on when he was sure that all was well with the girl, "Susan bound up my leg for me and made me comfortable. But I was stuck! I couldn't get out from down here. My leg is going to take weeks to mend, and I need to be out and about long before then."

"No," he continued, sensing the unspoken question, "I couldn't teleport myself out. It doesn't work on living beings without some rather specialised equipment. The dead are a different matter. Don't ask me why. I have no idea, but that is how we were able to 'tidy up' upstairs before you came."

"And how did you know we would come?"

This was the first time that Jamie had spoken and it caused Ken to remember his illness and cure, questions tumbling over themselves in his mind.

Donald held up his hands.

"All in good time," he said to Ken, and then to Jamie, "Why, we sent for you, of course! Thoughts can be transmitted only over a very limited distance, but feelings, for some reason, are a very different matter, particularly if more than one person is projecting. Susan and I joined forces and projected our need. We were not sure whether or not we had succeeded until you actually turned up, but we had to go on trying. Susan found the process absolutely exhausting, and I had to go on alone from time to time to allow her to rest. Only hours before you got here I sent her off to get some sleep in her own quarters. That's rather a grand name for a curtained-off area of the cellar, but it does give the illusion of privacy. That's where she was when you arrived, but you must have been in range of my unaided efforts by then. We just went on and on hoping you would respond. There was nothing else we could do. I think that your feelings towards Susan probably helped the urgency of our call, Ken, but

I have no proof of that."

This time it was Ken's turn to blush.

"As for Jamie's recovery, well, we are able to control many bodily functions within ourselves and in others, particularly if we have physical contact with them. I was able to locate the particular disorder in Jamie's pancreas and initiate his own natural defences that his body had failed to send into action. Once this was set off, Jamie's body healed itself."

"Then why didn't you heal your own leg?" asked Ken.

"Different process, I'm afraid," Donald responded. "A broken leg will heal itself in time. I can simply initiate the healing process, not make it work faster. Jamie's body needed insulin. I allowed his pancreas to start producing it again. The sugar in his system was neutralised and Jamie was well on the way to recovery. Bones cannot be knit together again in so short a time."

The explanation was at an end, and though each one would probably think of more questions later, they all had enough to digest at the moment. The silence was long and thoughtful.

"Right," said Donald cheerfully, when he judged that the silence had gone on for long enough, "if we're going to sit here and mull things over we can at least enjoy some of the good things I've stored down here. Ken, there's a bottle of excellent malt on that rack behind you, or some brandy if you prefer."

"Malt will do fine for me." Ken reached behind him and found what was a most palatable distillation. He then turned to the girl.

"And for you, Susan?"

It was the first time he had actually used her name, and it sounded good in his ears.

"Some Irish Cream I think, but it's OK, I'll get it. I know where it is."

Ken felt glad that she was not a 'pint of bitter' girl, but then, he had known she would not be. She disappeared into the shadows between two of the racks and reappeared a moment later with a bottle of Irish Cream, and a small bottle of Coke for Jamie. "I'll join you in a glass of Scotch," said Donald, leaning towards Ken with two good size glasses in his hand. The movement caused him to wince, and Ken was immediately by his side to see if he could help. He took the glasses from him.

"Ease over a bit, old son." he said to Jamie who was still lying on the mattress next to Donald. There was absolutely no response. Totally drained by the events of the day Jamie had fallen fast asleep as soon as the explanations were over.

"Right," said Donald seeing Jamie's sleeping form, "before we settle down to pleasantries we'd better sort out one of those extra provisions I spoke of a little earlier. Over there by the wall Ken, you'll find another mattress. If you can manage in that chair for tonight, Jamie can sleep on the mattress. I didn't know about him until just before you got here, and Susan was asleep then. We can easily get one for you tomorrow from one of the rooms upstairs."

Ken was quite agreeable to this. If it had not been for the boy relying on him he would probably have given up long ago, and now, glancing across at Susan he was so pleased that he hadn't. After laying out the other mattress, he carried the sleeping boy across to it and gently set him down, covering him with a duvet he found stowed on top of the mattress. He then went back to join his new friends. His feelings were indescribable. He had been with them now for slightly less than three hours, but he knew them better than anyone he had ever known in his life, and for the first time ever he knew, with absolute certainty, that at last here were people he could trust implicitly.

Susan had just finished pouring the drinks as Ken eased himself into his chair again, wincing as every muscle registered its protest. After passing Donald his glass she drew her chair very close to Ken's and as they sat sipping their drinks, she quietly took his hand with both of hers and looked directly into his eyes.

"I'm glad you came back."

She smiled at him and he found it a very pleasant experience.

Chapter 9

"...that ye be not ignorant of this mystery."
Romans 11:25

Long after his three companions had fallen asleep, tired though he was, Ken sat and mulled over all that Donald had spoken of in the flickering light of that dim cellar. The thought of his new powers excited him and he had been eager to try them out all evening, but had been occupied with other matters, but now at last he could see what he could do. Looking down upon the laces of his shoes, he concentrated hard upon trying to undo them. It was a strange sensation to see them move slightly as if stirred by a light breeze and then start to writhe like snakes. He stopped; somewhat scared by his own powers, but realising that he had not chosen a particularly easy task to begin with. There were too many movements to handle. He therefore undid the shoe by hand and placed it on the floor in front of him. This time he concentrated upon moving the shoe forward, and to his amazement it slid easily across the floor for about a metre before he could stop it. Immediately there was a flashing pain behind his eyes which settled down to a dull persistent throbbing. Ken realised that what Donald said was true. His powers were still very weak, and they would need that specialised training which Donald had spoken about before they could be of much use to him.

Satisfied that he had at least succeed in testing his powers, if only in a very minor way, Ken settled down to sleep, but found that his aching body was unable to relax enough in the camp chair for sleep to come. He therefore bunked down alongside Jamie and spent a peaceful ten hours in completely restful oblivion.

He slept late the next day, not that they could tell the difference between night and day in this windowless cellar and on awaking he was immediately aware of the tension in the air. Pushing himself upright he looked across to where the others were sitting grouped on Donald's mattress. Susan rolled her eyes heavenward as Ken met them and he was silently informed of the problem. There was someone prowling around in the rooms above them. Heavy footsteps dragged across the floorboards above their heads, as if searching for something. They paused for a second and then resumed their progress across the room. Ken, groggy from sleep, failed to see why the intruder posed a problem. He looked across at the trapdoor. The heavy bolts were firmly in place.

"What harm can he do us?" he thought at the others.

"He can set fire to the place. That's what harm he can do! You just can't predict their actions any more," came the immediate response from Donald. It was automatically assumed that the intruder was a man!

"We'll just have to sit tight and hope he goes away."

"If the worst comes to the worst, there's always the loading bay," Susan contributed.

"But we can't get Donald out that way in a hurry," Ken replied silently.

"Let's hope it doesn't come to that," was Donald's reply.

The footsteps retraced their original route and then came back across the floor towards the trapdoor. There they paused again, and they could all imagine the intruder looking down upon the freshly made scars around the lock. There was the sound of the ring being lifted, and a grunt as the intruder pulled at the ring. When the trapdoor would not lift the man above stood up again and crashed his foot down heavily upon it. The trapdoor was good and solid, and though it vibrated it showed no signs of any weakness. The intruder seemed to recognise this immediately and the footsteps retreated to where the front door of the inn was located. There was a crashing of glass heard through the floor as the man angrily threw an almost empty vodka bottle he had been drinking from back into the room. Taking a packet of cigarettes from his pocket, he idly lit one and

117

then threw the still burning match into the room after the bottle. It landed quite close to the flammable liquid, but died and went out before the vodka caught. The occupants of the cellar were not aware of what was happening up above until there was the sudden cough of a car engine being started. Ken grabbed his coat hanging over the back of one of the camp chairs and desperately felt around in the pockets.

"The car keys!" he gasped in a whisper, "I left them in the car door last night."

The sound of the engine rose in a crescendo and then started to decrease as the vehicle was driven quickly away from where it had been parked.

Words were unnecessary as each looked at the others in turn. In an emergency they may need to get away from here rather quickly, and they now had no means of doing so. Whether they liked it or not they were stuck here until someone was willing to venture out on foot to find another vehicle.

Eventually it was Ken who broke the silence.

"I suppose it's not as bad as all that, really. I mean, it would take a very determined effort to get at us down here, and as no one seems to know we're down here, then, barring accidents we can just stay put."

"I'm afraid one person might just know about this bolthole," broke in Donald, looking at Susan.

"Yes," she responded quietly, "I never actually saw what had happened to Dad up there when I went up to direct Donald's 'tidying up' operations. We only assumed that he had been killed somewhere else, but he could still be around, and if he is, he knows we're down here. At least he knows about two of us."

"Not only that," Donald added, "but I need to contact our people fairly soon to let them know that I survived, and about you three."

"And just how do you set about that?" Ken wanted to know. "Have you some sort of radio transmitter hidden somewhere?"

"Oh, it's slightly more than that, and it's not really hidden," was the reply. "It's always been in plain sight." He smiled to himself as if at some private joke, but the thoughts behind the words remained masked.

"I suppose now is as good an opportunity as ever for more explanation."

Here Ken broke in. "If you don't mind, I've only just woken up, and there are one or two things I have to attend to before I can sit still and listen. You three seem to have been up and about for hours."

The others understood perfectly well what Ken meant and waited while he disappeared into the darkened area beyond the stillage. When he returned, there was a steaming cup of coffee and a bowl of cereal waiting for him. He sat down in the chair next to Susan and prepared to listen whilst he ate.

"When our ancestors first visited this planet, it took them many years of travel across the depths of space to get here," Donald began, "but once they had landed they were able to set up a system for much faster communication and travel between their home world and this one. Since way back in their history they had known that certain crystals helped to concentrate and amplify their minds' power, and if these crystals were present in large enough quantities and in the correct configuration, then almost instant communication and even teleportation were possible for those whose minds were correctly trained. On arriving here they found that the crystal existed in abundance, and so they set about building their communication and travel centres. We too, on this world have discovered that crystal, and we too have discovered some of its potential, although only a fraction of its true worth. That crystal is quartz.

"The first visitors dug deep into the earth to set up the quartz configurations required, and when they were completed they joined them to the transmitting system on the surface. These systems were connected to the underground crystal system by a network of cables and wires, although they could never be identified as such by anyone of our world who might come across them. The systems were built to last, but even so only a few have survived until now in anything like good working order. The ravages of time and the natural destructive tendencies of our own forefathers destroyed more than a few of them. There are very few still in reasonable working order in these islands. By far the most effective one is what we have come to know as

Stonehenge, and that is where I need to head for if we are to come out of this in one piece."

Ken knew that the people of this world had always been fascinated by, and felt drawn to, these ancient stones, and some of them had even professed to feel a power flow when they placed their hands on them. It caused him to wonder if some of the mutants still retained a vestige of their inheritance, and whether racial memory actually existed.

"The answer in both cases is yes," replied Donald. "Many of the 'earth energies', as they have been called, can be put down to a sensing of the power systems installed so long ago by our ancestors."

At the mention of earth energies, the thought "ley lines" sprang automatically into Susan's mind.

"Yes, leys are also attributable to those who set up this world," responded Donald. "The major centres were scattered about and useful for movement between the home world and this one. The leys were for local traffic. I suppose we could compare it to our own rail system, except that this one is based on veins of quartz buried deep in the ground which provided the power to move about the surface of this world. Our more recent ancestors could sense the power that existed in these areas, but were never able to use or understand it. The places therefore became centres for superstition and magic."

"Can't you use the leys to get to Stonehenge?" This from Jamie, who seemed to be absorbing it all, probably better than the two adults.

"No. I just haven't had the training, and I don't know if staying here on this world has enabled me to develop enough if I could get the training. All I can do is use the communication boost at Stonehenge when I get there."

"Can't someone else go?" asked Susan simply.

"If you mean one of you three, I'm not sure that your minds are mature or powerful enough yet. You've all only just begun to develop your powers. As for others of our kind, well, there is no certainty that anyone else has survived. I certainly can't sense anyone else in the vicinity. No, I'm afraid that I have to go there personally, and I'm going to need a lot of help because of this leg."

Again there was a silence while they all considered what Donald had just told them, but there was a mutual feeling that they were all in this together and each was willing to play a full part in whatever course of action was decided upon.

Eventually the silent conclusion was reached. Stonehenge it had to be, and the sooner the better for all of them. Once the decision had been reached (in reality it had only taken a few seconds) they all felt better and soon they were deep into planning their next move. Donald's leg posed the first problem. Strapping both legs together was a useful first aid technique and was quite all right so long as he lay on the mattress and did not move, but it was not sufficient to stand up to a potentially hazardous journey. The leg had either to be splinted correctly, or set in plaster. Equipment for neither of these operations had been included in Donald's provisions. To obtain the correct equipment, a visit to a local hospital was necessary, but now that the Range Rover had gone they had no means of accomplishing that objective. Obtaining another vehicle therefore became their top priority.

Their watches told them it was well after mid-day and so they decided to eat before setting out to find transport. It had been assumed that this task would fall to Ken, but Susan insisted on accompanying him because of her knowledge of the local area. Ken tried to persuade her to remain in the relative safety of the cellar, but she would not hear of it. The gentle Susan also had a very determined streak.

Before setting out they crept upstairs and checked on the weather. It was a wet blustery afternoon, guaranteed to keep anyone with any sense under cover, but sense had long since vanished from this world, and so they took every precaution not to be seen when they left. They had chosen warm clothing from Donald's store, although it was a slightly tight fit for Ken. Good green cotton waxed jackets provided proof against the rain and were not too conspicuous.

They let themselves out through a rear door and, crossing the small garden behind the inn, passed through a gate in the hedge onto a path beside the river. With the rain, the river was in full spate and the noise it made drowned the sounds of their progress as they walked hand in hand, but watchfully beside it towards the village.

Eventually they reached a bridge, which carried one of the village roads over the river, and it was here that Susan suggested that they venture into the village to look for transport. Emerging onto the hard surface, she indicated that they were to turn right and follow the road away from the direction of the inn. Away from the sound of the rushing of the water the village was an eerie place, magnifying the mournful sighs of the buffeting wind, and any noise which they accidentally made, a hundred times in their ears; the echoes ringing back from the dead walls often startling them and causing them to duck into whatever cover was available. Wherever possible they kept away from the houses bordering the road to lessen the chance of ambush, and because there was a distinctly unpleasant odour in their vicinity. Ken kept his thoughts well away from whatever might lie within. Towards the far end of the street was a garage which Susan thought might have a selection of vehicles in the yard to the rear. It lay on their left, nestling into the crook of a road coming in from the hills and their view of it was blocked by a high wall, bordering the side road. Crossing to the right hand side of the road, they approached the garage slowly, giving themselves as wide an angle of view as possible without getting too close.

They were soon able to see that the forecourt was deserted, although the side gate which gave access to the rear of the premises was still hidden behind the high wall which curved protectively around that corner of the premises.

Signalling Susan to remain where she was, Ken sprinted across the road and pressed himself against the stonework at the end of the wall. Having risked a fast peek around the corner and seeing no one, he motioned to Susan, indicating that it was safe for her to join him.

"Don't you think you're being rather too cautious over all this?" she asked.

"Better be safe than sorry," was all he would reply.

The tension she could feel behind the words communicated more than the words themselves, and she remained silent. He was obviously worried about the prowler who had taken the Range Rover.

The high, wire-mesh gates between the wall and the side of the building were flung back, and Ken could see that there were indeed vehicles to the rear of the premises, although he doubted that any would have the keys in them. A visit to the garage office was called for.

Just beyond the gate there was a door in the side wall of the building and Ken cautiously made his way over to it, moving with his back to the garage wall, rather than making a direct approach. Still pressing back against the wall he tried the door. It was unlocked. Cautiously he gave it a push and then waited until it had swung fully open. Listening intently, all he could hear was the sighing of the wind as it gusted around the building, and so after a short pause, he moved in through the doorway. The dim interior of the garage was filled with vehicles in various states of repair and he could see the office on the other side of the workshop. After taking three steps into the building, a sudden movement slightly above and to his right caught his eye, and Susan's sudden scream from outside caused him to duck, but he was not fast enough. The blow, which caught him on the side of the head, felled him almost immediately, and the last thing he heard before the world went dark was a second terrified scream from the girl.

***

When Ken and Susan had left the cellar, Jamie, on Donald's instructions, began to gather together those things that would be needed on their forthcoming journey. It was a wonderful opportunity for him to be a boy again as he investigated the contents of Donald's stores, while at the same time being occupied in a role which he felt to be useful.

As Jamie pottered about, investigating the contents of mysterious packages and curiously examining those that he found most interesting, Donald busied himself with an attempt to plan their route south. From what Ken had told him, the journey would not be an easy one, and major roads as well as centres of population would need to be avoided both from the point of view of blockages and the danger of attack. It was also becoming apparent that places where there would be a high concentration of bodies would hardly be very pleasant or hygienic in the not too distant future. It said a lot for Donald's planning that he had included a number of firemen's breathing apparatus units in his provisions.

Jamie had just discovered these and was examining them with wonderment when there was the sound of a car engine from the car park outside.

"They've been quick! I hope they got a good one!" cried Jamie, projecting pictures of high-powered sports cars.

He ran across to the ladder and began to draw back the bolts in order to go and investigate their newest acquisition.

"No!" The warning thought came from Donald and the bolts moved back into position under the boy's hand.

Jamie dropped back down to the bottom of the ladder, startled by Donald's reaction.

"Think," came Donald's continuing thought. "The way those two broadcast when they are together, we should have heard them coming. It's not them!"

The urgency of the thought caused Jamie to creep away from beneath the trapdoor and crouch down on the mattress beside the man.

Up above the door of the inn was thrown back on its hinges with a crash that reverberated throughout the walls of the building. They heard a muffled snarl as the intruder thumped his way across the floor to the bar. Crashing glass seemed to indicate that he was in the process of searching for something to drink. There was a loud thump as something hard and heavy was dropped onto the floor above.

***

He stood at the bar, his wild staring eyes darting about the room, not resting upon anything for more than a second or two before they moved on. Murderous, unreasoning rage seethed within his skull as he smashed his way through what was left of the bottles behind the bar. His clothes were dirty, ragged and torn and his hair and skin, where it showed, were caked with dirt, mud and blood, which the rain had caused to smear and mingle together. His smell, if there had been anyone else around to bear witness to it, was appalling. Somewhere on his body, wounds from past encounters were obviously badly infected. With every movement his body seemed racked with pain and he needed constant drink to dull it. His eyes mirrored the madness, which was inflamed by the alcohol in his system.

He was totally unrecognisable as one of the bikers Ken had encountered in this very bar before the madness struck. At his feet lay a heavy axe that he had just dropped. He had been in the bar earlier searching for hard spirits to deaden his suffering, but there had been little left. He had noticed that an attempt had been made to hack into the cellar, and this, his fevered brain had told him, was where the best stuff would be. He had been unable to lift the trapdoor on that occasion and had taken the Range Rover outside to go in search of tools. He had now returned with the axe, but needed to bolster himself up with the small amounts of spirit he could find before he started to exert himself.

As he had entered the bar he had reclaimed the almost empty bottle of vodka he had discarded on his last departure. Finishing the last of it, he threw the bottle to one side and bent down to pick up the axe. The action obviously caused him some pain and he had to rest for a moment or two with the hand containing the axe resting upon the bar top. He shuddered and snarled as the pain racked his body, driving his mind deeper into its madness; then, hefting the axe in his right hand, he drove it down upon the trapdoor, screaming in pain as he did so. It bit deep into the wood and stuck fast, and the man had to employ his left hand to help to free it. This obviously caused him more pain, and made him even more determined to reach the Aladdin's cave of alcohol which he imagined to be below his feet. Again the axe bit deeply into the timber of the trapdoor, and again it took an effort to free it, but free it he did. On the third stroke a large splinter flew from near to the lock, leaving a prominent lighter scar in the wood. Each of the blows cost the intruder a great deal of pain, and he had to rest frequently. It was going to take some time for him to break through, but he seemed determined enough to make it eventually.

Down below, Donald and Jamie could only sit together and watch as the trapdoor rattled and shook under the onslaught. Sooner or later it would give and Donald knew that they had no defence once that happened.

**

Slowly and painfully, light filtered back through Ken's closed eyelids. Something cold and damp was draped across his forehead and he could hear the sound of sobbing as if echoing from far away down a long corridor. Gradually, as his senses returned, the sobbing grew closer until he realised that he was lying on his back with his head cradled on Susan's lap, and it was her sobbing he could hear. As his eyes fluttered open, a wave of relief swept though him, emanating from Susan.

"Thank God! I thought they'd killed you this time." Her thought caused a wave of pain to pierce his head, and he put his hand up to it to feel the stickiness of blood there.

He groaned, and then asked, with a distinct lack of originality,

"What happened?"

"Someone booby-trapped the place. I thought they'd killed you," she repeated, aloud this time.

Looking up he saw a car engine block swinging on a chain above him. It had probably been released by a trip wire as he entered the workshop. It had only caught him a glancing blow, but he wondered how much more punishment his head could take. If it had hit him directly he knew that he would not be alive now. Movement was excruciating, but he knew that every moment he lay here brought danger that much closer. Whoever had rigged the trap obviously intended to return, and Ken did not want to be around when he did.

Forcing himself to his feet, and still holding the damp cloth, which Susan had supplied, to his forehead, he stumbled across to the office he had noticed before entering the building, with the girl supporting him as best she could. On the wall behind the door was a board containing what were obviously sets of car keys, each with a label attached with the number of the car printed neatly upon it in pencil. Ken helped himself to all of them and set off to find the cars to which they belonged. Some, the ones in the workshop, were not in working order, and he discarded the keys to those as he passed them, but out in the yard there were a number of vehicles from which he could choose.

When it came down to it, the choice was obvious, for there standing in plain view, was a powerful, and almost new breakdown truck, with the words "WE MET BY ACCIDENT" emblazoned along the sides. With this vehicle they would not need to skirt some of the more minor blockages on their route, but would be able to clear them enough to get by.

"But why do we need this?" Susan asked "I understood Donald to say that we could now move things by the power of our minds."

"We can, but it's a pretty painful business at the moment. I did some experimenting last night and I am not sure that we are up to it just yet. I think I'd rather rely upon the old way of doing things, at least for the time being."

On examination, the keys to the truck were not amongst those taken from the board, and Susan ran back to the office to see if she could find them whilst Ken leaned wearily against the side of it, keeping his eye on the gate and the roadway beyond. Susan returned after what seemed an eternity, gleefully holding aloft what were obviously the missing keys.

"In the office desk," she said by way of explanation. "I'll drive. You don't look up to it."

It had been Ken's intention to seek medical equipment from a nearby hospital once transport had been obtained, but now Susan would not hear of it, insisting that they return to the inn immediately to attend to his injuries. Ken had no objections to this change of plan, and meekly climbed into the passenger seat, once Susan had opened the door for him, closing his eyes and allowing his head to rock back against the headrest when the vehicle was in motion.

He was aroused by being jerked forward into his safety belt as Susan slammed on the brakes, and he caught the fear which

127

was filling her head. Looking around for the cause of that fear he saw the Range Rover parked once more in front of the inn. The intruder had returned and must be inside even now. He strained to let Donald know they were back and was relieved when the answering thoughts returned. He was apprised of the situation inside very speedily, although at first no solution was apparent. It was Susan who did what had to be done.

Throwing the truck into gear she roared onto the car park blowing the horn. Ken saw what was in her mind and he did not approve, although he could see no alternative. Susan knew that the man inside had a wild compulsion to kill. Whom he killed mattered not at all to him. Hearing the truck outside he would not be able to resist the urge to come out and deal with those in it, thus leaving his assault upon the cellar. What Ken did not like was the thought of Susan putting herself at risk by acting as decoy and drawing the man off. He knew what a liking these people had for shotguns.

***

Donald and Jamie had been distinctly worried by the determined attack upon the trapdoor. The axe was obviously good and sharp, and although the blows were slow in coming, they were quite efficient when they arrived. There were already splinters beginning to hang down on the underside where the odd blow had penetrated. Donald knew that once the breakthrough came the axe would be turned upon them.

He tried to influence the direction of the axe's downward swing with his mind, but he only had limited success. Most of the blows still hit the trapdoor. It was, at the most, only going to delay the intruder for a matter of minutes.

Suddenly Ken's voice was in his head, and he quickly apprised him of the situation inside the inn. There was the sudden harsh sound of a car horn blaring and the roaring of an engine from outside. The axe blows stopped immediately and heavy footsteps stumbled across the floor above towards the front door. They both sensed Susan's plan, such as it was, even as it formed in her mind, and before Donald could stop him,

Jamie was up the cellar steps and throwing back the splintered trap door. If the man turned back now they were both done for. It was with great relief that Donald heard the second vehicle roar off in pursuit of Susan, but his relief was immediately replaced by worry for Ken and Susan. He knew that, if they were caught, they would be incapable of defending themselves. Their one hope would be to outrun their pursuer and lose him before they returned, and he was not at all sure that they could pull it off.

***

The first part of the plan worked perfectly. As the man stumbled out into the open, roaring like an animal, Susan gunned the truck into motion and shot away from the car park, showering him with gravel thrown up by the spinning rear wheels. Incensed, he clambered into the Range Rover and set off in pursuit. He obviously had difficulty in controlling the vehicle as it swung from one side of the road to the other, but being faster than the truck he soon began to gain on them.

"Now what?" yelled Ken over the roar of the engine.

"I don't know," she cried in despair. "I haven't thought that far ahead."

"Well we'd better think of something soon. He's nearly on us."

The Range Rover drew steadily closer and was soon alongside the rear of the truck. Looking back Ken could see their wild-eyed pursuer, screaming and yelling as he edged alongside. To Ken's relief the man did not appear to have a gun with him. Instead he seemed intent on using the vehicle as a weapon, and as Ken watched, their pursuer swung the wheel over towards them and tried to ram them off the road. At the last moment Susan swung the truck away and somehow coaxed a fraction more speed out of the pickup. The wildly veering Range Rover missed their rear bumper by millimetres and then started to draw alongside for a second attempt.

As the two vehicles shot across the river bridge Ken realised that he need not remain entirely passive and concentrated hard upon the steering wheel as the madman tried to steer towards them once more. He was relieved to see the gap between the two vehicles widening as the Range Rover pulled away from them, but the stab of pain which shot through his head caused him to relinquish his efforts and the other vehicle veered towards them once more. It had been enough, however, for the surprise at feeling the steering wheel move against his will had caused the madman to brake slightly and the front of his vehicle just clipped the rear bumper of the truck but inflicted no damage on them. Even over the sound of the engine Susan and Ken heard his wild scream of rage as he accelerated alongside for another attempt. Ken tried again but this time he was not so successful. The man was ready for any unexplained interference with his steering and his strength was too much for Ken's mind to overcome.

The two vehicles came together with a dull crump and both veered wildly, the truck half mounting the pavement from the force of the impact as Susan fought to keep control. Suddenly she noticed that the road ahead was partially blocked by a bus half slewed across the carriageway. With great presence of mind she swung the truck further onto the verge beyond the footpath and shot past the obstruction on the inside. The other driver opted for the other side of the wreckage and at greatly reduced speed only just managed to squeeze past the mangled tractor which lay beyond the bus. This put the truck ahead of the Range Rover once more and gave the two fugitives a breathing space. But a further hazard now presented itself in the form of the rain, which had been threatening all morning lashing down upon them.

"We were lucky that time." This from Susan as she frantically sought the wiper switch. "What's going to happen when we meet a blockage we can't get around?"

Ken knew that he was not experienced enough at mind manipulation to influence matters much more. His head ached abominably.

"Perhaps Donald can help," he muttered

"I'll try." The words were in his head. "But I can't really see what's going on. Your pain is forming too much of a barrier, and we need to develop more co-ordination together."

There was no time for more. The other vehicle was drawing alongside again and this time Ken concentrated on the brake pedal of the chasing car. Once more pain lanced through his head but it bought them more precious time as the Rover dropped back, skidding into a spin on the rain-slicked surface.

"Oh-oh. Trouble." Ken felt the fear forming in her mind even as she mouthed the words.

Up ahead they could see a roundabout, the entire left hand half of which seemed to be blocked by a tangle of wreckage. Looking back Ken saw that the other driver had righted his vehicle and was just resuming the pursuit. An idea began to form in Susan's thoughts.

"Hold on!" she cried, and swung onto the clear right hand road, going around the island the wrong way. "When I meet the blockage I'm going to cut back across the centre of the roundabout and go back the way we have just come. When we get to the bus crash we can use the truck to pull the wreckage right across the road – if I can gain us enough time."

She sounded doubtful but as the truck bumped onto the soft earth of the roundabout they could see the Range Rover just entering the system. Unfortunately for them their pursuer, despite his crazed condition, was a quick thinker. Perhaps this was why he had survived for so long. He did not try to follow their route but as the truck thumped back onto the roadway he swung his vehicle into a handbrake turn and resumed the chase.

"He's too close. We haven't gained enough time." Ken's despair was almost tangible.

There was nothing else for it and so Susan nursed the breakdown truck past the bus for the second time and squeezed as much speed as she could out of the vehicle. As he looked back Ken could see the driver behind them apparently having some difficulty with his car. It seemed to be dropping back. The relief he felt was short-lived, however, as the man appeared to sort out whatever the problem was and he began to overhaul them once more.

Both Ken and Susan knew that sooner or later their luck would run out and they would be forced to stop. They both tried not to think about what would happen then. They were approaching the bridge which led back towards the village and the inn when the madman made his most determined attempt. Ken tried to control the other vehicle but the pain in his head was too great. The Range Rover caught them a mighty sideswipe pushing the rear of the truck sideways, and causing it to skid to a halt sideways on across the road. Both occupants thought that it was going to roll, but the centre of gravity was low enough to pull it back onto its wheels.

The Range Rover was not so lucky. The impact with the truck caused it to bounce back and hit the kerb on the far side of the road. The damage inflicted by Ken's earlier crash with the petrol tanker and the severe punishment it had been subjected to since had weakened part of the offside front suspension. The impact with the kerb proved to be too much and the whole of that front corner of the vehicle collapsed. The forward momentum caused the Range Rover to cartwheel. Smashing through the wooden fencing that ran alongside the footpath, and narrowly missing the cornerpost of the bridge parapet it somersaulted some fifteen feet to land on its roof in the river below.

For a while they both sat there, Ken with his head in his hands, Susan shaking, eyes wide with the shock. The horror forming within her head blotted out all other thought.

"I never meant for that to happen," she whispered, and then the tears came.

"Of course you didn't," responded Ken, putting his arm around her shoulders. "It was he who rammed us. There was no way you could have prevented it. If he had succeeded in stopping us the outcome would have been very different, and it was essential to keep him away from Jamie and Donald. There was no aggressive action on our part. Everything that happened was a direct result of his actions, not yours."

She saw that what he said was true, but he could still sense the burden of guilt within her mind. Only time would remove that once she had recovered from the shock.

"Just sit quietly for a moment or two, and I'll go and check on him," he continued.

Despite his fiercely throbbing head Ken forced himself to

climb down from the cab and walk back in the cold rain to look over the parapet of the bridge and as he did so he was dimly aware of Susan informing the others of the outcome.

The Range Rover lay on its roof in three feet of swirling water. The cab had been crushed by the impact and there could have been no room for any air pockets. A muddy streak, tinged with red, extended downstream from the disturbed river bottom, swirling and eddying on the rain pocked surface. Ken stood there for some considerable time. There was no other movement from around the wreckage, but as he stood there, gazing down into the water he could feel an idea forming in the dim recesses of his mind.

When he returned to the truck, Susan was more composed. The tears had been the release she needed, allowing her to rid herself of the pressures which had been building within her over the past few days. Now that the dam had burst she would feel better. She insisted that she was still in better shape to drive than he was, and so being in no fit state to argue, he reoccupied the passenger seat and allowed her to drive slowly back to the inn.

Jamie, despite Donald's protestations, had been standing in the inn doorway, and on seeing their return, ran to meet them riding back the last few metres hanging onto the rear of the truck.

Once inside, and having removed their wet clothing, each was brought fully up to date with the day's events, during which Susan expertly cleaned and bandaged Ken's latest set of cuts and abrasions. The booby trap had caught him a glancing blow on the head, leaving him with a thumping headache and a bloody, but superficial, scalp wound. After treating this, Susan dispensed two painkillers, and sent him to lie down.

They had had a number of very lucky escapes that day, firstly Ken with the booby trap, secondly Jamie and Donald with the intruder, and finally Ken and Susan at the bridge. If they had not returned from their expedition earlier than expected things could have turned out very differently.

It was decided that, in the light of all that had happened, they ought to delay their departure for Stonehenge no longer than was absolutely necessary. Ken had gone out like a light as soon as he had lain down, and so Susan joined Jamie in sorting through what should be taken with them.

The breakdown truck, whilst being a totally suitable vehicle for removing minor blockages, would not accommodate all four of them, and so a second vehicle would be needed to take the stores and extra passengers. Ken would have to drive one and Susan the other. She decided that procuring this second vehicle should be their first priority as soon as Ken felt up to it.

After a couple of hours sleep he felt much better, the pain killers and rest having all but removed the headache, and he awoke feeling ravenous. It was dark again outside, preventing any further forays, and so they decided to hold a dinner to celebrate their respective deliverances and to commemorate what would probably be their last evening in the cellar. Tomorrow morning, once a second vehicle had been obtained, they would splint Donald's leg using a floorboard and try to visit a hospital in the course of their journey to obtain proper equipment, rather than delaying their start any longer. The intruder had proved to them that the cellar was as much of a trap as a refuge, and they now preferred to take their chances in the open.

The evening proved to be just what they all needed. Susan and Ken cooked a most excellent meal, using some of the steaks and vegetables from the inn's deep freeze, which had not been opened since the power failed and had thus retained the food in a frozen condition. The wines and spirits from the racks in the cellar provided enough alcohol to relax tense muscles and calm stretched nerves. It was the best meal Ken had eaten since his first evening in Kelden, and he appreciated it, but most of all he enjoyed the company.

By the end of the evening they had worked out a plan of action for the morrow. An alarm was set for an early start so that at first light Ken and Susan would be ready to take the breakdown truck and find a suitable second vehicle, and as much fuel as possible. They would then return immediately to load up and depart, hoping to be on their way by mid-day at the latest.

This was the plan, but Ken knew only too well how easily plans could be disrupted. The wine, however, served to put them in an optimistic mood as they cleared away and prepared for bed, each one determined to get a good night's sleep before facing the unknown rigours of a new day. They had considered taking turns on watch in case of any further visits, but decided against it on the grounds that it was unlikely to happen at night, and there was little they could do about it anyway. Thus it was that no watch was kept, and as it turned out, none was needed.

Chapter 10

"We looked for… the time of healing, and behold trouble!"
Jeremiah 14:19

The alarm proved to be unnecessary, all three adults being up and about well before dawn. A good night's sleep had eased Ken's head considerably, although a dull ache behind his eyes served as a constant reminder of the previous day's mental and physical exertions. With the arrival of first light Ken and Susan were ready for their excursion in search of a second suitable vehicle. All the stores had been moved to stand below the loading bay doors, Donald's leg was freshly bandaged and splinted with a board removed from one of the upstairs rooms, and each of them had a substantial breakfast inside to sustain the morning's activities. The weather had deteriorated yet again, with a cold blustery wind lashing the heavy rain across the car park away from the front of the building.

Ken drove the truck, and not knowing for how far the main road to the north remained clear, he headed south towards Rowsley. He had already travelled that route and knew it to be fairly passable. They spotted a number of suitable vehicles parked in front of various houses and buildings which bordered the road, but were unable to find the keys for them within the houses or in the vehicles themselves. Ken drew the line at searching the pockets of any bodies they saw, as there was now a distinctly tainted smell apparent whenever one was near.

Eventually having reached Rowsley, they turned northwest, and on the outskirts of Bakewell they located what they were looking for. Parked outside a small shop, with the door left open, and the keys in the ignition, was a white Transit delivery van. The driver had obviously not intended to be out of his cab for long, but had never returned. On turning the ignition key, the starter gave a quarter of a turn and died. The interior light operated by the open door had been burning for almost a week, and though it drew only a small amount of power, it had been on for long enough to completely drain the battery. With the truck, however, it was a relatively simple matter to tow-start the van, and they were soon bowling along at a good pace back to the Shipley Arms.

Susan unlocked the doors of the loading bay into the cellar, and daylight flooded down upon the pile of provisions and equipment standing below. Donald was the first to be moved, being manhandled towards the opening and then dragged up the ramp on his mattress using the winch on the back of the truck. Once out in the open, despite the rain, he insisted on sitting for a while in the lee of the building to 'clear his lungs' as he put it. He had spent long enough cooped up within the confines of the cellar, and wanted to enjoy the freedom of being out under the open, albeit somewhat forbidding, sky.

The rest meanwhile set to with a will, loading the readied equipment into the back of the Transit. Before long, Susan insisted that Donald sit in the passenger seat of the truck, out of harm's way. By then the cold and damp was beginning to penetrate, and he willingly complied, allowing them to lift him in and surround him with warm blankets.

It took them somewhat longer than expected to transfer all that Donald had stockpiled into the van, and it was well past midday before they took a last look around and prepared to leave. Susan after saying her own private farewells to her home, taking the wheel of the Transit with Jamie by her side, and Ken accompanied by Donald who was to be their navigator, leading the way in the truck.

At first they were able to make good progress as Ken had already covered the route south as far as Belper albeit by making sometimes tortuous diversions. Some mistakes were made as Ken decided to clear minor blockages rather than head into a lengthy diversion, only to find that there was an impenetrable blockage a little further on, causing them to backtrack and take the diversion they had hoped to avoid. Once they reached

Belper, however, they were breaking new ground and their progress slowed to a snail's pace.

Just to the south of them lay Derby, and it had been decided that they would need to enter the town in search of a hospital to obtain medical supplies for Donald's leg, in order that he might be more mobile and feel less of a burden. The prospect was not one that any of them relished, but the sooner it was accomplished, the sooner Donald would feel a useful member of the group, and the less chance there would be of his leg sustaining permanent damage.

Before reaching the outskirts of the town, they pulled onto a well-shielded sideroad near the settlement of Quarndon and squeezed into the cab of the truck, out of the rain, to consult the map.

"We seem to have the choice of two hospitals," Donald explained. "One here," he indicated a large complex in the south-eastern quarter of the town, "and another, smaller one, here, on the northern side. The large hospital would certainly have what we need, but it would mean either skirting the town and coming in from the other side, or going through quite close to the town centre."

"I can't say that I am looking forward to visiting either of them," broke in Ken. "Those who have survived for this long would probably have been the most aggressive and violent types and I am sure that they would have headed for the hospital complex to find drugs and medication – just as we are doing. If I had been one of them, I would probably have moved in there."

"Always provided they are still capable of rational thought, which I very much doubt," Donald rejoined. "There are probably quite a few loners left, wandering around, as yesterday's encounter demonstrated. It would be far too much of a coincidence for him to have been the last. I reckon the odds are about even on someone else being there. It all depends on which one was the nearest one for any dominant survivors to get to. To them a hospital is a hospital. I don't think size would come into it. Personally, I favour the nearer of the two. The less of the town we have to go through the better I will like it."

"Do you think we shall find what we need at the small

one?" asked Susan.

"I should think so," Ken replied, "after all, our requirements are not very exotic, just bandages and some plaster of Paris, and maybe crutches."

It was agreed that the nearer of the two hospitals appeared to be their safest bet. The other one remained an option should circumstances dictate, and they spent a little time discussing whether they should all go, or whether Susan and Jamie should remain on the outskirts while Ken and Donald went in. Eventually it was decided that there was nothing to be gained by their splitting up. If the going proved difficult they could remain in the town, making the hospital their base for the night.

Turning off the bypass at the large roundabout to the north of the town, having driven across the centre of it to avoid the wrecked vehicles, they headed towards the town centre, finding much the same pattern which Ken and Jamie had seen in other places repeated here. The sight of so many bodies lying around shocked Susan and Ken sent her a thought to warn her that the sights in the hospital were likely to be just as harrowing. From what Jamie had told them about Kelden, even the sick were not immune to the madness.

The journey to the hospital was uneventful, save for a few minor obstructions, caused by only one or two vehicles slewed across the road. These they were able push aside using the reinforced front bumper and grillwork on the truck, the road being wide enough for them to get by at that. In this they were assisted by the slippery, wet road surface as the rain continued to lash down from leaden skies. Twice a movement caught Ken's eye and he tensed, ready to race away from trouble if need be, but on both occasions it turned out to be packs of scavenging dogs, slinking away from the noise of the group's passage through the rain-soaked, echoing streets.

Ken felt his responsibility for the group very keenly, and by the time they pulled up outside the hospital building, his shoulders ached from the tension of leading them through the wreckage of the town, while at the same time keeping constant watch for any signs of movement which may herald a sudden, murderous attack.

The hospital had been easy to locate, being well signposted, and turned out to be a tall, red brick building, standing halfway down a small sideroad only a relatively short distance into the town. It was not at all what they had expected, standing in an area dominated by long rows of terraced housing and corner shops. The surrounding streets were double lined with parked cars, the road surfaces littered with the fragments of headlights, windscreen glass, and torn off fittings, left by the crazed vandals who seemed to have swept through the area. Many of the houses, and indeed the hospital itself, bore the scars of their passage in the form of splintered doors and shattered windows.

They parked on the clear stretch of pavement immediately outside the frontage of the building. An entrance labelled 'Enquiries' was located dead centre, and was reached by half a dozen or so concrete steps which ran up the front wall to the left of the door, parallel to the pavement, from which they were separated by a red brick wall which rose in height along with the steps. To the left of them a sloping tunnel ran down, directly into the building, and what seemed to be a decorated wall was dimly discernible at the far end of it. To the right of centre, a ramp running in the same direction as the central steps, also parallel to the road, was crowned at the top by a set of double doors marked "Outpatients."

During the drive in, Ken had worked out a strategy, which, having gathered them together in the cab of the truck, he put to the others.

"Our main problem is to find what we need without exposing ourselves to unnecessary dangers," he explained, "so what I propose is this. Susan, you stay here in the truck with Donald and Jamie."

This provoked an immediate protest from the boy that he was being left out again. Ken however was adamant.

"No, you must stay here. If anything happens to me in there, Susan is going to need all the help she can get with Donald and his leg. If all goes well, I can locate the fracture clinic and then I'll come out and get you all. It will be faster than trying to carry Donald through the hospital and search at the same time. Susan, give me the keys to the van."

With some difficulty, because of the confined space within the cab, she extracted them from her pocket and handed them to him.

"If there is any sign of trouble while I am inside, let me know and get out of here fast. I shall try to get to the van and meet up with you later. We can rendezvous back at Quarndon, where we stopped before coming in. If I don't show up before dark you will have to find a safe place to spend the night and then go on in the morning without me. I'll keep you in touch with what is happening inside. If anything at all should go wrong, whatever you do don't come looking for me. If I don't get back to you just go."

Before any of them could protest, he was out of the truck and running for the hospital entrance, taking the steps two at a time, head bowed against the rain. In his mind he could feel the mixed emotions of frustration, annoyance and concern emanating from the cab of the truck, and he tried to radiate feelings of love and confidence as he disappeared into the building. He was not at all sure that he succeeded with the confidence.

The interior of the building was heartrending, with corridors and wards of what was obviously a children's hospital, decorated for Christmas, now looking rather forlorn and pathetic in the dim grey light of the late afternoon. The popular cartoon characters, which decorated the walls, were intended to generate a friendly atmosphere in normal times, but now the whole building felt cold and hostile.

Located on the left, just inside the double doors, was a small enquiry office, which appeared to be deserted. Beyond, corridors led off to the right and left, while immediately in front of him the available light came tumbling down a staircase, which led to the upper floors, the wooden steps turning right and disappearing from view before reaching even the first of the higher levels. He turned right at the intersection at the foot of the staircase and found himself pushing through a pair of double doors into the outpatients department. Plastic chairs were scattered about the area, and the shop which lay on his right as he entered, had been ransacked, the brightly coloured wrapping papers and ripped open bags of sweets strewn about the floor. Behind the reception desk, which was on his left, lay the first bodies. Averting his eyes he passed on. Beyond the reception desk he turned into a corridor which ran towards the rear of the building. He tried to avoid looking too closely into the wards as he passed down the echoing corridors, but it was obvious that death had stalked this building. The odour was unmistakable. Taking out his handkerchief he held it over his mouth and nose as he progressed deeper into the complex, occasionally skirting or stepping over a small body which lay in his path. The mayhem, which had been wrought in the outside world, had not spared this former place of comfort and healing. He soon came to the realisation that, if possible, this would have to be the last excursion into what had been densely populated areas as the risk of disease would soon be a very real one, and the experience far too unpleasant.

Eventually, by trial and error, he arrived at his destination, and, after a careful check inside, pushed his way through the double doors into the plaster room. Again he was appalled by what he saw. Two young nurses had died in here, apparently having fought to the death using some of the horrific looking equipment scattered about the floor of the room. The victor had died of her wounds as she had attempted to crawl to the door. Skirting the edge of the room, Ken checked the examination cubicles, which bordered the right hand side of the room, to ensure that no one was hidden there. Only one was occupied. The body of a young girl lay upon an examination couch with the handles of a large pair of scissors protruding from her chest. During his search he had, as promised, kept his companions outside informed of his progress, without letting them know what he saw. His revulsion however was difficult to mask, causing them some apprehension as they sat awaiting his return.

Forcing himself to press on with his search, he eventually discovered a storeroom containing what he needed. The door was located on the wall directly opposite the examination booths. It was not locked, and within stacked neatly on the shelves, he discovered boxes of bandages already impregnated with plaster of Paris used for encasing broken limbs.

The room was not large. It was obviously a much later, one-storey addition to the old building, using up some odd corner, but it had the distinct advantage of having no windows, being lit from above by a skylight. There was also a stout lock on the door. If only the key could be located this could be their refuge for the night should they decide not to move on. It would be quite spartan, but they would at least be able to stretch out on the floor, and they should be safe from any surprise attack. All that remained now was to bring in Donald and attend to his leg.

Before returning to the truck, Ken risked another attempt at telekinesis, moving the two bodies in the main room into one of the examination cubicles and drawing the curtain across the doorway to hide the grisly remains. It was easier this time, and the resultant headache soon faded back into a dull throb. It was at this point that he realised that he no longer needed a key to open and close locks. Given that he had some knowledge of their interior workings, he decided that he should be able to manipulate the mechanism with very little trouble.

Back in the corridor he took possession of a wheelchair which had been standing in the doorway to a ward. If he cleared away the obstructions as he retraced his route, this could be used to transport Donald. By the time he reached the main entrance he was feeling well pleased with himself. Everything seemed to be going smoothly for a change.

The feeling of relief which came from his companions as he emerged from the building was almost tangible, and the air when he removed the handkerchief from his nose, smelled fresh and clean, washed by the steady downpour. All were pleased to see that he was safe and he quickly explained what he had found, warning them to be prepared for an unpleasant walk through the inhospitable hospital.

Before entering the building they reached the conclusion that, as no one had any idea how long the plaster would take to set properly, and even if they left the area immediately after completing their mission, there would be very little daylight left, the heavy cloud bringing forward the onset of evening, it would be best to remain in the hospital until morning. They therefore took their sleeping bags in with them in case they could not locate a bedding store, also filling a rucksack with enough food, drink and supplies to see them through the night. After Donald had been transferred to the entrance in the wheelchair, by way of the outpatients ramp, and Jamie given strict instructions to be on his guard, both vehicles were moved to a less conspicuous position in the deserted roadway behind the hospital building, and secured for the night.

***

Once installed in the storeroom, they all felt a great deal less vulnerable, and Jamie was set to work making the room a little more habitable whilst Susan and Ken made a start on Donald's leg. There was still water in the taps, the hospital having large storage tanks to supply its copious needs, and, most luxurious of all, the toilets still functioned!

Ken soaked some of the plaster-bandages while Susan took off the old splints, slit the seam of the trousers over the injured leg and applied fresh bandages to the skin. Some bruising was present, but the leg appeared to be positioned correctly. They could only go by common sense, but they worked out that if they applied dry bandages first to stop the plaster adhering to the hairs, then wrapped these over with plaster-soaked bandages, while Donald himself held the bones in the correct position, they would not be far out. They also built up a thicker layer of bandage and plaster underneath the heel to take the strain when weight could be put upon it.

By the time they had finished, they were both spattered with spots of white and there was a liberal coating of plaster over the treatment couch upon which they had carried out the process, and over the immediate floor area. Despite this, they were well pleased with their efforts, although they had to admit it was not the neatest job they had ever seen. Donald too confessed that he was pleased and that the leg felt comfortable.

By now the cold within the building was beginning to seep into their bones, and so Ken went off in search of crutches so that Donald could be moved as soon as the plaster had set sufficiently. Again he was lucky, finding a selection of adjustable crutches in a corridor cupboard just outside the door. Taking these back in, they found that, on maximum extension, there was just one pair which would do. Fortune was indeed smiling upon them.

As they had worked, the light had faded fast making the interior of the building very gloomy, with the only sound to be heard, other than those which they made themselves, being that of the rain as it lashed around the outside of the building, throwing itself against the windows in a frenzied attempt to gain access. The heavy grey sky had brought an early darkness.

What they had seen of the wards as they had passed along the corridor decided them against entering them to collect mattresses to sleep on. Each preferring to sleep on the floor rather than face what must lie inside those wards. Along with the food, they had brought two small camping lights, run from gas canisters, and a small camping stove from the van. These they set up in the storeroom. After covering the skylight with a blanket they had removed from a cubicle, the lights were lit, and their cheery glow filled the small room. The lights and stove, on which a pan of soup was being warmed, served to take the chill off the air inside their refuge. Donald was carefully moved from the treatment couch and manoeuvred into his sleeping bag, and, once they were all settled inside, the door was closed and locked. At last they felt safe. They were certain that no one knew of their presence, and that they would not be disturbed during the night. Tomorrow Donald would be somewhat more mobile and they could begin their long journey south.

The hot soup served both to warm them and to lift their spirits, which the hospital had done much to depress. Here they had been reminded of the Christmas season, and its message of peace, goodwill, and hope. A message which now meant nothing to the world outside, where the only people still to survive were those who had thrived upon violence, and in whose heads raged the madness which would, sooner or later, lead to their own destruction. For these there was no peace, a total absence of goodwill, and certainly no hope! Within that small room, however, hope still burned, like a tiny candle flame in a world of darkness. For them, once they had made contact, there was the prospect of all that Christmas had ever stood for. An end to all violence and evil, and the prospect of such a peace as the world had never known since the beginning of history, and it was this which fed their hope and gave them the will to go on.

Once the lights were out, they snuggled down into their respective sleeping bags to conserve warmth, but the hardness of the floor made sleep difficult to come by, except for Jamie who seemed able to sleep anywhere. The adults envied him that, as they constantly adjusted their positions in a vain attempt to find a more comfortable one. Inevitably, their shared thoughts turned to the journey before them.

"How long do you think it will take us to get there?" Susan wondered.

"Difficult to say," Donald was non-committal. "It depends on the blockages we meet. I rather fear that they will get worse the further south we go. The traffic always seemed worse in the south to me."

"If only we could get some information on what lies ahead," mused Ken, "it would save us hours in going back along roads we have already covered in order to get around a blockage."

"We don't seem to be getting very far very quickly." Susan again, "It reminds me of when Daddy and I took a narrowboat from Nantwich to Llangollen. It took us four days to cover a distance which would have taken an hour in a car, but compared with this even that would have seemed fast."

A picture of a sunlit canal threading through picturesque countryside filled the room before slowly fading away.

Donald agreed, nodding uselessly in the dark.

"It's going to make it worse having to avoid large conurbations," he thought, "and the fast major roads are the ones which are likely to have the most blockages. I suspect that we're going to get through quite a lot of fuel, so we'll have to spot our chances for filling up, and take all that come along."

"I suppose, if we have to, we can get it from other vehicles," Susan thought, "after all, they won't need it any more will they?"

The conversation continued, in thought, between Donald

and Susan for quite some time, but Ken lay quietly, busy with his own private thoughts. Something that had been said had rekindled a vague idea, which had stirred briefly in his mind the pervious day, but he did not want to raise their hopes until he knew whether or not it was possible. He therefore kept the thoughts hidden from them until he could obtain more information.

"Ken, what's the matter?" The worry was apparent in Susan's mind as she noticed his absence from the silent conversation.

"Nothing."

They knew it was not the truth.

"Ken?" she returned, scoldingly.

"It's all right, there's nothing to worry about."

This time they knew what he said to be true and respected his privacy, each of them retreating into the private areas of their minds as they sought elusive sleep.

It was not the most comfortable or restful of nights, and all three of the adults awoke feeling little refreshed, cold, stiff and sore. Jamie alone seemed to have spent the night in comfort and appeared well rested. Dawn was just breaking when they removed the blanket from the skylight, and it could be seen from the hint of blue in the sky that the weather had at last improved somewhat. They hoped it would last. The room was bitterly cold, and the lights and stove were again employed to supply a little warmth and hot water for coffee. Holding a steaming mug in cupped hands, Susan asked Donald how the leg felt.

"Pretty good!" was the reply, "but a bit cold. I reckon that will get better as the plaster dries out more. How are your cuts and bruises, Ken?"

"Still rather sore and stiff. This hard floor didn't help, but I'll be OK once we get moving. A warm, restful night's sleep would do us all good."

Donald nodded

"I'm afraid there doesn't seem to be much prospect of that until after we have made contact," he said.

Ken wasn't so sure. If what he had in mind worked out, life could become somewhat less hectic in the very near future, but again he kept the thoughts masked so as not to raise false hopes. He could not, however, mask the feeling of optimism that lay within him, and Susan looked at him curiously.

"You're hiding something," she observed.

Ken grinned, "I can see that this thought sharing has its drawbacks," he laughed. "Yes, I've got a little secret, but don't press me just yet."

A thought suddenly struck him, and he consulted the date on his watch. "Do you realise what day it is?"

Jamie looked at his watch, as did Donald. Susan, Ken noticed, was not wearing one.

"It's Christmas Eve," whooped the child, and then in a more subdued tone, "but it won't be much of a Christmas for us, will it?"

"If things work out as I hope, I might just have a rather nice Christmas present for all of us," Ken tried to encourage them, "but we'd better get started as soon as possible if we want to get anywhere today."

They all agreed and for a while they bustled around packing up their belongings in preparation for their departure. Donald helped as far as he could, with Jamie assisting him. The two were becoming firm friends. Donald having helped the boy with his illness was now in return being helped in his disability by Jamie.

Soon they were ready, but before venturing back into the hospital, Ken went to the corridor doors, and, opening them very slightly, stood and listened for any signs of activity. He started as a slight sound reached his ears. It was very faint and seemed to be coming from one of the wards on the opposite side of the corridor, which they would have to pass on the way out. Signalling to the others to remain where they were, he slipped through the double doors, ensuring that they closed silently behind him, and crept towards the source of the noise.

As he drew nearer he saw that the door to the ward was slightly open and, as he paused, crouching down behind the doors before looking in, the noise came again. It was a slithering, rustling sound, as if someone were searching through a sack of shredded paper packing or dragging it around the floor.

148

He flashed a thought back to the others, to keep them informed, and with his heart pounding in his ears, he slid one eye around the edge of the door to try to see without being seen. As he did so the sound came again louder and seemingly very close. He snatched his head back and pressed his cheek close to the door, as if trying to merge into it and so escape detection. He had seen no movement. The ward appeared to be deserted, although there had been areas that were hidden from view. The noise came again, and Ken was relieved to hear that it was no closer. He had not been seen. When his heart had stopped thumping he risked another look, taking longer this time, and he almost laughed out loud with relief as he saw what was causing it. The Christmas decorations had been torn from the ceiling on one side of the ward and were blowing to and fro in the draught from a broken window. The foil and paper were scraping across the floor and furniture as the light wind blew through the broken panes. He realised that they had not heard it on the previous evening as it had been drowned out by the drumming of the heavy rain on the windows. It was only in the silence of this relatively calm morning that the sound was at all noticeable.

As soon as they knew that there was no danger, the others emerged through the double doors of the plaster room, Jamie pushing Donald in the wheelchair. Ken meanwhile had moved off to bring the tow-truck back to the front of the building. They had decided that they would leave the van where it was, and pick it up as they drove past on their way out of the town. Drawing up outside the entrance he saw that his three companions were waiting just inside the doors at the top of the ramp. On seeing the truck draw up they carefully wheeled Donald down and Susan helped him up onto his feet, she and Jamie supporting him on each side.

"We've forgotten the crutches!" Susan exclaimed as Ken approached them. "You and Jamie help Donald into the truck and I'll go back for them."

Ken saw that this made sense, as he was better able to cope with the insertion of Donald into the truck's cab than Susan was. They did not want him to put any weight on the plaster until it was thoroughly dry. They were not sure whether this was a necessary precaution, but thought it better to be safe than sorry.

Having safely installed Donald and placed their equipment, including the wheel chair into the back of the truck, Ken climbed into the driver's seat and sat to await Susan's return, keeping the engine running to warm up the heater. Jamie was content to sit in the rear with the equipment, swinging his legs backwards and forwards over the back edge of the vehicle.

When he thought about it later, Ken found it hard to decide the order of events which came next, everything seeming to happen at once.

As Susan emerged from the building she stopped dead and pointed. "Look out!" she screamed.

Ken twisted round in his seat and looked at where she was pointing. Down at the far end of the street, was an off licence, situated on the corner. From its doorway, a man was emerging at a shambling run. In his hand he held an automatic pistol which he was pointing directly at Jamie. Immediately Ken threw the truck into gear and gunned the accelerator, swerving the vehicle from side to side as he shot away. Jamie threw himself backwards into the rear and clung on for dear life as a shot rang out and a bullet whistled over him, flattening itself into the bodywork behind him.

Meanwhile, Ken was projecting to Susan.

"Get out of here! Run! Back to the store and lock yourself in!"

Reaching the main road, the truck swung right, ignoring the one way system and as it disappeared from sight the last fading thought she caught was:

"I'll be back for you…!"

Then nothing.

She had been rooted to the spot as the action unfolded before her, but now she turned and dashed back into the building. The man, his attention caught by the sudden motion, got off a shot in her direction just as she disappeared through the doors. The bullet buried itself in the wall close to her shoulder. This man knew how to use a gun. Susan gave a sob as she sped off down the corridor, the man crashing through the doors in pursuit. She had never been so frightened in her life. Yesterday's incident had been bad enough but at least then she had had Ken's companionship and the illusory protection of the truck cab around her. Now she was alone! She knew that if he caught her there would be no time to reason with him. Murder was the only thing on his mind.

As she turned off the main corridor into the one on which their refuge was located, another shot rang out and she thought she felt a slight tug at the arm of her coat. An attempt to glance over her shoulder caused her to stumble, but she was able to recover her balance and continue down the corridor in headlong flight, not knowing how close behind her pursuer was. If only she could make it to the plaster room before he came around the corner, it would give her a small, but absolutely vital, chance. She just made it.

Panting and sobbing in fear she dashed back into their storeroom, pushing the door closed behind her. As she collapsed into a heap, with her back pressed firmly against the door, a sudden realisation almost caused her to panic. She had no idea how a lock worked, and try as she might her brain could not manipulate its intricate mechanism. There was no way she could lock the door between herself and the gunman.

***

As the truck sped away from the hospital, they could all feel the thought contact with Susan fading, until all they could sense was her fear. This proved an agonising situation for they had no way of knowing what caused the fear to peak at certain points. All they knew was that Susan felt herself to be in imminent danger. Ken waited for the fear to subside a little, which would indicate to him that she had succeeded in reaching the storeroom, but when the reverse happened, and her fear rose almost to panic pitch, he surmised that something had gone wrong. From what he had observed of the 'mad death' he knew that the people affected killed without thinking, but perhaps this man was an exception. Perhaps this one would not kill Susan immediately…! He tore his mind away from the thought and slammed his foot on the brake pedal as he swung the truck over to the side of the road. The sooner he got back there the better it would be for Susan, and the better he would feel.

Both Donald and Jamie knew what he felt, and sought to assure him that they would cope alone, staying in the locked cab and keeping well out of sight until he returned. Immediately on receiving that assurance Ken was out of the cab and sprinting back towards the hospital as fast as he could go.

***

Susan could hear the madman coming down the corridor, bellowing in anger and frustration at having lost sight of his quarry. Suddenly the noises grew less distinct although the ferocity of them seemed to increase. She guessed what had happened. Seeing the door lying open, he had thought that she had taken refuge in the ward with the blowing decorations, and she could now hear the crashes as he overturned beds and threw lockers aside in his fury, seeking to discover her hiding place. There was the crack of a pistol shot as he fired at something which attracted his attention. The smashing of furniture continued, giving Susan valuable minutes in which to control her sobbing and quieten her breathing.

Eventually the crashing stopped, and she could hear screams of rage as her pursuer realised that she was not to be found in that ward. He was back in the corridor again! Would he come into the adjacent room? She tried to hold the doors to the corridor closed with her mind and heard him grunt with surprise as he pushed against them. He pushed again and she found her control was just not good enough. The doors gave, and he was through into the room next door.

"Ken, oh Ken, where are you?" her mind cried, and then retreated into a terrified gabble as she heard the gunman searching the outside room and adjacent cubicles.

"Oh, I can't lock the door and he's coming! What can I do? I can't lock the door. Oh Ken, where are you?"

By now her pursuer was outside the door behind which she was huddled, so close that she could hear his breathing and muttered curses. In her mind's eye she could see him reaching for the door handle and wondered if her death would be a quick one. She fervently hoped that there would not be a lot of pain. She hated the thought of pain. Suddenly her body jerked as a shot rang out immediately followed by the sound of retreating footsteps. At the same time there came the click of the door lock shooting home, immediately followed by a shower of dust as the skylight above her opened and Ken's head and shoulders appeared. She scrambled up from her position behind the door.

"Quick, up here," came the silent instruction. "Hurry though, he won't be fooled for long.

He reached down for her and she put up her arms towards him. As she did so she noticed blood on her coat sleeve, and when Ken pulled her up through the skylight a cry escaped her lips as pain shot through her arm. The man outside, hearing the cry, ran back to the door, crashing into it and rattling the handle frantically in his fury. Lowering the skylight down into place and manipulating it into the locked position once more, Ken pulled Susan back away from the opening and then unlocked the door below, just as the madman threw his weight against it. The gunman crashed into the storeroom and sprawled onto his face on the floor. Immediately Ken closed and re-locked the door.

Pulling Susan, who was by now very close to collapse, to her feet, he half dragged half carried her to the fire escape ladder by which he had gained access to the roof. Her legs could hardly bear her slight weight, and he saw that she would never manage to descend it alone. Without hesitation, he bent down and hefted her onto his shoulders, taking her in a fireman's lift and unceremoniously carrying her down to the safety of the ground.

As he ran along the back of the building, still carrying her, he could hear the sound of gunfire as the man tried to weaken the door lock by firing at it. Running alongside a high wooden fence on his left, Ken realised that this was the fence which bordered the rear of the hospital, and they were in fact quite close to the van, parked on the road outside. He lowered Susan to the ground as quickly as he could and, finding that there was nothing that they could use to help them climb over, he took a hefty kick at the upright planks, which stood between them and the outside world. The fence was well made, the vertical planking being attached to horizontal members near the top and bottom, and it took four more good kicks before the first plank gave, clattering away into the roadway. Once the first one had gone, those on either side offered little further resistance, and the gap was soon wide enough. Scrambling quickly through, Ken ensured that the road outside was clear before helping Susan out after him.

"Can you manage now?" he asked.

She nodded, and Ken saw the tears streaming down her cheeks.

"Are you hurt?"

She nodded again.

"It's not much," she whispered, "please let's get away from here."

"Come on, then!" He grabbed her hand and pulled her after him, steeling himself against the flood of emotion which accompanied her tears.

As they ran across the road and headed for the van, Ken frantically searched his pockets for the keys, before remembering that Susan had kept them after parking it here on the previous evening.

"The keys!" he gasped. "Have you got the keys?"

Susan searched in her right-hand pockets but they were not there. An attempt to use her left arm caused her to cry out again in pain. Ken fished them out of her left pocket for her, opened up the passenger door and helped her in. He then climbed into the driver's seat, started the engine, and, with the tyres protesting against such treatment, he threw the vehicle into a tight u-turn to head back to where Jamie and Donald were waiting for them.

The moment the van drew up behind the truck, Jamie leaped from the cab and ran back towards them. Susan threw her right arm around Ken's neck and hugged herself close to him, with tears of relief coming thick and fast.

"I thought he'd got me," she sobbed, "I didn't know where you were. I didn't hear you coming."

"Of course you didn't," he tried to sound comforting, "you were projecting so powerfully yourself, there was no chance of hearing anyone else. I tried, but you blocked me out."

"He was so close," she shuddered. "If something hadn't caught his attention for a second he would have been in before you could get to me."

"I know, that's why I distracted him."

"You? How?"

I made one of the cubicle curtains rattle, and he thought it was you."

By now Jamie had Susan's door open and was examining the blood on her sleeve.

"Did he shoot you?" he asked in wonder, eyes wide at the thought.

"I think he must have done," she replied, pulling herself together, "although I didn't really notice it at the time."

"I think we have been incredibly lucky," Ken broke in, "but we'd better not stretch it by hanging around here any longer. Do you think you are up to driving?"

"I'll try," she replied, looking uncertain.

As it turned out she was unable to manage the gear change on the van, but Jamie came to her rescue.

"I know how the gears go," he offered, "if you just tell me when to change I'll do it."

There seemed to be no alternative and the boy was so keen to help that it was decided to give it a try. They were still much too close to the hospital for comfort. Once away from here they could pause for breath, attend to Susan's wound, and then decide on their next step.

They headed out of the town by the way they had entered, to rejoin their original route south. The arrangement between Susan and Jamie worked well, with only the occasional clash of gears to indicate slight lack of co-ordination. The contact between minds made it easier than it otherwise might have been. The exit from the town took less time than their entry, although some mistakes were made, it being difficult to recognise road junctions where detours needed to be made when approaching them from the opposite direction. There was, however, still much of the morning left by the time they regained the spot from which their expedition into the town had been planned.

The day, which had started with only a hint of blue in the

sky, had improved and the morning sun, still quite low in the sky lifted their spirits without doing the same for the temperature. Here on the outskirts of the town the air felt crisp and clean as they gathered to examine Susan's arm. The tug on her sleeve, which she had felt as she fled down the hospital corridor, had, in fact, been the slight impact of a bullet passing through the flesh of her arm. Again luck had been on their side as it had missed bone and major blood vessels entirely, leaving a neat but nevertheless painful entry and exit wound on her lower arm, just below the elbow. This was soon cleaned and bandaged, leaving Susan much more comfortable than she had been, and ready to resume their journey.

Major blockages on the bypass caused them to swing to the far west of Derby, and then, inexplicably, Ken cut back to the east, arriving at the village of Findern a few miles to the south of the town some two and a half hours later. Just south of the village, he stopped the truck on a bridge and carefully scanned the area to left and right. Not seeming to be satisfied, he moved on again, threading his way tortuously through the roads in that area as if searching for something. After twenty minutes of twisting backwards and forwards, they rounded a sharp bend and Ken let out a cry of triumph.

"There it is! That's what I'm looking for!"

The road, they saw, now ran alongside a canal, and there, directly before them lay a number of cruisers and narrowboats moored by the towpath. Now, at last, his plan was apparent. Their progress to date had been painfully slow as the roads were virtually unusable, but here they had an alternative. The canal system, largely restored for leisure traffic, could take them a long way towards their destination, with he hoped, relatively few blockages, and more importantly, keeping fairly clear of built-up areas.

Chapter 11

"Horror hath taken hold upon me…"

Psalm 119:53

Upon examination, the cabin cruisers proved to be rather too cramped for such a prolonged journey, Donald's leg making them all somewhat impractical. Although they would probably have been faster, it was decided that the extra space and comfort afforded by the narrowboats was well worth a couple of days added to the trip.

A cursory examination of the three other narrow boats berthed there revealed little, being locked and shuttered against vandals and the elements, but once they had managed to manipulate the locks and gain entry to them, one stood head and shoulders above the others. So it was "Rachel II" that was adopted.

She was a beautiful little boat, well equipped and well maintained, and had obviously been lovingly cared for. The panels on the tumblehome, hatches and doors were colourfully decorated with traditional canal-folk paintings, lovingly executed, each one a work of art in its own right.

"This is wonderful!" exclaimed Susan in delight, as she examined each new facet of the boat in turn. "I never expected to be able to enjoy the comforts of home and travel south at the same time!"

At the front of the boat was a well-appointed saloon, containing a solid fuel stove, electric lighting, and a colour television – now totally useless. The galley, with a fridge and a full size cooker, both of which ran on propane gas, was located immediately to the rear of the saloon, and directly behind that they discovered a cosy bedroom. This lay in front of a bathroom, holding a short bath, a shower, wash hand basin and, much to their surprise, a real flush toilet. Right at the back of the boat was a traditional boatman's cabin, containing a boatman's stove, by which the helmsman could warm himself during his long stints at the tiller. Sandwiched between this cabin and the bathroom was the engine room, where the powerful, four-cylinder Thornycroft diesel engine was to be found. The whole boat was immaculate, but it was this engine, lovingly polished and obviously very well tended which drew a long low whistle of admiration from Ken.

"This is really something," he breathed, as he stood in the narrow corridor that ran down the right hand side of the boat from saloon to the boatman's cabin, "I knew these boats were good, but I never expected to find anything like this!"

Spaced along the corridor were doors which closed off all the sections from each other, and running along the wall were large diameter copper pipes.

"It even has central heating!" Susan exclaimed, pointing to the pipes, and the radiator in the bedroom.

It was discovered later that this heating system could be run from either the engine or the solid fuel stove in the saloon, with a gas fired boiler in reserve should the other two not be in use. The boat's owners had planned for every contingency. That they were all-the-year-round canal people was borne out by the fact that the boat was fully provisioned and ready to go. Both the fuel and water tanks were full. They even discovered a generous store of anthracite beneath the seats up in the open bow area.

"That front section is called the cratch," Susan informed them, showing off the knowledge she had gained from her holiday, "and the deck at the rear is the counter. That large wide step there is where the driver" (here her knowledge let her down) "stands".

Further investigation revealed that the seats in the saloon converted to a second double bed, while the boatman's cabin held a small bunk, and a foldaway single bed which, when extended for use, lay across the boat. The craft could not have been better suited to their purposes if they had designed it themselves, the whole of her fifty-five foot length being crammed with all they could possibly require. Ken had intended to cannibalise the other boats to make up any shortcomings, but this proved to be unnecessary.

They helped Donald to settle into the saloon where the first thing to catch his eye was a set of waterway guides, but before turning to them he set about lighting a fire in the stove, while the others brought aboard all the provisions from the van, stowing them, temporarily in the saloon, to be dispersed at their leisure.

When the task was almost completed, Ken called them together.

"There are still one or two items I think we need to get," he began, hesitantly, not knowing how what he had to say would be received, "but I don't want to hold things up unnecessarily."

He took a deep breath before continuing, holding up his hand to counter any objections before they could be voiced.

"I want you to make a start without me and head south," he pointed out the route on the guide that Donald had found. "I shall try to meet up with you here, at Fradley Junction, where you turn onto the Coventry Canal, but failing that I shall make for Huddlesford Junction, here."

Again he pointed.

"If I fail to make that, this looks like a good place to moor for the night." He indicated a spot where the canal was bounded on one side by a wooded hill and on the other by a river. "Moor here, and that is where I shall head if I can't make the other places in time. If I am not at either of the junctions when you get there, leave one of these in a prominent place on the towpath."

He hoisted a couple of the half dozen or so traffic cones that had been in the back of the tow truck.

"That way I shall know that I've missed you, and I won't hang around needlessly. Your only problem area on the journey would seem to be Burton-on-Trent. There appears to be a lock to negotiate in the town. That will be where you will be most vulnerable. Just keep your eyes and ears open and get through it as fast as you can and keep going. As with the roads, settlements seem to pose the main danger as that is where the hostile survivors seem to have headed, possibly in the hope of meeting, and dealing with, other survivors. Their tactics don't seem to be very sophisticated – just seek and kill – as directly as possible. Every day that passes will mean fewer of them. Eventually we won't have to worry about them, but for the time being, remain vigilant. If you do meet any insurmountable obstructions, just moor in the centre of the canal, batten down the hatches, and sit tight, sending out a call like you did back at the inn, and I'll get back to you as soon as I can with the truck. I would expect," he concluded, "that the waterways are much clearer than the roads at this time of year, and this boat is probably powerful enough to nudge any small obstructions out of the way."

"I'm not so sure that this is a good idea," objected Susan. "We ought to stick together now that we've got this far. Why can't you stay with us and try to get what you need in Burton if they are really essential?"

"First," he counted off the points on his fingers, "I don't want the boat to stop in a town for any longer than is absolutely necessary. Second, I want to make use of the truck while we have still got it, rather than searching around for more transport. Third, I don't want to hold you up; otherwise we probably won't make what looks like the safest spot to spend the night. It's a good distance ahead and you will have to go as fast as you can to make it before nightfall. And fourth … Well, fourth is still secret," he concluded lamely.

"But what else do we want? We've got all we need right here on the boat."

She was determined not to let him go without a fight.

"Well, not quite," was all he would say. "I promise to be very, very careful and not to take any risks."

He could see that they thought the excursion itself was an unnecessary risk and that they were by no means convinced about the necessity for it, but he refused to allow them to penetrate his thinking behind it.

Susan made one last try.

"At least let me go with you."

"No, you are needed here in these early stages, to help get the boat through, and I really do want to do this alone."

The disappointment, which showed on her face at this remark, made him add, "It's not that I don't enjoy your company, but this is something that I would like to do alone. Trust me. Please?"

Nothing they could say could deter him, and Susan looked on in frustration as he went back and started the boat's engine. After leaping onto the towpath, he untied the mooring ropes and threw them aboard.

"Now get moving," he called, making his way towards the truck. "The faster you go, the sooner I shall meet up with you again."

Susan saw that there was nothing for it but to do as he said, and so, taking a firm grasp on the tiller, she revved the engine and began to move the craft smoothly out into the centre of the canal, as Ken drove off in the opposite direction.

"Please be careful," she thought at him.

"Don't worry, I'll be back before you know it!" came the fading thought as the truck disappeared from sight.

Once they were well under way, Donald called up to her.

"Are you quite happy up there, or do you want me to come and take the tiller for a while?"

"I'll do it."

Susan tried to hide her disappointment by her terse answer, but her mind was broadcasting loud and clear what she felt at leaving Ken behind.

***

Jamie took responsibility for working the locks, taking charge of the windlass, jumping off well in advance and running ahead so that the gates were ready and waiting by the time the boat arrived. Susan thought that they could probably work the mechanisms by mind control without even getting off the boat, but the work made Jamie feel useful, and he probably needed the exercise, so she held her peace.

To begin with, their route took them westwards along the Trent and Mersey, as Ken had indicated, and Susan knew that she had to look for a junction to take them south, but she had no idea how long it would take them. She felt totally inadequate for the journey ahead, and wished with all her heart that he had not

161

dashed off in such an irresponsible manner, leaving her with the responsibility of coping alone. It was true that she had Donald and Jamie for company, but if the worst should happen, Donald was handicapped by his leg, and Jamie was still only a child…! She shook her head, half in frustration and half to rid herself of thoughts of what might happen, and attempted to concentrate solely on familiarising herself with the boat's controls.

Pushing Rachel II on as fast as possible, they were approaching Burton after about half an hour. Just before entering the town, the canal crossed the River Dove on an aqueduct, which made Susan feel particularly vulnerable perched up on the rear deck. Looking around, she could see no signs of life anywhere. The only movement in the whole dismal landscape was that of their own boat, and the irrational loneliness at having left Ken behind returned with piercing intensity.

Concentrating on the way ahead, she noticed something which she had previously missed. A thin wisp of smoke was rising from amongst the buildings, and this served to increase her apprehension at entering the town to a point where her nerves were stretched to the maximum. The fact that most of the built up area lay to the left of the canal did little to relieve her anxiety, and she found herself gripping the tiller with such ferocity that her knuckles stood out whitely against the back of her hands.

As they approached the town, the canal was paralleled on the right by an elevated section of the – in former times – busy A38 trunk road. To the left of them the black, empty windows of grey apartment buildings stared down like dead eyes across the strip of intervening wasteland.

Immediately beyond the first of the bridges in Burton, the waterway opened out on the right into a wide basin where boats were moored. A bright mural depicting aspects of canal life adorned the concrete wall which supported the road high up above the back of the basin. Within the water of the canal basin lay death. A southbound juggernaut had penetrated the roadside barriers, and crashed down upon the craft moored below, reducing them to matchwood. The wreckage now lay on its side in the water, almost blocking the waterway. Only a narrow gap near the left-hand bank remained open. Susan was not at all sure that it was wide enough to allow them through. She thought that perhaps Ken had been a little over-optimistic about the state of the waterways…!

Throttling back the engine she slowed the boat's speed to a crawl, and pointed the bows at the centre of the gap. The surface of the water was totally covered with the debris from the splintered boats; plywood and irregular white slabs of polystyrene being shouldered aside as the narrowboat approached the constriction. It was a near thing. At one point the sides of the craft actually scraped both the stones of the canal wall and the metal of the lorry cab, but she applied full power, churning up the water under the stern of the boat, and just squeezed through into the wider waters beyond the wreckage, trailing a retinue of flotsam behind her.

If the gap had been any smaller there would have been no way through, but now the canal stretched out before them once more, beckoning them on, and Susan maintained speed, forging ahead away from the wreckage. The lock Ken had mentioned lay up ahead, hidden from sight somewhere around the next bend. Squat factory buildings sat beyond the towpath hedge, blocking off the view of the town.

Such was her tension that a sudden movement at the front of the boat startled Susan, and her left hand flew to her mouth to prevent a cry escaping her lips. The source of the movement turned out to be Jamie, preparing to jump off to run ahead and open the lock as usual. She steered towards the left hand bank, throttling back so as to cut down on the noise made by the engine, at the same time flashing a thought in Jamie's direction as he nimbly leapt onto the towpath.

"Be careful. I saw some smoke as we came in. It could be from someone's campfire. Make as little noise as…." The thought was cut off as she saw Jamie freeze in his tracks, his fear stabbing back into her head. She pulled the boat over to where the boy was standing, and as she did so she too was able to see around the bend to the lock. A short distance ahead, looming blackly over the water, lay the square slab of an iron-sided bridge, carrying a road out of the town over the canal. The lock seemed to lie directly under this bridge, occupying only a small portion of the span on the right, but it was the bridge itself which caused her to bite at her bottom lip. This time both hands went up to her mouth. Hanging down from the underside of the bridge a number of bodies swung and twisted in a gruesome dance. Whoever had been the victor in this particular area had hung up his victims like trophies.

"It's like they did to the vicar," came a small, frightened thought from Jamie, and Susan caught a flash of the inside of a darkened church as seen by the boy back in his home village.

"It's all right, Jamie," she thought at him, trying to exude a confidence that she did not feel, "They can't hurt you."

She felt his courage returning at the contact with her.

"Do you want to come back on board and we'll open the lock when we get there?"

"Noo…" came his hesitant reply, "I think I can still do it."

"Well, just remember to be extra careful at this one."

Her thought followed him as he resumed his forward progress.

Jamie needed no second warning, and she could see him creeping about up ahead with over-exaggerated caution as he carefully avoided the bodies and began to work the paddles. She gently coaxed the boat forward again, but even with the speed kept to a minimum the noise of the boat's passage sounded deafening in her ears echoing back from the lock walls.

Donald had appeared alerted by their thoughts, and had been standing at the front of the boat to see for himself what lay ahead, adding moral support by his presence, his leg ruling him out of any practical action.

"Don't worry," he thought back to her, "they seem to have been there for some time. It's not likely that there is anyone left around by now."

His attempt to reassure her was a total failure, the incident at the hospital still being all too vivid in her memory.

As they drew nearer it became more apparent that some of the bodies had indeed been there for a considerable time; others apparently had been added later. They had been hung from the metal rods which tied together the girders directly underneath the main span, some by the neck, some by meat hooks embedded in solid flesh or ropes tied around the torso, others by an arm or a leg. Pools of congealed blood lay beneath those with obvious gaping wounds, while others displayed no obvious signs of the cause of death. The first of them, which hung over the centre of the canal directly in front of the lock gate was that of a woman, suspended by the ankles, arms hanging downwards, long blond hair streaming in the breeze. Her throat had been cut.

Jamie had moved on and was waiting by the second gates, which stood some thirty or forty feet beyond the bridge, in the open. As Susan eased the boat forward, she was unable to avoid the gruesome carcasses and they scraped and bumped horribly along the top and sides of the boat as it slipped into the gloomy lock. The powerful stench of death beneath the bridge caused them all to hold their breath and clasp their hands over their mouths and noses. Susan crouched down as low as possible, but even so, the one which had been directly ahead, having scraped along the top, cleared the rear of the tumblehome and swung in, directly towards her. For a brief moment she found herself face to face with the bloody, eyeless, inverted face of the woman. The empty eye sockets gazed into her own, and just for a second, Susan, transfixed by the horror of it, thought it was going to touch her, but suddenly it was gone, swinging wildly behind the boat as it moved deeper into the lock.

She pulled up as near to the forward set of gates as possible, but even so, the rear, where she stood was still under the bridge amongst the dead. A sudden clatter from behind caused her to whirl around, and but for her fierce grip on the tiller arm, she might have overbalanced and fallen into the icy water. Donald grabbed her arm as she looked wildly for the source of the noise.

"Sorry," he whispered, "I should have warned you. I was only tying to speed things up a little."

He had used his powers to manipulate the rear gates closed, and the paddles slipping back into place was what had caused the clatter.

As the lock was not a deep one it did not take very long for the water levels to equalise, but to Susan it seemed an eternity. She half expected a murder-crazed face to appear from over the parapet of the bridge or from behind one of the supports. As she stood looking around, she could see that there were many more bodies, hanging from every concievable place. To the left lay the old lock keeper's cottage, carcasses hung from the window and the gutter supports just below the roof. The trees on the right hand bank also held their fair share. Someone had spent a lot of time, and gone to a great deal of trouble to try to satisfy some unimaginable, insane compulsion. It was like the web of some gigantic spider, with the bodies of the victims stored until they were required. Susan shuddered at the thought and it was with considerable relief that she saw the gates before her swing open, and she was able to guide the boat out of the confines of the lock and into the open waters of the canal beyond.

Small patios with wrought iron seats and white painted chimney-pot planters marked where the back gardens of the houses met the canal on the right, while another factory, storage yards piled high with wooden pallets, kept them company on the left. The occasional body adorned both banks, strung up from any convenient gibbet. A footbridge crossed the canal ahead of them, leading to a sports ground beyond the gardens. The last of the bodies hung here, one from the bridge itself, and the rest from the trees and goalposts of the sports ground. In all they reckoned that they had seen well over a hundred and fifty victims in just this one small area.

Beyond the footbridge the bodies ceased, and Susan, realising that she had been holding every muscle in her body taught, almost collapsed as the tension drained out of her. With this release came an uncontrollable trembling, and Donald, noticing her distress, had to grab the tiller, calling to Jamie to come and help, until she was able to regain control.

"I don't think there can be anything worse than that," she gasped when she was able to speak again.

"Wholesale slaughter is one thing, but to glory in it, and display the victims to advertise the victor's prowess just shows how sick the mind became at the end. It seems that people were capable of some very terrible things," Donald responded. Then, as if to clear the subject from their minds, "Would it help if I took over from you for a while?"

This time Susan was more than willing to relinquish the tiller, and Jamie helped her down the steps as she went below to recover her composure.

It was some time later, just after passing Wychnor Church on the approach to Alrewas, that Donald thought he heard the sound of the truck approaching, and slowed the boat, cutting the engine in order that he might hear better. Jamie, who had been sitting at the front, suddenly jumped up and pointed ahead.

"Another boat!" he called out.

Donald looked towards where he was pointing, and saw a small cabin cruiser up ahead. She was bobbing and rocking curiously, but otherwise seemed to be stationary, with no apparent forward motion. He flashed a thought towards it, asking if there was anyone aboard. There was no response.

"I just wondered if there were more of our own kind around," he thought to the others by way of explanation, "I can't imagine that any of the 'others' would have bothered to take to a boat."

"They don't seem to be the least bit predictable or at all rational," Susan responded. "Perhaps one of them uses it to live on. Someone must be aboard otherwise why is the engine running? We shall just have to go ahead and be ready to push it away should anything happen."

Donald restarted their own engine and moved warily ahead, keeping to the right hand bank, as far away from the other boat as possible. Jamie and Susan stood in the bows, each holding a long pole from the top of the cabin, ready to fend it off should the need arise. As they drew closer the problem became more apparent. The source of the noise was not an engine as Donald had first thought, but the sound of rushing water as it tumbled over a weir. The waters of the canal joined forces with those of the River Trent, sharing a mutual course for a short distance. The two bodies of water parted company at this point, the Trent, swollen by the recent rains, bidding a noisy farewell to the more placid canal, roaring and tumbling over the edge, onto a lower level. The small craft was now trapped by these waters, held tightly against the top of the weir, rocking precariously. Whether it had broken loose and drifted, drawn by the current to this place, or whether some hand had guided it this way to be taken unawares by the rush of water there was no way of knowing, but the passing of Rachel II proved to be the last straw.

Despite her low speed, the wash angling out from her bows raised the small craft those extra few inches needed. Slowly she lifted and edged further over, and then, as the wash and surging river water continued to lift her near side, she began to topple, slowly at first but with ever gathering momentum until with a final roll, she turned completely over and disappeared with a splintering crash down the far side of the weir, the turbulent waters continuing to roll her over and over as she was washed further and further downstream.

"Shouldn't we go back?" Jamie asked, when Donald, rather than stopping, urged the boat on, fighting against the flow of the river.

"There's no point. If anyone is still alive in there they can't be one of us or they would have responded to my thought, and if they are not of our kind we would only be endangering ourselves," Donald answered.

Susan agreed with him. What had happened had been unavoidable. They had passed as slowly as they could, but even the gentle wash from their passage had proved too much. There was nothing to be done now but press on. There was no sense in imperilling the lives of them all by taking risks that could be avoided.

Passing the point at which the Trent flowed into the canal, under the white-railed towpath walkway, beyond which they could see dark birds circling the tower of Alrewas church, the craft surged forward again towards Alrewas lock, and the picturesque thatched cottages of the village beyond.

The journey to Fradley continued well, and the sight of many crashes on the road which had paralleled their course for much of the way, immediately on their left, confirmed the soundness of their decision to take to the waterways despite their recent experiences.

Their approach to Fradley Junction was a gloomy one, being dominated by the castle-like appearance of the bridges with the lock gates immediately behind them, and the scene of carnage which greeted them at the junction itself did little to lighten their spirits. The once thriving Swan Inn, which faced the narrow entrance to the Coventry Canal, stood as yet another reminder of the change that had come upon their world. Ragged curtains flapped from smashed windows and the sturdy wooden tables, which had once fronted the inn, lay overturned or upended by the canal side. In the recessed arches to the left of the main entrance lay ragged bundles of clothing concealing the remains of what had once been happy, living human beings. Susan could imagine chattering children dining with their parents at those now scattered tables, and now...! She quickly put the thought from her mind.

Directly ahead of them the Trent and Mersey canal was completely blocked by a jumble of burnt-out narrowboats that had been moored up for the winter, some of the rusting hulks having settled deeply into the water. Two boats which had escaped the fire had slipped, or been released from, their moorings and had drifted out to sit squarely across the junction, totally blocking their access into the canal to their left. It was with considerable difficulty that these were pushed out of the way before they could make the turn, slowing down what had been, up to this point, an excellent rate of progress.

Susan, who secretly welcomed the delay, was bitterly disappointed that there was no sign of Ken by the time they had finished, but duly left the marking cone below the canal side fence directly opposite the junction before turning into the surprisingly narrow entrance, and pushing aside the small swing bridge which marked the beginning of the Coventry Canal.

Some time later she was disappointed again as they had to leave another marker on the towpath at Huddlesford Junction, and thirty-five minutes after that they were tying up below the hillside of Hopwas Hays wood. There was still no sign of the truck or its errant driver.

As soon as the boat was secure, all three of them gathered at the rear, Jamie standing on the top of the boat, looking up and down the towpath for any sign of Ken.

"Are you sure this is the place?" Susan asked impatiently.

"The precise spot," replied Donald, firmly.

"Maybe he's waiting a bit further on. Shall I go and see?"

Jamie suggested.

"You can if you want to, but I don't think it will do any good. This is where he said he would be." Donald was convinced he had it right.

"I'll come with you." Susan was obviously anxious to be doing anything rather than just wait.

"It will be getting dark soon, so don't go out of sight," advised Donald. "I don't want to lose you two as well."

It was already gloomy in the shadow of Hopwas Hill, a condition which closely matched the mood of all three of them, as Jamie and Susan set off along the towpath ahead of the boat. In front of them they could see a bridge. Perhaps Ken would be waiting on the stretch beyond it.

Passing under its arch they saw that the towpath beyond was as deserted as that which they had just left. Again Susan experienced bitter disappointment.

A short distance ahead, the canal swung sharply right, passing under yet another bridge and their view was impeded. Susan was in a dilemma. She badly wanted to go and look at the next stretch, but she knew that she ought to stay within sight of the boat. She came to a decision.

"Jamie, you stay here and keep the boat in sight, and I'll just go on and look under the next bridge."

"And what will you do if he's not there?"

"I suppose that we'll just have to go back and wait. Oh, why did he have to go off like that!" she burst out, clenching her fists and venting her worry in an angry outburst which brought her to the verge of tears.

"Now don't go getting all steamed up, I'll be with you in a little while." The thought stopped Susan dead in her tracks and she looked around wildly.

"Ken," she called, "Oh Ken, where on earth have you been?"

"I'll explain all that later. Now, where are you moored?"

"Exactly where you said." Donald had now picked up Ken's thoughts.

"Right. Now things are pretty bad on the roads around here, and the bridge in Hopwas is down. I'm going to have to make a bit of a detour. You say you are moored in the place we agreed?"

"As near as I can tell."

"OK, I'll meet you at the bridge which is in front of the boat as soon as I can. See you soon, I hope." His thoughts faded as he headed away from them.

Without a word, Susan and Jamie returned jubilantly back to the bridge to await Ken's arrival and before very long they heard the sound of the truck's engine drawing ever nearer. As it approached they could hear that it sounded terrible, grinding and crunching its way down the track, and they could see steam coming from beneath the bonnet. The bodywork was crumpled and gouged all down the side nearest to them, but as they watched, Ken's arm appeared through the driver's window to give them a cheery wave.

The battered truck drew to a creaking halt on the track by the bridge and, as Ken jumped down from the cab, the other two ran down to him, all three clinging together in a communal hug as they met.

"Where on earth have you been?" Susan gasped as soon as she could speak. "We've all been frantic with worry."

"Sorry, but things were worse out there than I had anticipated, and as you can see, there were a few problems with the truck, but I'll tell you about that when we've got everything sorted out. Come on, hop in and we'll try to get this wreck a little closer to the boat so that we can unload before it gets too dark."

It was indeed now becoming quite dark and Ken would have been very cautious about using lights, if there had been any lights left on the truck to use. Tamworth was only a couple of miles away across the river, and any light would have been visible for miles in that direction.

Donald was waiting for them on the cratch, as Ken, Jamie and Susan carried a number of mysterious-looking cardboard boxes, which Ken had brought back with him, from the truck to the boat. These were stowed in the saloon where Ken gave strict orders that they were not to be touched for the time being. He then went back to the truck and returned carrying a pair of short crutches, which he handed triumphantly to Donald.

"Try these for size," he said. "They should help you to get

around a bit better."

Donald accepted them gratefully, and as he stood trying them out, with Jamie helping to make the adjustments, Susan appeared from the direction of the galley, carrying an enormous mug of coffee, which she handed to Ken.

"You don't deserve this after what you have put us through, but I expect you need it. Now, explain yourself."

Ken felt like a schoolboy standing before a strict headmistress, but he could feel in their minds the distress he had caused them. It had seemed like a good idea at the time, and he was so used to only having himself to think about. It made him realise anew that they each had a responsibility towards the others. From now on he could not afford the luxury of being a loner.

"I just wanted to make this a real Christmas," he explained, limply, "and I felt particularly bad at not having any crutches for Donald. I just went back into Derby to get him some. I thought this shorter type would be best on a boat. More manageable. Once I had found those I was able to pick up a few things for our Christmas dinner."

He directed Susan and Jamie towards the other boxes he had brought with him, but kept one of them back for himself, explaining that, just for the moment its contents were secret. There were cries of delight as they unpacked a Christmas pudding, mince pies, crackers, an assortment of chocolates and nuts, and even a small turkey!

"I found that in a butcher's cold store," he explained. "The power supply must have lasted longer in Derby, and things were only just beginning to thaw out, but I'm afraid it will only be tinned meat after this, unless anyone fancies hunting. The world out there is rapidly falling apart, and many things are going to be harder to come by from now on."

"Unfortunately, the situation on the roads is far worse around here than I expected, and it took me much longer than I had anticipated to find a way through to get back to you. There's an army camp on the other side of this hill, and the soldiers who were based there seem to have used all the weapons they could lay their hands on when the madness struck. The village up ahead is just rubble and the canal bridge seems to have been dynamited. I don't know how much of it is in the water, but we shall have to take a look at it in daylight to see if we can still get through that way."

As he spoke, he had been cutting up the cardboard of the boxes into shapes to put over the saloon windows, so that no lights could be seen from the outside. Once the windows were covered he pressed the switch, and they all blinked as light dispelled the near darkness within the cabin.

"Tamworth is rather too close," he explained, "and I don't want to attract any unwelcome visitors."

As a further precaution he took Jamie back outside and they moored by driving pegs into both banks of the canal, passing the mooring ropes through the eyes in them and securing the loose ends back on the boat. Thus they were able to manoeuvre the craft directly in the centre of the waterway, making access for any would-be intruders that much more difficult. Looking towards Tamworth they could see only blackness. There was no indication that there was any life where the town lay.

By the time he had firmly secured all the hatches and made his way down to the cabin, the fire had been stoked up and a plate of warm mince pies sat on the tiled area upon which the stove stood. Their aroma, mixed with the fragrance of hot coffee filled the small compartment. There was no sign of the goods Ken had brought, all having been stowed neatly away, and the cardboard boxes folded out flat and cut to size for blanking out the rest of the windows. Susan and Donald had clearly been busy while Ken and Jamie had been mooring and securing the boat. The one box which Ken had reserved for himself still stood, untouched on the floor. He picked it up and took it to his cabin. On his return he was greeted by Jamie.

"These are great," was the boy's opinion as he munched his way through a mince pie. "A pity we've got no cream."

Ken had to admit that cream and bread were about the only two items on his list that he had been unable to procure.

Once he was comfortably settled, Susan turned to him.

"Did you see anyone else on your travels?" she asked.

"Not really. I left the truck some distance from the hospital and walked in so that I could approach it quietly. That way I was able to get in and out without being seen. I did see one man in the distance, but was able to keep out of sight until he disappeared. As I said before, road conditions were a lot worse than I had expected, and I spent a lot of time trying to get round obstructions. I eventually took to using the truck as a battering ram to get through some of them or I would never have got here before dark. That's why it's in such a state. I don't think it would have got me much further. The final straw was having to find a way to get around the bridge up ahead."

If he had had any close encounters, Ken was keeping them to himself.

Seeing that he had finished, Susan quickly recounted her own experiences of the day, bringing a flush of guilt to Ken's cheeks that he had left them to cope alone with such a gruesome situation, and his admiration for his new friends grew when he heard how they had come through. Both of them were now more than happy that they were reunited and that the day's events were behind them, and Ken made a secret resolution that, as far as it lay within him to ensure it, from now on they would all stick together.

After the difficulties of the past few days, the home comforts of the narrowboat seemed very close to heaven. The sense of relief at being surrounded by the trappings of civilisation in their own self-contained little world was indescribable. The hot running water in the shower, hand basin and galley were especially luxurious to them all, and the generator, operated by the powerful little engine, provided them with the electric lighting, the power being stored in a bank of heavy duty batteries secreted away in the depths of the boat.

During the evening, over the best meal any of them had eaten for quite some time, they sorted out their sleeping arrangements and their course of action for the future. Donald was to have the bed in the saloon, Susan the proper bedroom, and Jamie would occupy the boatman's cabin with Ken for company.

The route they had planned kept clear, as far as possible, of any large towns. Where towns had to be negotiated it was decided that, whenever they could, they would spend the night outside them, and then move through at dawn, hoping to pass before anyone still living there was awake enough to be aware of their presence. They assumed that even madmen still needed sleep. As for tomorrow, Christmas Day, they decided that it was still a national holiday, and that they all wanted to make the most of it, trying to make-believe that there was a normal world still out there.

"I think we all need some time to recover from the events of today," Donald had said, and Ken, whose bruised body had begun to stiffen up again as the evening wore on, agreed wholeheartedly.

They spent what remained of the evening, warm, dry and comfortable, each of them using the hot water to indulge in the luxury of a hot bath or shower.

"This is absolute decadence," Susan confessed as she sipped at her sherry and snuggled deeper into the warm white towelling bathrobe she had discovered. "I had almost forgotten what it feels like to be properly clean."

Her wounded arm seemed not to trouble her any longer, and Ken wondered about it. He did not realise that he had broadcast the thought until Susan answered, quite naturally,

"I seem to have learned to block out the pain. It must be one of our new abilities."

She demonstrated by waving her arm around before taking another sip from her glass.

"If it is, then I haven't mastered it yet," replied Ken, wincing as he tried to ease his aching body into a more comfortable position.

Donald was, at that moment, attempting to shower himself and keep his plaster cast dry, while Jamie was exploring his own sleeping quarters back in the boatman's cabin. Susan and Ken were alone in the quietness of the saloon.

Ken thought how fortunate he had been to find this gentle-eyed girl again when the rest of the world had been collapsing around his ears, and he looked across at her, sitting with her legs tucked under her, gazing into the depths of the fire, lost in thought. He was full of admiration for the way she had coped with all that life had thrown at her since that evening when they first met, and now he could feel that admiration turning to something deeper as he watched her sitting there looking very feminine and vulnerable.

He was just about to try to put his feelings into words when he heard the sound of running footsteps clattering along the corridor, and the next moment Jamie hurled himself into the room, shattering the calm with excited boyish chatter.

"This boat is great!" he enthused, "I've even found a secret drawer in our cabin. Come and see!"

Ken found himself grabbed by the hand and pulled towards the rear of the boat. The moment had gone now, and so he allowed himself to be led down the corridor, past the bathroom where Donald was towelling himself vigorously and singing a negro spiritual in a pleasant soft baritone, and on to their cabin.

"Look. It's here. See, this table pulls out from here," he demonstrated, "and the drawer comes out underneath it."

It was not really a secret drawer, but Ken, remembering how children liked to dramatise, said nothing.

"That's called the crumb drawer."

Susan had followed them softly down the corridor and was standing in the doorway.

"It's traditional on one of these boats to have one of those," she said. "Now that's enough exploring tonight. Donald is out of the bathroom, so now it's your turn, young man."

She smiled as Jamie pulled a wry face.

"It's been a long day, and I want to sit and talk with Donald and Ken for a little while before it gets too late," she said

She turned and led the way back up the corridor, followed closely by Ken. Jamie, after tucking away the table and drawer, also followed them back into the saloon, and was shooed out again by Susan.

"Go and get clean, so I can tell what you really look like under that grime," she scolded, "and don't be all night about it. Ken still needs to shower before he goes to bed."

Reluctantly the boy plodded back to the bathroom and disappeared from view.

"Now," she continued, closing the door and turning back to the room, "let's get a fresh drink each and decide where we go from here."

Both Donald and Ken elected to have a glass of the Scotch, which they had found on board, while Susan stayed with sherry.

"I think we should remain here and relax, at least until after we have had our Christmas dinner," Ken offered, once the glasses had been filled and passed around. "I, for one, need a rest and a time to myself before we go back into the world. Many things will have changed for us, and we need just a little while to think things through and readjust. It is somewhat different for you Donald, but much of what is happening to us is very strange and new, and I need time to adjust to it all."

Donald nodded.

"I can sympathise with you there. Don't forget that I've also been through some of what you have experienced. I remember when my brain first triggered, I thought I was going mad. Luckily, I had the sense not to speak about it to anyone at the time, and so I survived. It was two years before someone like myself contacted me. That two years was hell on earth, so I do understand your feelings.

"I've tried to help you through this first stage by explaining much of what I know, but I realise that you have had to come to terms with the drastic changes in the world, as well as the enormous changes within yourselves, and all in a very short time. You have had to cope with everything, from the horrific to the unexplainable, and I am sure that there is much that we still don't know, and probably new horrors still to face. I, personally, am eager to press on as soon as possible. The sooner we make contact the sooner we shall be safely out of all this, but I recognise that you need time to prepare for what lies ahead. Tomorrow, Christmas Day, has always been a rather special day, so I see no reason why we shouldn't take some time off, but we mustn't delay for too long. There are still many miles ahead of us. Now, let's enjoy what's left of Christmas Eve, just spending time quietly together if that's what you want, and we'll move on from here when it seems right to do so."

As the evening wore on they became more and more deeply engrossed in their own private recollections. They had all learned the trick of thought shielding fairly quickly, otherwise their situation would have been impossible to tolerate, but from time to time a wave of emotion would sweep through the warm cabin engulfing them as each remembered happy occasions, or experienced a particularly poignant memory, or a possibility which aroused fear or anxiety. At some point Jamie had returned freshly scrubbed, damp hair clinging closely to his scalp. Immediately sensing the mood of his three companions, he remained silent and was soon deeply wrapped in his own private thoughts.

Eventually it was Susan who came to with a sudden start.

"Come on now. We're keeping Donald up, and you, Ken, are still a member of the great unwashed. It's time we made a move."

It was, Ken saw as he looked at his watch getting quite late, and as Susan had said, there were still things to do.

"Right!" he said, draining the last of his glass and getting wearily to his feet, his battle-scarred body protesting against any sort of movement, "I'll sort out Donald's bed here, while you two go to yours."

Susan and Jamie needed no second bidding and disappeared as Ken began to make ready Donald's bed. Before wishing Donald a good night's rest, and leaving the saloon, he checked to make sure the fire was safe, although he did not make it up, being uncertain how long their stock of fuel would last.

After a very welcome and thoroughly enjoyable shower he emerged from the bathroom and called a soft "Good night" to Susan, but there was no answer from her curtained off room. The day had been long and eventful enough to tire her out and she had fallen asleep the moment she had got into bed.

Returning to his own cabin he found that the bed had been pulled down for him, and his sleeping bag, with the top folded neatly back, placed upon it. When he climbed in he found a hot water bottle had been pushed down inside it to take the chill off. Susan and Jamie may have been very tired, but they had taken the trouble to see that he had a cosy bed before they, themselves, turned in. So it was that Ken, his heart full of gratitude for these his fellow survivors, gave up his weary body to the healing hand of sleep.

Chapter 12

"...a time of war, and a time of peace"

Ecclesiastes 3:2

Christmas Day dawned crisp and clear, and although Ken was awake bright and early, it was apparent the moment he opened his cabin door, that Susan had beaten him to it by quite some time. The aroma of cooking bacon wafted down the corridor towards him, causing his mouth to water. By the time he reached the galley the turkey was ready for the oven and all the vegetables prepared for their Christmas dinner.

"Merry Christmas!" she called as he stumbled down the corridor towards the galley. Old habits die hard.

He rubbed the sleep from his eyes and stood at the entrance gazing in at her. She appeared blissfully unaware of his tousled appearance, giving him a beaming smile.

"Merry Christmas," he mumbled, tongue-tied at the sight of her. She had obviously brought along some of her favourite clothes, and there she stood, looking exactly as she had on the night he had first seen her.

"You've just time to wash and dress before breakfast is ready." she advised, "Provided you're quick, that is."

He shambled back to the bathroom, where he deliberately washed in cold water in an attempt to shock his system into action. Since leaving Kelden he had been unable to shave regularly, and his stubble was now a few days old. Shaving therefore brought a great feeling of normality back into his life, and he felt greatly restored and invigorated as he re-emerged into the corridor. The familiar smell of coffee and bacon met him and reinforced that feeling of normality, as did the sound of Susan's singing from the galley.

179

She interrupted the chorus of the carol she was singing to pop her head into the corridor and call, "Breakfast!"

The door to the rear cabin immediately crashed open and Jamie tumbled out, anxious not to miss out. At the other end of the boat, the saloon door also opened, in a somewhat less boisterous manner, to reveal Donald, already dressed.

"I've put the table up in the saloon," he called, "so that we can all sit down together."

Susan immediately scooped up all four plates, carried them expertly into the front cabin and laid them on the table, returning to the galley to pick up the coffee.

"I won't be a moment," called Ken disappearing into his own sleeping quarters.

By the time he returned his three companions were seated and waiting for him.

"Come on, we're starving," Jamie urged, as he re-entered the saloon.

Susan indicated the place next to her by patting it and he sat down, very conscious of her clean, feminine scent.

The cardboard had been removed from the windows, and the low sun was streaming into the saloon, casting a golden glow over the morning. Breakfast in sunlight made a most refreshing change from the conditions they had all endured over the last week, and they made the most of it, enjoying a slow, leisurely meal.

When they had eaten their fill, Ken replenished the coffee cups and then came back into the cabin with the armful of parcels he had so carefully wrapped and hidden in secret the previous day.

"A Happy Christmas to you all," he said quietly as they gazed at him in amazement. "I thought I ought to take this opportunity of showing how much you have all come to mean to me."

He handed the first parcel to Jamie.

"This is for giving me a reason to go on in those first few days."

The boy took the parcel eagerly, excited anticipation written all over his face.

180

It was Donald's turn next.

"For calling me back to you and for taking care of Jamie."

He passed a parcel to him.

"And for being there when we arrived." He smiled at Susan as he handed over her present.

All three protested the unfairness of such gifts as they were unable to return the gesture, but were somewhat mollified when Ken produced a final parcel for himself.

"Don't worry, I haven't left myself out," he laughed, "and I knew exactly what I wanted."

Each set to, enthusiastically unwrapping their parcels in their own particular way. Jamie, with the impatience of youth, stripping the wrapping from his in a matter of seconds, while Susan savoured the moment by removing the paper slowly and methodically. Jamie was delighted to find that his parcel contained a pair of high-powered binoculars and a superb Swiss Army knife. For Donald there was a silver hip flask and bottle of fine old malt whisky, while Susan discovered a magnificent gold bracelet along with a large box of chocolates. For himself, Ken had duplicated Donald's presents.

"I tried to choose things which didn't rely on batteries or need servicing," he explained, "and luxuries which may not be around later. I also felt they should be small enough to carry with us should the need arise."

"I think they are beautiful presents," whispered Susan, holding out her arm so that she could admire the bracelet she had put on, from a distance. "Thank you, Ken, for a lovely thought." Her voice was husky and there was a hint of tears in it.

"And so say all of us," cheered the other two, diverting attention away from Susan's embarrassment.

"Right," said Donald briskly, "it's about time I tried to help out a little. If you will just clear the table and bring the dishes to the galley, I'll wash up."

He would not allow any argument and hobbling to his feet, he used his newly acquired crutches to make his way to the galley. By the time the others arrived, bearing the breakfast dishes, he had propped himself on a high stool he had discovered, and was filling the sink with water. Much against everyone's wishes, Susan insisted on wiping and shooed Ken and Jamie out of the galley. Jamie immediately went outside to try his binoculars, while Ken explored some of the areas of the boat he had not already looked into.

One of his main worries was in the problem of waste disposal. The toilet, he knew, would last for a little while, but would eventually need emptying. Susan had told him that there were pump-out facilities sited at centres along the canal, but he did not think there would be any power available to run them. He was therefore relieved to find, on examination of the bathroom, that this excellent little craft had its own pumping facilities. The problem, which had occupied a considerable space in his mind during his lone expedition of the previous day, simply did not exist, and he was able to cross it off as one less thing to concern him.

Continuing on towards the rear of the boat, he noticed hinges on the steps leading up to the counter and on examination discovered that they lifted to reveal the space underneath the rear deck, below which lay the waters of the canal. The bright sunlight threw flashes of brilliance back from the gently-moving surface, lighting up this hidden recess, and causing Ken to shield his eyes from the shimmering glare. The reflection also illuminated the water below the boat, unusually clear now that the sediments had had time to settle. Just below the surface he could just make out the dim outline of the propeller.

He was slightly puzzled at the presence of a large bread knife lying on a ledge close at hand. He could not imagine why such a knife could be here so far from the galley.

A call from Donald soon put that particular puzzle out of his mind. Carefully swinging the steps back into place he went up into the galley to see what was wanted.

He found that the washing up was completed, and Donald was anxious to try out his new-found freedom which the crutches had brought to him. Susan was busying herself in the saloon, while Jamie was still occupied with his binoculars up on deck.

"What do you say we take a stroll along the towpath and have a look at that bridge you say is down?"

It sounded like a good idea to Ken and he said so.

"OK. But we ought to let the others know."

Jamie was eager to accompany them, but Susan restrained him, saying that she had other things for him to do.

"And I don't want you two wandering off too far, either," she said, making them promise that the damaged bridge would be the far limit of their excursion.

She was not completely happy about their going, but she knew that Donald was in dire need of exercise and fresh air, and was longing to test his new-found mobility. Besides this, she had a small venture of her own in mind.

Ken released the two rear ropes and hauled the stern of the boat over to the towpath, leaving the bow fastened in mid-canal. This allowed them easy access but would enable them to regain the relative security of a central mooring more quickly should the need arise.

As they walked slowly along the towpath towards the bridge, Donald breathed deeply, filling his lungs with the crisp winter air. The sun was still shining although a threatening bank of cloud had appeared on the horizon and was attempting to overtake it.

The silence was intense. For all they could tell, they might by now, be the only human beings left alive in the whole of England.

Eventually, Donald broke the silence.

"How bad was it at the bridge?"

"I only saw it from the road, but it seemed to have been blown up from below. If that proves to be the case, I expect most of the debris will have been blown clear, although I suppose some must have fallen back into the water."

Donald nodded.

"Won't be long before we're there now, then we shall have a better idea."

He resumed his previous silence, conserving his breath for walking.

The area around the remains of the bridge was littered with stones and earth thrown around by the explosion. It appeared that the charge had been laid under the arch, as Ken had surmised, and whilst this section had been blown upwards and scattered, some of the side walls had slumped and slid down towards the water. On their left, the towpath had held much of it back, but to the right the rubble sloped down into the water, reducing the width of the already narrow waterway by at least a half.

"There's no way the boat will get past that lot," was Ken's opinion of the situation.

He bent down and grasped a large coping stone which was sticking up out of the water by the towpath, grunting as he tried to pull it clear. The stone lifted slightly but then rolled over and disappeared below the surface. Ken released his grasp, just in time to avoid following it in.

"Absolutely hopeless!" he commented, as he stood up and watched the ripples spreading out from the point where the stone had disappeared to wash against the bank of rubble on the opposite side.

"It is, that way," said Donald, "but you keep forgetting about the power of your mind."

"Surely I can't handle something that large just by thought?"

"You managed to move your car when you saw the light didn't you? And anyway, who said you had to do it by yourself? This leg may stop me doing some things, but I can still think. Now, let's start with that stone you just lost. We know where it is, so reach out and let your mind feel it. Got it? Good, now think of it lifting and when it comes clear roll it onto the bank."

Ken did as he was instructed and watched in awe as the heavy stone broke the surface and, defying gravity, rolled easily up to lie on the canal side, water streaming from its craggy surfaces.

"It's easy when two combine their efforts isn't it?" He commented.

"It certainly helps," Donald replied, "but you did that on your own! I just watched."

Ken could hardly believe it, and felt around on the bottom of the canal with his mind for another stone to raise. It was a peculiar sensation, not being able to see the underwater objects, but being able to determine their size and position by sensing their presence and 'feeling' around them with his mind. He fixed on another large object and effortlessly brought it onto the bank.

"We should plan this properly," said Donald. "Not everything needs to be pulled out. Remember that the boat has a very shallow draught, and all we need to do is spread the rubble around the bottom so that we can get over it. If this canal is ever to be used again, it can be cleared properly later, when the others arrive. Now, you take this side and spread towards us and I'll spread the other way with the rubble on the far side. Only lift out the larger pieces."

Ken was astounded at how quickly and seemingly effortlessly the task was accomplished. Fifteen minutes later they were heading back along the towpath, the obstruction cleared. The headache, which had originally accompanied such mental activities, was but a slight presence behind his eyes, and had all but disappeared by the time they regained the boat.

As they walked slowly along, Donald answered Ken's unasked question.

"Yes, we could have cleared the road blockages like that, but they would have been far more involved and frequent. After three or four such actions you would find it very hard to stay awake. It may not tire you physically, but overdo it and you will really know what mental exhaustion is! As for helping you manipulate the controls of that madman's car back at the inn, everything was changing position far too quickly in relation to me. I just didn't have time to feel out where things were, and I'm not as expert at this as it may appear to you. There is much that I still can't manage."

As he helped Donald back on board, Ken called to Susan to let her know that they had returned. There was no reply. Ducking down into the saloon, he was met by a pleasant warmth and aroma of cooking turkey, but of Susan and Jamie there was no sign. He ran the length of the corridor looking into every compartment. The boat was deserted.

Leaping up onto to the rear deck he called to Donald, informing him of the situation. He then climbed up onto the roof and scanned the surrounding area for any signs of the missing pair. At first he saw nothing moving in the countryside around them, but then, just as the thought sent out from Donald calling to the other two flashed by him, his attention was caught by a movement on the towpath in the opposite direction from that taken by Donald and himself. An answering thought came from their direction, assuring them that all was well. Ken thought he could detect a certain amount of smugness behind the thought. The two small figures heading for the boat appeared to be carrying something between them.

"Panic over," he pointed, unnecessarily, in their direction as, equally unnecessarily, he called back to Donald, "they're here!"

Their new telepathic powers may have rendered speech unnecessary as a form of communication between them, but talking was a very difficult habit to break – in addition to being a great source of comfort, keeping the silence at bay in times of stress.

Impatiently he waited for them to arrive, eventually clambering down onto the towpath and running to meet them. As they drew closer he could see that the object they were carrying was a fairly heavy bucket.

"We've solved the milk problem," called Susan, when they were close enough for speech, proudly indicating the bucket.

She passed it to Ken when he reached them, grateful for his help, and he turned and walked back with them.

"How did you get on at the bridge?"

"Oh, we soon cleared that," and he opened his mind to her to show her how it had been done.

"I can see that this mind control has a lot of advantages, but some things are still best done the old way. We found a field of cows and just helped ourselves," she continued. "I used to help out on one of the local farms when I was a girl. It was all mechanised then, but occasionally I tried it by hand. I never knew how useful it would be." She was obviously very pleased with herself.

On reaching the boat, Ken placed the bucket carefully on the rear deck before helping them both back aboard. He then handed it over to Jamie to take down to the galley.

"It was dead easy, once we got the hang of it," Jamie

enthused, carefully manoeuvring the bucket down the steps, "and now we've got some cream to go with our Christmas pudding."

The state of his jeans testified to the fact that 'getting the hang of it' had not been as easy as he made it sound, but Susan let it go at that, not wishing to deflate him after he had been so enthusiastic over helping her.

"It will need skimming off when it's all settled down," she called after him as he disappeared.

"It gave us quite a start to find the boat deserted when we got back..." Ken began.

Susan cut him off.

"If you and Donald can go walking, so can Jamie and I. Besides we needed that milk. We can't just go down to the shops and buy it any more. We have to make use of what we find around us."

"I suppose there is a lot we shall have to get used to doing for ourselves," was all that Ken could reply, having had the wind taken out of his sails somewhat, and for a while they stood there silently staring into the deserted distance, each with their own thoughts.

"Our world is quite different now, isn't it?" Susan mused. "I just can't get used to the changes. Some of them I really don't want to think about yet." She paused for a while before continuing. "What bothers me most is the silence. All my life there has been the noise of other human beings around me. Even on the quietest of days the underlying rumble of traffic on the roads around was always present, a constant background to all we did. Even at night it was there, the indefinable sound of people living out their lives in ordinary, humdrum, everyday ways. But now it's gone! We still have the natural sounds of wind and water, and the animals and birds are still there, but the sounds of humanity are gone, and I miss them."

"Silence takes a lot of getting used to," Ken responded, taking her hand. "Modern man seems to have been afraid of it, going to almost any lengths to block it out of his life. I suppose that silence allowed a man to think and gave him time to reflect upon the state of the world and his own position. His thoughts naturally turned inwards, and to the closed, 'unenlightened', mind that exercise was just too painful. What he saw there, within himself, was not very pleasant."

They stood together a while longer, listening to the small natural sounds around them before Susan suddenly gave a small shudder and broke away. The chasing clouds had finally overtaken the sun and the day had taken on a gloomy aspect.

"We can't stand here all day," she said, gently disengaging her hand from his and disappearing through the hatch, "or lunch will never be ready."

Ken stood for a minute or two before turning to follow her. He had always enjoyed silence, or so he had thought, but now it was beginning to get to him too. It served to emphasise the finality of what had taken place.

Christmas dinner was a huge success, and everyone had to admit that Ken's lone expedition had been worth it – as a one-off. No one wanted to repeat the experience.

The galley was too small for them all to be able to help with the washing up, and so Ken and Donald volunteered while Susan was given a well-earned rest after her morning's work. It also gave the men a chance to talk things over together.

"So how long do you think it will take us to reach Stonehenge?" asked Ken, deftly handling the tea towel.

"I reckon that in normal times we could do it in about a fortnight," Donald gently eased himself into a more comfortable position on his high stool by the sink, "but of course we are now at liberty to exceed the waterways speed limit, and I notice that there is a good spotlight up front, so if conditions are right we can travel at night."

"Is that going to be safe?"

"That rather depends upon where we are. I suspect that any survivors will be in the towns by now, seeking out the last of their victims. So in country areas we should be fairly safe. I think we should stick to our original plan for going through built-up areas, though. We shall also need to keep an eye out for any more blockages like the one we cleared this morning."

"So how long?"

"Well, we should be able to manipulate locks so that they are ready for us when we reach them, and if some night travel is possible, we might be able to manage the canal trip in about nine or ten days, barring accidents. With luck we could reach Stonehenge in one more. Mind you, we shall all be pretty well shattered when we get there. Not that it will matter because that will be the end of our worries. Once the 'Other Worlders' arrive we can relax."

"What are they like, our other race? I mean, will they accept us? Won't they be wary of us?"

"They are very much like we are, now that our brains have fully opened up, but they have much greater control over their powers, and no, they won't be wary of us. They know that our 'enlightenment' renders us harmless to them, just as they are incapable of harming us. There is therefore no reason why they should be wary of us.

"There are, inevitably, ways in which we are different. Their spoken language, for instance, is almost unintelligible to us, having developed along different lines from our languages, but the roots of our languages and theirs are the same, and the odd word here and there has a familiar ring. We are still basically the same race, and with the change, we are now closer to them than we ever were to man here on Earth. The language barrier isn't a problem," he continued, anticipating Ken's question, "because they have taken the trouble to learn all of our languages so that they can still communicate with us, and anyway, languages are much less of a barrier when the thoughts behind the words can be discerned."

"Do these people have a name for themselves?"

"Yes, they call themselves the U-Morn, and their home planet is A-vern. Both these words have similarities in our own language. 'Human' and 'Haven' or even 'Heaven', I'm not sure which. These were obviously words which meant a great deal to our early ancestors, and they have survived in a slightly altered form."

"So. How do we set about contacting them?"

It was obvious that the time had arrived for Ken to be given more information, and for him to know just what to do – should they become separated, or worse, before they arrived at their destination, and so Donald took the opportunity.

"Unenlightened man has long suspected that some sort of power flows through the stones," he explained, "and some dowsers have claimed to be able to detect that power, both within the stones and in flows emanating from them. Some people who have touched them have felt strange sensations of movement – within their own bodies, and within the stones themselves. I tell you this because you will be acutely aware of these sensations and power flows when you touch them, for that is all you have to do. Place both hands upon any one of them and call for help, focussing your mind upon that call as hard as you possibly can. Ideally, I should be the one to do it. I have been trained in the techniques needed to make the contact easier, but if I can't manage it for any reason, then I suggest that you get Jamie and Susan to join forces with you. You can each take a different stone, or all touch the same one, it makes no difference. The call will be automatically amplified and directed in the right direction. I don't know how effective it will be as it has never been tried with untrained minds, but if it does work, help should arrive within eight hours. If someone else has already made contact, there will be no need for any of this. They will be there waiting for us."

"You said earlier that they set up and used leys for getting around."

"That's right."

"But that you haven't been taught how to do this?"

"Right again."

"Do you know why?"

"Not entirely, but I do know that when the leys are used on the few occasions when they visit us, they are only good for short hops, as it were. The person wishing to travel any distance flickers into existence at regular intervals as he proceeds along the ley. In the past this has given rise to all sorts of legends about ghosts, dragons, UFOs. and the like at various places along the leys. Gradually as the population increased there was more chance of being seen, and I suppose they did not want to give themselves away or to perpetuate superstition as far as it could be avoided. It also lessened my risk of detection, living among you, if I had to move around just like everyone else. If I couldn't use them there was no way I could give in to that particular temptation."

"But all that has changed now hasn't it? Do you think they will teach us to use them now that that particular risk has disappeared?"

Donald shrugged his shoulders.

"I'm afraid I just don't know the answer to that one. We shall just have to wait and see."

"Do they look any different from us?"

"Bodily, no, although they do dress somewhat differently. The materials are very similar, as they have passed on their scientific advances in that direction to us for our comfort. We are, after all, their offspring, whom they always hoped to restore to full 'enlightenment' some day. They have not, however, tried to influence our development in other ways, allowing our fashions and arts, and, to some extent our sciences, to follow lines which have diverged from theirs as time has passed. Everything they have done or refrained from doing has been for the good of our common race. They have never hated or even disliked us for what we were capable of doing to each other. They have always seen us as their children, whom they hoped would one day grow up. Only a very few of us ever did."

The thought of so many wasted, crippled minds saddened them both, but by this time the washing up was finished, and the two men became aware that Jamie was calling them from the front of the boat. Donald took up his crutches and nimbly followed as Ken led the way forward.

The boy was sitting on the top with his new binoculars up to his eyes, staring intently at something in the sky in the far distance, ahead of the boat.

"It seems to be an enormous cloud of birds," he said as Ken emerged from the saloon, "all wheeling and diving. Whatever can be attracting so many of them?"

He passed the binoculars over to Ken who focused on the birds once Jamie had directed him where to look. There was an unusually large number of them, as Jamie had said, soaring into the sky and diving to disappear from view below the tops of the intervening trees. Even with such powerful glasses it was impossible to make out what all the birds were, but he thought he could make out the distinctive shapes of gulls and perhaps crows amongst them.

"Scavengers," he thought. "I hope whatever is attracting them is well out of sight from the canal."

The boy caught the thought.

"Why?" he asked.

"Because whatever it is that is attracting them won't be too pleasant to look at or to smell by now. And, by the size of that flock, there are quite large pickings to be had."

Susan appeared on deck, alerted by the flow of thought between them. She too observed the flock through the binoculars and agreed that whatever had attracted them couldn't be too pleasant.

"Are you sure we have to go in their direction?"

"From what I remember of the map, I am pretty certain they are on our route. One problem about canal travel is that not many diversions are possible. We just have to press on."

"Speaking about pressing on," she said, "I know that you said you wanted to make this day as near normal as possible, and that we all agreed, but as I have spoken to each one of you today, I have received the distinct impression that we all really want to be on the move, and that we only agreed to remain here because we each assumed that that is what the others want. This morning has given us the breathing space we needed, but I think we ought to ask the others what they really want to do with the rest of the day."

Susan's observations had been correct, and as he started up the engine to resume the journey, Ken made a note to try to pay more attention to the mental, rather than verbal, output of those around him, as Susan seemed able to do.

Donald was up front with Jamie as they approached the ruined bridge. They would now see how successful their clearing operation had been. Throttling back the engine, Ken moved ahead cautiously, keeping the boat as near to the towpath side as possible, as that is where the rubble had been least. There were a few minor grating sounds from below, and at one point the boat lurched slightly to the right as it scraped by a large object hidden beneath the surface, but there was nothing that caused them any serious anxiety. They appeared to have done their job well.

Donald and Jamie disappeared below as Rachel II picked up speed once more, leaving Ken alone with his thoughts. It occurred to him that, though they may be able to share much through thought, each of them remained quite individual in the way they were able to use their new powers. Susan, for instance, seemed to be much more receptive to the 'feelings' of others than he himself was, but she seemed to have difficulty in 'manipulation', whilst his own manipulative skills had developed early, and made rapid progress. Jamie, on the other hand, seemed to have no 'natural' abilities as yet, although Ken was sure that he would develop his own particular skills given time. Donald was on an entirely different level, already having displayed some skills that the others could not hope to emulate without proper training. As the boat chugged along, Ken became engrossed in speculation as to what he might someday be able to achieve.

His reverie was interrupted by Jamie, calling from the front of the boat.

"The birds! This is where the birds are!"

Ken immediately became aware of his surroundings, and realised that he had been steering on autopilot for the last couple of miles, and that they were now approaching the outskirts of Fazeley, where the Birmingham and Fazeley canal left the Coventry canal to swing into Birmingham proper. The birds, however, had no interest in the junction, but rather in what lay in the fields and outlying buildings to the north of Fazeley.

The discipline of the army seemed to have held for a while, even after the mad death had struck, for here was evidence that they had launched a full scale military attack upon the civilians of Fazeley, using whatever weapons they had been able to lay their hands on. The buildings had been reduced to rubble and many civilians slaughtered before the soldiers had turned their weapons upon each other. The resultant carnage was what was now attracting the attention of the scavenging birds. Great flocks of them arose from the ground, darkening the sky as the narrowboat approached. Their departure revealed that the fields were littered with the corpses upon which they had been feeding. Dogs and other, smaller carnivores held their ground and snarled or bared their teeth at the boat as it passed by, unwilling to give up what they saw as theirs. At one point Ken was certain he saw larger, cat-like animals crouching over their meal. Perhaps there had been a zoo nearby from which they had escaped. As the boat passed by, the wheeling squadrons settled once more, covering the ground with a black and white mottled mass. Fights broke out as the animals defended their territory against the descending hordes.

Then came the smell, borne to them on the westerly wind. It was almost unbearable and Ken slammed the rear hatch shut to keep it out of the boat as far as possible. He clasped a handkerchief over his nose and mouth, at the same time urging the boat on as fast as it would go so as to pull clear of the stench of death as quickly as they could. Unfortunately for them, the canal swung east just beyond the junction, and then north again, keeping them in the flow of foul air, and they immediately had to abandon their plan for passing through towns. This was no place to spend the night.

The locks in Tamworth would have proved especially difficult under the prevailing conditions, but here Donald came to the rescue, passing out one of the sets of breathing apparatus Jamie had been so interested in back in the cellar.

"We've only got two of these," he said, "so we'll reserve them for those who have to be out in this stench. Those below will have to make do with wet cloths." So saying he disappeared again, tightly closing the hatches behind him.

The breathing apparatus was a lifesaver making it tolerable to work in the noisome atmosphere. There was absolutely no human movement to be seen anywhere around. If there were any survivors of the battle, they were keeping well clear of the area, giving Rachel II an unhindered run through the town. It was not until they had turned south again, and were clear of Polesworth, that they were able to breathe freely again, stowing the breathing equipment away again for possible future use.

Their mooring for the night lay just south of the village of Grendon at the foot of a flight of locks leading up to Atherstone.

They could have gone a little further, but the light was beginning to fade and they thought it better to remain where they were and make an early start on the locks the following day.

***

In the cold, grey light of dawn, Jamie leapt nimbly onto the towpath and sprinted off to the first of the locks to have it ready before Ken got the boat started. He had his procedure all worked out and knew exactly what to do, but on this occasion, just as he was opening the first of the lower paddles to empty the lock, the windlass slipped from his grasp, and the descending paddle whirled the windlass round before it slipped off the end of the spindle and clattered onto the lock side, teetering on the edge for just a second before disappearing into the dark deep water. In dismay Jamie watched the spreading ripples centred on the point where the windlass had entered the lock. When the boat arrived at the gates to find they were not open and ready to receive them, Ken drew into the bank and jumped onto the towpath. Quickly securing the boat to a mooring ring he hurried to where Jamie stood, staring into the disturbed waters.

"I'm sorry," called Jamie, apprehensively, as Ken drew near to him, "The handle dropped in! It just slipped off and disappeared, but I should have it again in a minute."

The boy was obviously concentrating very hard. Ken stood quietly by to see what would happen.

By now Susan was hurrying along the towpath towards them, obviously concerned at the unexpected delay, and Donald was standing in the bows. Ken, not wanting Jamie to be disturbed, and not being sure how thought messages might affect the boy's concentration, held up his hand to warn and reassure them. As the morning was cold, Susan had draped a cardigan about her shoulders and now, as she approached cautiously, she pulled it on and stood quietly by as Ken turned his attention back to Jamie who was staring at the icy water.

"Ah!" the boy exclaimed quietly. "There it is, lying in the mud at the bottom. Now, come on, come on, up... up... up... here it comes."

195

Another ring of ripples spread out as the handle broke the surface. Astonished at what he had done, Jamie almost lost it, and the windlass dipped under, only to rise to the surface once more as he regained control. Both of the adults remained silent as they stood by, watching intently.

"Steady now, stay there! Now, come on, come on," Jamie murmured softly to himself.

The windlass glided in smoothly towards the lock side and Jamie scooped it up and clutched it tightly against his chest, but quickly pushing it away again as it left a large wet patch on his anorak.

"I did it!" He whooped. "It's the first time it's worked!"

"You could have brought it right back to your hand if you had tried," Ken observed, "but I suppose what you did was enough for the first attempt."

"You're dead right there," muttered the boy. "My head's killing me!"

"Don't worry, that will soon pass, and it gets easier the more you use it."

"I suppose I could work the locks like that, instead of using the windlass." Jamie mused, already alert to further possibilities. "I wonder if I could….?"

"Don't try to run before you can walk," Susan advised as she and Jamie returned to the boat. "Practise on small things to begin with, and give yourself more time to get used to it."

The boy was looking very thoughtful as he jumped back aboard and disappeared below to tell Donald what he had done, and Ken knew that Jamie's emerging powers would come on in leaps and bounds now that he had flexed his mental muscles.

Ken's brow was creased in thought as he opened the lock gates and nudged the boat in. Seeing the metal windlass floating there in the water had struck a chord in his memory, and for the life of him he could not think what it was. Once inside, he manipulated the lock gates closed operating the paddles by thought control, and when the levels had equalised, he nosed the boat forward into the placid waters before him.

For the next few miles, as they ascended the locks and passed through Atherstone without incident, he racked his brain, trying to recall what the lock windlass had reminded him of, but the harder he tried, the more frustrated he became as the elusive memory remained just beyond the edge of recall, refusing to come any closer. Eventually he gave up and turned his mind to other matters.

There were a number of problems concerning this trip which would arise sooner or later and it would be better for all concerned if they were ready for them. Although they had started off with an almost full tank of fuel, he was not sure how far that would take them, and so they needed to keep an eye open for an opportunity to replenish their tank and take such opportunities whenever they arose. The same applied to their water supply. He knew that there were taps at regular intervals along the canals, and he thought that the supply was gravity fed. If this was so, and if the reservoir serving them had not run dry, then all would be well, but again the position needed to be kept under observation and their supplies replenished as frequently as possible. Next there was the matter of more fuel for the stove in the cabin, and he wondered if it would burn logs...! At the thought of logs the elusive memory slipped into place!

It had been one of those Old Testament prophets, Elisha. Or was it Elijah? He could never remember which was which.

"Elisha," he decided, "had been with a party of men who were cutting down trees by the side of a river. One of the axe heads had worked loose, and as the user swung the axe the head had come off and flown into the water. The workman was most concerned because the axe, a valuable tool in those days, had not belonged to him but had been borrowed. The prophet had come to the rescue by causing the heavy metal axe head to float to the surface, just as Jamie had done with the windlass."

People like themselves, as Donald had said, had been around for a long time.

Just at that moment Susan came up from below for a breath of fresh air and to keep him company for a while. In her hands she bore two steaming mugs of coffee and a plate of hot mince pies which she set down on top of the hatch. Sounds of happy laughter drifted up through the opening as Jamie and Donald kept each other amused with one of the many board games which they had found tucked away in a cupboard in the front saloon. Jamie's headache seemed to have cleared up very quickly.

"Is everything all right?" she asked, noticing Ken's preoccupation immediately.

He nodded, absent-mindedly, still thinking about the windlass incident at the lock,

After finishing the last of the pies, Ken was just downing the remains of his coffee, when he turned to Susan.

"Can you just take over here for a second? I won't be long."

So saying he disappeared into the boat, and could be heard making his way to the front cabin. A few moments later he was back again, a small black book in hand.

"Now let's see…" he murmured, leafing through the pages. "Ah yes, there it is. I was right. It was Elisha."

The book he held was a copy of the Bible, and he was pointing to a passage in the Second Book of Kings, Chapter six. Susan read it out.

.". 'And the iron did swim..' Why!" she exclaimed, "That's what happened with Jamie."

"Precisely," said Ken. "'There's nothing new under the sun' seems to have been a very true statement. It makes you think doesn't it? A great deal of all of this seems to be tied up with Biblical language and religion. I wonder how much more we have yet to find out?"

He left it at that, determined to enjoy Susan's company to the utmost while he had her to himself.

The weather had turned out cool but dry that morning, though it had rained during the night. This had tended to freshen the air somewhat, and the sun though it lacked warmth, brightened the landscape each time it broke through, although Ken suspected it was not just the appearance of the sun which lifted his spirits.

Their conversation was light and happy, and it wasn't long before they were sharing together those fondest childhood memories which play such a basic part in moulding the individual. Susan remembered the magic of Christmases gone by, sitting beneath the tree and looking up into its glowing, present-laden branches, while the gathered family sat in the candlelight, quietly humming or singing carols. To Ken it was the excitement of waking very early on Christmas morning to find a mysteriously bulging stocking, hanging from the bed head, which rustled in a most exciting manner when touched. Now that these memories could actually be shared along with the feelings they evoked, rather than just related by word of mouth, it was an exceptionally intimate experience for both of them, and one which they enjoyed immensely.

Eventually their thoughts returned, as was usual, to more recent events, and what the future might hold for them.

"At first I thought it was the end of everything," Susan confided. "But now I see it as a brand new start. A new and better beginning. A chance the world has never really had before. Donald said that it had been brewing for a long time, and that you had noticed it. I hadn't. I suppose that that could have come from your being in close contact with children, or maybe I had just closed my eyes to what was going on around me. All I knew was that the world seemed like an awful place, and that I didn't fit in."

"Donald tells me that there have been quite a number of people like that down the ages." Ken replied thoughtfully, his mind returning to Elisha and the axe head. "Many of those who have 'seen the light' simply chose to leave this planet and go back to A-vern with the Other Worlders. To live here became too painful for them. A fair number of mysterious disappearances can probably be accounted for in that way. But some, that very special few, chose to stay to help in any way they could. These were the hidden men and women in history. They were never recorded because mankind simply didn't know they were there, but there do seem to be clues, once you know what to look for. Remember Saul, on the Damascus road? He saw a brilliant light and it completely changed his life. And what about Joan of Arc? She heard voices that no one else heard, just as we do, and she was burned at the stake for it. And remember those beautiful words in the Church of England prayerbook – 'Lighten our darkness we beseech thee Oh Lord...' I wonder just how much old Archbishop Cranmer knew when he wrote them?

And of course there are other indicators in our everyday speech. 'Seen the light', or 'it came to me in a flash', being two which spring readily to mind, and mankind has always made reference to 'The Other World,' not really knowing what was being spoken of. Man in general has always failed to read these pointers correctly. Indeed, how could he succeed? They were referring to something which was, for the most part, outside his field of experience and so, beyond his comprehension. This was something which was just not available to him."

"And yet there has always been an inkling that there was something which escaped him," burst in Susan excitedly. "Couldn't that explain his searching for mind-changing experiences through drugs?"

"I suspect that all of these 'inklings' were deliberately planted," continued Ken, nodding in agreement.

"How do you mean?"

"Well, Donald says that some of those who were born here, like us, chose to remain after they had changed, and live amongst those whom they loved, rather than go back to the original world where they would always be strangers."

"Wherever they chose to be they would be strangers once the change had taken place in their brains," she responded.

"Yes, I know that," he scolded playfully, "but the choice to leave must have been a difficult one for anyone to make. I mean, we have each other, but the world we grew up in, and the people we knew are gone forever. It makes little difference either way to us. For them to stay and possibly help others, perhaps even their own loved ones, to make the change might have seemed like an attractive option."

"But to go on living in a world where their very 'difference' could make them targets of hatred should it ever show! I don't think that I could have done that."

"But some of them obviously did. They couldn't force the change to take place, but they seem to have dropped hints all down the line to try to spur as many others as possible into opening up to their full potential."

"All that is over now though, isn't it?" Susan pondered, wistfully. "So where does it leave us? Where do we go from here?"

"I don't think we know enough about the options open to us to make any sort of decision on those questions yet."

Susan turned to look him directly in the eyes.

"Whatever my future holds, and wherever it may lie, one thing is certain. I want to be with you."

At last it was said. Both had instinctively known that their futures lay together, but this was the first time it had been put into words. It was as if a final barrier had gone down between them. Ken reached out and put his arm around her, drawing her in to his side, and there was a deep contentment shared in silence together as the narrowboat chugged on through the cold English countryside.

Chapter 13

"But there went up a mist from the earth…"

Genesis 2:6

After negotiating the sharp bends and the historic stop lock at Hawkesbury Junction, they were able to replenish their supplies of water and diesel at Brinklow marina, and finding the junction with an arm leading to Stretton Wharf to be wide enough to allow them to moor in such a position as to make access difficult for unwelcome visitors, they decided to call it a day. The weather had grown steadily colder as the afternoon wore on, and a bank of solid grey cloud, building steadily from the north had eventually blanketed the sky. Closing the rear hatch as the early darkness began to gather, Ken noticed a slight dusting of powdery snow on the rear deck.

"It looks as though the weather might be taking a turn for the worse," he commented as he joined the others in the cosy saloon. "There's snow in the air."

"That shouldn't worry us too much, unless of course it freezes hard," said Donald, pausing to look up from stoking the stove with logs they had gathered from a pile found by one of the lock cottages.

"Will the canal freeze solid?" Jamie asked, pictures of speed skaters flashing from his mind.

"No, although we might get a covering of ice on the top." Donald laughed. "The boat could handle that, provided it doesn't become too thick. What would stop us is if the lock mechanisms ice up badly enough to stop us getting through. I don't know if it does ever happen, but I suppose it could."

"I think we ought to worry about that if and when it happens." Ken again, "For the moment it's just a little snow flurry."

They spent the evening in pleasant conversation; warm and dry in their self-contained little world, oblivious to the ever-thickening snow outside.

Just before turning in, Ken opened the doors onto the rear deck. The snow whirled before him in the rising wind, blocking off any view of the surrounding area. He quickly shut the hatch again and dusted himself down. This was no night for a stroll in the open. Stoking up the boatman's stove he undressed in its glow and climbed into bed. Before sleeping he lay awake for a while listening to the gusting wind, thankful for this haven of peace in a seemingly hostile world.

He awoke the following morning thoroughly refreshed, but with the uneasy feeling that something was wrong. The wind had died away during the night, and silence had returned to the world. The stove had gone out in their cabin, and the air felt cold and damp. He pulled his sleeping bag up around his head to retain as much warmth as possible while he gathered up enough courage to get out of bed. Listening intently to the boat he realised that no one else had yet found the courage he was seeking. He sent out a thought, wishing them a good morning. There was no response. Everyone was still asleep. The life afloat, with all its fresh air, was tiring and one slept well.

With a determined effort he sat up swinging his legs over the edge of his bed, still cocooned in his sleeping bag. It was then that he realised what was wrong. The boat had a distinct list to the left. The corridor side was noticeably higher in the water. His first thought was that the snow of the previous evening had piled up on one side and the added weight of it was causing the imbalance. Steeling himself against the cold of the cabin he quickly discarded the sleeping bag and pulled on the warmest clothing he could find, briskly massaging his upper arms to restore some warmth into himself.

Unbolting the rear hatch doors, he opened them slightly and peered out. A uniform greyness met his eyes. The temperature had risen during the night, and a fast thaw had set in. The relatively warm air over the cold blanket of snow had given rise to a thick fog. Scrambling out onto the rear deck, he looked forward down the length of the boat. The front was hidden by the fog, but it was obvious that snow was not the cause of the problem, most of it having disappeared.

"We've got a leak!" The half thought came from Donald who had awoken to find himself lying at an angle.

"It probably happened when we scraped over the remains of that bridge." Ken thought at him. "What do we do now?"

Donald didn't know.

"I suppose we'll sink eventually, although we don't seem to be in any immediate danger." Ken hated the thought of having to transfer everything to another boat. Rachel II had seemed so ideally suited to their purpose. "Let's see what the marina has to offer before we wake the others."

He manoeuvred the boat over to the side by once again slackening the ropes on one side and using those on the other to pull them across. The resistance to such movement was noticeably greater than the last time they had tried it, the boat sitting deeper in the water, but he eventually managed it, by putting the power of his mind behind his physical efforts.

The marina was a disappointment. After a careful inspection Ken ascertained that, of the boats moored there, only a few proved to be as well appointed as their own craft, and none of them was as ready for the off as she had been. Water, fuel and provisions would all need to be transferred. It made him realise just how fortunate they had been to come across her in the first place, and he wondered whether anything could be done to effect a repair, rather than change to another one.

Throughout his inspection he kept careful watch for any movement which would indicate the presence of others but his eyes were unable to pierce the fog for any distance. He took comfort in the fact that if the fog hid any enemies, it also served to mask his own movements.

"If I avoid making any noise I should be fairly safe," he thought.

Occasionally a half-discerned movement caught by the corner of an eye caused his heart to pound, but each time it turned out to be the deceptions of the mist as it wreathed and curled over the waters of the canal basin. By the time he returned to report his findings to Donald, he was in a very gloomy state of mind indeed.

Susan was just emerging from her sleeping quarters as he swung down through the rear hatch.

"What's wrong?" she called to him, shaking her hair back into shape as her head appeared from the top of a thick Aran sweater.

Donald stood framed in the doorway beyond her.

"We seem to be sinking. Ken thinks we might have holed her on the ruins of that bridge in Hopwas."

"It can't be all that bad if it's taken two days to show." Jamie, disturbed by the discussion now stood at Ken's elbow. "Can't we get the water out? Don't these boats have pumps or something?"

To everyone's amazement, Susan burst into peals of laughter, and they all stared at her, waiting for her to explain what had caused her amusement.

"What an idiot I am!" she was able to gasp when her laughter subsided. "We haven't got a leak, at least not one to worry about."

"You mean this always happens?" asked Ken, irritated, indicating the slope of the floor.

"It does if you forget to pump the water out of the bilge." she replied. "I never thought about it until Jamie mentioned a pump. All these boats leak a bit," she explained, "and the water gathers in the space under the floor. You are supposed to pump it out every night. I completely forgot about it. I suppose the weight of the snow and the pressure of the wind against the side of the boat last night caused us to lean over to one side a bit. All the bilge water would have run to that side and caused us to list that way. I bet when we pump it out we'll be all right again."

"I certainly hope so. There's nothing around here anything like as suitable for us." Ken's hopes were rising. "How do we start this pump?"

Susan had to admit that she did not have any idea.

"There must be a switch for it somewhere," she surmised, lamely.

Ken went back to the controls and tried each switch in turn.

On the third attempt, there was the sound of running water. Jamie rushed to the side and hung recklessly out over the canal.

"That's it. There's water gushing out of a hole down here," he cried, pointing.

Ken immediately turned the pump off again.

"What's wrong?" Jamie wanted to know, "Why have you stopped it?"

"Too much noise." Ken threw back over his shoulder as he headed for the mooring ropes; "It'll give our position away to anyone who may be out there. Come on; help me get her back to a central mooring. We should be a bit safer then."

Gradually the craft was eased back into position in the centre of the junction and the pumps restarted. Even with the boat in a less vulnerable position Ken was very apprehensive and kept a careful lookout, as far as the fog would let him, for any suspicious movement.

After what seemed like hours of pumping, Rachel II began to settle back onto an even keel. When at last the pump was sucking nothing but air, Ken heaved a great sigh of relief and turned it off. The descending silence was intense, and the thickness of the fog seemed to increase, wrapping them in the cocoon of their own tiny world.

For a while they simply stood and listened, wondering if the noise of the pumps had been loud enough to attract unwelcome attentions, but the fog seemed to have deadened all noise, and, for all they knew, they could now have been the final survivors of the catastrophe which had befallen mankind.

"We seem to be alone," Susan whispered, "but I wish we could see a little further. This fog gives me the creeps."

She shivered. It was possible to imagine that the fog masked too many horrors, the imagination being, all too often, worse than the reality.

"I think we are pretty safe here," Ken replied, "but I don't see how we could move in any case. We can't even see the front of our own boat!"

"We could try."

They all turned to look at Donald.

"We don't know how long this fog will last, or how

widespread it is, and anyway it's so frustrating just sitting around here doing nothing. If we kept our speed low, one of us could sit up front and act as lookout. We have pretty detailed maps and so we should know when locks are coming up, and we have the perfect method of communication. I would certainly be happier to be on the move, and I am just as happy to be the lookout up front."

The maps showed a good stretch ahead with only three locks before they reached the next junction, and so it was agreed to give it a try.

Donald, wrapped up warm against the penetrating cold and dampness positioned himself in the bows while Ken coaxed the engine into life. Susan and Jamie busily applied themselves to coiling the mooring ropes back on board.

Ken found it an eerie sensation, nosing the boat slowly into the greyness, but he soon got the hang of steering from Donald's received instructions. The fog swirled around them as it was disturbed by their passage, only to close behind them like a silent curtain, cutting them off from the rest of the world. Almost immediately after setting off, the fog in front darkened perceptibly, growing steadily darker until the shadowy outlines of a bridge appeared, only to disappear in like manner as they passed under and left it behind.

Only the excellence of the communication between minds enabled Ken to steer the boat through the constriction beneath the bridge without mishap, as the bows of the boat had already passed through before he had any visual confirmation of the location of it. About a mile and a half further on a sharp right hand turn caused a little difficulty and Ken ran the boat into the bank, both going into and coming out of the bend, although the speed was low enough to avoid any damage. Even with the excellent communication which thought contact provided, bends were a problem. A second problem soon became apparent.

Staring into the blank greyness was hard on the eyes, and before long both Donald and Ken found themselves imagining shapes looming up at them which caused them both some anxiety. It soon became clear that whoever was steering or on lookout could only operate effectively for a short while before the strain on the eyes became too much.

There seemed to be only one solution, and that was to work as two teams, one pair operating the boat while the second pair rested their eyes. They tried this for a while but the changeovers began to occur more and more frequently. Obviously the time spent resting was not long enough for them to recover. The darkness of the Newbold tunnel brought slight relief, but it was over far too soon.

They passed to the north of Rugby without really being aware of the town, eventually reaching the winding hole at the foot of the Hillmorton Locks by mid-afternoon. It was there that Susan, who was at the helm, called a halt.

"It's no use," she thought at them. "We can't go on like this. Just look at us."

They were all red-eyed from the strain of peering into the greyness.

"I don't think it's worth it."

They could see that she was talking sense, but Donald, in particular, did not want to stop.

"There is another way."

His thought was a very quiet one, but it caught the attention of the others and they waited for him to continue.

"There are really two problems here. The first is that the resting time is not long enough for our eyes to recover, and the second is that there is conflict between what the lookout observes and what the helmsman can see. It is difficult to steer if you can't see the front of the boat. We therefore need to attempt a different technique."

There was a sensation of puzzlement from the other three, but it was Ken who formed the question.

"What other technique is there?"

"From what you have told me I know that each of you has received quick flashes of one of the other's experiences. You, Ken, saw the inside of the church when Jamie remembered it, and you, Susan, told me you saw the movement inside the garage when Ken was caught by the booby trap back in Calver, your scream jerking him into the action which probably saved his life.

This 'picture sharing' is just another of your new abilities which can be developed. I was hoping we could leave it for the time being as you all have enough to cope with, but we obviously need it now. It requires the helmsman to close his eyes, and concentrate upon what the lookout is seeing. If it works, this will help in two ways. Firstly it will enable the helmsman to 'see' further ahead through the lookout's eyes, and so control the boat more accurately, and it will also give us all longer rests from being on lookout duty."

It was decided to give it a try with Donald at the helm, and Ken acting as his eyes.

Ascending the three locks gave them all a brief respite, but this was not as long as they had expected as the narrow chambers filled and emptied much faster than any others they had encountered. At the top lock Ken took up his position in the bows while Donald manned the helm. The extra height gained as they had climbed through the locks had caused the fog to thin slightly and this raised their hopes that they might soon be clear of it. The thinning however was not enough for them to abandon their experiment. With his eyes tightly closed, Donald urged the boat into motion.

Progress was good while Donald was in control. He was obviously more experienced at it than the others, but it served to show what could be done. Each of the others tried it in turn, with varying degrees of success. They found it difficult to keep their eyes closed while steering and so a blindfold became a necessity. Susan proved the most adept of them, reinforcing Ken's theory that they all had their own 'specialities'. Speed gradually dropped as they found the effort of concentration far greater than they had anticipated, and they had only gone a mile or so beyond the Braunston Turn when they decided to call a halt.

The fog was noticeably thinner with a slight hint of a breeze promising clearer weather soon as they moored, as was now standard practice, in the centre of the canal.

By the time darkness fell they had secured the boat and were enjoying their evening meal, after which they settled down in the saloon to enjoy each other's company.

"So what other hidden talents have we got?" asked Ken,

carefully balancing a generous glass of amber liquid on his knee, and looking directly at Donald.

"I think that I have mentioned them all by now, unless there are some that I haven't been told about," Donald replied. "We all have the same talents to a greater or lesser degree. It depends upon how each of us chooses to develop and use them. You have seen how we have been able to make use of what we have here. Ken seems to be good at manipulation, but you, Susan are better at linking up with the senses of others. Jamie on the other hand has not shown a particular strength yet. He seems to be an all-rounder. With the proper training, and in some cases, the right equipment, we can all become better. The one thing we don't seem to be able to manage without training and the proper equipment is bodily teleportation along the ley lines. If that were easily managed we wouldn't have needed to embark upon our present journey."

"What sort of uses do the other people of our kind make of their powers?" asked Susan. "The Yomorns, I mean." The word felt strange on her lips.

"Control of disease for one," Donald explained. "Some of their specialist 'doctors' can achieve the most amazing results, making what I did with Jamie seem like very basic first aid. Their control of plant life is also something to behold, making farming a very simple matter. They don't know what it is to have too much or too little of anything they need. Production always exactly balances demand. I mentioned before that birth control is as natural to them as sex itself. No child is ever conceived unless both partners want that. Hatred doesn't exist and wars are unknown on their world, and yet they have not lost that vital spark needed to continue the quest for new knowledge. Their society has not stagnated.

The most significant advantage, though, is that of being completely at ease with each other, as we are here. There is no envy, no malice, no jealousy or hatred, just a comfortable knowledge that no one is in danger from anyone else. They are completely at peace with each other. That is what we feel here. That is what makes these evenings together so enjoyable."

"Don't they ever compete for partners?" This was Susan

again.

"Compete yes, but never in such a way as to make that competition unbearable. Once the choice has been made the marriage is for life. Everyone knows when the right choice has been made, just as you and Ken know now."

Susan blushed. "Is it that obvious?"

"To us it is. Right,, Jamie?"

"'Course it is. You've been broadcasting it for ages. Everybody knows!"

As the four of them may possibly have been the last people left alive in England, Jamie's last statement, was no longer the wild exaggeration it may once have been, but was probably very close to the truth.

Just before turning in that night, Ken went back up on deck to check on the weather. The wind was rising, and he could see the fog being torn apart by it, curling and streaming between him and the high moon which occasionally disappeared as thicker rags of the mist were blown across its face. In lighter moments he could see grey streamers trailing across the canal as the water vapour ran before the wind. The world beyond was dark.

For a while he stood, thinking over what had been said that evening. It was true that he and Susan knew how they felt about each other, and if they had simply been the last survivors of any other catastrophe, they would probably have come together as man and wife, but this wasn't quite the end of all things. They faced a future together in a new civilisation, not a world where civilisation had disappeared altogether. There would still be an opportunity for a 'proper' wedding, and besides, a cramped narrowboat with two other people on board was no place for a honeymoon! Glancing again at the silver shards of mist in the moonlight, he wondered if the home world of A-vern had a moon. With this thought, and shivering as the damp atmosphere pierced his clothing, he turned and went back inside.

The following morning they were away again at first light. The day was cold and overcast, but so far the stiff westerly wind, which had dispersed the last remnants of fog, had kept the rain at bay. The countryside through which they were passing was deserted, with hardly a house in sight, and away to the south was a thicker dark horizon, hinting at a backdrop of hills.

During the morning the threat of rain materialised, but even this failed to dampen their spirits. The mood of the previous evening had continued, and there was a mutual feeling that a deep bond now existed between them; a bond of trust and shared adversity. They all felt that the worst was over, and it was just a matter of time before they could summon help.

Ken wondered just how far he could develop his new powers, and he spent a happy morning seeing what he could and could not manipulate. One experiment was to try to prevent the spots of rain from hitting him, and he was amazed at how successful the exercise turned out to be. When Susan brought him his mid-morning coffee, he proudly showed her his almost unspotted anorak as the drizzle came down around them.

Each new day brought them nearer to their destination. There was no indication that there were now any more survivors. Countryside and town alike appeared deserted. Day by day Ken's practice paid off, and he became ever more skilful at manipulating objects around him. Jamie too was obviously practising and spent long periods alone, sitting in the bows whenever the weather allowed. Thrown stones would deviate in flight to hit an impossibly distant target, or suddenly skim away into the air a second before they were due to hit the canal water. Occasionally a passing bird would perform an astounding aeronautical manoeuvre before streaking away in a startled flurry of wings. The boy, though never particularly garrulous, seemed to become somewhat introspective. Ken simply put this down to his concentration upon his newly discovered abilities and left it at that.

"He's coming to terms with all that has happened to him," he told Susan when she spoke of it.

The canal side settlements with their picturesque names slipped by one by one, Napton, Marston Doles, Cropredy. All now lying silent and deserted. Ken too spent a considerable amount of time in silent thought. For some days now he had had the uneasy feeling that all was not as it should be. At the back of his mind he could sense a thin stream of anxiety and deep sadness which he knew was not of himself, but try as he might he could not determine from which of the others it emanated. In addition to this something he had seen or heard had disturbed him. He could not, for the life of him, put his finger upon the cause of it, but he was sure that something, somewhere was wrong, and the more he thought about it the more his unease increased. He found that he was unable to dispel the unease that dogged his mind like an unseen shadow, and a great sadness, often tinged with an inexplicable sense of fear lay like an unseen aura around the whole party.

It eventually became apparent that each of them was experiencing similar feelings and at first they each thought that the source was one of the others, but the further south they progressed, the more the feelings intensified and it eventually became clear that what they felt came not from within themselves, but from some outside source.

"There can be only one explanation for it," Donald confided one overcast afternoon when they were all gathered together at the rear of the boat, Jamie at the tiller, "There is someone of our own kind somewhere up ahead of us, and these feelings are coming from them."

"But surely if we can sense them, they can sense us, can't they?" Jamie wanted to know.

Donald pondered for a minute before answering.

"Not necessarily. If this person is newly triggered then they won't be aware of what they are doing. There is obviously a great deal of fear and confusion in their mind, and any of our thoughts that may get through will almost certainly be put down as hallucinations. After all, remember how each one of you felt when it first happened to you. Whoever it is is feeling dreadfully alone and vulnerable. They are frightened by their own feelings and even more terrified at what has happened to the world, and all of these feelings are coming through to us."

"Why don't we try to draw them to us like you did with Ken and Jamie?" Susan wanted to know. "If it worked with them, it should work now."

"Not yet," explained Donald, "as far as I can tell, we are approaching him or her, and I think it will be best to wait until we are closer and we can then give them a stationary rather than

213

a moving destination to aim for. Besides, they are still some distance ahead and the closer we can get to them the quicker they will be able to get to us."

It made sense, but Susan found it hard to leave it at that.

"Can't we at least try to comfort them?"

"We can try, but they are so terrified that we may not be able to get through." Donald replied.

"Well I'm going to try now! The rest of you can either join me or try to see if you can detect any response – however small that response may be," she added.

So saying she wrapped her anorak more firmly around her and disappeared into the depths of the boat where she could concentrate in comfort out of the thin drizzle which had started while they had been speaking. The two men followed her while Jamie struggled into his waterproofs to continue his spell at the tiller.

As their journey progressed the thoughts of the other person grew steadily stronger but there was no indication that he or she was aware of their presence. All efforts to contact or comfort their unknown compatriot appeared to have little effect, with the fear and intermingled sadness waxing and waning in a most irregular and puzzling manner.

Banbury came as something of a shock. Ken remembered it as a bustling little market town, with its famous nursery rhyme cross, lying on the main road between Oxford and Coventry. He knew that the cross was not really the original one, but he always liked to think that it was. He had often made a point of stopping there whenever he passed that way, enjoying the charm of one of its tearooms or hotels. Such places were now a thing of the past, gone forever along with the vanished population.

Fire had ravaged the town, sweeping through unchecked, devouring all before it, leaving behind only the blackened skeletons of what had once been buildings, with distorted girders and shattered brickwork, sometimes topped by a lone, pathetic chimney pot, silhouetted against a grey mournful sky.

The cries of disturbed birds echoed back from fire-hardened surfaces, all the soft, absorbent materials having been consumed by the cancer of the inferno which had swept mercilessly through the town. The heat had been so intense that there were even signs of charring on the woodwork of the lock gates, where the ancient enemies of fire and water had fought another skirmish in their age-old battle for supremacy. Luckily for them, water had been the victor on this occasion and the sodden wood had resisted. The gates had remained firm. All of them felt happier when this disturbing reminder of the insanity which had struck the world was well behind them.

"It's so easy to forget what must have happened, living here in our own self-contained little world," whispered Susan watching the smoke-blackened ruins fall behind as they pressed on toward Oxford.

Chapter 14

"...lest I sleep the sleep of death."

Psalm 13:3

Their continued journey southwards, had it been undertaken in any but the circumstances in which they found themselves, would have been a most refreshing experience, but the sight of what had once been Banbury had cast a pall over the expedition which was difficult to shake off. The villages of Somerton and Upper and Lower Heyford, lying cold and deserted in the countryside to the north of Oxford, idyllic though they sounded, only served to remind them of the catastrophe which had overtaken mankind.

Ken found that he was unable to dispel the unease which dogged his mind like an unseen shadow. He was aware that the external feelings which they all felt were affecting him, but this, he knew, was more than that. Susan, aware of his preoccupation, sensed that something extra was troubling him but was unable to identify the source of his concern. Eventually it was Ken, himself, who broached the subject.

They were fast approaching Oxford and Susan was keeping him company on the rear deck. They had been indulging in their favourite pastime of sharing memories with each other. Susan had been telling him of her mother, who had died when Susan was eight. Her mother had known that she had not long to live, but both parents had kept it from her until just before the end. Conversations had ended abruptly when she entered a room, or people around her had been too bright and cheerful or over attentive. For almost a year she had been able to sense that there was something wrong within the family, but no one would tell her what it was. It had probably been the unhappiest year of her

216

life, and had culminated in her mother's death. Only then did she realise what had been the cause of her unease.

"I know how you must have felt," said Ken, softly, "that's just how I feel at the moment. There's something wrong, and I don't know what it is."

"Don't you have any idea at all?"

"No, I just get the feeling that something doesn't add up. I've seen or heard something that leaves me with a sense of..." his brow furrowed as he searched for a word,"... of 'wrongness' about it, but I don't know what it is. Haven't you noticed anything?"

Susan shook her head.

"Nothing, other than the emotions of the person ahead – and your preoccupation, and I can certainly feel your worry, but I have no idea what's causing it."

"And the others haven't mentioned anything?"

"No. Jamie was a bit down a few days ago, but you know about that, and he seems to be back to normal now. No, there's nothing I can think of. Are you sure you're not imagining it?"

"I don't think so, unless of course it's some sort of side effect from our new powers that we haven't been told about. I suppose I have been experimenting a lot lately, but I am certain Donald would have mentioned it if that were the case. No, I'm pretty sure it's not imagination," he concluded.Inside himself he was totally sure, and utterly frustrated. He knew there was something wrong, just as Susan had known when her mother had been ill, but he let the matter rest there. Thinking about it only seemed to push it further away into the deeper recesses of his mind. If past experience was anything to go by it would pop to the surface when he least expected it. He turned his attention back to the matter in hand.

"Oxford is up ahead, and the canal terminates there," he said. "Do you think you can fish out those guides so that we can see where and how we get onto the Thames?"

Susan ducked into the hatchway, to reappear a couple of minutes later with the canal guides.

Closing the top hatch cover, she laid them out upon it, open at the relevant pages, looking them over carefully for a while before speaking.

"There seem to be two connections between the canal and the river. The first is through Duke's Cut, just beyond the next lock, and the second is via Isis Lock, much nearer the centre of the city."

"I think I would prefer to avoid the city and get onto the river as soon as possible. Then the current should push us along a bit faster," he decided.

Unfortunately, the lock lying on Duke's Cut proved to be impassable. The bottom gates lay open and they could see the interior of the lock as they approached. From the look of it, a narrowboat had been passing through when the madness had come upon the world. The boat leaving the Thames to move onto the Oxford canal, and having entered the confines of the lock, had been tied up on one side when the lock was at its highest level. The owners then seemed to have opened the paddles in the lower gates to release the water.

From that point on things had gone disastrously wrong. The water level had started to drop, but the owners had never returned to untie the ropes. The rear of the boat seemed to have snagged on the lock gates behind it, while the mooring rope had pulled tight, stopping the left hand side of the boat from dropping with the water. Consequently, the narrowboat had turned onto its side, hanging there, supported only by its trapped rear and forward mooring rope. How long the rope had held was impossible to say, but eventually something had given, and the massive craft had come crashing down to lie on its side in the water at the bottom of the lock. The weight of the boat and the water inside her proved too much even for their combined efforts to move her with their new powers. There was no way that 'Maelstrom' would ever leave this, her final resting-place.

Had this occurred at any other lock on the canal, it would have brought their progress to an abrupt halt, but here they were fortunate – an alternative route was available. Reversing the boat back under the railway bridge, they rejoined the main waterway and set off to enter Oxford, fervently hoping that the City of Dreaming Spires had no nightmares in store for them.

The approach to the city was more pleasant than they had

expected, with small factories and warehouses giving way to the gardens of suburban houses on the left bank. The sun, which had been hidden behind the grey blanket of cloud all day, chose this moment to shoulder it aside and stream through the gap it had made for itself, low down in the west. The light it cast had a wateriness about it which promised rain, but for the moment it bathed the high towers and pinnacles of the taller buildings in a warm red glow, and highlighted the topmost twigs of the trees, making them appear to be touched by fire. By contrast, all that lay below its sphere of influence appeared darker and gloomier than it really was.

The secluded aspect of Isis Lock belied the fact that they were so close to the city centre, but the beauty of it was marred by the presence of a number of swollen bodies floating on the surface of the water, flesh standing out whitely against the dark water. Nudged along by the slight current towards the lock, they had congregated in this quiet, wooded area to await release into the further reaches of the waterways. The fact that a number of the corpses had their hands and legs bound bore witness to the fact that they had not entered the water by accident.

It was necessary for Rachel II to nose her way gently through them in order to reach the lock gates and it was during this delicate operation that the boat began to shudder perceptibly, and black smoke poured from the small chimney which was the exhaust. Finally the engine cut out completely, to leave her floating in a helpless, immobile silence.

"What's happened?"

Jamie looked at each of his friends in turn, only to be met by the same blank look of incomprehension from each.

Ken tried the starter, and, though he heard it engage, the engine failed to turn over. Something, somewhere had jammed solid!

Jamie meanwhile, having failed to elicit any response from the adults had been hanging over the side and peering down into the murky waters.

"There's something down there," he called, pointing just under the stern.

All four scanned the area he was indicating, trying to

identify the dim shape which lay below the surface. Unfortunately, the sun still cast a deep shadow over the whole area. Conditions which rendered it difficult to make out any more than an indistinct outline beneath the dark waters.

"We should be able to see more from down there," Ken said, indicating the steps leading down into the boat. "Those steps lift up."

He and Jamie swung down into the cabin, while Donald and Susan looked on from the deck. Turning back to face them, Ken lifted the steps to reveal the dark water of the canal. Taking the torch he kept by his bed, he shone it down into the water. His reaction to what he saw there was instantaneous. Starting back from the hatch, he slammed it down again, his face visibly turning paler as the blood drained from it.

"There's a body down there," he gasped. "It's all tangled up with the propeller, and it's pretty nasty."

He stood with his head protruding from the hatchway, breathing deeply until the nausea, which threatened to overwhelm him, subsided. Once he had regained control, he described the situation below their feet.

"The propeller's completely fouled," he said, "but it's not just the body or the clothing. Whoever it was had been totally enmeshed in a thick nylon net before being tossed into the water. It's that net which is the problem. It's wound round and round in a great tangle."

He didn't mention what this had done to the body, but the others could feel the revulsion in his mind.

"OK Ken, you just take it easy and I'll see what can be done." Donald's tone was comforting, and Ken felt a wave of relief that he was not going to have to face the mess below the hatch again. Donald looked down at the deck below his feet and closed his eyes, concentrating hard on the grisly task. They could all sense that he was attempting to reverse the direction of the propeller and so unwind the tangle. They felt it give a little and start to turn backwards, but then the motion ceased again as the blades caught in the net in the opposite direction and became even more firmly enmeshed. Clearly that approach was not going to work.

"It's no good," he said, opening his eyes and massaging his temples, "I can't shift it. It's too firmly caught up. We shall have to cut through the netting. Susan, have we got a good sharp knife in the galley?"

Susan nodded and turned away to fetch it. Ken stopped her.

"There's already one down there," he pointed, "I saw it when we first came aboard, and I wondered then why it had been left there. Now I know, although I doubt whether the previous owners had to remove anything like this from a fouled prop. It's not a job I fancy doing either."

"There's no need," Donald told him. "Manipulating a knife isn't difficult. Just tell me exactly where it is."

Ken told him, and immediately the small sounds of metal against metal were transmitted to them through the deck beneath their feet as Donald set about his work. Looking over the stern the others could see the frayed fibres of blue nylon cord floating free as the knife sawed its way through them. After a few minutes the small noises stopped and there was a slight clatter as the knife was laid down again.

"That was quick!" Ken exclaimed. "Do you want me to try the engine?"

"Not so fast," Donald replied quickly. "It isn't free yet. I just had to put the knife down for a moment while I feel around to see where to cut next."

He concentrated for a few seconds and then the sawing resumed.

It took a quarter of an hour of concentrated effort before Donald was satisfied that the last remnants of the net had been removed, the waterlogged body having sunk out of sight some five minutes before that. At long last he gave the signal for Ken to try the engine. It started without too much trouble, coughing the remnants of the smoke from the exhaust, and seemed to be none the worse for its sudden stop once this had cleared.

As they edged into the tiny lock, with Donald at the helm, Ken, Susan and Jamie, each engrossed with their own private thoughts about this new development, held the barge poles down into the water as near to the propeller as they dared, hoping to fend off any further entanglements, and it was not until they had cleared the lock with its grisly entourage and passed under the low railway bridge into the River Thames that they felt able to breath freely once more.

Once out on the open river, the light was better, and being assisted by the current, their speed increased. Immediately to their left lay a row of terraced houses, fronting onto the towpath, all of which bore the usual signs of the mayhem which had ensued when the 'mad death' struck. Many of them had their doors ripped off and windows gaped blackly through a necklace of jagged glass. The towpath was littered with the personal bric-a-brac of human lives, plundered from the houses in an orgy of killing and looting, and then abandoned as crazed minds switched to new diversions. Again there were bodies, lying on the towpath and in doorways. The air was tainted with death.

Donald asked Susan to move up to the bows to keep a look out for any more corpses in the water, but had there ever been any, the current had carried them away. They had not travelled far, however before an obstacle presented itself in the form of Osney Lock.

Up to this point on their journey, one lock had been very much like another, but that which now presented itself before them had an unfamiliar 'feel' to it when they reached ahead with their minds to prepare it. The mechanisms which operated it were different from those previously encountered, and they felt that it was desirable to stop and make a visual examination before attempting to manipulate them. Susan elected to stay with the boat, tying up opposite the weir, which, they were to discover, accompanied all of the locks they were to encounter on the Thames. She kept the engine running while the men went to investigate the workings of the lock, as there were buildings very close by from which danger might erupt without warning. Although it had been days since they had seen any indication of other survivors, Susan believed in playing safe, keeping a careful watch for any unexpected movement.

It took Ken and Donald a little while to figure out what needed to be done in order to work the lock, while Jamie stared at it fascinated. Compared with the ones they had so far encountered, this was gigantic. He guessed it was about twice as long, and three times as wide as Rachel II was, and looking over the far gates he estimated the level to be about two metres lower than their present position. That represented a great deal of water. He could see that getting through these locks was not going to be a speedy operation, but as luck would have it, this first one had been left full, and was ready to receive their own craft once the top gates had been opened.

By the time Jamie returned to them, the two men had achieved that aim, and Susan was already guiding the bows through the gates. Seconds later, the gates swung closed, and as they clambered back on board, Ken and Donald manipulated the sluices, and the lock walls began to rise above them.

Throughout their passage so close to the centre of Oxford the external emotions they were experiencing had grown very strong and the consensus among them was that they were very close to the unseen sender, but the circumstances in which they found themselves had prevented them from concentrating upon any but their own problems. Now that they had reached clearer waters they were able to discern that, instead of being ahead, the emotions were now coming from slightly behind them. At their closest position the surroundings had been far too intimidating for them to consider stopping for any longer than was absolutely necessary, but now the need to find a safe mooring was top priority.

They were able to manage one more, even larger, lock that day before tying up on what the map indicated was Rose Isle, situated on a dogleg in the river, still within the southern suburbs of the city. Although being reasonably well removed from any buildings, it was still closer to Oxford than they would have liked, and the air held the tainted smell which they had now come to expect from urban areas, but the greatest need now was to keep the distance between themselves and their unknown contact as short as possible, and anyway darkness was almost upon them and the current was far too strong, especially around the weirs at locks, for them to take the risk of proceeding any farther that day.

After mooring they all met in the comfort of the saloon to consider what was to be done about their new discovery.

"Whoever we can detect is obviously in Oxford and is now reasonably close to us." Donald opened the discussion.

He paused to let the implications of what he had said sink in.

"Does that mean." Susan asked warily "that we are going to have to hang around here until they can come to us?" Her dislike of the idea was openly apparent. In the light of the day's experiences, this was far too close to the city for any of them to feel comfortable about it.

" I'm afraid so. We have to give them a chance to get here." Donald replied. "It's either that, or abandon them in the hope that we can come back later, but just feel their emotions. Whoever it is has no idea of what is happening and is obviously terrified. I should think that if we start projecting towards them right away, they should get to us sometime tomorrow."

"Do we all need to project or can we take it in turns?" Jamie wanted to know.

"I think they are probably close enough for any of us to manage it alone." Donald reckoned, "In any event the sooner we start the sooner we can get under way again."

It was agreed that they take two-hour turns throughout the night, and as Donald was fairly exhausted from his mental tussle with the fouled propeller, Ken would go first. Jamie, insisting on playing a full part, was given the second watch, Susan was to take the third, and Donald the last one. The pattern was then to be repeated until the newcomer arrived.

Ken decided to keep watch on deck for his stint, partly to make sure that they hadn't been spotted by any would be attackers and partly in the hope that their call would be answered promptly and there would be no need to wake the others. He learned very quickly that he was able to send out his mental call almost automatically and that the rest of his thought processes remained unaffected by it.

At first he was jumpy, alert to every tiny sound, but gradually he was able to identify them as natural. When his hearing grew accustomed to it, he was amazed at how noisy nature could be. The overriding sound was that of the river, chuckling and gurgling as it sucked at the banks, swirling imperiously past them on its way to the sea, while small water fowl rustled in the undergrowth, calling to each other from time to time, their plaintive 'peeps' echoing away into the darkness.

Away in the suburbs dogs barked or howled miserably, sounding distant as their cries spiralled away to be absorbed by the streets of the city, and once quite close by, a fox barked distinctively. The wind too added its voice as it sighed and gusted through the nearby trees, shaking twigs and branches together in a percussive backing. Somewhere on the island one branch creaked against another, occasionally producing a high pitched squeal, but these were the natural sounds, sounds which belonged, having always been here since the dawn of time.

Man had drowned them out with harder, harsher noise of his own during his temporary occupation, but then man had been like that, subjugating nature for his own selfish ends, unthinkingly mutilating his environment, destroying the planet upon which his very existence depended, climbing to ever higher pinnacles of self gratification, totally uncaring as to who or what he trampled underfoot in the process. Now he had been removed from the equation, and the natural sounds were returning, triumphantly, to reclaim a domain which was rightly theirs. Man's passing would not be mourned by nature. He would, in all probability, never be missed.

A sharp screech startled Ken out of his reverie, causing him to cast around in the darkness for its source, but it was only some bird or animal entering the next phase in the food chain.

"Yes," he thought, "nature is not always kind, but it is never vindictively cruel, as man was."

He shivered as the cold of the night air, having penetrated his clothing, seeped into his body, and so, satisfied that their approach had not been observed and they were not in imminent danger of attack, he slipped quietly below into the warmth of the rear cabin where he was able to settle more comfortably into his transmission. Two hours later he was startled when Jamie called him in to hand over. As he drifted into sleep, he could feel the call Jamie was sending out, and knew that the stranger would be experiencing that same urgent pull which he had felt on his journey to meet up with Susan and Donald.

***

When he awoke the following day, Ken was immediately aware that the call was still being transmitted, but now recognised Donald's particular thought patterns behind it. Obviously their efforts had not yet brought any reward, the feelings of great fear and sadness had not changed in the slightest, but now there was a hint of frustration there too. Disappointment surged through him again at the thought of their journey being delayed, but he knew that, having been through the experience himself, he could not leave the stranger behind to face their terrors alone.

Donald was alone in the saloon when Ken joined him.

"No luck yet, I'm afraid." he said unnecessarily, as Ken entered gripping two mugs of coffee. "As far as I can tell there had been no response so far. The feelings faded down to a bare minimum from time to time during the night when the 'sender' seems to have dozed off."

He took a grateful sip from the brimming coffee mug as Ken asked,

"Can you tell anything about the 'sender'?"

"I think she's female, but impressions are terribly indistinct and very, very jumbled. She seems to have no idea what's going on and feels very much alone in it all. Her mind seems to be teetering on the brink of insanity."

"Let me take over then while you rest." Ken offered, "The sooner we can get her here the better for all concerned."

"No, I am puzzled that there seems to have been no response. Perhaps we ought to join forces for a while to make the call more demanding."

Ken complied immediately and joined Donald in sending out the call, while he took the empty mugs back to the galley and set about preparing breakfast for the two of them.

The smell of cooking aroused Jamie, and he too joined the transmission as they sat together eating a casual breakfast in the saloon.

It was approaching mid-day when Susan reappeared. Sleep had eluded her for much of the previous night, but when it had at

226

last been attained, it was deep and seemingly dreamless. Now she was awake however she was immediately aware that the call was having little discernible effect. The group had known for some time that Susan was more adept than the rest of them at linking with others, and she was now able to detect more about the stranger than the others had been able to.

"She is certainly female," she confirmed, "but I can't really say how old she is other than getting an impression that she isn't a child. Her frustration tells me that she is receiving our call and feels a compulsion to come in our direction, but for some reason she is unable to respond to it. Her overriding emotion, however, is sheer terror. She feels that her life is in imminent danger."

"Can you tell where she is?" Donald wanted to know.

"Only that she is somewhere over there," She gestured towards the centre of Oxford, "and not too far away, either."

Jamie, who had been deep in thought for the past few minutes, suggested quietly, "Do you think we can 'see' where she is through her eyes, like we did in the fog?"

Donald looked at him, astounded. "Out of the mouths of babes and sucklings," he breathed, and then, "Susan, you are best at that sort of thing, you concentrate upon her, and we'll try to see through you."

Susan closed her eyes and concentrated hard upon the thought patterns coming through to her while the others focused upon what she might receive. For a while there was nothing but an unrelieved blackness, but the impressions of great sadness and extreme fear were far more distinct to the others, channelled through Susan, as was the fact that the thought patterns had a specifically female 'flavour' which had not been apparent to the men before.

Just as Ken was about to suggest that they stop and try some more positive course of action, Susan gave a small cry and the black turned to grey. Within it indistinct shapes could be seen as if through a thick mist. Slowly the details sharpened until they could make out what appeared to be a highly decorated wall to the left of the viewer. Indeed it seemed that the woman's head was immediately alongside the wall, the side of her head resting against it. Directly in front were three ornate structures of what appeared to be heavy pierced metal, apparently arranged in a triangle where they joined the wall, and stretched out horizontally at right angles to it. Two of these structures about half a metre apart were approximately one metre in front of the viewer, whilst the third one lay between these and about half a metre further away.

None of the four could remember ever seeing anything quite like it, although, to Susan, there was something oddly familiar about it. Before they could discuss what it was they might be seeing, the view before them started to change as the woman or girl, responding to a sudden pain in her legs, looked down towards her feet. All four of them let out a gasp of surprise at what they saw. The woman was seemingly suspended in mid air, with nothing whatsoever beneath her. Her feet just dangled over empty space. Her ankles however were chained to something out of sight behind her and the red raw wounds where the chains bit tightly into her flesh were what was causing her the pain. She was shoeless and the blood from her wounds was welling around the chains. These chains however did not appear to be the source of her support. The wall to her left continued down until the grey haze enveloped it. More of the metal structures could be seen jutting from the wall in the same groups of three.

The scene before them suddenly disappeared, blackness enveloping it. Waves of fear and unhappiness washed over them as the woman lapsed into unconsciousness. Even in her unconscious state she still emanated her distress although at a much lower level. Here was the reason for the inexplicable changes in intensity which they had felt.

Opening her eyes, Susan was the first to speak.

"What on earth did you make of all that?" she asked.

The others looked blankly from one to another.

"Could she be hallucinating?" Ken ventured.

"It seemed real enough to me, and I was the one in closest contact," responded Susan. "I certainly picked up no sense of illusion. To that girl it was all too real!"

"But it couldn't be," Jamie chipped in, "She couldn't just hang there like that!"

"You're right. She couldn't. Therefore we must be missing something," Donald offered, "so let's go back over what we saw, or thought we saw, and see if we can't make some sense out of it. Now what do we know for certain?"

"She's in Oxford."

"She's very scared."

"She can feel our call."

"But she can't come to us because she's chained up."

"She's a prisoner!" This last from Jamie in a burst of triumph.

"If she's a prisoner," Susan offered thoughtfully "then her captor could possibly be the source of her fear."

"You're right of course, but what about what we all saw? Does it give us any clue as to where she might be?" Donald directed their thinking.

"She was in a place that can't exist!" retorted Jamie, exasperation obvious in his tone.

"But it must," responded Ken, emphasising the last word, "therefore we can't be seeing it right. Let's just close our eyes and see if we can't re-picture it."

It was surprisingly easy to recapture the scene with all of them having an input. There before them were the strange metal structures springing from the curiously decorated wall to the immediate left.

"They look terribly familiar, but I can't for the life of me say why," whispered Susan. "It's so frustrating."

The scene before them shifted and once more there were the woman's feet hanging over that mystifying abyss.

"It's like Ken said, we can't be seeing this right," said Donald, "What's keeping her up?"

"And look at the blood from her ankles," Jamie pointed out, "it's soaked into the wall."

Susan gave a sudden start. "That's it!" she cried, "try this for size."

Slowly the scene before them rotated. No more was the woman hanging in space alongside an ornate wall but lying on her side upon a highly patterned carpet. The structures which had lain before her now became the cast iron legs of the type of

229

table used in public bars!

"We assumed that she was upright and her emotions blocked out all her other senses so that we couldn't feel the pull of gravity upon her." Susan explained unnecessarily.

It was now laughably clear to the others how their senses had been fooled.

"She must actually be chained to a wall or radiator or something, which is behind her back." Jamie added.

"Well, one thing is clear. She can't get to us. We must therefore go and get her." Donald again. "She must be in one of the numerous pubs in Oxford; no wonder those table legs were oddly familiar, Susan."

"Not being the boozy type, I have never seen them from that angle before." The relief was obvious in her voice, but then a tinge of apprehension crept in. "This means an expedition into the city, doesn't it? And we know that there is still at least one mad survivor left, don't we, otherwise who could have chained her up?"

"He or she may not be around any longer." Donald surmised, "The woman's fear may spring from being chained up and the world she knew collapsing around her. She is facing a slow death by starvation – or thirst."

"No, I sense there is more to it than that. She is afraid of something much more violent." said Susan. "I can feel it."

"So what are we going to do about it?" Ken brought them back to the subject of rescue.

They all knew what he meant. They had vowed to stay together since Ken's lone venture into Derby, but now circumstances were dictating otherwise. They knew that it was not practical for Donald to go into the city as he would slow down the expedition and probably hamper any retreat which they may have to make. Susan on the other hand, being the most attuned to the woman, would have a distinct advantage in locating her. Ken's strength could be needed to help release her bonds and to get her back to the boat.

Much to the boy's dislike it was decided that Jamie should remain with Donald in case the boat should come under attack. They felt that, under the circumstances, despite their earlier resolution, this was the way it must be.

"Why don't we take the boat back nearer to Oxford?" Jamie inquired, "That would save time."

It was a sensible suggestion, but Ken decided that he did not want to risk leading any madman who may be on the loose back to their place of refuge, in addition to which it would probably be easier to plot a more direct course to the woman's location if they went on foot. The boat however might be needed to bring the woman out should she not be capable of walking.

"No," he said, "If it should be that we need to get you closer for any reason then we'll give you a call. At this stage I would prefer to keep Rachel II out of harm's way."

They still had the two sets of breathing apparatus and though these were not absolutely necessary they would make life a little more bearable within the contaminated city, but it was decided to save them until the air became totally unbreathable and improvise until that time arrived.

It was early afternoon by the time they completed their preparations, rather later than they would have ideally liked, but Ken reckoned that, given the predicament of the woman, and the fact that she was now drifting in and out of consciousness, all contributing to a very confused state of mind, the sooner she was rescued the better. It was therefore with hurried stride that they stepped ashore and made their way towards the unknown dangers of the once great centre of learning.

They kept to the river bank for the first two miles and then, before the waterway passed under St Aldate's, they struck off across Christ Church Meadow, turned left when they encountered Broad Walk by which they gained access to St Aldgate's. Here Susan indicated that they needed to turn right and head for the city centre. Progress by road was easier on foot than it had been by car but they had to remain alert, watching for any signs of movement which might spell danger. Before long Susan indicated that they needed to turn right, off the main thoroughfare and thread their way through the lanes and alleyways which lay between Cornmarket and The High.

Rounding a final corner, she indicated that their destination was very close. Her lower face was swathed, as Ken's was, in a thick towel to counteract the smell, but when she turned her head towards him Ken could see the excitement in her eyes. A number of hostelries lay down both sides of the street and it was now only a matter of determining which was the correct one and effecting a rescue. Up to this point all had gone much more smoothly than any of them had dared to expect, but events were soon to take a sinister turn.

Susan paused for a moment, trying to see through the woman's eyes, standing motionless on the pavement with Ken slightly behind her. Dusk was fast approaching and the room where the captive lay was dark and gloomy with little detail discernible. The two rescuers were feeling the tension both from the woman and from within themselves. Susan now had good contact with the woman and was fairly certain of her location. She motioned towards Ken pointing to a small inn about fifty metres away on the left-hand side. They tried to contact the woman again, Ken 'seeing' through Susan's eyes, and it was while they were thus distracted that their world fell apart.

Susan had just started to move towards the inn when a sudden flurry of movement slightly above and to their right caught both her own and Ken's attention. Before either of them could move there was a flash and the loud report of a discharged shotgun. Susan just had time to scream briefly and throw up her hands to her head before crumpling into a huddle on the pavement alongside the wall of the building to her left. At the same time Ken felt the surge of terror and the searing white heat of pain which radiated from her before all faded into deep velvety blackness, and his heart turned to stone as he realised, with absolute certainty, that he had just experienced the pangs of death which had emanated from Susan's mind.

***

Back on the boat both Jamie and Donald reeled as they too experienced what Ken had just felt.

"Something's happened!" yelled the boy, "It's Susan!" and Donald had to restrain him as he sought to rush off madly towards the city.

"Wait!" he cried, "Ken's got enough on his plate at the moment without having to worry about you. Stay here and let's wait for him to tell us what's happened."

"You can feel what's happened." He was very close to tears. "Susan's dead!" The dam burst and the boy collapsed into Donald's arms, deep sobs wracking his body. The man held him, stroking his hair, but unable to offer any words of comfort. They had both felt that dreadful cessation of the workings of the brain as the life force had ebbed away. What comfort could he possibly offer in the face of an experience like that?

***

For a second Ken was paralysed by what had occurred, but he was jerked back to reality by the sound of a second shot and he steeled himself for the impact, jerking himself towards Susan's inert form, but no such impact occurred. He realised that this time he had seen no flash and he looked towards where he had seen the last one. There was no sign of any attacker! Surely the killer would not give up so easily!

And what, or who, if not Ken, had been the target of the second shot? There could only be one answer. The victim of the second shot must have been the other woman. But the shot had come from the wrong side of the street for that! Ken's mind was in turmoil trying to make some sense of what was going on. He sought to make contact with the other woman, but met nothing but blackness, and then, wonder of wonders, he felt the faint tendrils of thought coming to him – from Susan!

Quickly he dragged himself to where she lay and his amazement was intensified when he saw that there was no blood, and that the sound of her breathing was steady and regular. Before he could take any more action, his mind was overwhelmed by her emerging thoughts.

"Oh that poor woman, that poor, poor woman! Did you feel her die?"

"Feel her die? We all thought it was you!" His relief was obvious – even in thought. "But how could it have been that? We both saw the flash from the gun."

"Of course we did! I was seeing through her eyes and you were seeing through my mind. We only saw what she saw. I suppose that I was in such close contact with her at the moment of death that I was totally stunned by it. My mind must have shut down completely as a defence mechanism against the horror of being present in her dying brain."

While this mental conversation was taking place Ken helped her onto unsteady feet, but she was still too shocked to support herself so he swung her up into his arms and made his way as swiftly as possible back to the head of the street and around the corner, seeking to put some solid cover between themselves and the scene of the slaughter.

Once they had reached comparative safety of a secluded doorway, Ken stood her back onto her feet and supported her by hugging her closely to him until she was able to draw from his strength and stand unsupported once more. Even so, he did not release her immediately. His relief and deep affection were obvious and he needed the comfort of her nearness to reassure him that he had not lost her forever.

Their journey back was slow and cautious with many pauses to ensure that they were not being followed. Ken insisted that Susan derive some extra comfort from the use of the breathing apparatus to block out the all-pervasive stench of death from her nostrils.

**

On Rachel II both Donald and Jamie had picked up Susan's seemingly miraculous return to life and the ensuing conversation. Jamie's tears had stopped but immediately started again as a great wave of relief engulfed him. Donald continued to hold him, and, if the truth were known, his own eyes were not exactly dry.

**

An hour and a half later the four were reunited in the relative safety of their own little world. Stiff drinks were willingly accepted as they sat once more in the comfort of their boat. There was no need to explain what had happened, all of them were well aware of the facts, and a sense of gloom hung in the air, but there were still one or two unanswered questions.

"Why did the murderer kill her at that moment?" Jamie wanted to know.

"I think that a more revealing question would be – why did he keep her alive for so long before he finally killed her?" Susan put in thoughtfully.

"You are rather assuming that it was a man rather than a woman, aren't you?" It was a statement from Donald rather than a question. "After all you didn't see them, did you?"

Susan admitted that this was so, but said that she found it easier to think of it as a man's act rather than a woman's. Donald decided that this was too small a matter to take issue on and passed quickly on, after all, male or female, it made absolutely no difference to them now.

"All this is pure speculation, but from what we have seen of this madness it seems to take over absolutely and the killing goes on until there is only one survivor," he said. "And from what Ken tells us the killer then turns his rage upon himself. So far we have accepted that, but on occasion we have seen things which don't entirely bear it out. Those people we saw hanging under the bridge in Burton. I suspected at the time that most of them were hung there before they were killed and then disposed of one at a time. Suppose one or two madmen are able to cling to a vestige of sanity for at least a while longer than the rest, and realise that when the killing stops then they too must die. Would it not make some sort of twisted sense therefore to provide themselves with a store of victims to be disposed of when the urge becomes unbearable, and thus postpone their own death for as long as possible? Intelligence may be a factor in this survival technique and Oxford had no shortage of such people."

"You mean she was kept alive in order to be killed at the right time? But that's horrible!" Susan shuddered in revulsion.

"At the present time the whole world is horrible. We have to face that." Donald whispered gently.

"Do you mean that there could be more people in that pub?"

asked Jamie.

"Either in that pub or somewhere round about." Donald went on. "It depends upon the whim of the madman. He doesn't necessarily have to keep all his victims together. There were certainly no other victims that we could see."

"That would certainly explain her distress – and her terror," Ken put in, "and if she were the last victim it would explain the second gunshot too!"

"You mean that he turned the gun upon himself once he knew that he had run out of victims?" It was Susan's turn to question.

"I think we ought to keep an open mind on that," countered Donald. "That madman could still be on the loose out there, and I for one won't feel safe until we are well away from here."

Chapter 15

"then sudden destruction cometh upon them
...and they shall not escape."

1 Thessalonians 5:3

The following morning, just as the first grey streaks of light were appearing on the eastern horizon, Ken stood and listened as the sounds of night gave way to the sounds of day. He paused for a moment before starting up the engine prior to moving off, reluctant to disturb the slumbering countryside with the unnatural noise of man's machinery once again, no matter how necessary that noise might be to their progress.

Susan, noticing the delay, popped her head out of the rear hatch.

"Is everything OK?" she asked.

Ken gave a sigh,

"Yes, but I'll be glad when all this is over," he said quietly, and leaned forward to start the engine. "The sooner we can put a good distance between ourselves and Oxford the better I shall like it."

The memory of their latest encounter hung like a pall over the whole party seeping into their innermost beings and colouring their every thought. They had done what they could to push it to the back of their minds, but that night the scenes from the inn had invaded all of their dreams and disturbed their sleep, consequently they were all at a low ebb as they resumed their journey south.

Progress was good during the morning. The winter rains had swollen the waters of the river, and the current was swift, pushing them onwards towards their destination, although the pull of the weirs at each lock they came to called for extra alertness from whoever was at the helm. Each of these weirs held its own captives and told the tale of events upstream. Any boat not firmly tied had been dragged along to finish her journey, either clasped tightly to the top of the weir by the possessive waters, or coming to grief on the far side of it. The dead had gathered at them to await the next rains, which would raise the level a little more, allowing them to slide over and move on to their next stopping place.

Many of the locks were primed for them, already filled with water when Rachel II arrived, making progress even more rapid. Although a couple of them had boats already in them, the locks were large enough for their own craft to get by without the need to disturb either the boats or any dead occupants they might have contained.

Abingdon Lock, however, proved to be an exception, the water there being at the lower level when they arrived, and Susan, taking Jamie with her once more, made good use of the extra waiting time by replenishing their milk supply from a nearby herd of cows.

By mid-afternoon they had just negotiated Mapledurham Lock, west of Reading, and were heading for the Kentwood Deeps. The fast current which had sped them along had also brought its dangers, and they had experienced one or two near misses with buttresses on bridges, and one extremely close shave at a weir. The pace had called for vigilance on everyone's part, and not a little last minute fending off using the barge poles. All of this proved exceptionally tiring, and Ken had promised them that he would tie up early for the night once they were off the Thames and clear of Reading on the Kennet and Avon navigation.

"Another hour should do it," he promised himself, as he pushed the rudder hard over, at the same time revving the engine in order to avoid being driven onto a small island which lay in his path.

He urged the boat on, heading north east, away from the railway lines that had paralleled the river for the past couple of miles, towards Caversham. Ahead he could see the river swinging east once again just beyond what the map told him was

St. Mary's Island. Another mile after that would bring them into Reading. Had he not been so intent upon negotiating the swirling currents at that point, he might have glanced across towards the town and perhaps been a little more prepared, but he didn't, and so the sight which met him, as the boat rounded the last bend and entered the straight run in towards the first bridge, took him completely by surprise. It was not until they drew close that any detail could be made out, however.

Ahead of them lay chaos. The wreckage of demolished buildings was strewn about the landscape. Huge slabs of concrete with the spider legs of reinforcement mesh clinging to them had been tossed aside to lie haphazardly on the bank and surrounding area, some of them projecting from the surface of the water, causing swirls and eddies in the current as it surged around them. Piles of rubble spilled across the riverside appearing to have been cast there by a giant hand. Timbers and girders had been shattered and buckled, tossed around like straws as if by an enormous explosion. To their right, and running at an angle towards their path lay a gigantic furrow, with great banks of earth and rubble cast up on either side, and directly in front of them lay the cause of such devastation.

A massive airliner, seemingly on route for Heathrow, had come down on Reading. Miraculously, it had not dropped onto the town directly, but had approached low and flat, ploughing into the fields adjoining the river. Its landing gear had been retracted. In the course of its headlong career it had scooped out an enormous furrow which now lay to their right. The fuselage of the plane had passed directly between two buildings that had bordered the river, and it was the wreckage of one of these buildings that was scattered around them. Evidently, at this point, the wings had been ripped from the fuselage, the right hand one burying itself within the fabric of the riverside inn that had stood there. As the debris, loosened by the impact, had showered down, the fuel tanks, contained within that wing, had exploded, completing the demolition started by the initial impact. The left-hand wing had been severed by contact with a sturdy tree, the splintered remains of which bore witness to the impact; the wing itself lay embedded in the wreckage of a blue and white painted wooden boathouse. The fuselage had ploughed on alone, miraculously untouched by fire, careering into and across the water.

Having narrowly missed the bulbous central pier of the bridge, its headlong passage had finally been brought to an abrupt halt when the nose compressed into the angle where the north end of the Caversham Bridge met the bank of the Thames, thus effectively blocking that side of the waterway. The exploding fuel tanks had torn one of the mighty jet engines from its mounting and tossed it high into the air. It had landed on the bridge itself, bringing down the right hand span.

The traffic on the bridge had tumbled into the waters below, filling the river with a tangled mass of metal and concrete, making any further progress by their present route totally impossible. The tail fin, bearing the B.A. coat of arms and the stylised union flag above the enormous engine, had come through completely unscathed and stood out colourfully against the slate grey sky.

Throttling back the engine, and throwing the screw into reverse to counteract the flow of the river, they slowly approached the wreckage, staring ahead, aghast, unable to comprehend the size of the disaster. Jamie's head appeared up at the front, as he clambered out to see why they had slowed down. He immediately disappeared again, and could be heard calling urgently for Donald to come and see for himself.

"It's a plane," his voice drifted back to them. "Looks like a Tristar, and it's crashed right across the river. Come and see. It's huge!"

The last word was dragged out, at some length, to emphasis the enormity of the disaster.

The wreckage did indeed appear to be gigantic, dwarfing the narrowboat as it towered above them, with the jagged edges of torn fuselage dipping low to meet, and in places, disappear below, the surface of the water. As Donald's head appeared alongside Jamie's, Ken noticed the small, poignant reminders of the cost in human life. The flotsam and jetsam caught up in the wreckage told the tale of travellers returning home or coming to England for the Christmas holiday, with the brightly coloured wrapping paper caught on sharp edges of twisted metal showing where luggage had burst open, spilling the contents into the disturbed waters. Thankfully there were no bodies in sight, but tucked in under the bank, and caught in an endlessly circling eddy, floated a small family of yellow plastic ducks.

No one found it easy to break the silence, which hung like a pall over the river. Of the river birds which had once thronged the area there was now no trace, and even the sounds of the water as it gurgled and sucked at the wreckage seemed muted, as if in reverence of those who had died.

"It must have been terrible."

Susan was shocked at the scale of it all.

"Many would have been dead long before the plane came down," responded Ken. "Maybe all of them. Once the mad death struck, there would have been absolute chaos in the passenger areas, with everyone trying to slaughter everyone else. The pilot may have been disciplined enough to resist it for a while."

"I hope so," Susan came back, "I would hate the thought of him being the first, and crashing the plane on purpose to kill them all."

"We'll never know without going to look inside and maybe not even then," this time it was Donald, "and I am sure that none of us particularly wants to do that. Speculation is useless. I suggest that we need to concentrate on our own predicament. Namely, where do we go from here?"

Ken edged the boat towards the wreckage, stopping just short of the overhanging bodywork, to get a closer look at the situation. It was immediately apparent that there was certainly no way that the boat could be taken any further and an alternative had to be found. They had intended to continue through Reading and link up with the Kennet and Avon, which would carry them westwards north of Stonehenge. This was still a possibility, provided that another craft could be found on the far side of the ill-fated airliner.

"I don't like it here at all," thought Susan. "I keep feeling that the whole thing is going to topple sideways and crush us. Please can we go back?"

Her fear was a tangible thing, communicating itself to the

other two adults, but Jamie was quite disappointed when Ken reversed the boat away from the plane and swung her around to head back upstream. He wanted to stay and take an even closer look at the wreckage, standing at the stern and gazing, wide eyed at the massive body, as the boat, fighting the current, pulled slowly away.

Safely moored out of harm's way, they gathered in the forward cabin, and after the stove had been stoked to warm their bodies, chilled by the raw breeze, Donald spread out the local map on the floor. They grouped around him, watching as he smoothed out the creases.

"We are here," he pointed, "and this was to be our route." He followed the blue line of the river with the end of a ruler he had picked up, tracing it through the town until it met the River Kennet.

"At the moment we are heading east, but once we leave the Thames we will swing back westwards until we have to take to the roads again somewhere here."

Ken noticed that the end of the ruler now hovered above a name he recognised from the past. Hungerford, north of Salisbury! This was the place he had been thinking of which had received a foretaste of what was to come. A gunman running amok and killing people at random. The memory reminded him of his cottage hideaway so far to the north, where he had remembered Hungerford (although his recollection of the name had been inaccurate), and he wondered if he would ever again see the sunlit hills from its doorway. For what was probably the first time in his life Ken Howard felt homesick, and wished that the world could return to normal so that he could go back there to share the places he loved with Susan. His reverie was interrupted, and he was jolted back to reality by Susan's question.

"So what options do we have?"

"Well, I suppose that we could still carry on this way if we can find another boat on the far side of this wreckage," Donald replied, "but I doubt whether I would be the fastest person to go and look."

Ken realised that, once more, the responsibility fell to him, but thought that the other alternatives should be considered first.

"If we go back upstream a little way," he said, calling their attention back to the map, "until we are clear of the built-up areas, we could pick up a car and head south, keeping to these minor roads."

He waved his finger over the map to indicate the area he meant.

"Then, depending upon how bad the roads are, we could either take to the water again, here," he indicated the snaking blue line of the River Kennet near to Woolhampton, "or continue westward by road to Salisbury Plain."

"It hardly seems worth picking up another boat once we have left the waterways," Donald chipped in. "After all, it will only mean another lot of unloading and loading."

"I agree. I think we should go back to the roads," was Susan's opinion. "After all, we are now much closer to our destination."

"I think we ought to make sure that we really can't get past the plane wreckage before we come to any final decision," said Ken.

Jamie was dying to get a closer look at the plane crash. Airliners had always fascinated him, and he longed to get close enough to touch the giant at the bridge, even though it was a total wreck.

"I'll come with you, Ken."

His enthusiasm was irrepressible.

The boy had been so disappointed when he had been left behind at Oxford that Ken did not have the heart to refuse him again. Besides, he reckoned that as this was only a short trip to reconnoitre the far side of the bridge it would probably be safe for Jamie to accompany him. After being cooped up on the boat for so long, the boy needed a chance to let off steam. Susan said that she would stay and keep Donald company. She was only too happy not to have to go anywhere near the carnage ahead if she could possibly avoid doing so.

After the warmth of the cabin, the air outside felt chill despite their warm clothing, and so Ken walked at a brisk pace along the riverbank, Jamie running and leaping with the exuberance of youth, ahead of him. They had disembarked on the side of the river which was nearest to the front end of the wreckage, intending to pass round the front of it, rather than have to scramble over the rubble to the rear. Clambering up the embankment to the road over the bridge brought them level with the flight deck.

A section of the fuselage on the side nearest to the bridge had been peeled back by its contact with the masonry, exposing some of what lay inside. It was not a pleasant sight. The aircraft seemed to have contained its full complement of passengers and a jumble of bodies, seating and luggage could be glimpsed through the opening. Although the nose had been compressed by the impact, the flight deck above it, despite being badly distorted, had survived. The crews' seats were unoccupied. Whether the crew had been hurled through the shattered windscreen on impact or whether they had not been at the controls when the plane came down was a matter of no consequence. It had all come to the same thing in the end.

Standing on the bridge and looking at the scene around them confirmed their fears. There was no way they could go any further. This was indeed the end of the road, at least as far as Rachel II was concerned. A few pleasure boats were moored around a small island on the far side of the bridge, but close examination showed none of them to be as well equipped, or in such a state of readiness as their own fine little craft had been. If they were to continue by way of their original route, much hard work transporting necessary supplies lay ahead of them, and as it would only take them a few more miles south, Ken doubted whether it was worth the effort.

As they walked back, Jamie wanted to climb in and examine the flight deck, but, in Ken's opinion, the wreckage was far too unstable. The disturbed current had undermined the riverbed on the upstream side of it, with the water there muddy and turbulent, churning gravel from the bottom. He did not want either of them anywhere near it when the aircraft shifted position. From where they stood they could see the instability, as the giant cylinder rocked too and fro, buffeted by the water from below, and the stiff breeze catching the fin sideways on, from above. The tortured metal of the compressed nose screeched as it grated against the masonry of the bridge, setting Ken's teeth on edge, and making him more determined than ever to put as much distance as possible between himself and the ill-fated airliner.

Returning to the narrowboat they broke the news to Susan and Donald, although those two had already guessed what the verdict was from the disappointment which both Ken and Jamie had been projecting.

"That's it then," Ken called as he climbed back aboard. "This is as far as we can go by this route. There's no way past, and nothing very suitable on the other side. It's back to the open road for us, I'm afraid."

The prospect was not a happy one for any of them after their life afloat and the security it had offered. They would all find it a wrench to say goodbye to Rachel II, for she had been their floating home, a warm and comfortable refuge from grim reality, since they had boarded her at Derby. But for the tangled wreckage now lying in their path, they would have stayed with her, a mobile sanctuary in a vastly changed world, for a few more miles yet. Fate, however, had decreed otherwise and they now had no alternative but to bow to her wishes.

For the moment, however, they decided to maintain that illusion of normality and put off their return to the roads, spending the small amount of daylight which remained in preparing for what remained of their journey, and relaxing for the night just one last time in the security of the boat they had all come to love. Procrastination, they decided, was a luxury they had earned.

***

The wreckage ahead of them prevented them from bringing a vehicle close enough to the river to take off supplies, and, they reasoned, they were so close now that, even travelling by road, they should be able to carry what was needed, living out of rucksacks and foraging for any extras. At first light they completed their packing. Warm, waterproof clothing and nourishing lightweight food were given priority. There was little room for anything else, although Ken did notice Donald stowing his bottle of Scotch into one of the side pockets. Seeing Ken's eye upon him, he winked conspiratorially.

"For purely medicinal purposes."

Ken nodded and patted his own bulging rucksack.

"You can't be too careful. Mine's wrapped in a sweater."

They both laughed, and carried their loads out onto the front of the boat, where Jamie and Susan were waiting for them, their breath clouding in the cold grey of the morning.

"Come on!" Jamie cried as they emerged. "What kept you?"

"Essential medical supplies," they chorused, grinning like a pair of schoolboys at the private joke.

Ken helped Donald with his rucksack before taking up his own, and they prepared to disembark.

"Bye, old girl, and thanks for the ride."

Donald patted the side of the boat as they helped him ashore, the others making similar remarks as they followed him onto the bank.

Finding a gap in the hedge, bridged by a short length of weathered wooden fence, they climbed over, and with one last look back at their home for the past fortnight, they turned and trudged off southwards towards the nearest road.

The soft ground made the going difficult, especially for Donald, his crutches sinking into it each time he put his weight on them. Progress was therefore somewhat slow, and they were all relieved, and more than a little mud stained when they reached the hard surface of the roadway. Pausing to catch their breath after the difficult start, and stamping their feet on the paving slabs to rid their boots of as much mud as possible, they all looked forward to putting this stage of the journey behind them and arriving at Stonehenge.

Using past experience, they had little difficulty in locating and fuelling a suitable vehicle. In this case it was another Range Rover, it being large enough to carry the four of them, and versatile enough to handle soft ground should the need arise, and Ken's sadness at leaving the narrowboat was tinged with anticipation as he gunned the motor to set off on the last stage of their journey.

Their return to the road system was as dreary as they had expected it would be, with interminable backtracking and detours causing a great deal of frustration. The canal journey south, whilst being slow, had been steady, and this had given each of them an important psychological boost, in that with each passing mile, they had felt that they were drawing just a little closer to their goal.

Back on the roads, they had no such feeling, as often as not, driving directly away from their intended destination, as they sought yet another way around some blockage or other. Frustration increased as the miles clocked up on the trip meter, and the distinctly gloomy atmosphere within the car deepened considerably, when, just as they were passing through East Chisenbury, only a few miles from Stonehenge, the persistent mist which had been their companion since they had skirted Newbury, thickened into a full blown fog. Driving with extreme caution, they were able to proceed a few more miles to Netheravon, but here their advance was finally halted.

Major blockages on the A345 could not be penetrated, and ruined buildings cut off all the other possible detours that they had tried. It had taken many more hours of intense concentration than it would under normal conditions, and Ken estimated that they must have covered five or six times the normal road distance in their efforts to get through. Now, after getting so very close, they were unable go any farther!

If it had not been for the fog, he would probably have retraced his route northwards and attempted to approach from a different direction, but that had not the slightest appeal under present conditions. At this stage in the day, all four of them were tired and bored.

Sitting there, gripping the steering wheel and staring out at the tangle of interlocked vehicles stretching away into the greyness before him, Ken voiced their mutual thoughts, with the key question, "What now?"

They had, with any luck, around two hours of daylight left, and none of them wanted to prolong the journey by yet another day if it could possibly be avoided. This left only one possibility.

"We'll just have to walk the rest of the way." The

suggestion came from Donald.

The others had not dared to make this proposal, as it was Donald who was going to experience the most difficulty. There were perhaps, four or five miles left to go, providing that they cut across country and only Donald knew whether he was up to that distance, given the state of his leg.

"I can do it. I know I can," he said, sensing their reservations. "My leg has mended well, and the plaster gives ample support. I could probably do it without my crutches if I had to."

The others could see that he believed what he said, but were not so sure that he wasn't fooling himself.

"Come on," he said, "I'm sure I can do it, and even if I'm wrong, we should be close enough for you to leave me for a while, go to the stones for help, and then come back for me. We must make it today!"

He sounded desperate, and Ken suddenly realised how he must be feeling. Donald was the one who was supposed to be the rescuer, and here he was, feeling himself to be a burden to them all. He wanted to get this over and done with.

"OK," Ken decided suddenly, "we'll try it. But you must say if you find the going too tough, or even too fast."

Before leaving the car, Ken dug out a couple of compasses and took a bearing, then, with determination showing on all their faces, they set off into the grim greyness towards Stonehenge.

Chapter 16

"...full of dead men's bones."

Matthew 23:27

As dusk began to gather the fog had, if anything, thickened, and navigation became even more difficult. After abandoning the car they had managed to cover the remaining miles in a little less than two hours on foot. Because of Donald's leg the going had been slow but now, according to the map and compass, they were within a few hundred yards of their destination. Had visibility been good, they would have been able to see the megaliths. This area had been a centre of mystery and speculation for centuries, now the full mystery was about to be explored, and the stones put to their intended use.

Jamie, who was a little way in the lead, suddenly stopped as a large indistinct shape loomed up out of the greyness ahead of them. Susan and Ken, following along behind with Donald, drew up beside him, trying to make out the shape of what stood before them.

"What is it?" He whispered.

The shape bulked large in front of them, and Ken edged a little closer to try to observe some details.

"It's a tank!" He exclaimed, "and rather the worse for wear, too."

Together they approached the tank – or rather what once had been a tank, for now it was nothing but a rusting shell.

"It must have come from one of the army bases around here," Donald observed, "and it seems to have been knocked about a bit."

Jamie, who had climbed up onto the turret, looked down into the open hatch. He immediately recoiled.

"Ugh! There are bodies in there. They're all burned!" He exclaimed in disgust, wrinkling his nose as he jumped down.

They moved on, away from the tank. The ground ahead seemed to be rather uneven, with large mounds and ditches scattered across their path. In the poor visibility, it took a little while to recognise them for what they were.

"They're shell craters!" Jamie's voice was incredulous.

It was obvious that he was right, and, as they moved carefully forward, stumbling around the deeper craters, dark blotches loomed up out of the fog, indicating the presence of more tanks. All were lifeless, and all bore the heavy scars of battle. The bodies which hung half out of hatches or lay scattered over the torn ground all wore the battledress of what had once been a proud regiment. Tattered, bloodstained and muddied, it was still recognisable as being the uniform of the British Army.

"It looks as if there has been a full scale war around here," Ken remarked as they passed on, picking their way carefully.

The further they progressed, the worse it became. Larger and deeper craters, often interlinking in wide sweeping arcs blocked their path with increasing regularity. Looking down into them they could see twisted wreckage, rusting as it lay there, contrasting starkly against the white of the bedrock chalk. Such obstacles had to be skirted around and it became difficult to know if they were still headed in the right direction.

It reminded Ken of an experience he had had some years ago, when walking on the moors in the North of England. Gaining the top of a ridge he had been confronted by the sight of a gigantic quagmire of mud and clay. A motorway intersection was being constructed and his path lay directly across it, although all traces of his route had been totally obliterated by the construction work. It had taken quite some time to locate and gain the path on the far side, making him late in arriving at his Youth Hostel.

When he eventually arrived, he found that the warden had been on the verge of contacting the rescue services, and was not at all pleased with him! Here he faced the same situation. The pathway before them which had seemed so plain had suddenly been obliterated, and they could see no way forward. When the madness had struck, the army here, as they had further north, had gone to war – against each other! The results had been disastrous.

In the gathering gloom, they crossed the hard surface of a road, almost immediately stumbling upon the remains of a chain-link fence, half buried in the churned earth. Somewhere beyond this fence, not far in front of them, lay the ancient stones they had travelled towards for what seemed a lifetime. As they approached, carefully crossing the outlying ditch, indistinct outlines began to appear, and the deep foreboding which they had begun to feel dispersed slightly, only to clamp down upon them with renewed intensity as they saw that the shapes were not the stones, but those of wrecked missile launchers and allied support equipment. Just beyond this wreckage they stopped and peered ahead into the gloom. This was where the megaliths should have been.

Just for a moment a gap in the gloomy greyness appeared in front of them, and then the tendrils of fog regrouped in an ever-thickening curtain. The moment, though, had been enough. Where the stones should have stood lay total devastation. A huge crater lay in their path, the white of the underlying chalk showing palely, with no sign of the famous landmark except for a few shattered, blasted rocks, tossed aside by the force of a mighty explosion, or lying shattered within the crater itself. Stonehenge was no more. The historic site, which had more significance for mankind than he could ever have imagined, standing here on this wind swept plain since the dawn of history had gone for ever. Obliterated in a few minutes of madness.

The four stood on the brink of this discovery stunned into immobility. They were thunderstruck. Over two hundred miles of often-difficult travel had brought them here – and now it appeared that it had all been in vain. Their contact station was gone. They felt totally drained. Furthermore, the fact that there was no one here to meet them or no indication that anyone had yet arrived told them that no contact had yet been made by any others of their kind who may have survived.

"Now what?" was all that Ken could think to say when he

could bear the absolute silence no longer. "Where do we go from here?"

"There is nowhere else." Susan was on the verge of tears. "You said that this was the only place left in this country, didn't you, Donald?"

"Well, yes." He replied. "And strictly speaking it is, but there is one other place where we might manage to make contact. No promises mind."

"And where's that?" There was hope in Ken's voice.

"Callanish."

"Callanish? Wherever's that?"

"Lewis, in the Western Isles of Scotland."

The hope was dashed.

"But it will take forever to get there. Won't any of the other stone circles do?"

"I don't think so. Stonehenge was always the main centre. Others were never powerful enough to rival it; they were simply built as booster stations for surface travel, and some of them were never genuine in the first place, being erected by the first generations on this world. The mutants sensed the power in Stonehenge and tried to copy it. Callanish was built as an emergency backup, but I am not absolutely certain that it has retained enough of its power to get through."

As they stood there mulling this over, a sudden gust of wind tore the mist apart, swirling it into strange grotesque shapes before it died away, and the uniform grey, now very dark in colour as the light ebbed away, returned.

"It's a long way to go, only to find it won't work." Susan whispered. They could feel the great sadness in her.

"What other alternative do we have?" Ken's question was an answer in itself. "Anyway, we can't do anything tonight, and if we don't get under cover soon we won't be in a fit state to accomplish anything tomorrow either."

The damp fog had begun to penetrate, chilling them to the bone as they stood there on the edge of the crater. It seemed to make their disappointment even more bitter.

As they turned to seek shelter, helping Donald over the rough ground, Susan caught at Ken's sleeve.

"Where's Jamie?"

They stopped to allow the boy to catch up, but there was no movement to be heard.

Donald sent out a call.

"Jamie. Over here."

The silence remained unbroken.

"Maybe he's out of thought range," said Susan.

"Surely not in such a short time. He was with us a moment ago," Ken responded.

"Maybe he fell into the crater." She clutched at straws.

"Surely then we would have heard." Ken again.

"Let's at least try calling him," Susan needed to be doing something.

They tried, automatically increasing the intensity of their thoughts by calling aloud. Old habits die hard. Their voices, echoing back with a strangely muffled quality from the depths of the crater, drifted away, absorbed by the mists around them, into an unbroken silence.

"We've got to face it. Either he can't or won't answer. He's either decided to strike off on his own for some reason, or someone's got him. I don't see any other alternatives," was Donald's opinion.

"Wouldn't he have shouted or thought a message at us if he had been grabbed by someone?" asked Susan.

"Not if he was suddenly knocked unconscious." Ken did not mention the other, worse, possibility, but his companions read it nevertheless.

"But surely we would have heard something, like we did in Oxford." Susan would not give up.

"We should have done, but the fact is we didn't," Ken said simply, stressing the last word. He was at a total loss to understand what had happened to the boy.

"We can't just leave him here!" protested Susan.

"There's nothing else we can do. We can't find him if he won't answer, and we certainly can't just stand around here all night. We'll be lucky if we can find some shelter from this lot now." He indicated the darkness around them and, coming to a sudden, difficult decision, he turned and reluctantly led them back away from the mighty crater that had once been Stonehenge.

They spent a miserable night huddled in the shelter of the shattered ruins of the visitor's centre. None of them slept, and from time to time they would unite in sending out a thought call for Jamie, spending the following minutes straining to receive a reply. Each attempt caused their hearts to grow heavier as it was met by a deafening silence.

They were out again as soon as the sky began to lighten. The fog had given way to a thin grey persistent drizzle, which at least gave them more visibility. The scene before them confirmed their worst fears. The megaliths had indeed been completely annihilated. Each of them had clung desperately to the hope that they had not gone far enough in the fog, or had somehow missed it. Daylight dispelled all such false hopes. The stones had been in the very centre of the battle and their destruction had been total.

For some time they wandered around searching for signs of the boy, finally returning to the spot that he had occupied when they had last seen him. There they found traces of his footmarks at the edge of the crater, but beyond that, nothing. Jamie seemed to have disappeared into thin air.

After an hour's fruitless searching, they gave up, and cold, tired, wet and bedraggled they decided to leave and find a place of refuge where they could rest before deciding what their next move should be. Throughout the previous evening and during the search that morning, Donald had insisted on playing his part, but it was becoming increasingly obvious to both Ken and Susan that he could not go on much further. His recent exertions had taken their toll. His leg seemed to be giving him trouble, and the crutches had apparently chafed his arms. Their main priority now was to seek out some form of transport, and to this end they examined every vehicle they came to. On the fourth attempt their luck returned, finding an army lorry, which, except for numerous bullet holes in the cab doors and a shattered windscreen, appeared to be in working order.

Ken approached the driver's door and snatched it open, jumping back out of the way as he did so. The putrefying body of the driver tumbled out sideways and hit the tarmac of the road with a sickening thud. Checking the ignition, he saw that the keys were in place, and, wonder of wonders, the ignition was off!! With any luck there would be enough left in the battery to start the engine. He did not fancy trying to push start a lorry.

The back of the vehicle held weapons and ammunition, but tucked into one corner was a pile of blankets which the driver had had the foresight to provide for himself.

Taking one of the blankets, Ken wiped as much of the dried blood as possible from the steering wheel and the seat. He spread out a second one across the seat before the three of them climbed into the cab.

Although the driver's body had been somewhat gruesome after it had sat there for three weeks, the smashed windscreen had kept the air in the cab relatively breathable. Even so, no amount of fresh air could completely remove the smell of death from the upholstery. Susan had wrinkled her nose as she had climbed in but said nothing,

"Keep your fingers crossed." Ken reached for the ignition key. The dashboard lights glowed and then dimmed as he tried the starter. The engine turned over slowly a few times but failed to catch. He tried a second time, and again it refused to start.

"Come on... come on..." He coaxed, as he tried for the third time.

The engine turned again, more slowly this time, and then with a roar it burst into life. A cloud of blue smoke plumed from the exhaust. Carefully he brought the engine speed down and allowed the accumulated fumes to clear from the exhaust system. Selecting first gear he depressed the accelerator and let out the clutch. With a lurch the lorry bounded forward, jerking them all backwards and forwards as he struggled to control the unfamiliar vehicle. Smoothness returned as he depressed the clutch and managed to engage second gear, heading away now from Stonehenge, with their new destination, as yet, undecided. The lorry had been pointing west when they found it, and, for want of a better direction, that is the way they continued.

Two hours later they were safely ensconced in a small bungalow on the western edge of Salisbury Plain. They had chosen carefully, and Ken, remembering his earlier experiences, had picked a place with a propane storage tank standing to one side of the building, ensuring that warmth was available. Thus it was that they sat in the comfortable sitting room with heavy curtains masking the windows, warming themselves in front of a cosy gas fire.

The warmth however failed to dispel the chill in their hearts, caused by Jamie's disappearance. Before going in they had made a careful observation of the area, even going so far as sounding the truck's horn and waiting to see if it elicited a hostile response. No response had been forthcoming. Even so they could not be entirely sure that the area was clear, and the uncertainty made each of them jumpy and on edge, especially as they had found no reasonable explanation for the boy's disappearance.

During their journey west this had been the sole topic of conversation, their talk going round in endless circles. In the end they were no nearer an explanation than they had been when they started, and even now they could not leave the subject alone.

"Surely if he had been attacked we would have heard something." Susan went over the same ground again, blaming herself for not keeping a closer watch on the boy, as indeed they all did.

"We've been over this a thousand times," said Donald. "It's almost certain we would have heard something."

"But we didn't." She stated the obvious. "Therefore he must have gone off by himself."

She was clutching at straws again, refusing to believe that the boy was dead.

"But it's not like Jamie to have done that," Donald came to the boy's defence. "I've spent a lot of time with him during the last few weeks, and I thought I had got to know him pretty well."

Ken, who had appeared to be dozing in the warmth of the fire opened his eyes and looked up.

"But there has been something wrong recently. Something has been bothering me for quite a while now, but I haven't been able to pin it down. I'm fairly certain it's something Jamie said or did, but I can't for the life of me think what it was!" he said quietly.

The others confirmed that they had felt his unease, but they had witnessed nothing odd themselves and had put it all down to the Oxford incident.

Susan had a sudden alarming thought.

"Do any of us ever revert?" There was fear in her voice.

"No. I'm pretty certain the change is always permanent." Donald tried to sound confident, but they knew he was not certain at all.

"Look, this is getting us nowhere, and we need to concentrate upon our own problems." Donald saw the need to change the subject, and they had to admit that he was right. Idle speculation, with no facts to go on was a waste of time.

"So, if we have to go to Callanish, how are we going to get there?" Ken asked. "Shall we take Rachel II back north?"

Susan however, had been thinking along different lines. She had sensed something when Donald had been explaining about the stone circles. She turned to face him.

"You said that some of the circles were fakes?"

"Yes."

"And that the real ones were built as booster stations for surface travel?"

He nodded.

"And you mentioned earlier that these booster stations are, or were connected in some way, along leys?"

"That's right, but I don't see what good that will do us."

"It may do no good at all, but let me finish. Now, are any of these connections still there?"

"Yes I think so. I believe that some have been disrupted by deep mining or earth tremors, but a good number of them are still intact."

"Do you happen to know where the stations which are still operative are?"

"It's difficult. I have never been able to use them, so I never really paid much attention to where they are, or which are genuine and which are not. But just give me a minute, and I might be able to help."

He closed his eyes, and his body seemed to become stiff and immobile, as if his mind had drawn far away from it, drawing in upon itself. Ken wondered what sort of memory searching techniques were being employed, for this state was something quite outside his experience.

Donald's breathing became deep and regular, and but for the stiffness in his body he might have been asleep. Suddenly his eyes opened and he sat there, unseeing, seeming to stare right through them. Then he blinked rapidly a few times, and the life appeared to re-enter his body.

No one spoke until Donald, seemingly having collected his thoughts, began again.

"Now," he said, "the only times I have had occasion to discuss such matters with the U-Mornz has been when they have come to pick up one of the newly enlightened, and of the four or five times that has happened in my lifetime I can recall only two sites, other than Stonehenge and Callanish, being mentioned. Boscawen-Un, in Cornwall, and Castlerigg in the Lake District."

"But they're both miles away!" exclaimed Susan, exasperated. "Surely there must be some that are closer than that."

"I'm sure there are, but I don't know which of them are genuine, and which were copies made by our early ancestors. There is, however one other place which, I am fairly sure is still active. I was once speaking to another of our kind who, like myself, had stayed behind to help. He was a Welshman, and I remember him speaking of a group of stones in Wales which had been used when one of his 'charges' had been taken back to A-vern. They stood on a headland overlooking the sea at Penmaen-Mawr."

Susan groaned.

"But that's still an awful long way away."

"What does it matter? We can't use them."

"I've an idea. Bear with me for a moment," she continued. "The power of the stones and the ley system is all based on some of the peculiar properties of quartz, right?"

Donald nodded again.

"Yes."

"And somehow that boosts the power of the mind and

enables them to travel along those lines of quartz buried deep underground?"

"That's right."

"Well then, if it can boost the power of their minds to make travel possible, couldn't it do the same for thought communication, especially if the three of us combined in it? Can't we direct a message through the system and on to Callanish, without having to go that far?"

Donald was astounded. He shook his head in disbelief.

"You know, it could just possibly work," he said incredulously. "It's never been tried as far as I know, but then, there has never been reason to!"

"It's worth giving it a shot," Ken added his support. "We can't lose anything by it, and if it doesn't work we can still go on to Scotland."

He looked at Susan with new respect. There was more to this girl than met the eye. With renewed hope in their hearts, they dug out the maps and started to plan again.

Boscawen-Un was much further south and west of them, carrying them further away from Scotland. The Welsh site however, had distinct advantages. Road travel, they had discovered, was painfully slow and difficult, while the waterways had been somewhat easier, but not all that much faster.

"The sea," Donald said, "probably offers a far faster alternative and now that I come to think of it he also mentioned another group of stones on the coast, near to Haverfordwest. Both sets of Welsh stones are possibilities, and both are on the coast, and if we find that they don't work, we can still go on by sea to Castlerigg. All the time we would be getting closer to Callanish, and could carry on to that station if we don't have success anywhere else."

It sounded simple enough, but Susan had thought of a snag.

"How will we know whether it has worked or not? After all, we can only cry for help, not send messages. If they do get our SOS it will have gone out through Callanish. They won't know where we are."

This time it was Donald who had the answer.

"Once a call has gone out they usually arrive within eight hours," he said. "I am sure that if this works at all then they will be able to trace us if we stay in contact with the system. We will just have to remain in each place we try for long enough to be sure they haven't heard us, with at least one of us in contact with the stones at all times."

"How long do you think that should be?" Ken wanted to know.

"I think that if they haven't arrived within twelve hours of our call, we can move on."

"Why can't we just go to the nearest sites, and try them all out in turn?" Susan wanted to know.

"Because we would have to wait for twelve hours at each one, not knowing whether we had been successful or not, before moving on to another. Counting travelling time, it could take us well over a fortnight to visit half a dozen sites, and if we had no success, we would still have to get to Callanish, but would not have got much nearer to it. This way we can go to sites that were known to be active and head for Callanish at the same time. I personally have high hopes for the Welsh sites. The first one is quite close to the Prescelly Mountains, which is where the stones for Stonehenge came from. I reckon those stones will prove to be from there too, and should give us a good chance of making contact," Donald explained.

This sounded reasonable to them. The cold water Susan had poured on their new hopes evaporated, being replaced by the warm glow of hope.

The Severn Bridges, with their tollbooths, would be prime areas for major blockages, they reckoned, and anyway, road travel, as they had discovered, would be far too slow. They considered going north and picking up the Kennet and Avon waterway to take them westwards, but they were not sure that it was completely navigable. Eventually it was decided to strike west and make for the coast, somewhere near Burnham-on-Sea, where they could pick up a boat, cross the Bristol Channel, and then, depending on the weather, either hug the Welsh coast round to the stones, or take to the roads again.

By this time, the room was pleasantly warm, and not having

slept the previous night, they were all having difficulty in keeping their eyes open. They therefore decided not to set out immediately, but to rest for a couple of hours first. Before settling down, Susan had tended to Donald's injuries. The recent activity had caused the plaster to rub off the skin where the leg emerged from the top of the cast, and she bandaged the area as well as she could to protect it from further damage. His arms too were somewhat sore, where the crutches rubbed against them, and these she treated in the same way.

"You'll have to keep off them as much as you can for a while." She smiled at him as she packed the first aid kit back into her rucksack. "No marathons just yet."

The treatment obviously made him much more comfortable, for he was peacefully asleep almost as soon as she had finished speaking.

Three hours later, they were back on the road. Their sleep had done little to refresh them, and with their tiredness, the depression at having to resume their trek returned, bolstered by the fact that there was now no guarantee that the outcome would be successful. Heading for Stonehenge, they had been certain that their journey would end there, and contact would be made. That certainty had driven them onwards, giving them a positive goal to aim for. Now there was no certainty, only a vague hope that eventually they would win through. It was a far less attractive prospect, and much less of a spur.

The lorry proved to be a reasonably successful vehicle, with the extra height afforded by it giving a good view over roadside hedges, enabling them to avoid at least some of the blockages. Others they cleared by telekinesis. Minor obstructions were simply pushed aside. Although the higher pressure inside the cab, once they were up to speed, kept much of the wind out, it did not exclude the rain. They had discovered this problem on leaving Stonehenge, and by now, they were prepared for it. Donald and Susan sitting under a polythene sheet they had brought from the bungalow, and Ken dressed in waterproofs he had found there. He had also discovered a pair of swimming goggles, which he now wore to keep the rain out of his eyes. Despite her worry about Jamie, Susan found the combination amusing, and could not resist a quiet smile each time he put them on.

By nightfall of the second day they were still ten miles short of the coast, having met the usual scenes of carnage and destruction. They had not, however, encountered another living soul, although they had seen many forms of wildlife on the move. At one point they had witnessed a pack of dogs hunting, although they did not get a clear sighting of the quarry. It appeared to be a small horse, or perhaps a deer. The animal instinct to survive had soon reasserted itself, and the law of the jungle was returning to the British countryside.

The weather had cleared on the second morning out from Stonehenge, and the day had been clear and crisp. As darkness fell, so did the temperature. The lack of human sightings helped them to decide to take the risk of travelling in the dark and press on. Three hours later they reached the coast, somewhere between Burnham-on-Sea and Watchet. Ken heaved a great sigh of relief as he turned off the engine, and they sat for a while, staring out at the absolute darkness ahead of them.

Somewhere out there in front of them lay Cardiff and its outlying towns, but for all they could tell, they might have been sitting on the edge of the world, with nothing before them but an abyss of aching emptiness. Ken had pulled off the road facing the open water, and the headlights shone out over it, their beams picked out by droplets in the vapour that was rising from the slightly warmer water, until they were overwhelmed by the darkness and died away to nothing. He turned off the ineffectual lights and stared out into the void. He had never seen such unrelieved blackness.

Even on their journey there had always been the light of the moon, and when fog had shrouded the landscape it had still been there, lightening the mists, making it easy to imagine that the lights of civilisation lay just beyond the limits of the eye, but here, there was no deception to be had. The moon, if there was to be one that night, had not yet risen, and the darkness was absolute.

For a while they sat in silence, hugging their warm garments around them, huddled together, listening to the eternal pounding of the waves as they continued their relentless attempt to invade the land. Out there were all the basic primeval fears which had plagued man since the dawn of time, and now, faced with a situation, which must have been all too familiar to their ancestors, they could feel those fears causing their skin to prickle. Within each of them was a deep longing to be out of this situation. Here lay danger. If only Stonehenge had been intact...! Anywhere would be better than this. Perhaps they should return even now and look for Jamie again? Fear was welling up from deep within them.

It was Susan who broke the spell.

"Look at the stars," she whispered.

Simultaneously, Donald and Ken lifted their eyes from the vast blackness before them and gazed towards the heavens. The splendour was breathtaking. Countless points of light blazed in glorious display in every colour imaginable, some hard, blue and bright like diamonds, while others twinkled and flickered like far away candles, soft and yellow, or glowing red. The last of man's pollution had stopped contaminating the atmosphere of his world some three weeks ago. Even the most persistent of the fires he left behind him had died out by now, and the world was climbing the long road to recovery, to which the clarity of the night sky bore witness.

It reminded Ken of a night in his boyhood, when he and a friend on a cycling holiday, had camped in a field on the Long Mynd in Shropshire. Sitting outside the tent on a warm summer's evening they had remarked on the absence of lights, other than the occasional passing car on a road far below them. The stars on that evening too had been impressive, but they paled into insignificance when compared with the grandeur of this display.

Opening the cab door, Ken climbed out, and with head tilted back, turned full circle. The others followed suit. Throughout the whole three hundred and sixty degrees the stars blazed down, and the fear which had been welling up within them only moments ago was replaced by a sense of awe.

"When I consider thy heavens, the work of thy fingers, the moon and the stars, which thou hast ordained;" quoted Ken, dredging deep into his memory.

"What is man that thou art mindful of him?" finished Donald. "It's not until you see something like this that you understand what the psalmist was getting at is it?"

"It certainly makes me feel insignificant," Susan whispered.

Again they stood and admired the vista around them, Ursa Major pointing their way north, whilst behind them Orion, with his jewelled belt, flamed in all his glory. Every second more stars appeared as their eyes grew more and more accustomed to the darkness.

"We'd better get under cover before we all freeze to death," Susan called them back to their senses, shivering suddenly as she realised how cold she was becoming.

Reluctantly they lowered their gaze from the heavens, and taking torches from the lorry, turned to examine the dwellings behind them.

The first three they tried all contained what remained of their owners, and were left well alone. The fourth appeared to have been unoccupied when the madness had struck and it was here that they settled for the night. Having been on the road for three days, snatching meals where they could and sleeping fitfully in makeshift quarters, they were all grateful that at last they had the major obstacle of the roads of southern England behind them, and sleep came quickly. Tomorrow, hopefully, they could find a fast, well-equipped boat and head north with far greater speed.

Chapter 17

"These are they which came out of great tribulation."
Revelation 7:14

They slept late the following morning, the tiredness and stress of the previous few days at last catching up with them. The clear night had deposited a heavy frost upon every available surface, and the morning, which turned out to be sunny and clear, still remained very cold. After a hurried breakfast they decided to head west along the coast in search of a boat, but the direct route was blocked causing them to make lengthy detours inland through the Quantock and Brendon hills. These took them well out of their way, and they finally approached Watchet, their intended destination, from a south westerly direction. Every road into the resort seemed to be blocked, with many of them being purposely barricaded using rocks and furniture from nearby houses. It looked as if some sort of resistance had been organised here, and Donald wondered if any of the 'enlightened' had been around to offer such resistance. A thought call into the settlement elicited no response. If there had been anyone of their kind here, they had either moved on, or perished.

The barricade, once approached, offered little resistance. After the largest of the rocks had been removed, mind control once more proving its worth in this, it was a simple matter to push their way through using the lorry. Timber cracked and splintered as it was brushed aside, the huge wheels making short work of the fragile material, which seemed to have been used as a deterrent, to slow down any attackers, rather than a serious attempt to keep them out altogether.

There seemed to be far fewer corpses lying around the streets than in most other towns they had visited, and far less damage, re-enforcing Ken's theory that there had been a mass exodus for some reason or other, while the few who remained behind had erected the barriers to try to prevent re-entry. This however was pure supposition on his part based only upon what they could see around them.

As they entered the town the sun disappeared behind banks of grey cloud, which were being driven across the sky by the cold east wind. The sunshine of the morning had cheered them considerably, but the returning cloud brought with it a corresponding gloom and foreboding. None of them could rid themselves completely of the depression caused by Jamie's disappearance, and Susan in particular spent much of her time in fruitless speculation as to the boy's fate. It had not felt right to leave the area without knowing what had happened to him, but as they had made a thorough but totally unproductive search before they left, it was difficult to see what else could have been done.

Despite this a persistent sense of guilt pervaded their thinking, which was accompanied by an irrational urge to return and resume the search, no matter how useless it seemed. Such feelings however were ignored, being replaced by their own sense of urgency as they sought for a boat to carry them across the Bristol Channel on the next leg of their journey. They had no idea how long the crossing would take them, there were too many imponderables, but they felt that if they did not get away fairly rapidly, they may well not make it to the Welsh coast before nightfall and none of them wanted to be still at sea when darkness fell.

It was therefore with a vast feeling of relief that they saw a number of likely boats the moment they arrived at the harbour. They eventually settled on 'Nomad', a 23-foot cruiser powered by a pair of seemingly enormous outboard engines. Compared with Rachel II she was rather cramped, but they hoped that, once they had reached the first stones, she would be surplus to requirements. She had been laid up for the winter and all her tanks needed replenishing, but this was soon accomplished from the many other boats in the harbour, and there was still a good hour and a half of daylight left when Donald finally edged her through the harbour entrance.

Although the temperature had risen slightly, the wind was raw and biting, and the grey waters of Bridgwater Bay were choppy, with the tips of each small peak of water showing flecks of white. Donald kept the speed down at first, getting the feel of how the boat handled, but once he felt comfortable with the controls he eased the throttle open until they were skimming across the top of the swell, the powerful craft leaping from the top of each small crest to bounce onto the next. At first, Susan was alarmed at the noise produced as boat and water met each other, crashing together at high speed, but Ken was able to re-assure her that this was quite normal for a high-speed boat.

Donald was thoroughly enjoying himself at the controls, at last feeling that he could make a useful, positive contribution to their progress, and he became so confident, that instead of cutting directly across the channel and then hugging the coast around to their destination, he swung towards the north west, to meet the Welsh coast further along. His intention was to shorten their journey.

"At this rate we might even get all the way to the stones tonight," he thought to himself.

It turned out not to have been the best decision he had ever made, as they were still well out in open channel when the storm arrived. Unnoticed by Donald, the ominous cloudbanks from the east, driven onwards by a steadily increasing wind, had thickened and darkened. He had insisted that Susan and Ken take refuge in the cabin from the biting wind.

"There's no point in us all freezing to death out here," he had said, "I'll call you if I need you."

They were unaware of the situation, therefore, until it was too late.

The first hint of trouble came when the Welsh coastline, which had been getting gradually more distinct, was obscured by a sudden flurry of snow. Donald, realising how vulnerable to the weather they were, swung the boat back onto a more northerly course in order to approach the coast more directly. It was then that he realised that he had left it too late, and that they had a problem. The cloud cover was now total, blanketing the whole

267

sky, and the wind was increasing rapidly approaching gale force. Up to that point they had been running at an angle to the wind direction, but turning north meant that they lay sideways on across its path, and both the wind and waves caught the side of boat, causing it to wallow and roll alarmingly.

Fear welled up from deep within Donald as he realised the severity of their position. This feeling of fear, along with the alarming motion of the boat brought Ken and Susan scrambling up from below, the erratic motion of the boat causing them some problems in this. As they emerged, the sky darkened ominously and driving snow lashed across the surface of the water, urged onwards by the fury of the ever-increasing wind. All sight of land had gone as the weather closed in, entombing them in a lashing whirling maelstrom of wind, snow and crashing water.

Ken grabbed the wheel and both he and Donald struggled to maintain control, attempting to turn the bow of the boat into the storm. This, they found, was not possible with the mighty forces of nature pitted against them. Each time they tried, the waves threatened to swamp them as the heaving water caught them sideways on. Any attempt to turn into the waves was foiled as the boat heaved and bucked like a wild thing, the engines screaming into a crescendo at the propellers rose clear of the water each time the bows dropped into a trough. This caused the craft to lose way and she spun around again when caught by the following wave. By this time there was a considerable amount of water inside the boat, and the pumps were fighting a losing battle. Their fear was an intense, tangible thing as they realised how helpless they were against such mighty forces. Their world was a mass of whirling white as the boat spun helplessly in the driven snow and wind-lashed spume.

There was little they could do, faced with such raw power.

"Let's try and run before it!" screamed Ken over the tumult, but as he and Donald fought to swing the boat around, even the small amount of control they had was snatched from them. A powerful wave caught the rear of the boat, and with a tearing crash, one of the outboard engines was wrenched from its mountings and swung crazily sideways. Below the waterline the spinning propellers of the two engines met, with disastrous results. The loosened engine was ripped completely out of its seating and thrown into the angry sea, whilst the remaining one battled valiantly on alone for just a short while longer, then with the final sound of tortured metal and plastic, it seized solid and died.

With the realisation that they were now totally helpless their fear deepened. All three of them clung to the useless wheel, as the deck below them gyrated wildly, and racked their brains furiously for some means of escape from this perilous situation, but with the boat now being driven further and further towards the mighty Atlantic Ocean they knew that their luck had at last run out and that their chances of survival were minimal and getting worse by the second.

"Why?" gasped Susan. "To come so far and end up like this! It's all so futile!"

She was angry, and her heart was in the grip of a deep dread, black fear threatening to engulf her.

A wave crashed down upon the stern and the boat settled ever lower into the water. By now they were soaked to the skin and freezing cold, the snow hitting their faces with stinging intensity. Death could only be a few minutes away in such conditions.

"It's all so unfair!" She was weeping now, as Ken clung to her to prevent her from being swept away. "To have come through it all like we have done. To have found each other – only to have everything snatched away like this."

The boat was wallowing heavily, the water within it swirling around their knees. One more wave over the splintered stern would send her to the bottom. The three of them clung together for mutual comfort and watched as the next wave approached, their minds linked as they stared death in the face, sharing their despair and fear.

The wave rolled remorselessly onward, and Susan stared in fearful fascination as it appeared to move in slow motion, surging towards them with malign intent. She gave a sudden start, cowering away from it, as it crashed in upon them and they could feel the boat shudder and start to slip away beneath their feet. With a forlorn cry she clung ever closer to the two men and prepared to be engulfed by the icy waters.

It came as a great shock to the system to find that, after the initial sliding motion, the deck beneath them steadied and inexplicably, began to rise again. The storm continued to rage about them with unabated ferocity, but the boat was steady as a rock.

Ken's first thought was that they had run aground, but the only place he could remember west of their position was Lundy Island, and they would have to have been incredibly lucky to have been washed up there. Nevertheless luck seemed to have been with them and renewed hope surged within their hearts, dispelling the fear which had paralysed their minds and allowing their heads to clear. As soon as the fear released its grip upon them they heard it.

"Hang on, we're coming. Ken! Hang on!"

They recognised the call immediately.

"Its Jamie!" screamed Susan, in disbelief. "Jamie! Where are you?"

"We'll be with you soon. Just concentrate on helping us keep your boat afloat till we get there."

"He said 'we'," Ken screamed over the howling wind. "There must be somebody with him."

"Never mind that now, concentrate upon the boat. Keep it afloat," Donald shouted, above the noise of the tempest. "We could have done that before if our minds hadn't been so frozen by fear."

Ken wondered whether even their combined minds would have had the strength to hold out against such raw power. He doubted it, but held his peace, concentrating instead on helping all he could.

The storm was as violent as ever, but it seemed to have lost its malevolence, and had returned to being a natural phenomenon. Wild, terrible, angry, but without the power to harm them, as they stood shivering on that firm oasis amidst the turbulent, churning waters.

Then the driving snow parted slightly to reveal an enormous dark shape gliding towards them. The wild waves had absolutely no effect upon it, remaining as it did, rock steady as they threw themselves against its sides, only to be rebuffed, falling back to regroup and hurl themselves yet again, with renewed force, against the immobile plating.

The craft glided to a stop between them and the storm, offering a little protection from the icy blast. She appeared to be a naval vessel, but what surprised them most was that the sound of wildly labouring engines, which should have been heard even above the tumult of such a storm, was most noticeable by its absence.

Looking up Susan saw a small, familiar figure leaning out over the side and waving furiously. Behind him she sensed more of their own kind – a good number of them. She could actually feel their presence.

"We're going to bring you aboard," thought the boy, and immediately they felt themselves being lifted, as if by some gigantic hand, from their own stricken vessel. Looking down they were just in time to catch a last glimpse of her as she slipped below the surface, finally claimed by the dark and angry waters. It dawned on them all, in the same instant, that there was nothing supporting them! Clinging together, high above the waves, they were rising towards the deck of the ship and the safety it offered, transported by the power of the mind – something which Donald had said was impossible with living creatures – and yet here it was, happening to them!

Ridiculously, it was at that moment that Ken realised what it was that had been troubling him about Jamie. It was the bird!

Back on the narrowboat he had watched as a bird had performed spectacular, impossible aerial manoeuvres before fluttering off. Jamie had been manipulating it. Donald had told them that such a thing was impossible without the use of very specialised equipment. But Jamie had been doing it!

"He's a very special young man is Jamie, and we're most grateful to you all for taking care of him. He has a lot to bring to our people."

The voice, which spoke within their minds, was warm and friendly, and came from one of the group before whom they were now coming to rest on the deck. Ken was amazed to realise that he knew from which of them the thought had emanated. As they drew near to the deck, the man who had been in contact with them stepped forward, and the moment their feet touched the deck they stumbled towards him, crumpling onto the deck as the control was released and the weight came back onto their leg muscles. Scrambling to their feet they joined together in a mutual bear hug with the boy, relief, joy and love overflowing in this act of mutual comfort. Eventually they broke apart and turned towards their rescuers. Many questions jostled for position in the minds of the three travellers, but the man nearest to them held up his hand.

"There will be time for answers later. First we must get you below where you can be warm and dry." His voice was warm and soft, as his thoughts had been, though the accent was strange and unfamiliar. All three knew instantly that here was someone who could be trusted. At last they were safe and amongst friends. The U-Mornz had arrived, and not a second too soon.

The boat was indeed a naval vessel, but she seemed like a floating five-star hotel to Donald, Susan and Ken as the three of them luxuriated in deep hot baths and warm fleecy towels, afterwards climbing into the strangely-fashioned, but familiarly-textured clothing which had been laid out for them. The moment each of them was ready they were visited by one of their rescuers and taken to a comfortably furnished cabin where they were provided with a good, hot meal. The food was not all familiar to them, but it was entirely delicious. Each of them was brim full of questions, but knew that all would be revealed when the time was ripe. Right now was the time for appeasing their hunger and such a feast demanded their whole attention.

As they pushed away their empty plates, their new friend handed them each a glass.

"Jamie has informed us of your tastes, and we took the liberty of bringing along something for you."

The glasses contained exactly what each of them had drunk on their first night together in the cellar. Jamie beamed as they expressed their appreciation of the gesture in turn and raising their glasses to him in a silent toast.

Taking their drinks with them and rising by mutual unspoken consent they moved to the comfortable seating at the other end of the cabin. Half a dozen of their rescuers joined them, filling up all the available seats, rescuers and rescued intermingling. There were no divisions amongst them. All were united in the common bond of true humanity.

The leader, or the man they took to be the leader, whose name was Keval, introduced the others. Their names, like his, were strange, but oddly familiar variations on names they knew; Joran, Namil, Grenda, Dachel, Jale, and Romas, four male and two female.

"Now for your questions," said Keval, once everyone was settled.

"What happened to Jamie?"

"How did you get here?"

"How did you find us?"

The three of them spoke simultaneously, each with a different question.

"It is possible for us to answer more than one question at a time," Keval laughed softly, "but I am sure it would be easier on you if we took them one at a time. We can see from your minds what you want to know, and so, if you will allow us, we will answer your unspoken questions in what seems to us to be the right order."

Immediately Jamie began to speak.

"As you noticed without noting, Ken, I found that I could manipulate animals, back on Rachel II. Donald had said that we couldn't do this to living things, and at first it worried me. I saw that it had disturbed you too, and so I only tried it after that when no one was around. I knew Donald hadn't lied when he said it couldn't be done, but I also knew that I could do it! I practised and I got better at it, but I never harmed the animals," he added hastily. "It wasn't until we reached Stonehenge that I tried the next logical step."

"You transported yourself?" Susan guessed.

"Yes. I could see how upset you all were when you found the stones were gone, and I just 'thought' myself away."

"But why didn't you come back and tell us?" asked Ken. "We were all worried sick about you."

"I couldn't. When I thought myself away, I had no idea

where I wanted to go. I just went away. I didn't know where I was, and I didn't know how to get back! There I was standing by myself in the middle of nowhere, completely lost! I immediately tried again, with the same result. Different place this time, but still no idea where I was. I suppose I panicked a little then and started flashing about from place to place more or less at random, hoping to get back to you by blind chance. It took a whole day of that, resting between jumps, before I was able to find out how to move in a given direction, but by then I didn't know which direction to go in!

Then I had some luck. I came to a place I recognised. I realised that I was at the Devil's Arrows quite near to my home. My mum and dad had taken me there on a picnic once. From then on I could feel the power beneath me, and I knew which direction to take. I had heard what Donald had said about Callanish so that's where I headed for. When I got there, I wrapped my arms as far around the biggest stone as they would go, and cried for help."

"We heard the cry and immediately put our rescue plan into action." Keval took up the story. "Jamie stayed where he was, and we found him when we arrived about seven hours later. When he explained what he had done, we like you, were amazed. What Jamie had achieved was entirely new to us. He had managed to teleport without any artificial help, because, with the destruction of Stonehenge, many of the leys in that area were dead. We too thought it to be impossible, but once we had examined how he achieved it, those of us you see here were able to master the technique. Like most things, it is surprisingly simple, once you know how. When he had arrived at the Devil's Arrows, Jamie found himself on a ley which was drawing power from Callanish and that made it easier for him. It was the initial leap that broke all the existing rules.

"The rest of our party, that is the ones who were unable to master the technique right away, dispersed elsewhere along the working leys, to try to locate other survivors. We went directly to Stonehenge, but of course you were no longer there, and we had no idea where you had gone. We tried to call you back, but if you heard us, you either didn't recognise the call, or you took no notice of it. Then yesterday evening we had our first breakthrough. We felt a touch of your fear. It's a powerful emotion, and travels well. That gave us the general direction of your whereabouts, but didn't last long enough for us to pinpoint you. It wasn't until your fear returned today that we got a good fix on your position. From then on we had to act fast, commandeering this boat and getting it out to you. The rest you know."

"So what happens now?" Ken asked.

"Well, as you know, there is a lot of clearing up to be done here, and you need to be trained to use your new powers effectively." Keval nodded towards Jamie, Susan and Ken. "We also need to see what other tricks this most unusual young man has up his sleeve." He placed his hand on Jamie's shoulder. "We therefore propose to take you back with us. When we have all learned what we can from each other you may do as you please."

"We're going to a different world." Jamie was excited at the prospect.

"Will we ever be able to come back here?" Susan wanted to know.

"As I said, you may do as you choose, once you know everything."

Susan was glad of that, for despite what mankind had done to it, this was her world, and she loved it.

"Shall we have to travel to Callanish to leave Earth?" Ken wanted to know.

"Yes and no," their host replied with a secret smile. "We do need Callanish as a departure point, but we don't need to travel there because we have already arrived. While you were cleaning up and eating, this boat had been heading north at speeds you wouldn't believe, under the control of our friends here." He waved a hand to indicate the others in the room. "We 'docked', for want of a better word, just before they came in to join us here."

They were astounded. There had been no sense of motion, no sound of vibrating engines, and no sense of stopping. All this activity around them and they had been completely unaware of it.

Suddenly their minds were filled with joy and laughter as the rest of their rescuers 'opened up' to them, welcoming them and sharing with them the loving experience of a completely open mind. They were amongst friends.

"If you are ready, then, we'll make a start," said Keval, as he turned and led the way out of the ship, and towards the mysterious stones of Callanish.

Chapter 18

"Blessed are the meek..."

Matthew 5:5

Ken and Susan Howard stood at the door of their cottage, hidden in the hills of the Northern Pennines near to where Skipton had once stood. It was July, and the warm summer sun was low above the tops of the hills to the west, casting long evening shadows over the landscape. They had returned to Earth only a few days before, and the renewed beauty of it still filled them with a sense of wonder.

A-vern had been beautiful in its own way and they had enjoyed their time there, but the sky had been a slightly different shade of blue, and the atmosphere of that world, although its chemical composition had been precisely the same as Earth's, had been intrinsically different. They had missed the scent of heather and of pine forests. It was not their world.

At first there had been so much to see and so much to learn that they had had little time to think of Earth, but gradually a deep longing to return had set in for both of them.

Not so for Jamie. He had taken to A-vern like a duck to water. There he had been a celebrity for a while, bringing as he did, his newly discovered talent to the world, and there were children of his own age – young girls who looked at him with more than a glint of interest in their eyes. He was young, and this was to be his world from now on, though he promised to visit Ken and Susan often, "once they had settled in."

Donald too had found his niche. Once his leg had healed he was taken on a lecture tour to describe what it had been like when the Earth went mad, and how he had brought the others out. Everywhere he went he was greeted as a hero, and given a

277

chair at one of the major universities. He too elected to stay, but again with the promise of frequent visits.

It appeared that there had been few other survivors of the catastrophe which had overtaken the Earth. The British Isles had escaped the worst of the excesses wrought by those who had embarked upon the final frenzy of mass destruction. In other countries awesome powers had been released by the crazed minds of dying men and countless millions had perished at the push of a button. The entire Japanese race had been wiped out when a hydrogen bomb had been dropped into the crater of Mount Fuji, the entire island of Honshu slipping beneath the waves in the ensuing earthquake and countless thousands of lives being lost as adjacent lands were swamped by the colossal tidal waves which followed.

The methods of destruction had been as varied as the warped minds of their perpetrators, with the result that many parts of the globe had been wiped clean of life within minutes of the onset of the madness. Britain had escaped by pure chance – the worst of the weapons had not been deployed there – and Ken often gave thanks for it,

During their two and a half years away, vast changes had taken place. The scars left by man had been treated and healed, although in every country, one town had been left as a memorial to those who had once lived in such great numbers on the face of this planet. In Britain it had been Stratford upon Avon. All others had been removed. The ley system had been repaired for use by those who could never master the new skills (both Ken and Susan were amongst this number), and a new 'Stonehenge' had been erected on the top of the more central Pendle Hill.

At Ken's request, the canal system had been restored, and was now maintained by robot workers, keeping well out of sight except when repairs were needed. Rachel II, fitted out with a new, emissionless engine, developed on A-vern, had been brought north, and was now berthed on the Leeds and Liverpool Canal, where Skipton had once stood. Of the town there was now no trace, but its ancient castle had been left to stand guard over the peaceful countryside. An ancient memorial to a branch of mankind which had ceased to exist.

Most striking however were the changes wrought by the Earth itself.

Now that man had been taken out of the equation, or at least reduced to an insignificant level, the planet had begun to heal. Acid rain no longer fell, and the foliage on the trees was green and wholesome. Depleted ozone layers had been replenished, and the whole balance of nature restored. The air was clean and crystal clear, as were the streams which cascaded down the hillsides to run free and sparkling into the clear waters of rivers and oceans. The weather systems too seemed to have reformed, with summer and winter returning to their rightful places. The Earth was once again a beautiful planet.

Ken put his arm around Susan, and breathed deeply.

"I've always loved this place," he said, "but I never realised how incomplete it was. It needed a woman's touch." He looked up at the windows where new curtains hung.

"I know they are unnecessary, but I do like them. A house looks dead without curtains at the window," Susan responded. She too heaved a deep sigh of contentment. "I'm glad we came back. This is where we really belong"

Ken had to agree with her. This was their rightful place. This was how it was meant to be. The medical science of A-vern now meant disease was a thing of the past, and all threat of hostilities had vanished. Stocks of food would last for many lifetimes, and there was ample room to grow more. Should something go wrong, A-vern was only a matter of hours away. All major factors which had blighted man's peace of mind throughout history had been removed. Eden had been restored.

"You know, the Bible was dead right," he said.

"What do you mean?"

"'The meek shall inherit the earth,'" he quoted, holding her close to his side and watching the sun as it slowly disappeared behind the purple hilltops.